THE LOST REALM BOOK 2

Sapphire Falls

AUDREY LYNN

THE MIDDENS
QUARTZ MOUNTAIN
LATIAH
DORFAREN LAKE
SUMMER ENCAMPMENT
BAYBERRY
OROFINE
PASS
AMETHYST PEAK
CALDERA
TOWERS OF NEPHEL
SAPPHIRE FALLS
NEPHEL
WASTEWATER
N
GOLDOTH
ONYX CAVERNS
DOMINO44 MAPS
AERITIS

To all the book girlies who dream of other realms.
You never know where your portal may be hiding.

Sapphire Falls depicts dark thematic material, including violence, battle scenes, explicit sexual descriptions, trauma, depression, slavery, pregnancy, and adult language. It is the second book in a series and ends on a cliffhanger.

Contents

The Prophecy

Prologue

Morgan

The cave floor was cold and damp, but that was the least of Morgan's problems as she lay covered in dirt and crusted blood on the hard rock surface. She needed to think beyond the throbbing injuries to her head and the bruising across her body, yet trying to think led to even more pain. Water splattered down on her shoulders from the low ceiling of the cave. As she tried to push past the pulsing ache in her head, she began to notice that this wasn't a cave at all. There were rusted old pipes in the corner of the small shaft. The tunneling cuts through the earth weren't naturally formed either. Morgan realized that she must be in an abandoned mine shaft.

The monster that brought her to this place had stepped outside just moments ago, and he would probably be back any minute now. For the last day, he'd hardly left her for more than a minute or two.

Morgan could only describe the creature that snatched her from the top of Quartz Mountain as a monster. The massive bear had grasped her head between his jaws as a ringing sound and blinding light filled Morgan's senses. After that, the pain of being dragged down the mountain in the maw of a bear's mouth had been too much for Morgan and she'd passed out.

She had no sense of how much time had passed when she woke up in the cave. The bear was over her body, sniffing at her clothes, and she knew that she wouldn't survive the attack. She'd been reassured to know that at least Avery wasn't being attacked any longer. Avery would get help and be back with her parents, comforting them after losing Morgan.

The bear's hot breath had been on her neck as she prayed that this would be over quickly and she wouldn't have to suffer much longer. Suddenly, the creature had lifted a massive paw and stroked Morgan's cheek with surprising humanity.

Then, it had stepped back from her and transformed into an enormous man. Morgan had thought she was hallucinating, but the hallucination didn't end. How could he be both a man and a bear? Her skin grew cold and clammy as she stared at the creature. There were so many things that weren't right about him. He was unnaturally beautiful, like he had been carved from stone, and his clothing was tattered. But it was his ears that made Morgan doubt her sanity. They were tipped to points.

As Morgan thought back to that first time the monster had transformed in front of her, she knew she needed to do everything she could to get away and find help. She'd noticed from the small cave entrance that the sun had set twice, and the creature that held her captive was becoming increasingly volatile.

Morgan's body was growing weaker, a feverish chill creeping across her skin. If she didn't escape from this creature, she would be dead from infection in a few days. This was it. The moment she had to make a decision before he returned.

She picked up a rusted iron pipe from the side of the tunnel. It was stuck in decades of mud and grime, and Morgan had to pry it out of the ground before she got a good grasp on it.

Silently, Morgan moved to the entrance of the tunnel. He was out there, growling and shouting in his strange language. He'd done that multiple times a day, and Morgan was beginning to suspect that beyond being an abducting monster, he was also losing his sanity in the tunnel with her. Something about her was making him angrier with each time he came near her.

Yet, he hadn't killed her. He'd been so close on more than one occasion over the last day. But, always seemed to stop himself and mutter something under his breath before he moved away from her, disgust glinting in his eyes.

Morgan held her breath as she heard his footsteps approaching. For being such a huge creature, his footsteps were nearly silent. It was as if he'd been trained to stalk through the forest silently. Or maybe that was part of his animalistic side coming through?

Now he was close enough for Morgan to hear him breathing, a steady beat that had her clenching her jaw. She tightened her grip on the pipe. This was her only chance at escape. If she didn't attack her abductor, she'd never get out alive. As he stepped into the tunnel, Morgan lifted the iron pipe sideways and swung it with all her might at the creature's abdomen. She wished she could have bashed him in the head with the pipe, but he was far too tall for that.

His breath escaped him with a wheeze as he bent his body forward, clutching his stomach. He hadn't seen her attack coming. That was the only way he wasn't ripping her to shreds. The monster gasped, trying to regain his breath.

Extending her arms over her head, she brought the pipe down with all her strength on the top of the monster's head. The bashing sound of metal on bone made Morgan flinch as she watched the creature drop to the ground. She didn't scream or shout out her fury at her abductor as she crushed his skull. She didn't even cry or curse. No, she put all her remaining energy into killing the creature that had left her hurt and alone. Lifting the pipe over her head again, she brought it down on her collapsed kidnapper. Again and again, she struck the creature as the tunnel filled with the iron-tinged scent of blood and gore. In the low light of the tunnel, Morgan could make out the black, frothing blood that seethed out of the monster.

This was her chance to escape. To get help and try to forget about what had happened to her after she and Avery climbed Quartz Mountain. As she ran for the tunnel entrance, she took one last look at the still form of the monster that had hurt her so much. Was this even real? She could see his corpse before her eyes, but at this point, she was beginning to think this was all a messed up hallucination.

The burst of adrenaline Morgan experienced as she raced through the woods in the setting sun wouldn't last for long, not in her weakened state. She didn't have any gear and wasn't sure how far away she was from the trail. If she didn't get help quickly, she would likely die of exposure.

Just as she expected, Morgan began losing her energy quickly. She couldn't be more than a quarter of a mile from the tunnel when she stopped running and leaned against a large pine tree.

It could have been only minutes, or maybe it was hours that she sat there against the tree, fever distorting her ability to think straight. Then she heard something.

It was distant, but unmistakable. People were shouting as they walked through the dense underbrush of the forest.

The air was still, so different from the windy morning that blew a warm breeze past Morgan and Avery as they had summited Quartz

Mountain. Morgan listened closely, thinking she must be hallucinating again.

She heard the sound again. Closer now, and clearer through the trees.

"Avery! Morgan!" the call rang out. Again, she heard it.

Morgan rose up on shaking legs and let out a frail shout for help. Over and over, she shouted for help as the rescuers called her name.

Finally, two men made it to her. She saw the horror on their faces as they looked at Morgan's broken body.

One offered her a drink of water and said, "We're with Search and Rescue. We're here to get you home."

Morgan wanted to cry, but no tears flowed down her dirt and blood splattered cheeks. "Is Avery safe? Where is she?" Morgan asked.

The man's answer made Morgan's stomach flip. "We haven't found her yet. We need your help to get her home. Where was the last place you saw her?"

Chapter 1

Avery

One and a Half Months Later

Avery held Morgan close. Her sister's wet body pressed against hers as she cried on her shoulder. Slowly, she pulled back and looked at Morgan. Her sister wasn't dead. A bear hadn't killed her over a month ago. Instead, she was here with her in Aeritis, wet and cold, but alive, and she'd saved Avery's life by shooting Jasper.

But what was more shocking was her sister's face. Her beautiful sister's round cheeks and big green eyes were now overshadowed with deep, ragged scars. Some were slightly purple while others made parts of her skin look punctured, like something had sunk its jaws into her flesh. The bear. It did this to her. Above the jagged scars were the same tiny stars that Avery now bore. The mark of the Premier Goddess of Aeritis, Althea.

It was all too much, having Morgan in Aeritis, alive even after such a horrible attack, and now marked by the Goddess. How did Morgan survive the attack, and how had she found her?

Tears streamed down Avery's face as her hand shook, clinging to her sister. "How are you here?" Avery asked. "Are you real? Am I dead or something?"

"Oh no, I'm here. I'm with you. But where the hell are we?" Morgan looked around the room as she asked the question, and Avery noticed how she flinched as she made eye contact with the Latian warriors in the room.

To be fair, facing a group of huge, ethereally beautiful men and women was intimidating. Avery had firsthand experience with it herself, after her traumatic entry into Quartz Mountain only a little over a month ago. She took a steadying breath. This was a chance to reassure her sister, give her the knowledge she'd so desperately needed after her own journey to Aeritis.

"You must have gone through a portal, just like I did. This is going to sound crazy, but you're in another realm. It's called Aeritis. But you're safe. We're safe now, thanks to you."

Morgan looked at Avery like she had lost her mind.

"Look, I need to talk with you privately. We're not as safe as you think we are," Morgan said as she subtly shook her head.

All around them were the Nepheli Fae who came to watch Avery showcase her magic at the dinner held for Jasper, the Latian King. The king who now laid dead under a table cloth. The king that her sister had shot with a gun. The room was in disarray, tables toppled and folk milling about, looking slightly confused about the events of the last hour. Somebody really should have told them to leave. Wasn't that the job of a king?

"I know this seems fucked up, but, we're going to be okay. You killed the bad guy, King Jasper. We're still being held by another bad guy, King Rylo, but I think we're going to be free now that Jasper is dead. How did you know to kill him anyway?"

Her sister didn't answer as she stared at the fae buzzing around the room, trying to clear away the chaos of Jasper's assassination.

Morgan had shown up out of nowhere, just as Avery had been trying to kill Jasper while she also attempted to pass the crown to the rightful king of Latiah, and her soulmate, Savine. She'd failed to do that one thing and had been near death, tortured by images of her sister being dragged away by a bear when Morgan had suddenly appeared and shot the king.

"Avery..." a voice said behind her, and she turned to see Savine standing close behind her. She should introduce him to Morgan. But, the look on Morgan's face as she glared at Savine, slightly coated in blood, essence slowly shifting under his skin, made Avery think Morgan must be in shock after all this.

"Savine. Come, meet my sister Morgan," Avery said in calm tones. She felt her sister tense up as Savine drew closer. "Morgan, this is Savine. He's the new king of the nation of Latiah."

Morgan shifted, scooting her body back behind Avery. She didn't say anything to Savine. Avery looked back at her sister as she shot him a death glare with her green eyes.

"Um, Avery. Will they let us talk in private? Can we do that, or are we... Are we captives?" Morgan asked. Her voice was hardly above a whisper.

Savine gave her a soft smile, and Avery's heart did a little flip at the kindness on his face.

"Avery, why don't you take your sister to your room? She looks like she needs some time alone," Savine said.

Just as Morgan and Avery turned around, Rylo, the king of Nephel, approached dangling Morgan's gun off his gloved hand. His haughty grin made a chill run down Avery's back. She had done what he asked.

She had tried to kill Jasper. Yes, she was unsuccessful, but he was dead now, anyway. What would he want from her now?

"Just a moment," Rylo said. "I agreed to return you to Savine after you assassinated Jasper. Unfortunately, things did not go according to my plan. Not only did you not kill Jasper, but your sister has inadvertently fulfilled a prophecy that I have been waiting to see come to fruition for quite some time."

Avery cocked her head as she waited for an explanation. She looked to Savine, and the calm, disciplined face told her right away that he knew exactly what Rylo was talking about. Avery recognized this stoic, secretive look on Savine's face by now.

"Savine? What's he talking about?" Avery asked, hoping he wouldn't keep things from her again.

Savine didn't speak right away. Instead, Rylo interjected, saying, "Now that I know Avery's true purpose in Aeritis is to fulfill the will of the goddess, should I keep the flower and the stardust? Or return the flower to you, Savine."

Avery felt her body stiffen. What in the actual fuck was this man talking about? Jasper's body wasn't even cold yet, and Rylo was up to some sort of trick again.

"They are both coming with me, Rylo," Savine replied. "I'm not negotiating on this."

Rylo's smile turned menacing and Avery felt a chill run across her skin. "Ah, well. We had a deal for Avery. The sister is another matter entirely. And now that I know she is also touched by the goddess, I have come around to the importance of keeping a witch on hand. Just in case events follow the trajectory foreseen by the prophecy."

Avery couldn't keep quiet anymore. She hated this horrible man so much. She hated his fae trickery and his selfishness. "You can't keep my sister here. I won't let you and I'd never leave without her."

Rylo grinned with a crooked smile. "Then it appears you will remain at the Towers for longer than I expected. But no, I will not allow the kingslayer to leave here. Not after I saw her display her magic. The way those shadows seemed to dance around her as she blasted Jasper was titillating. And to think her magic barreled out of her after only moments in Aeritis. How long did it take your magic to manifest, Avery?"

Avery scowled, but didn't reply as she thought back to the dark shadows that circled her and Morgan. They seemed almost sentient as they wrapped around her and her twin, like they were protecting them from harm. Of course Morgan would have instant control of her magic here. She was always the overachiever.

"Magic?" Morgan muttered as she looked at Avery, concern glimmering in her green eyes. "What are they talking about?"

Avery thought about the first time Savine had tried to convince her that she was a powerful witch, and all the doubts that had swam through her mind. "We're witches, Morgan. I know that's crazy, but look."

Avery tugged at her magic. It was all but depleted inside her, but she managed to form flowers in her hands and tried to pass them to her sister.

Morgan put her hands up to block the flowers and they spilled to the ground. "This is insane. Avery, I need to talk to you alone. And no, I'm not going to go with you," Morgan said, pointing to Savine before she turned to Rylo. "I'm not staying with you either. I'm getting out of here, even if I have to jump off that waterfall again."

"I'm afraid not. You will not be leaving Nephel anytime soon. As Avery already knows, you cannot return to your realm and I will not allow Savine to have you. I'm generous enough to offer to give him back his soulmate," Rylo drawled. He wore his typical uninterested expression, masking his true thoughts, as Avery knew all too well.

Savine stepped forward, drawing his sword. The fae around the room gasped. Nepheli warriors rushed forward. Out of the corner of her eye, Avery saw her friends move closer, drawing their weapons. She'd forgotten about everyone in the moments after Morgan's arrival. But there they were. Rue and Susan, Jay and Raikin, and somehow, Kyla, Garnel, and an entire group of rebel warriors.

Savine's voice boomed throughout the enormous room. "Morgan will be staying with Avery, and I will see you dead in your own nation before you keep Avery from me again, Rylo. Unlike you, I am more than willing to end you and worry about other nations later."

Nepheli warriors moved in around them from every side. Weapons were raised and Avery feared they'd cut Savine down just for raising his sword against Rylo. This couldn't be happening. She couldn't let Savine die now, not for her or for her sister.

Avery heard Raikin clear his voice and murmur, "Savine, don't act rashly. Not now that you wear the crown."

Savine looked at Avery, that hard, unreadable expression still on his face, and she thought her heart would shatter. They were finally getting their chance at happiness, but once again it hung in the balance thanks to Rylo's scheming. Avery couldn't let Savine kill Rylo, even if he deserved it. She wouldn't see him gain his crown only to be embroiled in war against other nations for killing a king, and she couldn't watch him be cut down by the Nepheli warriors surrounding them.

"I'll stay with Morgan!" Avery shouted. She turned to Savine and put her hand on the flat of the sword. "I can't leave her like this."

She looked at Rylo. He wore a triumphant expression on his face. "I'll make a bargain with you. Morgan and I will stay here for a month.

Savine, you can take the time to get settled into life at Orofine. After a month, Morgan and I will both go to Orofine. We can figure out how long we are there before we return to Nephel. I'd like it to be longer. Maybe six weeks?"

Savine scowled, but once again, Rylo spoke first.

"I can agree to this," he said, his wings slightly spreading as he spoke. "If after her time in Orofine, Morgan will return to me until I am finished with her."

"I can't agree to any of this," Savine interjected. "I'm not leaving my soulmate with you for a month." Savine turned to Avery, taking her hand in his swordless hand. "First, Rylo kidnapped you, Avery, then he forced you into attempting to kill my father."

Avery saw Morgan's eyes widen, and she looked at her sister with a shocked expression. She gave Morgan a quick nod. It was almost hard for her to hear what she'd been through. She couldn't imagine how Morgan was handling any of this.

"Then we are at an impasse!" Rylo said, his voice more shrill than normal.

"Stop arguing over me!" Morgan shouted before she turned to her sister. "Ave, this is madness and I have to talk to you alone. Please, let's get out of here."

"You are not leaving until we come to an agreement," Rylo said in a voice dripping in honeyed whiskey.

"May I interject, highnesses?" Raikin said, stepping into the small circle within the crowds of onlookers. "It would be wise of you to consider our strategy as we return to Orofine for the first time since the beginning of the rebellion. I think it prudent to hold off introducing Avery as your soulmate until you have had time to begin reuniting our nation. After a month, we can celebrate her arrival around the Night of Feasts."

Savine shook his head, but Avery placed her hand on his arm and looked into his dusky blue eyes. "I'll be safe here. Rylo already took an oath that he won't hurt me. Plus Raikin has a point. You've got a hard enough job reuniting your people without bringing in the woman who tried to assassinate half the population's ruler." Then Avery turned to Rylo. "You can't keep Morgan indefinitely. We'll both return to Orofine after a month. No way in hell am I leaving her alone with you."

"Avery, remember my generosity. I could end your soulmate just for threatening my life. I could lock him back into the Tower of Teeth. After all, he is an escaped convict. I have been hospitable beyond necessity to both of you. I mean it when I say that I will have this witch for myself. I do not want the soulmate of the King of Latiah in my home every other month. You have served your purpose and I will allow you to stay for a month and enjoy my continued hospitality, but after that time it will only be Morgan returning to Nephel. I am willing to let her return to you every other month, only if she is trained in her magic by the Bayberries, including your little witch friend."

Avery looked at Morgan chewing her bottom lip, a look of sheer confusion on her face. Despite what must be a frightening and bewildering conversation, she gave Avery a tiny nod in agreement anyway. Poor Morgan had no context to this whole world that she'd fallen into, and here Avery was, having to make a bargain with the devil incarnate for her freedom. "I agree to your bargain, Rylo Finnian."

She watched as Savine looked at her, the pain of her decision evident in the hard lines of his face. This must be torture, leaving her in this place that held nothing but terrible memories. But, she wouldn't abandon Morgan. If Morgan had to stay, then Avery would stay with her.

Savine turned to Rylo, but moved his arm possessively around Avery's shoulder, wrapping her into the warmth and hardness of his body.

"One month. That is it. If Avery isn't back by then, I will level this place to the ground. Make no mistake, Rylo."

Rylo grinned, showing his white teeth, as he reached out his hand and placed it on Savine's shoulder. "We have a deal then."

Chapter 2

Morgan

Morgan's head was spinning as Avery led her down a wide stone staircase. The last few hours made no sense, but nothing in her life had made sense after she and Avery climbed Quartz Mountain. The last month and a half had been filled with so much pain. Pain from healing from her wounds, pain at the loss of her sister, and the aching pain at the loss of who she once was. She couldn't go to work. Hell, she hadn't even returned to her condo after she was released from the hospital. Instead, she'd moved in with her parents and tried to help find Avery, even through her own agonizing recovery.

This evening she'd left her parents house and drove to a nearby waterfall to try and clear her mind. One moment she was standing on the platform overlooking the waterfall and the next moment her head was filled with her sister's voice, screaming her name. Somehow, she wasn't even sure it was possible, but the railing began to shake before it just collapsed and she was plummeting down the waterfall, still hearing nothing but Avery's screams.

Morgan hadn't been injured beyond a few scrapes and a lungful of water. She had followed that strange looking woman after she had pulled her out of the waterfall because she didn't know what else to do. The woman had touched her head and Morgan could suddenly understand what she said. It didn't go without notice that the woman looked similar to the monster who took her from Quartz Mountain, but she'd pushed down her fear and followed her. Kyla was her name, and she knew Avery and promised she would help her find her sister. There had been no reason to trust this woman. Every instinct in Morgan had been kicking and screaming to run, but she had a feeling that Avery must be hurt or in danger and this woman might be her only chance at finding her sister. Kyla said she'd get them to Avery quickly, but Morgan hadn't thought quickly would mean in the arms of some winged woman. Winged and with pointed ears. Fortunately, Kyla wasn't lying and Morgan had gotten to her sister as she writhed in agony on the stone floor.

Something erupted within Morgan when she had seen that man standing over her sister. As she prepared to shoot him, shadows had emerged around her and danced at her feet. Then, she'd pulled out her gun and shot him without question. All she had been thinking was that she had to save Avery, had to keep her safe, and it had felt as though the shadows were answering her deepest concerns.

"Are you okay, Morgan?" Avery asked as they walked down floor after floor of twisting stairs. Her voice was hesitant, like she already knew the answer to her question and regretted asking. The open air windows showed an inky black night, dotted with more stars than Morgan thought could be possible.

"I think I'm in shock. This can't be real. It's another one of my hallucinations," Morgan replied. She didn't fully believe this, but after there had been no body found in the tunnel, Morgan had begun to give the answer others wanted to hear. As the doctors said, the bear attack had caused a lot of trauma and her mind was trying to cope with what had happened to her. Hallucinating that the bear transformed into a giant man with chiseled features and pointed ears seemed to be the only reasonable explanation.

Morgan reached out her hand and stroked the back of Avery's green gown. It was like nothing she had ever seen. All subtle details of plants and forests in a form fitting dress. It felt *so real*, but her sister would never have had a reason to wear a dress like this in Montana. Avery turned on the stairs and took Morgan's hand in hers. It felt so warm, so lifelike.

"I know it sounds crazy, but this is real. We're in the fae land. We probably should have been more interested in fairy tales as kids because I've got so little baseline for the magic. It's been a struggle to comprehend this world."

Morgan tensed her shoulders. Maybe she actually was lost in a world filled with the nightmarish creatures that had caused her pain. Only now the creatures were willing to bargain for her life. She didn't want to admit it to her sister, because she knew nothing about the fae who held her captive, but she'd felt some relief when the shimmery winged man wouldn't back down on keeping her here. At least he didn't resemble her attacker. Her sigh came out more like a cry as she squeezed her sister's hand.

"I thought you were dead," was all Morgan could say as she walked hand in hand with her sister.

"Same. The last thing I saw was that bear dragging you away." Avery's voice shook with emotion as she spoke.

Her sister looked at her with such a strange mix of sorrow and delight. Morgan couldn't tell if her sister was happy to be in this alleged fae realm, or if she was suffering like Morgan.

"Here's my room," Avery said, unlocking the four locks barring the door.

As Morgan entered the room, she immediately noticed the unmistakably male clothing folded neatly on a stool in a corner. The rest of the room was white, fluffy, and overly feminine. It felt like Morgan was transported into a luxurious cloud. After all the fear, all the doubts about what had happened to Avery, here she was living in comfort and presumably sleeping with that creature that had called her his soulmate.

"What is going on here, Avery?" Morgan asked, pointing to the men's clothing.

Avery's face could never hide what she was thinking. She turned as bright as a cherry. "It's hard to explain. But I found my soulmate. Like a real, tangible connection that I can feel. Even right now."

Morgan's face hardened. Her posture stiffened. Only Avery would disappear into another world and find an alleged soulmate in a little over a month. It hurt Morgan, thinking about how hard everyone had searched for Avery. How much Morgan had worried that the monster who took her had gone back for Avery, killed her, and hid the body. How distraught her parents were, even putting up a missing person billboard on the highway.

"So we've been busting our asses off searching that damned mountain for you, and you've been up here playing princess in the tower with your supposed soulmate? Are you kidding me, Avery?" Morgan demanded.

Avery looked hurt. Her expression slipped from a grin to a scowl as she crossed her arms. "You have no idea what I've been through, Morgan. Or even why I'm in this tower. I was kidnapped by that horrible man Rylo! And so many other awful things have happened to me, like being forced to murder a man who was kind to me. I don't think you'll get what I've been through."

"Oh I get it!" Morgan snapped, bringing her hands to the jagged scars jutting down her face. "I absolutely *get it*! After all, *I* just killed a man!"

Avery's face softened. She uncrossed her arms and brought her hand to Morgan's shoulder. "I'm so sorry that you had to do that. But I wouldn't be alive without your help, and Savine—" Avery paused and looked at the stuff on the floor. It seemed like she was choosing her words carefully. "I wish Savine's stuff wasn't here right now. It's not something we need to talk about at the moment. You've been through so much, and I know how overwhelming this place is. Do you want to tell me how you survived the bear attack and how you got here?"

This was such typical behavior from her sister. One moment thinking only of herself and her needs, the next remembering that Morgan existed. It was always like that between them. Usually Morgan was okay to lurk behind Avery's shining personality, but not today. Not when they'd been mourning Avery. Not when Avery had been actually enjoying her time in this place enough to start a new life without Morgan in it.

"Do you really even want to know?" Morgan asked.

"Of course I do! I've been so worried about you. I've—I thought I saw you die in front of me and I've been worried about Mom and Dad." Avery's voice sounded rough and she slumped into the soft bed, exhaustion etched in her features.

Morgan's heart tightened. She had felt the same way. And now Morgan was with Avery, leaving their parents with two missing daughters. She didn't know how they could possibly cope with that loss. She'd seen the devastation Avery's disappearance had caused her parents.

"Yeah. Me being here is going to break them. You have no idea how hard your disappearance has been on them. On everyone, really. I'll tell you my truly messed up story of how I survived, but first can I get a shower or whatever is the fae equivalent? I'm still in these wet jeans and I'm freezing."

Avery's face looked like it was going to crack, like she was going to be spilling tears in a matter of moments. She'd always been able to cry at the drop of a hat. It was one of those things that drove Morgan crazy when they were kids. But this was different. These tears weren't over some petty argument. They were because her sister was hurting. Morgan moved onto the bed, damp clothes against the crisp, white bedding. She pulled her sister in close for a hug.

"Ave, how are we going to get home?" Morgan asked.

Avery just shook her head. After a long stretch of time, she whispered, "We can't."

Chapter 3

Avery

Avery sat in silence as her sister bathed in the other room. She'd set out a nightgown and underwear for her and placed Morgan's wet clothes out on the balcony to dry. Morgan had been so much angrier at Avery than she'd ever expected. She understood what it looked like. That she'd been actually enjoying a comfortable life in Aeritis since she disappeared. But that wasn't accurate at all. Her time in Aeritis had been mostly terrifying with moments of unexpected joy and love.

A knock at the door brought Avery back into the room. Deep down she hoped it wasn't Savine. She needed to actually talk with Morgan first before she brought him around her sister.

"Who is it?" Avery asked as she walked across the room to the door.

"It's Kyla. Savine told me where I would find your room," Kyla responded.

Avery paused before she opened the door. Savine's sister had healed her when she first arrived in Aeritis, and maybe she was the one who saved her sister? She wasn't sure on the details, but Kyla wasn't in Rylo's throne room when she'd attempted to assassinate Jasper. If she was the one to save Morgan and get her to Avery, then Avery was indebted to Kyla. Just as Kyla thought she was indebted to Avery for saving her soulmate, Garnel's life.

Regardless of what Kyla thought, Avery didn't fully trust her. Not after she realized Kyla could manipulate her emotions with a simple touch. It felt wrong that someone could do that. Kyla tended to act before she asked, and Avery didn't want Morgan's emotions manipulated without understanding what Kyla was capable of doing.

She opened the door and took in Kyla's immaculate Latian gown, similar to the one Avery wore. The forest green was the symbol of Latian royalty and like so many things in Aeritis, the gown seemed to tell a story within its stitching. But this story looked like a horrific battle laid out in red thread.

Avery caught Kyla's eye as she studied the intricate dress. "It's the story of the civil war. I've waited years to finally wear it, and have carried it with me everywhere I go, hopeful for the end of the war. I've added images to symbolize each year of the conflict. All twenty-five years of it. Nearly twenty-six if it wasn't for you and your sister. Now we can finally return home and I will add you and Morgan to the story. Thank you, Avery. Without you, this conflict may have never ended."

"No need to thank me. If it wasn't for you, I'd now be dead and Savine would be tortured for the rest of his life. I'm still sorry about your father's death. I know he never treated you or Savine as a father should, but he was still your dad."

"I mourned the loss of my father's love many years ago, Avery. Now is a time to reunite our nation and to celebrate the just and true King of Latiah." Kyla paused as she looked deeper into Avery's room. For some reason, Avery was still holding her back, still unsure if she wanted to welcome Kyla deeper into her private space. Kyla turned to the door before she paused. "How is your sister? I brought you both some food. Soups for warming up, some tea, and bread."

Kyla had brought her a similar meal the first time she'd eaten Latian food, helping restore her after the brutal bear attack on Quartz Mountain. Regardless of what Kyla's essence could do, she meant well. She was trying now, and Avery didn't need to push her away. She opened the door wide enough to allow Kyla to enter.

"Thank you. We appreciate your thoughtfulness. Morgan is in the bath right now. She hasn't told me much yet, but you found her, didn't you?"

Kyla nodded. "I did. I saw her at the bottom of Sapphire Falls and pulled her out. Just like with you, the goddess answered my prayer to communicate with her. I noticed that small black object on her waist, but couldn't imagine it had the potential to kill the king."

Avery poured a cup of tea for herself and for Kyla. She kept her voice low as she spoke to Kyla. "That's a gun. My sister must have gotten one after I disappeared. I never even knew she had an interest in carrying a gun." Avery shook her head. Her sister's behavior had been so out of the ordinary. Obviously, the bear attack had rattled Morgan to her core, especially for her to now be walking around with a loaded gun in a holster.

Avery needed to check on Morgan, but she couldn't resist finding out how Savine was doing. They'd been through a lot today, and she felt disjointed, not being able to check in with him.

"How is Savine coping?"

Kyla gave Avery a sad smile. "He's doing well, considering the circumstances surrounding Jasper's ending. Your kidnapping and Rylo forcing you to kill Jasper before you were ready shook Savine. I would have suspected that he wouldn't let you out of his sight for years to come. But, he's handling your decision to stay here with Morgan better than I would have expected. He has little choice in the matter, doesn't he?"

Avery wondered if Kyla was judging her for her decision to stay with Morgan in Nephel for a month. She suspected that Kyla would never abandon Garnel for an entire month, but this was her sister and she couldn't leave her alone. Not after what Avery had been through on her own in Aeritis.

"I want to see him soon. I know I need to talk with him, but not yet. Morgan's been keeping something from me, but I think she wants to tell me," Avery said, sighing. Suddenly, her whole body felt exhausted. Like the weight of everything they had experienced rushed at her, threatening to send her spiraling.

Kyla's eyes widened. She could sense Avery's emotions, no doubt. But she didn't say anything about her sudden exhaustion and overwhelm. "I understand. I need to be with the council. We are planning a quick departure for Latiah with our troops, cutting up to Orofine along the river valley. I hope your sister feels comfortable sharing her experience with you. If you need anything, I am here for you, always Avery." Kyla paused in the doorway. "Oh! I almost forgot. I have something of yours."

Kyla turned and picked up Avery's backpack from the hallway. It was repacked and the iron axe that Savine had gifted her was strapped to the outside of the pack.

Avery choked back a cry at seeing her bag. Yes, it was silly of her to care this much about her last items from Montana, but she couldn't help it. They'd helped her survive in this world and she felt empty without them. She gave Kyla a quick hug. "Thank you so much, Kyla."

After Kyla left, Avery heard Morgan getting out of the bath. The drain gurgled as the tub emptied and Morgan emerged from the bathroom wearing the formless nightgown Avery had left her. She made a dramatic twirl before she walked over to Avery's backpack.

"What's all this?" Morgan asked.

"Kyla, the woman who found you brought food and my backpack by. She's Savine's sister."

Morgan's face softened as she touched the bag. "You still have your bag."

Avery smiled at her, nodding. "I was really lucky to have it. It's been a lifeline to have a piece of our world with me. I even have a full external battery to charge my phone one last time. I've taken some pictures and I don't know what I want that last charge to be used for. Something fun or some way to remind me of home, I think."

Morgan pointed to the bathroom, her phone visible on the floor. "My phone isn't working. You're lucky you have your stuff."

"My clothes are ruined except for my fleece and my rain gear, but you're welcome to anything you need in there."

Morgan gave her a tiny smile, moving across the room to the food tray. "Thanks. Is this the food?"

"It is. It's safe to eat, but *never* accept food from a fae you don't completely trust. They can't lie like we can, but they love to bend the truth and extract truths from others. If you eat or drink something that a fae gives you, you're basically under their control. They can ask you anything and your body will force the truth out of you. Believe me, it's not pleasant."

Morgan poured herself a cup of tea and took a bowl of soup, still piping hot, thanks to the essence from a cook in the Towers. "I'm guessing you had to learn that the hard way."

"Unfortunately. And it wasn't only once. There's so much I need to tell you to help you adjust to this place, but first tell me your story."

Morgan sighed and took in a spoonful of soup. After she swallowed she said, "I'll just be direct. That bear wasn't any normal bear. He was some sort of a monster. He could transform from a bear into one of those elf looking humanoids. The fae."

Avery couldn't hold in her astonished gasp. The bear was actually one of the fae? If he was fae, then that means they could pass into their realm too. She didn't want to interrupt her sister further, so she held in her questions while Morgan continued her story.

"I don't think he wanted me dead, but I couldn't understand anything he was saying. I was getting an infection from my injuries, and I thought if I didn't get away I would die." Morgan sucked in a breath, her hands shaking as she continued. "As luck would have it, we were in an abandoned mine shaft and I found an iron pipe. I bashed him in the stomach with the pipe, then on the head. I kept bashing him until he was dead and I don't regret it. I did what I needed to get out of there, but when search and rescue returned to the cave, there wasn't a body. Nothing. People think I'm crazy or I hallucinated the whole thing. But I survived, and I guess that's what really matters."

Tears streamed down her sister's face, streaking down the raised purple scars on her cheeks. God, how could her sister have had to suffer so much? Avery scooted her chair to her sister and pulled Morgan into a hug as she let out a deep, mournful sob. Avery wouldn't let go while Morgan sunk her face into Avery's shoulder, her body shaking as she held her tight. Finally, Morgan let go, her face puffy from crying.

"I can't even imagine what you've been through. Did Mom and Dad believe you?" Avery asked.

The long sigh told Avery all she needed to know. "The idea of a pointy-eared shifting bear-fae, or whatever you called them, isn't exactly an acceptable explanation when it comes to a bear attack and missing person story. They were trying hard to support me, while dealing with your disappearance. They didn't believe me, but they did care for me. I think they needed me as much as I've needed them over the past few weeks. Since I got out of the hospital, I've been staying at their house. I wasn't ready to go back home yet."

Morgan let out another long sigh. Avery could see the exhaustion on her face. She should let her sister get some rest, but there were so many things that weren't adding up.

"Do you know how you got here?" Avery's voice was quiet as she asked the question. She thought back to her own journey to Quartz Mountain and the terror and confusion that came with her experience.

"I think so. Back at Quartz Mountain, the last thing I remembered before I lost consciousness was the bright light and the high pitched sound. I didn't see you disappear. Honestly, I thought I was dying when it happened. But, the sound and the light happened again this evening, and I knew at that moment it had to be linked to your disappearance.

"I went for a drive to get away from Mom and Dad. It's been... intense just seeing them band together and work nonstop to try and find you. I went over to Sapphire Falls and while I was looking over the railing I started to hear your voice. You were screaming for me and the next thing I knew I was falling down the waterfall with that bright light and ringing sound. When I came to, I was on the shore and Kyla was helping me up. She touched my head and I could understand her. But I'm confused by that. We're speaking English now, how can we speak another language?"

Avery shrugged. "I don't understand it either, but Kyla said she prayed to the Goddess for my ability to understand their language. I guess her prayer was answered, because I can read and speak the fae language."

Morgan's face looked puzzled, but she didn't say anything.

Avery thought of her parents, of how desperate they must be now that Morgan was missing. "I wish there was something I could do to help Mom and Dad. I wish I could let them know I'm okay. What I still don't understand, if you don't mind me asking, is how did you end up with a gun?"

Morgan's face looked stone cold as she turned her head and looked out the window to the balcony. She rubbed her neck, the tension in her muscles obvious even to Avery.

"I bought it after I was out of the hospital. After that thing's body wasn't found in the mine shaft, I was scared he would come back for me. So I've been carrying it everywhere I go. I want my concealed carry license. But until it comes in, I've been open carrying. I want it back as well. I don't trust these creatures."

In some way, it made sense to Avery that Morgan would do this. She'd always liked to have control over her life. Always calculating every potential variable to her success and comfort. So if she felt like her life was threatened, she'd do everything she could to account for that potential danger.

Avery wanted to reassure her in some way. "You don't have to worry about that, Morgan. The fae can't tolerate iron. If it gets in their blood, they die. The fae that attacked you is dead."

Morgan glanced toward the door, a cold look on her face. It sent a chill down Avery's spine and Avery felt her sister's cool shadows circle their feet. Did Morgan even know she was performing magic?

"We can try to get your gun back, but for now, I just got my axe back and this knife, if it makes you feel better." Avery took out her knife and gave it to her sister. It wasn't the same iron knife that Savine gave her, but it was better than nothing. "Keep it. Wear it on you if it makes you feel better. I have a lot to tell you too, but after the day we both had,

I think we need to get some rest." Avery looked down at the splendid gown she still wore. "Before I change and get into bed I should go talk to Savine. There's an insane amount of locks on this door, so just lock them behind me and I'll use my keys to get back in."

Morgan yawned. "Yeah, sleep sounds like a smart idea. This was a horrible day, but I'm happy I know you're alive now."

Avery smiled at her sister as she pulled her into a hug. "I'm so happy you're with me, Morgan. Things may seem messed up right now, but I promise we'll figure it out together."

As Avery left the room, she watched the fae lights dim and heard her sister sleepily say, "Goodnight, Ave."

Chapter 4

Savine

"We should make our way to Orofine as soon as possible," Raikin said for what must have been the fiftieth time since Jasper's death.

If it wasn't for everyone else, Savine suspected that Raikin would have them packed and traveling on their elk at this point. But, considering the events that unfolded, Savine had no plans on racing away from the Towers.

"Stop pushing the issue, Raikin," Savine growled in a tone that didn't even begin to show the extent of his irritation with his ambassador. "We are not going anywhere tonight. I wear the boughs and the antlers. Everything else will fall into place."

Savine had met with his council in a spacious parlor that Rylo had made a show of his alleged generosity in sharing with Savine and his advisers. The room was more ornate than Savine's tastes, with marble flooring and black velvet couches meant to accommodate wings.

"I, for one, would just like to know if I'm sleeping in a traveling tent, or if Rylo is going to bother with giving me accommodations," Garnel muttered from beside Kyla.

"I don't think it would be wise for you and Kyla to stay in the Towers. You need to stay with the warriors and the elk. If it wasn't for Avery, we would all be joining you in traveling tents. But I'm not leaving her in the Towers alone," Savine said.

Garnel snarled slightly, but didn't argue with Savine.

Jay stood and motioned to the room. "Then if we're done here, I'd like Raikin and I to join the warriors too. I've been gone from the elk for too long as it is, and with so many of them here, I need to make sure they're being cared for properly," Jay said as he stood and tugged on his mate's hand. Raikin stood up, his green eyes shining with disappointment.

"If we're not traveling tonight, could we not just enjoy an actual bed?" Raikin argued with his soulmate.

Jay just shook his head before he placed a tender kiss on Raikin's pale hand. "I've had my fill of the indoors."

Just then, Savine heard a knock on the door. Jay opened it and smiled in that broad, welcoming grin of his. His dimples popped as he let go of Raikin's hand and took Avery's. She was still wearing the same dress she had been wearing to the assassination attempt, and despite her disheveled hair and tired eyes, she looked every bit the queen he wanted by his side when he entered his kingdom.

His heart fluttered as he watched her search the room for him. Her sweet mouth warmed into a smile when her eyes met his. Despite all the odds, she was alive. His own witchy soulmate.

Savine crossed the room and pulled Avery into a hug. The bond was there, tugging and pulling at him to bring her as close to him as he could. "Little Flower," he murmured in her ear. "You look beautiful."

He felt her shift onto her tiptoes and he bent his head lower to hers. Her warm, small hands stroked the crown resting on his forehead. "You look good too, old man"

Savine couldn't suppress the smile on his face. "Let's get out of here."

Avery entwined her hand in his as she said, "Lead the way, your highness."

Savine couldn't get her close enough to him. He'd been patient as she took her sister out of the throne room and back to her bedroom. He'd resisted the urge to go check on her, to make sure she wasn't harmed by the ordeals she'd experienced that evening. But now that she was here, there was no resisting the need to hold her in his arms, to breathe in her honeysuckle and mint scent.

He reached down and scooped her into his arms. She melted into his embrace with such tenderness that he never wanted to let her slip away again. "I'm here, Savine. I'm safe and I'm yours," she whispered into his ear before she pressed her lips to the pointed edge of his fae ears.

Garnel looked at them with a smirk that in other circumstances he would have called him out for, but he had no desire to be the grumpy, brooding rebel leader now.

All that was in the past. He was king now, and he had his soulmate. For the first time in Savine's life he might actually have a chance at happiness.

He carried her to a large balcony designed for private rendezvous. He didn't want to point out how he knew about this place. Those old memories always threatened to push themselves forward, but now was not the time for him to think about his past and the hurt he'd experienced in the Towers.

Savine set Avery down on a low outdoor couch. A fire blazed in a large ring, keeping them warm as they sat in the cool night air. Overhead were the thousands of stars, brilliant and clear. This view was what the Towers were famous for.

Avery leaned her head back, staring at the stars. Goosebumps prickled her skin and he immediately went to retrieve a blanket for her. Avery was still transfixed by the night's sky when he returned. As he sat down beside her, he tucked the blanket around both of them.

"It's incredible, isn't it? I've never seen this many stars before," Avery said as she nestled her head against his chest.

"Do you see that constellation there?" Savine asked as he traced out a cluster of stars in a row. "That's Gaia, the premier goddess' twin sister. Legend has it that she was the goddess who ruled over the witches and the humans, and all witches were her descendants. She disappeared the day of the Cleaving."

Savine shifted his hand to their right, tracing a long line of stars. "This constellation is called 'goddess tears'. It's said to grow each year as Althea mourns her lost sister."

Avery leaned in closer to Savine, her cheeks pressed against the exposed skin on his chest and her hand made lazy circles, tracing the lines of his essence. "Why does everything here have to be so damn sad? Do fae have any happy tales?"

Savine chuckled as he kissed the top of her head. "Ours. Our tale is a happy one."

Avery smiled up at Savine, but it was laced in sadness. "It would have been a sad story if my sister didn't show up when she did."

"But she did show up, and that's what matters." Savine paused, thinking about Morgan and Rylo's insistence to keep her in Nephel. "I only wish I could take her with us. I want you to come to Orofine with me now. I understand why you want to protect Morgan, but it would make me feel better if you stayed near me." Savine's chest tightened as he spoke. He didn't want to make Avery angry about this matter, but it physically hurt his heart to imagine being without her at his side again.

Avery pushed herself up a little, leaning away from Savine. She still wore that same sad smile, but this time her chin was quivering slightly. "Knowing what you've been through here, I get it. I mean, hell, even knowing what I've been through! But that's why I can't just leave her."

Savine hated knowing that Avery was right. He wanted to flee with her, to leave the Towers and never return. But Avery was loyal to her sister, and Morgan must be distraught from the evening's events. There was no reason to make Avery upset with him by trying to convince her to abandon her sister.

"How is she taking all of this?" Savine asked

"Honestly, she's doing better than I did. But she told me something that's going to shock you."

Savine's essence squirmed. "Tell me."

"The bear that attacked us wasn't a normal bear. It was a Latian shifter. He took her to an abandoned mine shaft and she hit him with an old iron pipe." Avery frowned and ran her fingers through her hair.

"There is a way for us to cross into your realm? Why haven't we ever heard of such a thing?" Savine stared into Avery's dark eyes as she shook her head.

"Maybe they can't get back? It could be a one way portal on each side. But what I don't understand is how he could shift into fae form on Earth. We don't have magic. And how has nobody noticed fae warriors walking around? Are there ever folk who go missing here?"

Savine shook his head as he thought. "Folk go missing, but we live in a dangerous world. It's not out of the ordinary for someone to disappear."

"Well, it adds a whole other element to me being here, doesn't it? Morgan said she kept expecting him to kill her, but he didn't."

Savine thought about the prophecy. "I heard the prophecy Rylo mentioned the same night my grandfather gave up his essence and my mother was killed. I always thought I was the only one who heard it, and honestly I didn't give it much thought, with all that happened that night. But now we know Rylo heard it, that means others may have also. Rylo figured out it was talking about two witches. What if my father knew?" Savine felt his heart tighten. He couldn't risk losing Avery. Not now.

Avery sighed. "The prophecy and knowing that Morgan killed Jasper complicates things for us. I can't leave her, Savine. And Rylo made an oath not to hurt me. I'm probably safer here than in Orofine. At least until you gain control there."

Savine growled. He wasn't going to fight her, and yet he couldn't stop himself from saying, "You're safest with me. We shouldn't be apart."

She shook her head before leaning back into Savine. "I don't want you to think that I don't want to be there with you when you re-enter Orofine. I really do! But, I think it's a good thing for you to return to the city without me."

Savine felt a rise of frustration in him. He wanted to push it down. Everything she was saying made sense, but it didn't make it any easier for him to accept. Her words felt like a rejection.

"I have spent most of my life convinced I couldn't have a soulmate, that I was unlovable. And I only just found out all the lies I believed aren't true. There is someone for me. Letting you go after all that, even if it is for a month, hurts. It's not what I want and I'm afraid..."

Savine cut himself off. He couldn't say that he was afraid Avery would reject him and their bond, but that thought was at the forefront of his mind.

Avery slid back from Savine before she climbed into his lap, both legs hugging against his hips. The slit in the Latian green dress revealed her muscular thigh on one leg and Savine let his hand drift there, squeezing her soft body.

She looked into his eyes and all he could see was the reflection of starlight in those dark pools. "Savine, I want you. I'm not rejecting you or the bond. I just want you to have a chance to establish order in Orofine. And I need to be with Morgan."

Avery lifted her hands to his cheeks, playing with his beard before she pressed her lips to his in a kiss that was so tender it made Savine's heart pound and ache at the same time. Her soft lips brushed his, pressing deeper as he opened for her, letting her tongue sweep into his mouth in soft, languid strokes.

She pulled back and looked at him with a passion that took his breath away. "I want you to know that I'm not leaving you. Do you want to do the bond thing tonight?"

Savine twisted his fingers in Avery's wavy, golden strands and thought about their bond. Did he really want to take that step with Avery in this place that had haunted his past for so many years? The answer was a resounding no. He could wait. This was important enough to wait until they were both safely in Orofine. Plus, he needed her to understand how serious the soulmate bond would be. She seemed eager to accept him, but he feared she lacked an understanding of how life altering this choice would be.

"Not here. I—I don't want that moment attached to this place. And... I worry you don't understand how serious this choice is," Savine said, his voice not hiding his emotions. He wanted her. It nearly consumed him, this need to bond with her. But not now. He'd been patient and could continue a bit longer.

Avery pursed her lips. "This place holds a lot of terrible memories for you, and maybe you're right about waiting. I promise you I will be by your side in a month, and I won't leave you again. We'll keep

Morgan safe. I have no intention of keeping my promise to return her to Nephel."

Savine smiled. Of course she was lying about letting her sister return to Nephel. He should have known that was her plan. "My sweet little liar."

Chapter 5

Kyla

"Are you sure we should try for a child so soon?" Garnel asked, his hand stroking Kyla's thigh as they sat together on their sleeping mat in the traveling tent.

Kyla bit her lower lip. "This was always what we talked about. Once we were at peace, we would grow our family. I don't want to wait any longer to release my fertility."

Garnel shook his head. "Everything has changed so quickly. We're not even to Orofine yet. Why do this now?"

Kyla placed her hands on his, interlacing her smaller fingers with his larger ones. "Don't worry, Garnel. Inducing ovulation isn't easy. It will take several tries, and a lot of my essence, to make it work. I just want to try for the first time tonight. That's all."

Garnel pressed his lips to Kyla's. The tender touch made Kyla's heart beat like a drum. Would he agree to do this with her tonight? She'd waited so long, wanted more than anything to see peace in her nation and to finally begin a family with her soulmate.

And now it was here.

She didn't want to wait any longer.

Kyla thought Garnel felt the same way as she did. So many late night conversations about the child they would have together, about the life they would give that child.

"Alright, my love," Garnel whispered into her ear. "We'll give our child what neither of us had."

Kyla smiled up at him. "Love."

Kyla woke from her sleep and she could feel her soul traveling to another place. A mountain that was stiflingly hot, and yet the breeze around her cooled the flush in her skin. There was something pulling her to this place, and she could do nothing to stop the draw as she rushed forward into a dazzling throne room made of pure amethyst.

She walked around the room, taking in the beauty and riches in the space. A large, sparkling throne was carved out of the largest crystal Kyla had ever seen. The pure, clear stone allowed light to shine through the room. Surely this was a royal's residence, but who did this splendor belong to?

A woman's voice, deep and powerful, shook Kyla to her marrow. "You have done well, my daughter."

Kyla looked around the room. She couldn't find anyone in the glimmering space. "Hello? Where am I?" she asked, but nobody responded.

Kyla walked toward a tall, arched window and looked out to see a vibrant valley below with a wide river flowing through golden fields. Bright autumn colors shone, and even the larch were resplendent in yellow needles. Steam rose across the valley and water gushed forth from geysers. Far in the distance, Kyla saw a deep, tumultuous red stain flowing across the land. A lava flow.

Fire on the mountain.

A chill went down her spine as she realized where she was. There was only one place in Aeritis where lava flowed freely—the caldera near Amethyst Peak, the home of Althea with the entrance to the Abyss below her famed mountain.

"The False King is dead at long last. You have used my gifts wisely," the voice said, filling Kyla's every sense with pure, untapped power. Kyla reached out with her essence to find where the emotions from this being were coming from, but she couldn't sense any emotions in the room. All that was there was a void so expansive that Kyla felt it would devour her essence if she pressed it further.

She stumbled back as she fell to the floor, the emotionless, raw power thrumming through her.

"Where am I?" she said, barely above a whimper.

A woman appeared before her. Taller than any woman she'd seen, the deity wore nothing over her dark green skin. On her head grew the antlers of a great elk and her essence swirled in a brilliant mix of starlight and gleaming minerals. The woman's blue eyes seemed to roar with the current of a glacial melt river. Her clawed hands pointed down to Kyla, and Kyla shielded her eyes from the radiant brilliance before her.

Kyla knew without a doubt that she was, indeed, in the presence of the Premier Goddess Althea. She prostrated herself before the Goddess, fear and awe coursing through her veins.

"Mother Althea. I am blessed to be before you!" Kyla said, pressing her forehead into the cold crystal floor.

A chill went down Kyla's spine as a claw brushed through her hair. "Rise, my daughter," the Goddess said.

Kyla stood on shaking legs in front of her most sacred deity. She couldn't utter a word as the Goddess' power pulsed against her skin. The force of Althea's essence swirled around Kyla, making it difficult for her to draw a breath without choking on the energy surrounding her. She bowed her head low, her eyes burning from the sight of the Goddess' magnificence.

"I shall give you a blessing for your good faith, my daughter." Kyla felt a rigid, black tipped claw touch her chin as Althea raised Kyla's head to meet her icy gaze. A sharp-toothed smile met Kyla, beautiful and terrible at once, as the Goddess leaned in closer to Kyla's face. Kyla gasped as the Goddess brought her lips to her forehead. Warmth and bitter cold, pain and comfort, flowed from Kyla's face and through her body, sending her into a convulsion. With the tenderness of a mother, Althea drew Kyla close to her and helped her to the floor. Kyla's face burned as the searing mark made her vision blur from the pain.

"Go, my child. You have proved your worth in protecting the witches. Help them to restore the Divine Five and you shall be greatly rewarded," Althea whispered into Kyla's ear as Kyla drifted into a deep sleep.

"Wake up! Please, Kyla! Wake up!"

Garnel's muffled voice felt far away, like she was hearing his cries from underwater. Again she heard her name cried out, but this time it was from Jay. He spoke in a tone that Kyla didn't remember hearing from him before—desperate and afraid, like he was facing an unspeakable danger.

"Please, my love, please," Garnel pleaded. His desperation and the writhing bond between them snapped Kyla out of whatever held her back from her soulmate, and Kyla's eyes opened to Garnel cradling her body in his strong arms.

Her heart was racing and her body shook. Kyla gasped for a deep breath, looking at the fear in Garnel's and Jay's eyes.

Garnel's face turned ashen as he tentatively stroked Kyla's forehead. "You're back, my love. You came back to me."

Kyla just stared at him in disbelief. Back? She hadn't gone anywhere. She'd had a bad dream, that was all.

"I—I never left you," Kyla muttered.

Garnel shook his head as he invited Jay to sit in the tight space of the traveling tent. "You're welcome to wait with us for Raikin and Savine."

Concern etched Jay's face as he sat down beside Garnel.

"What happened to me?" Kyla asked. "All I remember is the nightmare."

Garnel shook his head. "You were in my arms one moment, and the next you were gone. Vanished into nothing. I searched for you, but you were gone. I ran to Jay and Raikin. Raikin went to get Savine while Jay and I looked everywhere for you, but you were nowhere. We returned to the tent and you reappeared before our eyes. But you were shaking so hard, your eyes rolled back in your head. And the mark—the mark was glowing like a hot coal on your forehead." Garnel choked out the last words, and all Kyla could do was stare at him in stunned silence.

Finally, Jay spoke, a gentle hand on hers. "You bear the mark of the Goddess now, Kyla."

Kyla's eyes widened in disbelief. "But it was only a dream. It wasn't real. *Nobody* but the minor goddesses and priestesses could bear to be in the Premier Goddess' glory."

The tent rustled as Savine asked, "Did you find her?" He looked at her, brows furrowed. "The goddess mark. Kyla, how?"

Kyla just shook her head and looked at the already too tight space. "We need to move inside the Towers. We can't fit four fae men in here."

Savine shook his head. "Rylo saw through Avery's glamour. He'll see your mark and have questions."

Raikin scowled as he took in their surroundings. "It's safer here. I'll glamour the tent to prevent our voices from carrying."

The four fae warriors and Kyla squeezed into the tiny tent as Kyla began her story.

It was nearly dawn when Kyla finished sharing the dream that appeared to be more than she expected. The four men, who she loved more than any other, stared at her, none daring to speak.

Finally, it was Garnel who cut the tension in the room. "We always knew there had to be more to the Goddess' unusually high rate of answering your prayers. Now she's revealed your calling."

"But what are the Divine Five?" Raikin asked, pursing his lips as he paused. "And why would she want these humans to find them for her?"

Jay laughed, shaking his head as he said, "One of us should have studied history more closely."

"We were otherwise preoccupied, I'm afraid," Raikin replied. "I'm sure that library of Rylo's has an answer, but do not speak of this to him."

Savine nodded. "I'll ask Avery how she could hide the mark. Humans must have some trick to hide things without an essence. This is going to change your role in Latiah's reconstruction. Althea herself has given you a task."

Kyla felt her chest tighten. All she ever wanted was to help her country return to the peace and prosperity that it had known before her father's reign. Now that he was gone, she thought it was finally time to see her dreams come true. But no, she could already see by the scowl on her brother's face that he was thinking of other plans for her. Plans, no doubt, she didn't want.

She pressed her hand to her lower belly. She'd released her fertility tonight. These sorts of things took time for fae to release, but there was a chance she could already have a child quickening in her womb. Why had she been so reckless? Why did she think now would be a good time to start a family, when there were so many unknowns?

And now this new burden—Kyla didn't even know where to begin to find out what the Divine Five were.

Chapter 6

Morgan

Soft, low sunlight drifted into the room as Morgan stirred. She realized that after Avery got in bed that she'd slept deeper than she'd slept since reducing her pain medication for her injuries. Next to her, Avery slept soundly. No doubt she was exhausted after the previous day.

Morgan slipped out of the covers and padded to the balcony door. Her breath caught in her throat as she felt the chill of a fall wind rush past her. Looking out across the morning sky, she saw just how high up in this tower she was. Far, far below her, down at least three hundred feet was the river that she had been transported to. The whitewater of the waterfall was nothing but a speck on the landscape. Would she return home if she jumped off the waterfall? Did this portal work both ways, or was she trapped in this place, like Avery claimed?

She had hundreds of questions for Avery about what she'd learned of this place and what her plan was to get back home, but she wasn't about to wake her sister up and badger her with her questions. Morgan suspected that her sister wasn't as interested in leaving this place as she had let on last night. She heard how Savine, that big, handsome man with the strange crown and tattooed skin, had called her twin sister his soulmate. Yeah, Avery was going to have to do *a lot* of explaining this morning.

Across the canyon, Morgan saw other towers jutting out of the landscape and winged fairies, or fae as Avery had called them, flying between the massive buildings. At least these winged creatures didn't remind her as much of the monster that had taken her on Quartz Mountain. If she didn't notice their pointy ears, she'd think they were angels. Super hot angels, with chiseled features and a strange glow to them, but angels nonetheless.

"Morgan!" Avery called out, her voice frantic.

She stepped back into the room to see Avery standing beside the bed, hair tousled into a mess of waves and tangles.

"I'm here. I was just checking out the view," Morgan said with a smirk.

"Oh, good. You scared me. Has Edet come by with breakfast? She usually does by now," Avery said as she walked to the door.

"Daily breakfast in bed? You really are becoming a princess, Ave. You'll never want to go home after getting used to this type of lifestyle." Morgan's words came out harsher than she intended. She wanted to joke with her sister, but there was an undeniable bite to her tone.

Avery sighed as she pushed in two trays of food on a cart, a tea set for two, and fresh juice. "Usually Edet comes in. She's a terrible gossip and likes to catch Savine and me..."

Avery's voice trailed off as she looked down. Morgan pursed her lips as she looked at her sister. "Savine and me what?"

"Oh, nothing," Avery said, her cheeks glowing crimson.

Morgan let out a huff as she removed the cover on her tray. The food smelled delicious, a mingling of rich, delicate flavors. It seemed to be some sort of egg dish mixed with sauteed vegetables and berries on the side.

Avery slipped into the bathroom, and Morgan noticed the red stain left on the bed.

"No!" Avery called from the bathroom. "I just started my period! I don't have anything in my backpack either."

Morgan grabbed a cloth napkin from the breakfast tray before bringing it to her sister. "Here, this isn't ideal, but it should help until you figure out something else."

"Thanks," Avery said, taking the napkin before Morgan left her sister alone. She kept talking, despite the door between them. "My period was late—I guess from stress. I knew it was late, but I was a little relieved it hadn't come yet. The fae have a freaky sense of smell, so this is probably going to be awkward for a few days."

Morgan grimaced. "I've never been so happy to have an IUD. I haven't had a period in over a year."

Avery came out of the bathroom, sitting beside Morgan at the table as she poured herself some tea and assessed the meal before them. "So hygiene wise: I have a feeling that having my period here is going to be horrible. Like medieval level."

Morgan shrugged. It seemed like they had bigger issues to deal with than her sister's menstrual cycle. Avery took off the lid of her breakfast tray.

"Just so you know, the Nephel eat all kinds of weird eggs. I think it has something to do with them being the sky kingdom and all, but that is definitely not made out of a chicken egg. In fact, they probably don't even have chickens here. I'm not up to date on all the livestock, but I do know there aren't any horses around here. The Latians ride around on giant elks and moose. Oh, and the Nephel ride on terrifyingly huge eagles called eagans. I got to ride on one too, but I was unconscious."

Morgan felt like she already had a headache coming on from the information overload, and they'd only discussed eggs and a lack of tampons in this world. "Giant elk and eagles? You were unconscious? What's been happening to you here?"

"I told you last night—I was kidnapped by Rylo and taken here. But I'm getting ahead of myself. I need to tell you everything that's happened."

"Yeah. I hope you've figured out a way to get us home," Morgan said as she took a tiny bite of the breakfast. It was more flavorful than she'd expected, like an explosion on her taste buds.

"I don't think going home is possible, but we'll be safe with Savine. Once we're in Orofine we won't have to come back here. The fae can't lie. They still seem to think we wouldn't break an oath, but obviously I'm not above breaking my agreement with Rylo if it means keeping you safe," Avery said as she casually sipped at her tea.

"Aren't you worried about going to Orofine?"

"Of course not. Savine saved me and his folk have kept me alive. He won't let anything happen to us. Meanwhile, Rylo is a crazy demon. I can't wait to get away from him. Are you worried?"

Morgan could feel herself losing patience with her sister. Couldn't she understand what she was saying? "Of course I'm worried! First of all, if there are those shifting bear people, I'm not interested in being there. I'd rather stay with the angel looking people. At least one of them didn't attack us and hold me captive. Second, I just killed these creatures' king. Shouldn't *I* be worried about going to their capital? They could take revenge on me."

Morgan shivered at the thought. She could tell, just based on how everyone was armed, that this was a dangerous place and she didn't want to be anyone's revenge kill. "Not only that, but I want to try and jump off the waterfall. I think I should be able to get home if I do."

Avery shook her head as her eyes widened and her mouth went slack. "Morgan, you can't jump off Sapphire Falls. It will most likely kill you, and there's no way you'll make it back."

Morgan went rigid. Avery was going to fight her on this. "Look, I want to try getting home. I don't care if you think you've found your alleged soulmate and don't want to leave. I can't stay here without trying to go home."

Avery reached over and squeezed Morgan's hand. Her sister's hand was rougher than hers, more calloused, but they always had been thanks to Avery's work outside. Morgan pulled her hand back and looked down at her plate, avoiding her sister's glance.

"I get why you want to try, Morgan. I really do. I even tried too. I returned to Quartz Mountain and tried to go through the portal, but nothing happened. It just broke my heart all over again. You—you could break your body in the process too. I can't watch you die all over again," Avery said with such gentleness that it caught Morgan off guard. "Besides," Avery continued, "Susan tried too, and she couldn't get back either. She's another human trapped here."

Morgan wasn't surprised. If she and Avery had managed to both fall into another realm, then why wouldn't others? "I was wondering how many people ended up getting stuck in this world."

"Maybe more than I thought. Anyway, I think you'll like Susan. She's more knowledgeable about this place and our magic, plus she loves researching the history of witches in Aeritis. Susan came through as a kid and got lucky enough to be adopted by kind folk. She hardly even remembers Montana."

"That's messed up." Morgan's body shook and Avery placed a reassuring hand on hers. Avery's hands were warm against her cold skin, but that was normal. She'd always felt like she had ice in her veins.

After a long silence, Morgan asked, "What do you know about the history of the witches here?"

Avery told Morgan how there were once humans in Aeritis. She shared how magical humans—witches—saved the human race by separating the two realms between Earth and Aeritis. That's when things started getting confusing. There were whisperings of humans in this realm. But, most humans had been killed or died in the journey through the portal. Avery even suggested that Morgan wasn't the first human to enter the realm through Sapphire Falls, and that the Nepheli king had been responsible for their deaths. However, she and Avery were inexplicably chosen by the goddess to fulfill some prophecy. It was all too much for Morgan to take in. She pressed the palms of her hands against her eyes, and sank back in her seat before she looked at her sister.

"So these people think we're here to destroy their land? They're going to kill us off," Morgan said with a heavy sigh. She couldn't believe that she and Avery were trapped in a land like this.

Avery's face flashed with concern. "No, it's not going to be like that. Savine will keep us safe."

"Savine? The supposed *soulmate,* Avery? You trust someone who isn't even part of our species with your life only after a little over a month of knowing him?" Morgan rolled her eyes. Avery had always been slightly gullible, but this was insane.

Hurt shone in Avery's eyes before she said, "You don't have to believe me that he's my soulmate, but I know what I feel, and it's real."

"I know what you feel! You feel good fucking a creature that isn't even human!" It was a low blow, but she still couldn't believe that Avery had spent her time here falling for a creature that claimed to be her soulmate instead of trying to get back home.

Avery stood, hurt shining in her eyes before she took steady steps to the balcony.

Morgan turned back to her tea, which somehow was warm long after it should have been cooled. Just like her bath the previous night. Avery stayed outside, and Morgan didn't bother to go to her. She'd let her sister cool off first before they talked again.

Eventually, she came back into the room. Her eyes were red lined and her cheeks puffy. Avery cleared her throat before she spoke. "You know, last night I thought that this was sort of a dream come true. I don't have to worry every day if you survived the attack, instead I get to have you here with me. But, we always have a way of getting under each other's skin. Even still, I love you. I love you in a way that I can never love someone else. And having you here gives me hope. So yeah, I may not have spent my time here researching how to escape or formulating some grand plan. Yeah, I found someone who I care deeply for, and I want to be happy about that. But we've got to be a team here. There's some messed up stuff in this world and I want to know you've got my back no matter what."

Morgan fidgeted with the cuticle of her nail as she looked at her sister. "Of course. You've got my back and I've got yours. We're not going to let this place tear us apart. I'm sorry I said that about you and Savine. It's just caught me off guard."

Avery came closer to Morgan before she pulled her into a hug. "Good. We stick together. We learn together. And we fight together."

Morgan let out a nervous giggle. "The Hollis sisters: badass fairy fighters."

Avery laughed in return as she pulled away. "Speaking of fairy fighters, we have to train. At least in our magic and self defense. Savine told me I'll never have to fight another battle, and I plan on that being a reality."

Morgan shook her head. A sense of dread coming over her. This was all too real, this nightmare she found herself in. It was easy enough to joke that they'd be fairy fighters, but the reality of that situation sent cold dread through her. "I'm still not ready to commit to anything crazy here. I want to try and get home. Nothing else is as important as finding a way back to Montana."

Chapter 7

Avery

Avery wasn't very surprised that she and Morgan were already arguing. Of course, she wanted to get along, but she was also overwhelmed with a strange mix of excitement mingled with dread that her sister was with her. And she wondered what sort of havoc Morgan would cause in Aeritis with that shadowy magic.

After breakfast, they got dressed in simple, soft tunics and leggings that Edet had provided. She'd had questions when Avery asked for something for her period, and Avery found out that the fae don't even menstruate. Great. Of course they didn't. This was going to be worse than she thought, but she figured she could discreetly ask Susan what she did.

Avery wanted to introduce Morgan to Susan and Rue right away. It would help Morgan to begin to meet fae who weren't a threat, and Rue was just that. Also, she knew Morgan would get some of her questions answered by Susan.

As they stepped into the hallway, Avery expected there to be a guard preventing her from wandering the tower. During the previous days, it was made clear that Avery wasn't being held captive, but she didn't have the freedom to wander without an escort. That seemed to lighten after Savine arrived, but she still felt like any wrong move could leave her trapped in the Tower of Teeth instead of living in luxury and comfort as a guest of Rylo's.

As Avery surveyed the hallway, Morgan looked at her with an expression that was pure fear. "It's okay, Morgan. We're safe. I promise." The jarring scars across Morgan's face seemed to darken as she took a small step out of the bedroom. Avery still couldn't believe that her sister had been so brutally injured and survived to share the story.

"Where do you want to go anyway," Morgan asked as she stepped into the hall.

Avery gave her a quick smile before she turned toward where she suspected Susan and Rue were staying. "I just want you to meet my friends. They've helped me so much here."

Avery's steady footsteps echoed across the red rock of the floor as she crossed to a door that had previously been guarded. She heard Morgan close behind her as she knocked on the heavy wooden door.

Dark skin and sleek raven-black feathers greeted her. Selene was in this room, not Rue and Susan. She'd never suspected Selene to be living in this part of the Towers. Selene, the woman who was responsible for torturing Savine's soul.

"Oh! Selene. I didn't expect to see you here. Sorry, I thought this was Rue and Susan's room," Avery said, feeling embarrassed for the mistake.

Selene just stared at her with violet eyes, a gaze that was cold despite the warmth in their color.

"Avery! In here. Selene, please let her in!" Rue demanded from the room. Selene pursed her lips and let Avery and Morgan in. Immediately, Rue was embracing Avery in a tight hug. "I'm so happy you're okay. Last night was—well it was something I never want to experience again. Seeing you down on the ground, tortured like that? The rest of us were in some sort of a frozen state. I could see everything, but I couldn't move. Only Susan was free, but I think she was too scared to act." Rue turned her head, tight curls bouncing as she looked at Susan, sitting quietly in a chair in the corner.

Avery noticed the pale color in Susan's skin, her glamour gone as she sat in her human form. Avery squeezed Rue's arm as she walked over to Susan. "Hello, friend," Avery said.

"I'm so sorry, Avery. I wasn't there when you needed me most. We could have stopped him together if we'd tried to combine our powers, and when you needed me most I froze. I—I understand if you can't forgive me for what I did." Susan's eyes were rimmed with red. She looked like she'd barely slept.

Avery squeezed her shoulder and knelt down beside her. Susan let her red hair tumble in front of her face as she avoided Avery's eye contact.

"Susan, you don't need to blame yourself! We didn't have time to form a proper plan and I was overwhelmed. If it wasn't for Morgan, we'd probably all be dead." Avery turned and looked at her sister, standing uncomfortably near Selene.

"I should have done something. Your sister just walked in and killed the Latian King without fear! That power she released wouldn't even let anyone near either of you." Susan looked directly at Morgan as she said, "We are honored to have you here, Morgan. All of us, Latian, Bayberry, and Nepheli owe you a life debt."

Morgan shrugged. "I was just trying to save my sister."

Selene made a small scoffing sound from where she stood. Avery raised her eyebrow and stood back up. "What exactly are you doing here, Selene?"

Selene's black wings tucked in tighter, as if she was insulted by the question alone. "I have orders to keep an eye on the Latians until they leave. I was merely doing my rounds."

Rue chirped in, "She was just about to leave, but she was kind enough to have tea with us." She moved closer to Selene, her pinky finger extended as she brushed against Selene's black feathers.

It was almost like Rue enjoyed Selene's company. But Selene was a torturer. She did whatever Rylo instructed her to do, and didn't question his orders. Worst of all, she seemed to delight in causing pain. No, surely Rue didn't actually want to be around Selene.

"I'll be going now. You are all expected to be dressed for supper with King Rylo by evening. Guards will escort you to his private dining room. Gowns, of course, will be provided as I dare say none of you have the appropriate outfits for supper with the king." Before anyone could reply, Selene expanded her wings and walked onto the balcony, leaping into the autumn sky.

Avery would never get used to seeing the Nepheli do that. Fortunately, in only a month, she wouldn't have to be around it.

"They are so weird. Do you think the Nepheli don't know how to say a proper goodbye?" Avery asked to break the awkwardness that settled over the room.

"What do you mean?" Susan asked. The other two women looked at Avery with confusion.

"You know, just jumping out of the building like that. Rylo's done that to me a few times. Anyway... I came over here so Morgan could meet you two."

Rue laughed. "I'd do that too if I could fly! I would never walk anywhere. It's so nice to meet you, Morgan!"

"Nice to meet you both," Morgan said in a monotone voice, not bothering to move from the wall.

"Morgan, Susan is the witch I told you about. And Rue is a shifter fae, but don't worry. She shifts into the cutest little fox!"

Rue batted Avery in the arm. "You may not know this, but calling a shifter 'cute' is considered bad manners. I may be small, but I'm powerful!"

Morgan didn't respond to the information. She was usually so thoughtful with her words and her actions. Now she stood, arms crossed near the door. Maybe it was a mistake to bring her here. She didn't want to make her uncomfortable, but it seemed she'd done just that.

Avery tried to move the conversation forward, but she could see Morgan didn't have much interest in interacting with Susan or Rue.

Finally, Susan caught Avery and Morgan's attention. "I think the three of us have to start training together. I've studied enough about witches that I think we can learn to use our powers together, and prevent ever experiencing something like last night again."

"What do you mean, use our powers together?" Morgan asked, stepping a bit further into the room.

"Well, from your display last night, you have potent magical abilities. You're a natural at wielding your magic. From my adolescence on, I've been reading everything I can on the ancient witches, and your natural ability with shadows was rare. Usually we are more connected to one of the elements—like Avery and her connection to the earth or mine to water. Anyway, when witches formed a coven and learned to wield their magic together, they were virtually unstoppable. That's who separated the two realms in the first place. Witches, like us."

Morgan cocked her head. "So you want us to learn to control our magic together and then what? Kick the shit out of these fae bastards?"

Avery winced as she looked at Rue. Rue had a funny smirk on her face. "Sorry, Rue."

Rue shook her head, "No it's fine. There are plenty of fae bastards who need the shit kicked out of them, and Morgan just took care of one of them. Who should be next? King Rylo? Or should you three head south to take care of King Maglar and Queen Mara next. I heard those cave-dwelling creeps are worse than Jasper."

Avery looked at the frown on Morgan's face. "Avery's right. Rue, I'm sorry. But... I was attacked by one of the fae in my world. They can get through and I don't want anyone else to experience what happened to me. If I can stop them from getting into Montana, I will."

Avery cocked her head at her sister. "I thought you were ready to throw yourself over the waterfall and try to get home."

Morgan crossed her arms across her chest. "Of course I want to go home. But, you said it's most likely not an option. So if I'm stuck here, I won't be spending my time cowering in a corner or looking for my soulmate. No offense, Ave. I want to use whatever magic that we've got to my advantage. I want to stop monsters like the one who attacked me from ever hurting somebody else again."

"I like you already!" Rue laughed. "Would you like to learn how to use a sword? Or maybe knives? No, never mind. You have that small weapon that you used on Jasper."

"I think I should focus on my magic. If that's actually what happened to me last night." Morgan shrugged as she turned her attention to Susan. "Susan, you mentioned studying the history of the witches? Do you have access to books? I want to be prepared for whatever this place is going to hit me with."

Avery couldn't believe her sister was already jumping into formulating a plan to train her magic. It had taken a lot longer for Avery to accept that she had magic. But, she hadn't manifested magic within minutes of landing in Aeritis.

"So you're cool with it here now?" Avery asked incredulously.

Morgan looked like she wanted to snap at her. "No, I'm *not cool with it*, Ave. I want to survive this place and learn everything I can to get home."

Susan tapped her fingers together, concentration on her face. "King Rylo has a vast library. Avery, didn't you see it?"

Morgan's attention snapped from Susan and back to Avery. Oh no. There'd be no stopping her sister if she knew she could get her hands on the information she needed to help her. "Yeah, it's huge. I don't know if Rylo will let us use it though."

"We have a month. We'll use it," Morgan replied. There was a gleam in her green eyes that Avery recognized. Morgan was planning. It was, without a doubt, her favorite thing to do.

Savine

Savine had hardly slept, knowing that he would be leaving Avery soon, and taking his place as the rightful king of Latiah. The irony wasn't lost on him that he'd spent over twenty-five years of having one purpose in life, and now he couldn't stand the thought of fulfilling that purpose if it meant leaving Avery behind. He still didn't like it, but he knew he had hard work to do and he wanted to make sure he set the groundwork for Avery's safe ascent as his queen.

Raikin, of course, had hardly left his side as they talked strategy and politics. The only time he could get Raikin to give him some space was when he had to take a piss. This would be his life from now on. No personal space. No private moments unless he demanded them. It was what he'd prepared for his whole life, but the reality of that new life weighed heavily on him.

Knowing that the Latian loyalists ensconced in Orofine would hear word of Jasper's death before too long, Savine agreed that they needed to leave after Rylo's planned supper between the two leaders. The route to Orofine wasn't nearly as long as traveling to Bayberry, but they still had several days of hard riding before they reached the capital city.

Raikin had managed to procure a fine suit of Latian green for Savine, and Savine sat in a chair as a manservant—perhaps from the far north based on the icy hue of his skin—added various beads to Savine's shoulder length hair. He hated being primped, but understood he needed to look the part of the king tonight. The gilded cedar boughs and crown of antlers wasn't on display at this moment. It was taking some time for him to get used to the sensation of withdrawing the crown into his essence and out of sight. The stinging sensation would probably never go away, but at least he no longer had rivulets of blood etching his head when he pulled the crown in or pushed it out.

Raikin answered a knock on the door. As Savine turned, he saw Avery pass through the doorway. She wore a dress in the Latian-style. The lavender dress was all tight lines and hugging curves on top before it opened into soft billows of skirts. Savine noted how Avery had lost some of her muscle mass since she had arrived in Aeritis. No doubt she hadn't been as active as she was working on trails in Montana. Instead she'd become leaner, thinner. This would need to change. He knew she had been happy and healthy in her former life, and he wanted to see her rounded cheeks and small, powerful muscles. There was no reason for his human to be looking fae thin.

Avery walked straight toward him as Savine stood. She smiled at him and he felt his heart pound in his chest. Goddess alive, he couldn't even look at her without having a physical reaction to her gaze.

"Out, Raikin. Take the others too," Savine ordered.

Raikin bowed, leaving them alone as Avery picked up her speed across the room, launching herself into his arms. Savine didn't hesitate to pull her up as she wrapped her legs around his waist, the layers of her skirt bunched between them. "I missed you," Avery said as she pressed her lips to Savine's.

"I missed you too. You look beautiful, Little Flower," Savine said as he pulled back to memorize her soft features, putting her back on the floor. He smelled the sweetness of her honeysuckle and mint scent—but there was something else there. Avery was injured.

His hand instinctively tightened around Avery's arms as he assessed her. "You're hurt."

Avery shook her head. "I knew your obscenely good sense of smell would catch that. I'm on my period."

A fresh fear built in his chest. What did she mean?

"Don't worry," Avery assured him, lightly placing her hand on his own bicep. "It's totally normal for humans. It usually happens every month, but I think my body's been too stressed, so my period was late. It's... um... Part of the female reproductive system."

Savine cocked his head at her. Was she ready to have his child already? Savine didn't even know what to think of that. He had been sure they weren't ready for a child yet, hadn't even considered it yet.

"Are you in heat, like animals? Or did you release your fertility? So soon?"

Now Avery looked at him with a baffled expression as she also let out a snorting laugh. "No, I'm not in heat like an animal! This is so awkward. Okay, I'm going back to seventh grade science here. Females ovulate typically once a month and if the egg isn't fertilized they have a period. Totally normal human biology here." Her cheeks were flushed with the most delightful crimson glow as she described how her body functioned.

"So you're not ready to have a child?"

Avery stepped back, alarm on her face. "Hell no! I don't want a child! But now that I know female fae don't spontaneously become pregnant, and you would have been completely unprepared for birth control, we're going to need to figure out an option soon. I can only assume you don't normally need to worry about that in the same way humans do."

Savine brushed his mouth against her hair "Just as long as you're okay. I can get used to your human habits. We can ask a healer for some suggestions on preventing a pregnancy."

Avery laughed again. "It's not exactly a habit. But yes, let's do that."

The bond between them grew taut, tugging and pulling for them to accept it, for them to finally be joined. He didn't know how in the Abyss he'd go a whole month without accepting their bond. Without feeling her wrapped in his arms each day.

But there was no sense in reflecting on that. What was done was done. She was staying and he couldn't change her mind. More so, he was beginning to believe keeping her from Orofine was a good idea. He and Raikin had spent the entire day preparing for dozens of scenarios, and there was not a single option that didn't put Avery at risk. Sending her back to Bayberry would have been ideal, but he knew Avery would refuse to leave Morgan behind.

"Enough about me. Haven't you cleaned up nicely? Now, let's see that sparkly crown," Avery said with a nod.

Savine drew his essence forward and in a pop of pain, the crown reappeared on his head.

Avery smirked as she said, "I can better understand how it's impossible to kill the king without retribution, when the damn crown grows out of your head. It looks good on you." Avery smirked and twirled one of her golden waves around her finger.

Savine shook his head. There was a lot that Avery would need to learn about Latian culture when she was in Orofine, but it could wait. He adored her carefree outlook on life, and he wondered if it actually mattered if Avery lacked reverence toward the crown. After all, his father had done an excellent job of making a mockery of the role of king.

"There's something I want you to have tonight. You're not wearing Latian green, but I wanted to remedy that." Savine picked up a box on the side table and opened it, showing Avery the contents of the box. A large, rectangular cut emerald necklace encrusted with smaller emeralds was nestled on satin. Next to it laid identical emerald earrings.

Avery sucked in her breath, her eyes wide as she looked at the jewels. "Oh Savine! They're gorgeous. But how did you get them here?"

"They were once my mother's and my grandmother's before her. Kyla brought them to me this morning. She took them when we fled Orofine and kept them hidden for my future queen," Savine said, his breath catching on his words. "I didn't even know she had them. All these years, she's kept them safe, waiting to give them to me."

Avery's big, brown eyes shone like orbs as he moved around to her back and draped the jewels over her neck. "Savine... Are you sure? I don't deserve to wear these."

Savine felt his essence whirl at the lie she muttered. He naturally felt on the defensive when she talked down about herself. "As my mate, you are the *only* one deserving to wear the queen's emeralds." Her chest rose faster as he led Avery to the mirror. He wanted her to see herself in splendor. Savine moved to her ears, placing the heavy jewels into her lobes. His fingers lingered over the shell of her ear. Goddess alive, he loved all her soft curves.

"But Kyla—" Avery hesitated, and Savine didn't let her get another word in.

"Kyla has no claim to these jewels." Savine pulled Avery close, pressing her back against him as they continued to look at their image in the mirror. He didn't mean for his voice to be so filled with emotion as he said, "Please. Accept them, as my queen."

The color drained from Avery's face as she nodded. "Your queen."

A queasy sensation roiled within him. Was she going to reject him? She looked as though she doubted her place with him, the old pangs of past rejection made him want to push her away and put distance between them before he got hurt again. But he didn't. Despite every instinct to guard his heart and soul, he stayed next to her.

He turned her to face him. "Avery, talk to me."

Her head dropped slightly before she looked him in the eye. "It's just a lot, you know. I'm not qualified to be a queen. Like, fuck Savine, I didn't even want a full time job back at home. And now I'm going to be a monarch? I'm not meant to be a queen."

Savine gently lifted her chin up. "I never thought I would have a soulmate. I didn't think that was even *possible* after what I experienced in the Tower of Teeth. But you're here, and our bond is begging us to complete it. You and me. That's all that matters. Nothing else. And if you don't want to be queen—if you want to spend your days making trails around Orofine, then so be it. If you want to learn to use your magic and find your natural place here, then do that. I will not make you be a monarch." His voice shook and he was overcome with emotion. "But please, do not reject me. Not until you have seen Orofine."

Avery placed her small hand in his. He felt her tremble slightly as she said, "I'm not rejecting you. But Savine, you're a king now. Not a rebel leader. Not a prince. You're king. You are going to have to make the best decisions for your country. What if that's not me?"

"Of course it is!" Savine's tone came out sharp, his own essence pumping in response to her doubts. "I would *never* reject you! You've made it clear that I need this month for my nation, but you will be mine. No more talk about it, let's go to dinner."

Avery shook her head. "Just think about where I'll fit in your new reality."

She turned and began making her way to the door. Savine took a deep breath, trying to keep the unease from devouring him. She wasn't going to stay with him. The woman he'd waited his whole life for was going to run, not because of his past, but because of his future. It was a cruel twist to what he'd always known about himself.

He wasn't worth loving.

Chapter 8

Morgan

Morgan walked up the endless stairs of the Towers corridor, following closely behind Avery's two friends, Susan and Rue. Her heart hurt that her sister had left her alone with strangers and went off to find that king. She felt queasy and sweaty as she tried to follow the others up the stairs. It had only been three weeks since she'd been discharged from the hospital, and she was still taking pain pills to deal with the agony of her broken body's slow healing. Fortunately, she'd had them in her jacket pocket when she went over the falls and had taken one around lunch. There were only six left in the bottle and she shivered to think of the kind of pain she'd be in when they ran out.

Selene had brought her a gown to wear to this supper, and it was the most gorgeous article of clothing that she'd ever worn. But, she felt like something smashed and half mended in the elegant gown. Her broken face could never look beautiful in such splendor. The harsh red lines of her scars hadn't fully healed yet, and the off the shoulder gown revealed her mangled neck and shoulders from where the monster had dragged her down the mountainside in his jaws. She didn't say anything in protest when the gown was brought to her, even when the sight of her reflection made her want to throw up.

"Almost there, Morgan!" Rue called out from a few stairs ahead. "You would think the Nepheli could be a little more hospitable and at least *fly* us to where we need to go. Or, you know, not put our bedroom in the middle of the tower."

Susan giggled and stopped to wait for Morgan to catch up to her. "Are you okay, Morgan? We can take a break if you need one."

Morgan nodded through heavy breathing. Her infection from the attack and her stay in the hospital had left her weak. She'd always been petite, smaller than her sister's muscular body, but after her hard recovery, not even her own clothing felt like they fit her anymore. "Just... give me a minute," Morgan rasped.

Susan nodded and patted Morgan's shoulder. "I'm from a community of healers. I don't know if Avery has told you that yet. I'm not a skilled healer, but I can try to help you. I'm sure Kyla brought some salves, and Avery has been showing a strong aptitude toward healing magically. We can help you recover from this attack."

"Thanks for the offer," Morgan said and paused. "I think I'll be okay." She passed Susan and continued climbing the staircase. She didn't want their pity or sympathy.

Two winged guards waited at the staircase to escort them down a long corridor, past other windows and open balconies. The open air windows exposed a sunset sky of remarkable colors—all pinks, oranges, and reds. The late evening light glimmered off the spires and peaks, revealing a beautiful alpenglow. For how many pane-less windows this place had, it still was a comfortable temperature. Morgan assumed, like her tea and bath, that it was magic that kept the rooms comfortable.

The guards motioned to a wooden door carved with a bas-relief of a woman receiving a shining crown on her head. The sun above sent rays down to her head and the obvious fae crowd knelt before her.

Susan nodded to the guards and Morgan followed close behind her as they entered a large and stately dining room. The long table stretched across the expanse of the room and there were many folk already taking their seats. A few looked up as Morgan and her companions entered, but she immediately put her head down to avoid eye contact.

The woman, Kyla, who had helped her find Avery, came over with an intimidating red-head. He had to be the tallest fae in the room and his body was ripped with corded muscles. The fur tattoo—no, essence—moved slowly under his skin. The sight of it sent a chill down Morgan's back. She felt herself growing clammy as she watched the towering man approach them.

"Morgan!" Kyla exclaimed. "It's so nice to see you again. I wanted you to meet my mate, Garnel."

Just being close to this man made Morgan want to scream and run from the room. He was too much like her attacker, and as she looked around the room, she saw there were dozens of men similar looking to the monster who had hurt her so badly. Morgan couldn't stop herself from shaking as Kyla put a reassuring hand on her arm. She saw Kyla mumble something to the enormous man, and he backed away slowly, turning to talk to a woman who resembled a fish out of water.

Kyla led Morgan to a spacious balcony just past soft, billowy curtains. "Morgan, I'm an empath. I can feel your emotions, and right now I can feel your fear. You don't have to return to that room. I can help you back to your bedroom if you prefer it, or I can help soothe the fear. I can give you some of my essence and change the feelings you are having. But only if you want that. It's your choice, Morgan, but I know this must be very frightening and overwhelming for you to be in a room with so many fae."

Morgan's breathing was still too quick—her heartbeat still too rapid—as she thought through her options. She didn't want to look weak in front of these monsters. Not after she'd already shot one of them. "I can't leave yet. Where's Avery?"

"She and my brother are sitting at the head of the table with King Rylo. Should I get her for you?"

Morgan knew Savine was leaving later tonight. Avery hadn't waited for her before coming to dinner, and she didn't want to bother her now. "No. You said you can remove the fear? How? What can you make me feel instead?"

"I can help you feel calm, happy, brave, whatever you need to get through the night," Kyla said.

Morgan nodded. She wanted to rid herself of the fear that was coursing through her. "Give me courage and confidence. If I'm getting thrown into a pit of wolves, at least arm me with the courage to make it through this meal."

Kyla smiled, showing remarkably white teeth for someone without access to modern dentistry. "Excellent choice. Take a deep breath with me." She laid her hands on Morgan's shoulders and the fear, uncertainty, and pain she'd been experiencing vanished. She felt stronger and more willing to face the room filled with monsters.

Morgan sighed with relief. "That feels good. Thank you, Kyla." As she spoke, she saw Avery pass through the sheer curtains.

"Kyla, please don't do it!" Avery said as she tugged Morgan from Kyla's grasp.

Morgan flinched. "You know she can change a person's emotions?"

"Yeah, it's wrong that she does it without asking." Avery turned to Kyla and snapped, "Kyla, you can't change someone's emotions without their consent." She actually looked angry at Kyla. Morgan noticed the sparkling emeralds that adorned her sister's neck and ears.

Morgan stuck out her hand, touching her sister's wrist. "It's okay, Avery. She asked me if I wanted her to change my emotions and I agreed. I feel better this way."

Avery frowned. "Are you sure you're okay with it?"

"Yeah, I didn't want to spend this dinner feeling terrified." Morgan shrugged and looked into the room. Most of the guests had found their places at the table.

"Okay. As long as it's what *you* want." Avery turned her attention to Kyla. "I'm sorry I jumped to conclusions, Kyla. That was wrong of me."

Kyla just shook her head. "It was me who was wrong that time. I know I've had to earn your trust back, but I won't do it again."

"Alright then. Let's get this dinner over with," Avery said as she walked toward the dining room. "Morgan, you're with me. Remember what I said? *Do not* eat or drink something from someone you don't trust. We can lie, but they can't. However, when one of them directly feeds us or gives us something to drink, they can control what we say. It's like a compulsion or something. You'll be forced to answer their questions."

How would she miss a detail like that? Morgan was already dreading how she'd eat since Avery shared that information. "I didn't forget."

Avery gave a tiny nod. "I'll put food on your plate and Savine will be serving me. Even the servants giving us the food could potentially force us to confess things. Savine won't force anything unwanted on me and I'll just pass some food from my plate to yours. Rue is giving Susan her food."

They slid into their seats, Avery next to Savine and Morgan next to a pale, slight built man with white hair and the greenest eyes she'd ever seen.

The man said, "What an honor to be placed next to you, Morgan." She was sure he was being sarcastic, but couldn't detect sarcasm in his tone. "We wouldn't be gathered here without your quick work. I'm Raikin."

"Thank you? The former king was my first gunshot victim, but maybe not the last here."

Raikin gave her a sinister grin, showing his white teeth. "You may be more useful than any of us realize."

Now it was Morgan's turn to smile. The sensation tugged at the tight skin around her healing scars. "Well, I don't plan to be useless here. That's not in my nature."

At that moment, Avery poured Morgan a glass of dark crimson wine and placed a bit of food on her plate. "Would you like more?" Avery asked.

Morgan shook her head and sipped at the wine. At the head of the table sat the Sun King, Rylo. His wings were draped across his low back chair, relaxed and gleaming gold. She hadn't paid close attention to him the other night, but now she noticed the slight golden glint to his face, almost like he wore makeup. It seemed to fade then grow more distinct as he talked with Savine, like the glow was coming in waves. He was, without question, the most beautiful man she'd ever seen.

From her angle, Savine seemed very uncomfortable. He was hardly eating and the strange marks under his exposed skin seemed to churn uncomfortably. Morgan couldn't make out what they were saying, but the gleam in Rylo's eyes and the frown on Savine's face told her they were arguing.

She watched as her sister put a protective hand on Savine's arm. Immediately the tension in his face relaxed a bit.

"Our king has many difficult memories from this place," Raikin commented. "It will be best for him and for the Latians to leave as soon as this farce of a dinner party is over."

Morgan nodded and took a bite of salad. "And what is your opinion on my sister and I being forced to stay here?"

"It will be easier to have them separated before the bond is accepted, and best for Savine to do the work he was born to do. You and your sister won't come to harm here. If Rylo wanted to harm Avery he would have done so already. Though what he wants with you is another question." Raikin stared at her, looking at the scars on her face and the damaged skin exposed along her neck and shoulders.

"You're staring," Morgan seethed.

Raikin nodded, unabashed. "You'll grow used to it, I am sure. But that rage you have for our kind? That should not be something you give up. Harness it, learn to use those dark shadows you displayed, and everyone will stare at you for your power, not your scars."

Morgan felt a strange sense of pride at his words. *She would become a force here.*

At that moment, Savine and Rylo's voices raised to a crescendo. "You dare to threaten *Avery?* After everything *you* have done to us?" Savine roared as he stood from the table. In far too quick movements, Savine punched the other king in the face, coming back for another strike. Light burst from Rylo and he stood to his full height. They were nearly equal in height, but while Savine was stacked with muscles, Rylo had a leaner build.

Avery grabbed Savine's shoulder. "No! Don't!" she shouted.

Savine froze, his attention drawn to Avery, but Rylo didn't hesitate to strike the Latian king. Guards from both nations moved forward, swords drawn, and Raikin jumped to his feet, ready to defend his king.

"Stop! Both of you!" Avery screamed, drawing Savine close. "We're leaving, Rylo." Morgan watched as her sister took Savine's hand and walked out of the room, side by side with this towering fae man. Morgan's chest tightened as she looked around the room at the folk left gaping. She'd need Kyla to take away the unease brimming at the surface soon.

Rylo stood, his cheek already swelling, and spoke in a voice that seemed equal parts bored and at ease. "It appears our Latian friends have become upset at the dinner conversation. Don't let this end the festivities." He lifted his glass to the guests and drank deeply before returning to his seat.

Raikin sat down again, his face drawn in a poisonous glare at the Sun King. Morgan turned to him and asked, "Should somebody follow them?"

Raikin's cocked his head in the direction that Avery and Savine went. "Savine is with the only person he'd want near him right now."

Avery

Avery and Savine stood on the top terrace of the Towers. The stars were shrouded in thick cloud cover and the scent of moisture hung in the air. Avery knew Savine needed to get outside and cool off after they stormed out of the dinner party. Since it was quicker to go up than down thousands of stairs, she chose to lead him to the place where they were first reunited after Rylo had taken her captive.

Blood spilled from Savine's nose as his breath came in shallow, angry spurts. "Breathe, Savine. It's okay. We're safe," Avery whispered as she pressed her hands to his chest, letting her magic build and flow into him. As her power moved through him, working to heal the obviously broken nose, Savine's breathing became more relaxed. The blood stopped flowing and he pulled Avery tight against his chest. His body wrapped around her possessively and Avery couldn't help but savor these last few moments in his arms.

After several minutes, he finally loosened his hold on her. "I don't like you staying here. Did you hear what he said? If you're not going to comply with your side of the bargain, then he will imprison you and your sister in the Tower of Teeth."

Avery felt queasy at the thought of what Savine had gone through in Rylo's prison tower. "It won't happen, Savine. It's going to be okay."

Savine gave her a gentle shake, his essence writhing. "Avery, you don't know what he can do to you!"

Avery stretched up, tilting her face up as she pulled Savine down and placed a tender kiss on his cheek. "Then I'll be a very good guest for a month and make sure he has no reason to do anything to hurt me or Morgan. But, I'm not leaving her here alone. Once we're in Latiah he won't be able to force me into our agreement."

Savine looked at Avery with skepticism. "There are consequences for not upholding an oath like what you took, Avery. I don't know what they are for a human, but for the fae it can be very serious. Rylo taking an oath to not harm you is the only reason why I'm even considering letting you stay." He paused for a moment. The cool fall air prickled Avery's bare skin as Savine pulled back from her, looking down to the ground far below them. "I told Kyla she needs to stay with you and Morgan. And I want you to ask Rue and Susan to stay too."

Avery nodded. "I don't think Rue and Susan had any plans of leaving me here alone. I'm fine with Kyla staying if she's willing. I know what you're thinking. She can manipulate the Nepheli if she needs to. It's not a bad idea."

Savine pressed his thumb and forefinger to the bridge of his nose. "I can't believe I'm leaving you tonight. This is the most foolish mistake in a lifetime of mistakes. Willfully leaving your side."

He huffed out a breath and pulled Avery close, kissing her hard on the lips. He kissed her like his very life depended on it. Punishing and bruising in its intensity, Avery opened to him and surrendered to his touch. It felt like he was trying to memorize every detail of her, to imprint her being onto his soul.

Finally they pulled back and Avery gasped at the emptiness that came from losing his touch. She felt the strange, coiling tension between them rise, like if they weren't melded together she would lose herself.

"This is going to hurt, isn't it? Being away from you. Damn, it's going to hurt me inside and out to not have you near me," Avery confessed.

Savine responded by kissing her again and Avery lost any thought of the world beyond this man and his embrace. He scooped her into his arms and she felt weightless as her dress billowed around them. She continued to kiss him, working her mouth down his neck as he carried her toward the stairs. With her hands she traced the lines of his essence, trying to memorize every curve and line of Savine's body for the month ahead.

Avery didn't stop him or protest as Savine carried her down all the thousands of stairs in the Tower of the Moon. As he held her, she whispered all the things they would do together once they were reunited. A slow, steady murmur of what they would become and the life they would share.

And she meant it—even if she wasn't sure how they could ever be together. He was a king. He had the weight of a nation on his back, and she had been a carefree girl looking for her next big adventure, with no plans of starting a relationship or looking for stability. Meeting Savine had transformed her life, and she wasn't willing to give up on sharing that life with him, even if all these feelings were terrifying. That was the reason why she hadn't said "I love you" yet. It felt too big and too final to say, and she wasn't ready yet. It was a relief that Savine hadn't asked her to reciprocate those words.

She wanted a life with him, but the barriers to get there felt insurmountable. Avery wasn't a queen, and despite what Savine said, she wasn't sure if she could give him what he needed.

Savine sat Avery down on the ground once they were outside the Tower of the Moon, and Avery realized that this was her first time outside since she arrived in Nephel. It had been the longest time she'd ever been inside, and the ground beneath her seemed to pulse in greeting.

All the Latian fae were assembled, and Avery saw Jay and Gaelyn in action, organizing the elk and gear. Savine squeezed Avery's hand before he let go of her, walking over to Kyla.

Instead of following him, she walked over to Jay as he saddled Jari, Savine's war bull elk. Jari gave a grunt as Avery stroked his black furred neck. "Jay, are you ready to finally go home?" Avery asked.

Jay gave her a friendly smile, "Anywhere I'm with the elk and Raikin, I'm at home. Orofine will bring its own challenges, but I'm not going there right away. Gaelyn and I are traveling back to Bayberry to move the warriors who stayed behind and any others over the pass before the snow falls."

"And Raikin?" Avery asked.

"He and Garnel will be at Savine's side when they enter Orofine. He needs them there, with the warriors to make a show of strength as he takes his throne. Also, I suspect my mate will soon be made Sage."

Avery paused, touching Jari's soft muzzle. "What is the Sage again? I think Rylo said something about it once."

Jay rubbed Jari's neck. "The Sage is the King's second in command, often the voice of the king when he's not available."

"Is that what you want?"

Jay's lip twitched, but that was the only thing that gave away his apprehension. "I want Raikin to be happy. When we accepted our soulmate bond, I knew that being bonded to someone as ambitious as Raikin would mean some sacrifice on my end. But, I've found my place and I support him in his. He will make a good Sage. I can't think of anyone better, and I don't say that just because he is my mate. Raikin has a way of making Savine see reason when Savine allows his demons to overshadow himself."

Avery nodded. She understood exactly what he meant. Savine had been so focused and determined to keep his people safe, to serve their needs over his own, that he had lost himself in the process. She could only imagine that there had been many moments when he needed Raikin's cool sense of convincing to get Savine to make difficult decisions. Even now, Raikin had been on Avery's side that she should stay in Nephel for a month.

Kyla and Savine approached her. They both looked tense, and Kyla's eyes were rimmed red. Kyla leaned in and gently touched Jari's head. "So, I'm to stay with you, Avery. My brother helped me under-stand the importance of my presence here."

Savine gave his sister a demanding look. "Your service here will be most helpful, sister."

"Yes," Kyla snapped. Avery hadn't heard Kyla speak so harshly before, not even to Savine. She turned and began walking to where Avery could see Garnel, laughing with a group of warriors.

"I guess that didn't go well?" Avery asked.

Savine shook his head. "You need her more than I do. She sees that now, but she wants to return home."

Avery sighed. She would never get used to how difficult decisions and actions were here. Life was simpler at home, when the biggest concern was figuring out how to make rent. She almost wanted to laugh at herself for how stressed she'd been when she asked Morgan if she could live with her.

"And you're about to leave?" Avery asked.

Savine nodded. The devastation on his face made Avery's heart ache.

"Avery, I can't—"

"Don't, Savine. Let's just say 'see you soon,' okay?" Avery tried to put on a smile, but it was strained. Damn, why did this goodbye have to hurt so much?

"Your face reveals what you really think, but alright. We'll say your human goodbye," Savine said, tilting her face up toward his.

Avery flung her arms around Savine as he bent down, kissing her. He pulled back sooner than she wanted and she had to keep herself from wrapping her arms around him tightly and refusing to let go.

"See you soon, old man," she said as a few tears escaped down her cheek.

Savine gently wiped them with a scrape of his calloused hands. "See you soon, Little Flower."

Chapter 9

Kyla

It stung, seeing Garnel and Savine leave her behind. She understood why Savine wanted her to stay. She could protect Avery and the others while they stayed behind in Nephel. Yet, it didn't make her feel any better to know that her brother and soulmate would be entering Orofine in triumph without her.

Being marked by the Goddess had changed everything. She now had a purpose that was separate from her brother's war or her father's oppressive rule. *She* was chosen, *she* was set apart by Althea herself to help Avery and Morgan in their journey through Aeritis. Together, they'd figure out what the Divine Five were, and locate them to better serve the Premier Goddess in whatever way she desired.

As she walked down the quiet, empty halls of the Tower of the Moon, she thought about the experience of seeing the Goddess in person. Althea's aura had been so overpowering, Kyla had been filled with a mix of awe and terror. She didn't know if she could be strong enough to encounter Althea again, and hoped that it would be a once in a lifetime occurrence. Perhaps if she fulfilled this task of finding the Divine Five, she would be blessed from afar.

Kyla knocked quickly on Avery's door. She hadn't had time to share the story with Avery yet, and wanted to begin searching soon. Avery opened the door, wearing a casual Latian outfit. Of course Savine hadn't left her without clothing. It was probably Raikin's doing, procuring an entire wardrobe for the women.

"Kyla! Come in!" Avery said in a cheerful voice. Kyla entered the small bedroom and noticed Morgan sitting at the table. Her feet were tangled in a dark shifting shadow, and her pain was palpable.

Kyla approached Morgan gently. Morgan looked up at her with an empty expression. "Morgan, would you like me to try and heal those wounds?"

Morgan shook her head. "I'm going to run out of painkillers. The skin around my scars hurt, but I'm trying to wean myself off the medication."

"There is no need for you to feel pain. I don't believe I have the capabilities to remove the scars, but I can help with pain. I can also give you a salve to treat the tightness around your scars," Kyla said, careful not to touch her, even though her fingers itched with the need to relieve Morgan's pain.

Avery joined them at the table. "I offered to try and heal her, but she said no. Maybe together we could make it better for you, Morgan."

Morgan shook her head. "Kyla, I'd appreciate the salve and if you could remove the pain. But the scars stay. I want to remember what I faced."

"Very well," Kyla said as she placed a hand on Morgan's shoulder. A rush of agony washed through her. The girl shouldn't even be sitting up with this much anguish coursing through her body. Kyla took it, wiping it clean from Morgan and replacing the emotion with peace and relaxation.

The tension in Morgan's body dissipated, and she sighed with relief. "Thank you. I think I'm going to have to keep you," Morgan said.

"Did you come to check in on us?" Avery asked.

Kyla shifted the headpiece she'd been wearing to cover the Goddess mark. "I came to show you this," Kyla said.

"You've been marked by the Goddess too! What does that even mean?" Avery asked.

"Welcome to the club," Morgan said, tracing the obvious line of stars and vines across her own forehead. Avery was the only one who had hers hidden beneath a glamour, and Kyla needed to figure out how to keep her own mark hidden from Rylo and the other Nepheli fae.

"Yes, I was marked. I appeared before Althea and saw her in her radiance. She touched me and left the mark, but not before ordering me to help you two find something called the Divine Five."

Both women looked at Kyla with confusion. Morgan glanced at Avery before she asked her sister, "Did you know their deity could appear in person? Like she's a real walking, breathing Goddess?"

Avery bit her lip. "Kind of... I asked Savine once and he said she was real, but I thought it was more in the sense that anyone religious says their god or goddess is real."

"Of course she is real," Kyla responded. "Althea formed Aeritis with her sister, Gaia. Althea's daughters are the minor goddesses we serve in temples around Aeritis. You can meet one here in Nephel if you're inclined, or in Orofine for that matter!"

Morgan pursed her lips. "Ave, you weren't more concerned that you were marked by an actual Goddess? What does she want from us, other than to fulfill that foreboding prophecy?"

Kyla responded, "She wants us to find something for her. I think we should go meet the minor goddess here and see what she might know about the Divine Five."

Avery worked her lip between her teeth. "You're right. Let's ask Susan what it might be as well. She seems to have a better grasp of history than we do, and we'll bring Rue as protection."

"I also came to ask if you knew how I could hide the mark in plain sight. Rylo can see through glamours, and it would be strange if I continued to wear a headpiece all the time."

Avery and Morgan talked between themselves in the language of their people, leaving Kyla at a loss of what they were discussing.

"Why don't we all get bangs?" Avery asked. "If anybody asks, we'll just say we wanted to share a human hairstyle with you. Then we'll all have our marks covered."

"Bangs?" Kyla asked, unsure about the strange word on her tongue.

"Yeah, we'll just cut the front of our hair short enough to cover our foreheads. It's not like the mark glows or anything, so as long as we just cover them up we should be fine," Avery continued, demonstrating what she intended to do by pulling the front of her hair across her face. "I've got scissors in my first aid kit."

Avery

Avery and the others were making their way through the Tower of Stars, a tower across the river from the Tower of the Moon. Of course, there was no bridge so they'd needed help flying over from the Nepheli guards. Which drew unnecessary attention from Selene, who showed up just as Avery was trying to convince the guards that they wanted to pray in the temple. The lies slid off her tongue so easily, even Selene seemed to buy Avery's sudden bout of devotion to the Aeritis religion. Unfortunately, Selene chose to join them, keeping her distance, but close enough to hear their conversation.

Just at that moment, Kyla came in close to Avery and whispered that she would sneak away to speak to the goddess. Avery nodded as she slid back to be closer to Selene.

This Tower didn't have all the windows and open air views that the Tower of the Moon had. Instead, it was a dark, windowless enclosure with a winding staircase. At the center of the room was a burning altar. The smoke billowing up from the altar seemed to sparkle like the night's sky. All around them, priestesses clad in black robes and wearing star-kissed masks chanted in a steady rhythm.

The sound of their unified voices made an enchanting and eerie echo across the walls of the enclosed space. Avery looked around for Kyla and noticed she was gone.

"Do you not plan to show your supplication before the altar?" Selene asked. Avery twitched as Selene's breath brushed against her neck. She was far too close for comfort.

"I don't know what to do," she answered honestly.

"First you must be deemed worthy by the pool. If you are not, you will be expelled from the temple. After that you will throw stardust on the fire and chant the song of intercession to the Goddess of the Stars. As Althea's second-born daughter, she holds great weight with her mother, but surely you know that if you are here?"

Avery lifted her chin, giving false confidence as she replied, "Of course I knew that. I wouldn't come in here without knowing how to show my respect."

Selene pursed her lips and began walking to a stream welling up from the ground. "Then wash. All of you," she said, pointing to Rue, Susan, and Morgan. "It does not go without notice that Kyla is missing."

As Avery approached the flowing water, she hoped with everything in her that she wasn't about to be caught for her sacrilege or lack of faith. She took a deep breath and rolled up the sleeves of her tunic as she prepared to plunge her hands into the water. Maybe the expulsion meant that she'd be thrown out of the temple, but things weren't typically that simple in Aeritis.

As her hands were about to touch the water, a sharp clang rang through the temple. Avery looked up to see hundreds of fist-size glowing balls tumbling toward the ground below. The chanting priestesses gasped and cried out as fireballs struck the hard rock floor of the temple. Cries of agony rang out across the tower, growing louder and more anguished.

Kyla was frantically running down the stairs as a glowing woman, so bright her essence burned Avery's eyes, chased after her. "Run! Now!" Kyla shouted as she hit the rock floor, skidding to the ground. Priestesses were closing around her as she pushed herself off the ground and ran towards their group.

Avery didn't need to be told twice. She sprinted toward the door, Morgan just beside her as she ran out of the Tower of Stars and into the crisp autumn evening.

They didn't stop as they made their way over to the waterfall. Without speaking, Selene scooped Rue into her arms and flew across the river, setting her down before she came back with two other Nepheli fae to grab Avery and Morgan. She didn't even seem winded as she set the sisters down. The two other fae landed with Kyla and Susan beside them.

"I should have let the goddess have her way with you," Selene said to Kyla. "I know you're keeping something from me."

"It is nothing concerning you," said Kyla, as she gritted her teeth at the other woman. It was possibly the harshest words Avery had ever heard Kyla use.

Selene rolled her eyes and spread her midnight wings wide. "It does not matter if you tell me *why* you left us. I know you were up to something, and I'm not keeping it from King Rylo."

Kyla kept her expression neutral, and Avery admired her dedication to keeping the information from the Nepheli Sage. Selene kicked off the ground and began flying up toward the Tower of the Moon. Once Selene was out of sight, Kyla turned to the others and began talking.

"She was unwilling to meet me," Kyla said, shaking slightly as she looked across the river. Avery reached out a steadying hand to support Kyla as she continued.

"I showed her the Goddess mark, and she became furious. She threatened to kill me for my sacrilege, for daring to imitate the mark, although I tried to explain that Althea placed the mark there herself. I tried to ask what the Divine Five were, but the Goddess of Stars slapped my face. When she struck me, the stars from the prayers began colliding and falling to the ground. That's when I ran. I'm sorry, the whole journey was a failure."

Avery pulled Kyla into a hug, knowing that Kyla needed comfort this way, before they began making their way back to the Tower of the Moon.

"We'll figure something else out," Avery suggested as they walked, arm in arm.

Chapter 10

Savine

Savine's stomach flipped in anticipation. He'd begun recognizing the landmarks and trees along the road nearly four hours ago. By his calculations, they must only be an hour's ride from the outskirts of Orofine—his former home and more recently the site of the loyalist stronghold. Fuck if he knew how he was going to convince his former enemies to faithfully pledge to serve him as the crowned King of Latiah.

What gave him encouragement was the response of the villagers and nomadic groups he'd encountered over the last few days of riding through the river valleys and woods of Latiah. Crowds of folk had come to see the procession of the new king, throwing late-season flowers and autumn leaves at his feet.

Many of the village folk were thinner than they should be, with the approaching winter, but it was the nomadic groups that made Savine grip Jari's reins tight, fighting the urge to lash out at a man that was now dead. Their essence was faded, even younger fae looked aged beyond their years. Many were wearing rags and begged his warriors for help. Raikin and Garnel spread the message that Savine would hold court in Orofine. All would be welcome and heard if they came.

Despite their condition, men and women had cried out to Savine, calling him the True King of Latiah, and prostrated themselves before him. Gifts of all sorts, from harvest produce to elk, and even inexplicably, furniture were brought forward. Not wanting to offend anyone, Savine quietly accepted all the gifts, knowing also that some of these gifts were all these folk had to offer. It left him with an uneasy gratitude.

Raikin insisted that Savine ride in the front of the procession, dressed not in his leather armor, but in an outfit of Latian green, reinforced with cleverly stitched protections from a particularly powerful Nepheli seamstress. On his back was a bear skin cloak, attached to his neck with a golden leaf clasp. The clothing was itchy and stifling in the mild autumn weather. Worst of all, he wore his shoulder length hair down, woven with beads and small braids that were constantly getting tangled in the crown of boughs and antlers. This, Raikin insisted on as well, stating that his hair down and crown displayed gave a more kingly image. When Savine had suggested that this wardrobe may bring about an attack by angry loyalists, Raikin argued that they would be attacked whether he was dressed in splendor or not, and as crowned King of Latiah, nobody but a fae with a death wish would dare assassinate him and risk an eternity of horrors in the Abyss.

As they grew nearer to Orofine, Savine felt his own anxiety about this moment rise. This was what he'd been fighting for. For over twenty-five years, he'd worked to free his folk from the tyrannical rule of his father and bring peace, unity, and order to all of Latiah. And now that it was happening, he felt a sense of dread. He should have liberated Latiah sooner. How could he be worthy of such praise when he had contributed to these folks' hard lives? Their sons and daughters had fought bravely against the rebels, even though many had been forcibly recruited. Most of the lower ranks of the loyalist military didn't have a choice to serve Jasper, and Savine had pardoned any loyalist deserters willing to join the rebel cause. Yet, he was still responsible for their poverty and their poor health. He had caused this war and sent the nation into a twenty-five year tailspin.

"Savine?" Garnel called out. Savine turned his attention to his general, riding slightly behind him and to the right. Raikin had stayed to his left through the long journey. Neither man had mentioned how they felt about being separated from their soulmates, but if they felt anything like Savine, they were torn in two at being apart from Kyla and Jay.

"You can come up here, Garnel," Savine replied.

"I believe we'll be in the outskirts of Orofine soon. I think we should move you into the center of the caravan, just in case we meet resistance from the loyalists."

Savine shook his head. "Let them see me first. I've been fighting this war at the front for decades. I'm not going to hide amongst the ranks now. Inform the back of the procession to have Jasper's body on display for those who wish to view their former king. I want no doubts about the legitimacy of the crown."

Garnel grunted, rolling his eyes.

"You're a stubborn ass, but you're right," Garnel choked out. "But don't think you're fooling me into believing that you're not anxious about this. I may not be an empath, but I know you well enough to see you're about to shut us out."

Savine gave his friend a hard glare, then softened, thinking about how this man was his brother, even before he'd become Kyla's soulmate. "It's—It's complicated coming back here after all that has happened. I knew the day would eventually come if I survived the war, but it doesn't make it any easier."

"I feel the same way. You're never alone, Savine. Try as you might to have kept yourself isolated all these years. I've always been waiting for you to let me back in," Garnel said.

Abyss damn him! Where was this emotional speech coming from? Savine felt like he was speaking to his sister, not Garnel.

"Yes, well. Thank you, Garnel," Savine said, charging Jari forward to put himself back at the front of the group.

They rode in silence until they reached the small communities outside the great wooden walls of Orofine. The walls were built through the sacrifice of trees that rose up and rooted themselves into place at the forming of the city, thousands of years ago. The king at that time had wielded such a powerful essence that the trees had willingly set down their lives in exchange for being imbued with some of the king's essence, keeping their trunks and branches in a permanent stasis. Even the palace was made from these trees, creating a baffling network of connecting stairways and bridges across and around massive trunks.

As they entered the first outlying community, Savine and his warriors were met with a throng of cries and shouts. Alarmed, Savine reached for his sword at his side before he eased, the tension in his body releasing as crowds of cheering folk parted ahead of him. Cries of "Long live King Savine" echoed through the narrow valley and up the steep peaks that protected the capital city. Savine waved and Jari let out a piercing bugle as the crowd grew tighter.

Then Savine heard the sound of bells. The bells of the nearby temples were ringing incessantly, bringing even more folk into the crowded streets. By the time Savine reached the cedar walls of Orofine, thousands of folk had filled the streets, chanting their welcome.

He never thought this would happen, never imagined that he would ride into Orofine as a triumphant king. He'd always assumed he'd have to take it by force, winning over the city bit by bit. But thanks to Rylo's trick, he didn't have to sack the city or force his way in like the brutal fae rebel he'd tried to portray himself as. No, he was riding into his city—his *home*—with a hero's welcome.

The only thing that could make this moment any sweeter would be to have Avery's small body pressed between his thighs, celebrating this victory with him.

As he neared the palace, Savine felt a prickle of nervousness in Jari, like the elk was preparing to enter the battlefield. Then, a powerful blast of wind struck Savine and knocked him to the ground. Only one fae could hit him with such a strike. Davian, his father's Sage.

Avery

Avery had slept later than she'd meant to. Savine had been gone for nearly a week, and she'd felt slightly adrift as she adapted to life in Aeritis without the threat of death at the hands of Jasper, Rylo, or some other awful fae. Add in Morgan's obsession with returning home, and Avery needed some time to herself. So she'd gone to Kyla that evening after supper. Avery hadn't planned on drinking with Savine's sister, but it seemed that they both needed a few too many glasses of wine.

Kyla had confessed to Avery how hurt she was to be left out of the return to Orofine with Savine and Garnel, and admitted that she'd resented Avery's decision to stay with her sister over Savine.

Avery understood how Kyla could feel this way. If anything, their evening together had brought them closer than she'd expected. She learned more about Orofine and the longing Kyla had struggled with, being away for so long. Kyla wanted to return. She wanted to help reconstruct Latiah, but now she had been excluded from that process.

Avery noticed Morgan's absence from the bed as soon as she stretched her arms across the soft linens. Most likely, Morgan was fine. She'd been making a deeper connection with Susan over the past few days, and was probably having breakfast with her. Regardless, Avery hurried to slide on something appropriate for the halls of Rylo's royal residence and headed to the breakfast room they shared with the other guests.

When she walked into the room, she immediately smelled the scent of eggs, tea, and oatcakes. Rue cracked a smile at Avery's disheveled appearance. "You look like you just got out of bed."

Avery frowned, pushing herself farther into the room. "Have you seen Morgan this morning?"

Both women shook their heads as Susan replied, "I haven't seen her since yesterday."

Avery tried to keep her beating heart from racing. Most likely, Morgan went to Kyla. Avery knew that her sister's wounds were hurting her, her pain medication gone. Kyla's fae salve had provided Morgan with temporary relief, but Morgan was growing increasingly restless with each passing day. Avery didn't know what to do to give her sister relief, or to help her find her place in Aeritis. She had even asked if she and Morgan could visit Rylo's library, but he'd emphatically refused to let them explore his books. She'd tried to help Morgan tap into her magic, but other than angry, dark shadows that seemed to uncontrollably fill a room, Morgan could do nothing.

Avery knocked on Kyla's door, and she could hear the bells and beads in Kyla's hair clink together as she walked to the door. "Have you seen Morgan?" Avery asked Kyla.

Kyla shook her head. "Not since yesterday afternoon."

A wave of fear crashed through Avery. Her chest tightened and an icy chill swept over her.

There was only one place that her sister would *want* to go on her own.

Sapphire Falls.

Avery rushed out of Kyla's room, but she chased after her. "Wait, Avery! I'm coming with you!" Kyla said.

"She's gone to the falls!" Avery tried to shout, but her voice came out hoarse and panicked. "She's going to jump!"

Avery ran through the Tower of the Moon, down flight after flight of stairs. *Where was a fucking flying fairy when she needed one?*

At one point, nearly a quarter of the way down, Avery went to one of the spacious balconies that the Nepheli used for flying between towers and floors. She looked down to the river, and saw in horror a small figure at the edge of Sapphire Falls.

"Oh God! She's there. She's at the falls!" Avery shouted, her feet already running toward the staircase.

Kyla strode ahead of her, her long fae legs and unnatural speed left Avery behind. As Avery flew down the stairs, trying to keep up, she prayed that her sister wouldn't jump off the rocky falls into the icy river below. It seemed impossible that she'd survived the first fall, Avery didn't see how Morgan could survive another jump off the falls.

And if she did get transported back?

Her sister would be leaving her without even saying goodbye. The thought that she'd do this was too much for Avery to bear.

Kyla paused at a wide, arched window. They were only about four stories from the ground now and Avery ran past, not bothering to look at what Kyla saw.

"Avery! Avery! It's Rylo," Kyla shouted.

Avery stopped in her tracks and ran back to Kyla's side as she let out a stilted gasp. The Nepheli king shot through the air like a rocket, flying directly toward the falls. He was so close to her now while Morgan was still on the edge. To Avery's horror, as Morgan caught sight of Rylo, she leaped from Sapphire Falls, plummeting from Avery's sight.

Chapter 11

Rylo

To say that Rylo was irritated to be dive-bombing through the crisp autumn air after some human girl was an understatement. He'd been enjoying a perfectly peaceful morning with a cup of tea and a decent book when his friend, Elio, had informed him that Morgan had been standing at the edge of Sapphire Falls for the better half of an hour.

He hadn't put restrictions on the two witches, trying to keep a semblance of respect between himself and the Latian nation. After all, he gained what he had set out to do and now he wanted to keep his plans for restoring Nephel to greatness in motion. Further, his nation was substantially smaller and the last thing he needed was a war against those Latian brutes for upsetting Savine's soulmate. It was one thing to push Savine into accepting his crown, but it would be another matter to push him into war. He'd even avoided the witches and their small posse of women as much as possible. There was no reason for him to interact with them. Not as long as Avery was here. Once she was gone he would begin training his witch.

But he couldn't have the one witch he had any interest in leaping off waterfalls. No, that just would not do. He knew he needed to make a power move as soon as he'd understood that these two unlikely foreign girls were the ones spoken of in the prophecy. He certainly had *no* interest in the whiny and weak Avery. Sure, she'd killed her guard, but she had made such a fuss about it. Plus her display in front of Jasper had nearly cost them all their lives. *She* would not be the sister to use to his advantage.

No, he wanted the scarred one with the billowing shadows. At least she had taken action with that odd weapon, ending that idiot Jasper's reign for good. And now that fool was trying to jump off his waterfall.

Rylo deepened his dive, tucking his wings to gain speed. He made eye contact with the dark little figure standing precariously close to the edge of the cold waters of Sapphire Falls just as she turned and jumped off the precipice.

Oh, *excellent*. Now he was going to have to get his feathers wet and retrieve the soggy woman. He *loathed* getting his feathers wet. They always seemed to dry in such a way that made them look slightly tattered and less dignified, like he was some sort of damp pigeon. Rylo banked down, just in time to see the girl flailing in the air, plummeting toward the rocky ground below.

He reached out, wings hitting the mist, and grabbed her around the waist just before she broke on the rocks. What a foolish woman. Sapphire Falls was often driest in the autumn when last year's spring snowmelt was long gone. The rocky basin was more exposed than usual, and she hadn't a chance of surviving the fall. Not to mention, if she had managed to hit the water, like she apparently had the first time, she would have been exposed to frigid temperatures.

He heard the woman gasp in his arms before she let out a sorrowful moan. "Why didn't you let me go?" she whined, writhing in his arms as he attempted to bank upwards on dampened feathers.

"Because I have use for you, and I don't want to see you dead or returned to your realm," Rylo said, trying to put as much sweet indolence into his voice as he spoke.

"Put me down!" the girl shrieked and Rylo tensed at the piercing sound. "I want to go home!"

"*Poor little Kingslayer.* Not getting to go home," Rylo mocked. "Unfortunately, we often do not get what we'd like in this world." He tried his hardest to keep up his insolent demeanor, but the woman was acting insufferably. Shouldn't at the very least, a *thank you* be in order for saving her life? "Now, if you try that again, I'll let you spend some time in the Tower of Teeth. *That* will teach you a thing or two about being thankful for what you have."

He felt the woman shake in his arms. He really should have paid better attention to her name, but her name seemed less consequential than getting her into his service.

Rylo landed on the balcony to his library and placed the Kingslayer firmly on the stone terrace. "Let me look at you, Kingslayer." Rylo said, cupping her chin in his hand. He saw the goddess mark, distorted slightly by a hard ridge of dark red scar tissue. "What did this to you?" he asked curiously.

"A fucking fae bastard. On my side of the portal," she said. A whisper of darkness bit at his ankles, cool to the touch.

"Interesting. Some sort of dark fae then? Must've had massive teeth or claws to do this damage," Rylo assessed, still holding her chin firmly between his fingers.

She yanked her head out of his grasp as she said, "It was one of those Latians. He was a bear, and shifted into his fae form after he'd dragged me nearly to death. The monster looked a little like Kyla's soulmate, with the fur tattoo."

Rylo knew from experience that plenty of humans had found their way into Nephel through Sapphire Falls, but he'd never given much thought to fae crossing the portal into the human realm. Perhaps because he'd killed several weak and dying humans who were broken on the rocks of the falls. Only one had been strong enough to keep, but his panicked screams and indecipherable language had given Rylo such a headache that he'd spared the man and ordered Selene to put him down after a thorough analysis.

"Rather strange to think a fae could travel to the human realm, but if you can travel here I suppose we could travel to your land. Now, come inside. I have a warm fire in here and can order some hot tea."

The kingslayer bit her lip and furrowed her brow. The tight, scarred skin hardly moved with the gesture, only giving her a hardened look to her already injured face.

"Why should I do that?" she asked. Ah, the girl was no fool. She already knew about Rylo's ability to pull uncomfortable secrets and truths from her through food and drink.

"You may pour your own tea. What is your name, pet?"

The tightness in her face grew. "I'm not your pet! You haven't even bothered to learn my name, King Rylo?" Her tone was sharp, like a knife's blade.

Rylo shrugged and turned to his library. "It was of little consequence to me what your name was, and I haven't had reason to learn it until you unceremoniously launched yourself off a cliff. Come inside and warm up, or stay out in the cold. The choice is yours, although I'd rather not make a servant nurse you back to health when you're sick."

He heard her slight footsteps behind him as she followed him into the room. She sat across from him in the same seat that her sister occupied only a little over a week ago. He gave an amused grin when the teapot appeared on the table. One of the greatest perks of his home was the way the Tower responded to his needs. The look of surprise on the girl's face delighted him.

"Your name, witch," Rylo said as he poured himself a cup of tea.

"It's strange being called a witch when less than a week ago I'd thought witches were only things in stories and Halloween costumes. I once dressed up like a witch for Halloween in college." She shook her head, lost in her own thoughts, before turning to pour herself a cup of tea.

"I'm beginning to wonder if you even have a name. Should I call you 'Avery's sister' or perhaps 'pet' would do."

She rattled the tea cup as he called her that. He loved to see her composure slide a bit. "Kingslayer has a nice ring to it. Maybe you'll be next," she said in mock sweetness.

"Perhaps I should pour a bit of that tea for you so I can learn all your little secrets, Kingslayer. Like why you had that weapon on you. I had it delivered to the Tower of Teeth and used on a particularly vexing prisoner. It was an interesting way to learn how it worked, with the brains and bits of bone of the prisoner splattering the wall. How did you come into possession of such a weapon?"

The woman just looked around the room, not answering him. She didn't even seem particularly phased by his description of the death of the prisoner. But no matter, he didn't need to know any of this. She'd already interrupted a perfectly relaxing morning and he may as well have a bit of fun seeing how far he could push this woman.

Finally she said in a soft, cool voice. "It's a gun and I'd like it back. Now, take me back to my room. Avery's probably panicking by now."

"You are much more interesting than your sister," Rylo said with a laugh.

"I think you're the first person to say that to me." She stood and headed toward the door, but Rylo stopped her.

"I'll fly you down," Rylo said as he grasped her wrist.

"I'd rather walk," she said, tugging herself from his reach.

"I insist, pet." He pulled her into his arms. She was all skin and bones, nearly no muscle to her and he briefly wondered if she was getting enough to eat. They leapt into the air as she continued to struggle in his arms.

Once they were airborne, he felt the tendrils of her dark shadows snake around his wings. The pressure of the shadows grew tighter as the woman's expression hardened.

"I didn't want to go with you!" she shouted.

Rylo felt a mounting panic in his chest as he pressed against the tethers on his wings, but still they wouldn't be released.

Down they plummeted toward the ground, picking up speed as the darkness entangled his wings. "Stop woman!" he shouted, real panic like he hadn't experienced in years began to build. She was going to smash him into the ground. He'd been a fool to think this kingslayer would stop at Jasper.

The rocky outcropping along the side of the Tower of the Moon was quickly approaching, and yet he could do nothing to uncoil her dark tendrils or slow their speed. His back muscles screamed in effort as he tried to work her magical bindings off him. The entire time the woman smiled at him like a cat toying with a mouse, delighted with herself.

Morgan. The damn woman was named Morgan.

"Now Morgan! Release me now." He put a honey-coated glamour into his voice and his wings sprang outward, slowing their speed merely feet from the rocky earth.

She began laughing with hysterics that made his heart speed up as he set her feet on the ground. On and on she laughed, shaking through what must be mild shock.

"Stop!" Rylo shouted, but the laughter continued. Putting glamour back into his voice, he ordered Morgan to stop laughing, but the small woman seemed to be beyond reason.

He couldn't stand the shrill sound of it and he struck her hard in the face. Immediately, her lip began to swell and bleed. The laughter ceased, and Rylo saw a strange gleam in her green eyes.

She grinned up at him, blood dripping across straight teeth. "Don't forget my name next time, asshole."

Avery

By the time Avery had run back up the stairs to Rylo's library, the only place she thought to look for him, her sister was gone. Rylo sat back in his chair, casually drinking a steaming cup of tea.

Rylo saw her walk in the room and shouted, "No! No more *humans* for me today. Go find your wretched sister and take care of her yourself!"

Avery stood aghast, not sure what to make of Rylo's loss of composure. "But—you caught her! Where is she?"

"I disposed of the nuisance down along the rocks at the base of the tower. Where she's gone from there, you know as well as I do," Rylo drawled, turning back to the book in his hand. He seemed to glow faintly, or maybe it was just the damp and dreary weather that brought out a brighter gleam to his skin.

"Why would you do that? She could throw herself off the falls again!"

Rylo let out a dry laugh. "I was trying to show a modicum of kindness to your injured sister by bringing her back to her room, and she was very ungrateful for my hospitality. Now go. As I have already said, I do not want to see another human again today."

"Um... Okay," Avery mumbled as she walked out the door. She shouldn't have taken his order. It wasn't very queenly of her to just go along with what a bully like Rylo said, but she was already in the long, dark passageway through the center of the tower that led to Rylo's private library. It would be best to just go to her room and see if Morgan made it back. Plus by now she was absolutely exhausted from all the stairs she'd climbed down and up and now down again. Her calves burned and she realized that she was losing some of her previous endurance with this life of comfort and luxury in the Towers. She'd need to start getting outside again, and if she was being honest with herself, Avery had been feeling increasingly restless with all her inactivity.

When she finally made it back to her room, she found her sister asleep in the bed, still in her clothes. Her lip was swollen and there was a bit of blood at the corner of her mouth.

Avery tried not to disturb her, but Morgan sat up and stared at her sister. "I'm not okay, Ave," she muttered before she sank back into the bed.

Avery stood by her side, gently touching her sister on the arm. "Morgan, what's happened?"

"All of this, starting from the attack. I've lost myself. And that magic that I have feels like a wild animal. It's like it's feeding on my fear.

I almost killed Rylo and myself, and do you know how I responded? I *laughed!* I fucking laughed and there was no way of stopping."

"What do you mean?" Avery asked. She kept her tone soft, like the voice she'd use for an injured animal.

"My magic came pouring out of me, or whatever those smoky shadows are. They wrapped themselves around Rylo and the feel of his panic rising was—it was intoxicating, like I could just swallow his fear and feast on it. Dammit, look at what this place and these creatures are doing to me! I'm already turning into a monster!"

Avery could see what her sister meant. Ever since arriving here, probably further back to the attack at Quartz Mountain, Morgan had become so far removed from herself that Avery hardly recognized her steady, thoughtful sister. Her sister who thrived on order was replaced with this woman who was letting herself sink deeper into a darkness that seemed to fester like a wound.

"And you tried to go home without saying goodbye?" Avery's voice cracked as she asked.

Morgan nodded, closing her eyes. "I *can't* stay here, Ave." She opened her eyes, shaking as she continued, "Every time I see the fae, I feel sick or full of rage. I'm not okay here, and I need to get home. I can sort of understand why you might choose to stay, but I can't do that. I'm not an angry or violent person! I'm helpful and practical and all of that has been turned upside down in this world. I just can't keep doing it. *Please,* help me get home."

Avery's stomach clenched. Her sister was hurting, and was desperate to get home. Just like she'd been. When she arrived in Aeritis she'd been alone and scared, desperate to get home. She remembered how broken she'd been when she couldn't get through the portal at Quartz Mountain, how she even begged Savine to end her suffering.

Now she knew returning home wasn't what she actually wanted. The thought of helping rule an entire country terrified her—she was *not* qualified to be a monarch. But, Savine had offered to let her play a smaller part on the sidelines, and she owed it to both of them to explore what was between them.

But Morgan didn't have a Savine here, and she had experienced trauma at the hands of the fae that Avery hadn't—not even being kidnapped and forced to kill Weston had been as horrible as what Morgan had experienced. To be trapped in Aeritis, experiencing the unwieldy magic that her sister possessed must be terrifying. Avery had no interest in seeing her sister die at Sapphire Falls, but she also couldn't let her suffer here if there was even a chance that she could get through the portal.

She nodded to Morgan. "Yeah, okay. We'll try and get you through tonight. Kyla and Rue have that crazy good fae vision and can keep a lookout, plus can see if you go through the portal. Susan can control water, so maybe she can direct you into the flow of the falls."

Morgan sprang up and wrapped her arms around her sister. Tears flowed between them, but Morgan wouldn't let go. Finally, she sank back onto her pillow, grief and exhaustion etched onto her face.

"Thank you," she whispered before she closed her eyes.

Chapter 12

Savine

Orofine residents shouted curses toward the source of the wind as Savine looked up from the ground. All around him, his followers were toppled over by the gale. Some of his warriors even had their elk toppled over on them, crushing them as the beasts struggled to stand. Savine leaped to his feet, drawing his sword with one hand and his essence with the other.

The King's Residence of Latiah stood up the steep and wide path that snaked through the residential streets and bustling shops of Orofine. Now that they were just outside of the interior walls to the building, Savine knew exactly who had dared attack his rebels. Davian was the cause of the wind that had knocked so many of his followers—and himself—to the ground. He'd expected an entire force of resistance as he strode into Orofine, and he wouldn't let one man stop him from claiming his throne.

"On your mounts!" Savine shouted to his disheveled rebels. *This* was not how he wanted to enter Orofine. Looking weak and powerless in front of the folk of this city. More so, he and Raikin planned to put Davian quickly in his place, dispelling him of the title of Sage and passing the honor to Raikin.

Around him, Savine's warriors got off the hard ground, dusting themselves off and settled back onto their elk. Only a few seemed injured enough to need medical attention, including a man who'd been stabbed in the side with his own elk's antler. Savine approached the man, murmuring words of comfort for the bleeding warrior. The man's eyes already had a distant glaze to them as he looked past Savine and up to the clear autumn sky overhead. Fortunately, a healer from the crowd was at the injured warrior's side in moments and Savine took his place on Jari's back.

"Do you see how the loyalists still defy their true king?" Garnel roared, and the crowd responded with jeers and shouts at the loyalists.

Savine squeezed Jari's side and the war elk was immediately running through the streets, the throng of the crowd separating as his rebel warriors reclaimed their city. Another bitter blast of wind threatened to topple them, but Savine cast his essence out, creating a wall of thick foliage that cut the wind.

From the King's Residence, Savine heard a jeering call toward him. "You are not welcome here, traitor! We shall not acknowledge you as king!"

Damn. Savine didn't want to cause more bloodshed. Already too many Latians had died in this bitter conflict, but he wasn't going to stand aside now and lose what was rightfully his.

At that same moment, a screeching groan came from the preserved trees of the building. Savine looked up to see the King's Residence *in motion.* An ancient branch came down at Davian as he stood guard at the edge of the King's Residence. A terrified scream echoed through Orofine as Savine saw that the very building itself grasped Davian in an ancient branch—a branch that had given its life to serve and protect the King of Latiah and this city.

It was yet another reason he'd never tried to attack Orofine. *If* the sentinels of trees that made up the city saw him as a threat, he'd be ripped to shreds.

"At least the trees took care of that threat," Garnel muttered. "Made things easier, and after that who would question your rule?"

"Whoever does will need to be more crafty than Davian if they want to survive the attack," Savine said.

And that was just what the trees in the King's Residence were doing now. Jari lightly snorted with nervous energy as Davian was tossed and shredded by the branches sworn to protect Savine.

Savine dismounted from Jari's back and immediately a steward—it had been so long since he'd seen a Latian steward— was at his side, taking Jari for him. Jari let out a reluctant huff as Savine began walking away from his side. Savine saw as the steward took a small treat of some kind from his pocket and gave it to Jari. The bull elk settled down, following the steward without protest.

Raikin and Garnel were immediately at Savine's side as they began walking up the cedar-planked stairs to his former home, stepping over what remained of his father's former Sage.

"Say something," Raikin muttered under his breath.

Savine gave the tiniest nod before he turned and looked at the crowd. The entire city of Orofine seemed to be staring at him, waiting for him to address them. Some had the whorls of essence like his own, others resembled fur, still others had that slight tinge of green to their skin, fae who drew their essence from grasses and underbrush. But they were all Latians, all looking to him to see what sort of ruler he would be. Finally, he let his voice carry over the crowd.

"Fellow Latians, we are no longer loyalists and rebels. Never again will brother fight against brother, sister against sister. Today is the day that tyranny ends. Today we are a united Latiah once again." Savine's voice rang out strong and proud. He'd always had this confidence buried in him. He'd mustered it out of the shadowy grave of his soul from time to time when his rebels needed it, but now he had to share that part of himself with his nation as their rightful king.

The crowd cheered and Savine felt the victory in this moment across the city. "Today we celebrate a new beginning. As your king, I vow to serve *you*."

Raikin gave a subtle brush of his hand to Savine's shoulders before motioning toward the imposing stairway that led to the King's Residence. Savine turned with his general and soon to be Sage as the crowd continued to roar.

The wooden stairs, carved into the mountainside, led them up to the cedar-built structure. It was all just as Savine had remembered it. Massive trees supported rooms interconnected by open air breezeways. On the lower levels were the king's administrative rooms, offices, and throne room, while higher up the network of trees held the residency for the king and his closest advisors.

"Home. We're home," Garnel said with a sorrowful smile. "I didn't think it would ever happen."

"Now the hard work begins," Raikin muttered, his face set into a stern expression as they walked past courtiers and servants on their way up the outer stairs to the throne room. They bent their knee for Savine, no doubt afraid the King's Residence would detect their traitorous actions or words.

The folk of the King's Residence had little choice but to accept his loyalty, or face death.

"Raikin, can we just enjoy this moment without your pessimism?" Garnel growled.

Savine let out a small chuckle. He was in Orofine, and it hardly felt real. As he walked, the sacrificed trees that supported the structure dipped in his presence. His hands itched with the urge to touch the bough and antler crown on his head, if only to remind himself that this was finally happening.

The halls were filled with Jasper's court. Some cried out in anguish as they held the bodies of slain loyalists. Bodies torn limb from limb by the trees sworn to protect him. Others bowed low, a look of distrust and awe on their faces.

A fae he'd recognize anywhere waited for them at the top of the stairs. He felt the lines of his face harden as he looked at the moss hued woman. She bowed low as he reached the top step.

"Your highness. It's my honor to serve you." Her expression was unsure. Fear twinkled in her eyes as she looked up to him.

"Darby," Savine muttered before his hard facade cracked. He couldn't stop the grin that spread across his cheeks. "Rise, old friend."

The apprehension faded and her face took on a crinkled smile as she stood tall and proud before him. She looked like she wanted to hug him close, but didn't dare.

Garnel didn't hesitate as he pulled the woman into a tight hug. "You made it through everything! I didn't know if we'd see you here."

She pulled back from his hug and gave a quick nod as the apprehension grew again over her face.

"I never understood why you didn't leave with us," Garnel said as he pulled back.

Darby wrung her hands as she turned her attention to Savine and said, "Someone had to stay with your mother." She looked at him with deep brown eyes. "I knew you couldn't do it. You had to get away before the king killed you, but I couldn't leave her without knowing she was put to rest properly. Then I suppose I felt I had an obligation to her memory and to preserving this place for you. I became a good loyalist, never sharing what was in my heart. I knew I'd have to if I were to survive," Darby said with a shrug, glancing at the mangled bodies being carried out of the hall.

"Where is she?" Savine asked with a frown. Darby had stayed to bury his mother, something he and Kyla should have done. She'd always been loyal to his mother, coming from the distant seafaring lands with Jasper's bride so many years ago. She'd been a second mother to him, always there to bring him comfort when his mother couldn't show it herself. So often, she'd been the one to tuck him in at night and read him stories. Yet after all these years, the sting of her perceived betrayal felt like an old bruise.

"She's up the mountain just past the springs. We took her body and buried her in secret. Jasper never noticed, but I knew you and Kyla would want her near the place that gave her such comfort. We can finally honor her memory properly."

Savine felt a knot form in his throat. His mother, who'd sacrificed her own life for his, was in an unmarked grave all these years. "We'll do it immediately. Bring me to her."

Raikin cleared his throat before he said, "There is much to do here, my king. Perhaps we should wait?"

"I have waited over twenty-five years to be at her grave. I won't wait any longer." Savine turned from his adviser and began making his way to the familiar path that led out of the residence and up to the hot springs his mother loved so much.

She'd never gotten over the loss of the sea. Orofine was far inland and high up a mountainous canyon. The water that ran through it was swift and shallow. He remembered her shifting into her finned form and splashing in the rapid's spring runoff before shifting back and seeking the comfort of the hot mineral springs. She and Darby had taught him to swim in those springs and in the high alpine lakes above Orofine.

Beyond the springs was a copse of red cedars, hemlock, and spruce. Trees that thrived in damp forests that not only called Orofine home, but also his mother's former coastal homelands. It's probably why she'd always been drawn to this place. The feel and scent of this forest was home to her. The aerated water coursing through the river made the air smell clean and pure.

In the center of a ring of trees, with scattered ferns and coral mushrooms growing, sat a large agate stone.

"Here is where she rests," Darby whispered. "The agate is from our nation, plucked from the ocean. I thought it would bring her peace to have part of our home with her."

Savine nodded. "Leave me," he murmured as he knelt beside his mother's grave.

Morgan

Morgan looked down at the dark precipice over Sapphire Falls. All down the stairs and across the rocky outcropping along the edge of the canyon, Morgan had been working up the courage to jump again. She had to go home if she was ever going to find herself again and let go of the angry, insecure person she'd become. Hell, she'd almost let herself smash into the ground today because she couldn't control the writhing shadows that threatened to overtake her and Rylo.

But knowing that this jump could hurt or kill her was terrifying. This morning when she'd tried, she'd been in a bad head space. She didn't want to die at the falls, but she also really didn't care what happened. Now she just wanted to be home, not dead, not here. Home.

"Morgan?" Avery's voice shook with concern.

Morgan snapped out of her thoughts and looked at her sister. Despite the small scar that she bore on her forehead, she looked unscathed by the bear attack that had mutilated her own body. Whether Morgan stayed or not, she knew Avery was going to be alright. She was building a life here—a life that didn't need to include Morgan.

"Yeah, Ave?"

"Are you ready? Susan and Rue just signaled that they're below the falls. We should do this before any of the Nepheli catch on to what we're up to," Avery said, stepping a little closer to her.

Morgan nodded before she moved to hug her sister. "I love you, Ave. You can go to Savine right away now and I'll let Mom and Dad know you're safe and happy."

Avery sniffled near Morgan's ear. "I love you too, Mor. Be safe." Avery planted a hard kiss on her sister's cheek before Morgan scooted forward toward the edge of the cliff.

Without hesitating another moment, she leaped into the darkness. Immediately, she felt the wind whip around her before the icy water pulled her farther into the falls. That would be Susan's help, Morgan knew. Down she tumbled as she held her breath through the cold pull of the falls. Her body slapped into the icy waters of the pool and she kicked up, gasping for that first breath as her body churned and tumbled through the thrashing current.

There was no bright light and no high pitched sound. She hadn't been transported, and she knew it immediately, even through the sting of being hit by such cold water. She swam hard, fighting the current, thankful that she wore clothes light enough to manage the thrashing rapids below the falls. Her muscles spasmed in the frigid water and her body shook, but she still took long, even strokes toward the shore. Suddenly, the water began to warm and gently pull her along. She flipped over to her back, letting her breathing steady as Susan's magic wrapped around her and brought her back to the rocky shore.

Susan was by her side, pulling her up from the water and giving her a steadying hand as Morgan found her footing. Avery and Susan were right. There was no way back home.

"I'm so sorry, Morgan," Susan said as she led her to the others. Rue was ready with a wool blanket that she draped around Morgan's shoulders. The length of it dragged the ground, but Morgan didn't care.

Rue handed her a warm mug. "Drink, friend. It will help you."

Morgan didn't argue, just mechanically sipped at the spicy liquid. Immediately her cold muscles began to thaw.

"Morgan!" Avery yelled as she ran down the steep canyon trail. She was by her sister's side in minutes, holding her in a tight embrace. "Are you okay? Are you freezing?"

Morgan was cold, but it felt like the cold had seeped deeper into her than just surface level. Even her insides felt numb. "Yeah, I'm okay. You were right though, Ave. We can't go home."

Kyla appeared behind Avery and Morgan looked at the tall, stately woman. "Can you take away the rest of the cold?" Morgan asked.

"I can warm you with my essence, yes. Do you want me to help you with what you are feeling?" Kyla asked, her hair tinkling as the bells and bobbles moved with her.

What was Morgan feeling? Nothing really, all the pain and sorrow that she'd felt was numbed. "No. Just warm me please."

Kyla nodded, but her face was turned into a frown as she touched Morgan's arm, sending a comforting warmth into her bones.

Rue and Kyla's eyes snapped up to the night's sky. "Someone is coming," Rue murmured. Morgan saw what Kyla and Rue had already detected. Wings like the depth of night glided across the starry sky, followed by others. Selene. She watched as at least a dozen Nepheli landed in front of them.

Finally, she saw the golden brilliance of Rylo's wings as he gracefully touched the ground, the others immediately moving to let him pass. The indolent expression on his face didn't give his thoughts away as he tsked before saying, "Now Morgan. I thought I made it clear that you'd be punished for attempting to return to your realm. Selene, bring her to the Tower of Teeth."

Morgan could hear her sister screaming in protest as she was wrapped into the arms of the woman and sent skyward.

The flight to the Tower of Teeth was short, just beyond the other side of the canyon and Selene didn't seem inclined to talk as they flew there. That was fine with Morgan. She didn't want to talk either. She didn't want to do anything but curl in around herself and be left alone. There was no way that was happening now that she was sent to Rylo's prison. They landed on the roof and were met by guards wearing leather armor and armed with long, sharp blades.

"This is King Rylo's wayward witch," Selene said. "I'll be handling her situation."

The guards let them pass without question. "What is he going to do to me here?" Morgan asked, smelling the metallic tinge of blood in the air.

Selene didn't speak as she led her to a room draped in darkness. "Sit," she ordered and Morgan didn't hesitate to heed her command. Fear crept over her as the fae reached a hand out and touched Morgan's scarred cheek. "Hold still. This will not take long."

A searing pain ripped through Morgan as the woman seemed to protrude into her very soul. Images of her life flashed before her like a movie and all the feelings she'd ever had before streamed through her in a burning, overwhelming rush. A life of diligence, of being a good student and employee, of always working hard for what she had. A childhood filled with happiness and peace, but always the feeling of needing to work hard to be good enough, to be perfect.

Selene continued to dig into Morgan's soul, searching for something until it seemed she found it. Buried so deep inside Morgan that she didn't even know where it had rooted itself in, was a growing kernel of darkness. Morgan felt Selene poke at the darkness until it felt like it would burst. She continued to scratch and prod at it until the darkness began to seep out and Morgan felt those twisting, coiling shadows circle the room. With it came a wave of jealousy. Never feeling good enough. Never being able to give enough, to work hard enough. Morgan screamed and the sound seemed to carry on forever, but Selene continued to scrape at that bitter darkness in Morgan's soul until a gleaming light poured from it. The light seemed to burn Selene and she flinched in pain before she removed her hand from Morgan's face and the searing pain vanished from Morgan.

Selene panted as she recovered from using her essence to probe into Morgan's soul. Finally she said, "I can examine a soul. Yours is... unexpected. King Rylo was right in choosing you as the witch for Nephel. While I haven't had the opportunity to examine it as closely, your sister has the soul of a child. *You* on the other hand have ambition and cunning. It's been wasted in such a frivolous capacity in your realm, sitting in front of that human device. But here? If you reach your potential here, you will be unstoppable. Did you know this about yourself?"

Morgan could barely make out the violet eyes shining back at her in the pitch-black room, but she felt those ever-present shadows coiling around her as if protecting her from another invasion. "What are you going to do to me here? Force that darkness out of me?" Morgan asked.

Selene let out a shrewd huff. "Dear girl, that darkness is *dancing* around you. No. All I believe you need is to become acquainted with your darkness."

At that she turned, opening the door as the muted light from the hallway entered Morgan's room. Without another word, she closed the door with a soft click. Morgan was enveloped in an ever expanding darkness.

Chapter 13

Savine

Strange rumors were circulating through the land of fae who were worn thin, as if their essence had been nearly depleted. Savine wasn't sure if they were just rumors, or if it was a remnant of his father's use of dark magic. Had his father been using that dark force against the Latians as well as the forest? The forest, drained of its essence like skeletons on the mountains, would forever haunt his dreams. There still hadn't been any explanation for what Jasper had done to the trees before that final battle of the war, but Savine knew there had to be some evidence of it here in the King's Residence.

Darby entered Savine's office, her pale green skin flush from rushing to his call. "I heard you needed me, my King. What can I do for you?"

Savine smiled at the small fae. She still wasn't as short as Avery, but she was petite for a fae. "First, I want to thank you for all your hard work during this transition. I know it hasn't been easy for you."

Darby's face lit up with a smile. "Thank you. It's what I've always dreamed of. Seeing you with the boughs and antlers on your head. Your mother would be proud."

Savine nodded, not letting his grief over her absence get to him. "I have a few things to speak to you about. Private matters that I don't want anyone to hear of."

"Of course," Darby said as Savine showed her to a set of chairs in the corner of the room. With high backs and sumptuous bison leather, they made a comfortable place to discuss daily business with Raikin or Darby. His office near the throne room was quickly beginning to feel like his own personal refuge. With a view of the city below and close proximity to the throne, Savine found himself spending most of his days in this room as he sorted through the mess of reconstructing his nation.

"Would you like me to get us anything?" Darby asked.

"If you would like a refreshment, please help yourself." Savine pointed to the sideboard with honeyed cakes and a pitcher of water. "I don't need anything."

"I'm fine as well. What would you like to discuss?"

Savine fisted his hands, thinking about the memories that brimmed forth with this conversation. "Two things. First, you know I have chosen to stay in my old rooms. I want them prepared for Avery's arrival. I've thought about it, and I cannot move into the king's apartment. It–" Savine's throat clenched as he worked to make the words come out. His father's angry face came into his mind, himself as a frightened child, facing his father's wrath in his study. "As you can assume, it holds many negative memories. No amount of redecorating will change that."

Darby's mouth drew tight. "Of course. I understand."

"However, I believe Jasper was hiding something. I know he was experimenting with magic somehow, possibly even corrupting deep magic. I could feel it in the trees Avery and I healed before the final battle. Do you know what that could have been?"

Darby scowled. "There were rumors that he kept a small bone near him. How he used it, I do not know, but I believe it was said to hold dark powers that no fae should have access to. No one dared to speak out against King Jasper, so everything is just whispers in the wind."

Savine felt a sense of dread come over him. What had driven his father to such dark magic? Was it all in the name of safeguarding his crown from Savine? Savine couldn't fathom how Jasper had let himself be degraded to such extremes. "Would you be able to search his personal effects and see if there is any evidence to corroborate these rumors? Perhaps he left the bone here. He had to have been using something powerful to destroy the forest in such a way."

"Of course. While we are on the subject of dark magic, I wanted to ask if you have heard the rumors of the young fae appearing with their essence nearly depleted. Do you suspect it is tied to Jasper?"

Savine pressed his thumb and forefinger to the bridge of his nose. Healing his folk from his father's disastrous reign was a burden he always knew he'd inherit, if he survived the war. But, the day to day work was exhausting and disheartening. If it was his father who caused these fae such extreme levels of harm, what were his motives? "I suppose it could be. So far it's only been rumors outside of Orofine, correct?"

Darby nodded.

"I'll let Garnel and Raikin know I'd like one of these fae brought to the King's Residence. I'd like to understand how a young fae can become so depleted."

"While I'm searching for the source of Jasper's magic, I'll see if there are any clues to these fae. May the Goddess bless their poor souls. Could you imagine being drained of your essence in such a way?" She shook her head, a sincere look of worry on her face.

"Thank you for all your help, Darby," Savine said as he stood and showed her to the door.

He sat in his chair, looking out over the city and yearned for Avery's company. The burden of the crown was heavy, its cold, gilded metal an ever-present reminder of his duty.

Morgan

Morgan's shadows danced around her, wrapping her in a cocoon of dark comfort. She'd lost all sense of time as she sat in the darkness, letting the encompassing silence draw all her previous fears out of her until she felt like she was being eaten alive by the terror within her.

Her mind kept spiraling to the horrible darkness of the mine shaft, to the fear she'd felt as that fae loomed over her, a look of angry hunger etched in his features. The memories left her soaked in a cold sweat, gasping for breath as shadows squirmed across her skin. She couldn't get them to stop, couldn't control how they seemed to suck all the oxygen from the room and left her struggling for some semblance of security in the deafening darkness. Even hearing other prisoners would have been better than the sensory deprivation she was experiencing.

When she wasn't trying to claw her mind out of that mine shaft, she kept thinking of what Selene had forced her to relive. She'd always tried to meet her high expectations she'd placed on herself. She'd always been convinced that if she wasn't perfect in everything she did then she wasn't worthy. Her parents never overtly said this to her. It was more in the way she was always praised as a child for her good grades, for her quieter demeanor compared to Avery's loud and rambunctious attitude. That praise had felt good and it had made her seek it more and more. Eventually, she'd convinced herself that being the sister with the perfect grades and the plans was who she was.

She could remember the first time she began hiding her slip ups from her family. She'd been a teenager and had an algebra test that she'd spent hours studying for. She'd studied so long that she didn't get enough sleep, and when it came time for her exam she couldn't concentrate, her eyes closing as she tried to think through the equations. So she looked at her classmate's test while her teacher did something on her computer, distracted from the seemingly quiet test takers. She was seated next to the smartest boy in their grade. They usually worked together to quickly find the answers to their daily classwork and she knew he would be a reliable person to cheat off of. She ran the calculation herself to check the answer, but it was correct and she spent the rest of the test checking her own answers against those of her classmate's. They both received a perfect score and the teacher hadn't noticed.

Then in college she'd found relief from the growing pressure she placed on herself in the bodies of strangers. It gave her a sense of power to have these fleeting sexual experiences without needing to be the perfect girlfriend or worry about making time for a relationship in her busy schedule. She'd never told Avery, only sending her location to a close friend. She was safe, always prepared with a condom and an IUD and she got tested regularly. Avery had always assumed Morgan was too busy to want a relationship, and while that was true, Morgan also liked the thrill of being with a stranger and knew her sister wouldn't understand.

There were more. Many instances of a crack in her perfect facade. Of the ways she'd let herself slide from perfection when nobody else knew. That was why she'd begun practicing yoga. She thought if she could just get control of her mind's desire to stray from perfection then she'd become her best self. Meditation retreats, daily yoga, none of it had relieved her of the need to keep herself in a tight, orderly box, only to let herself do something quietly reckless when the pressure became too much. The attack at Quartz Mountain had splintered that box, and she didn't know how to gain control again.

The darkness consumed her as she tried to let her mind be blissfully free of thoughts. She stretched herself out on the stone floor, the shadows licking against her cool skin. Selene said she had ambition and cunning. She looked into her soul, released the kernel of darkness inside her that she'd tried to bury so deeply.

Her shadows curled around her, and she willed herself to control their writhing movements. As she tugged at them, they bucked and expanded, making the room feel even more dark and more claustrophobic. Her vision was filled with the bear, pressing down on her before he wrapped his jaws around her head, and it was like he was in the room with her. She could feel the heat of his breath and the prickle of anticipation that came from knowing his maw would be on her next.

Morgan screamed as the shadows roiled and burst from her, tearing at her skin while her mind slipped back into the jaws of the beast that had caused her so much terror. The shadows were whirling around her, and she thought she'd be choked on their grip—a grip so reminiscent of the one that once surrounded her skull.

She gasped for breath and let out a fearful cry, but nobody came to help her. She was lost, alone in this darkness that would surely suffocate her.

The only thing that could save her from this heavy darkness was herself. She was the source of these smothering shadows, and nobody was going to help her escape that part of herself. As Selene had suggested, they were a part of her, and she wasn't about to let her own magic destroy her.

Morgan took a series of deep breaths, letting her mind travel to a place of serenity. A place she often let her mind wander to while meditating. She opened her senses to a place with cool, streaming water as she let her racing heartbeat relax. The shadows loosened around her and she sat up, crossing her legs. With eyes still closed, she envisioned a fern-covered forest with a creek flowing through carved stones. The shadows swayed with her steady breathing as she visualized them becoming a part of her, a part of her that would *never* harm her. The heaviness like a dark mist in the room began pulling back, slowly sinking into her. Her arms lifted and her body began floating in a sea of shadows. The sensation was soft, delicate. The shadows didn't fight her or suffocate her. Instead, they responded to her mind's grasp on them. Gently, she went back to the ground, her magic pulling into her as she continued to visualize that peaceful location.

For the first time since she entered this cell, her shadows weren't writhing and blustering around her. Morgan controlled them. They were a part of her, just as her arm was a part of her, and she'd never let them overpower her again.

Chapter 14

Avery

Edet tutted as she tried to comb out Avery's unruly waves. The woman's sandpaper rough hands worked their way through Avery's hair before she set the comb down with a sigh. Avery studied her roughened, reddish features in the mirror. She still didn't know what kind of a fae Edet was, and thought better of asking her. She clearly had some sort of rock essence. Sandstone if Avery had to guess, since she so closely resembled that type of rock. Avery sighed, but didn't say anything as Edet returned to prodding at her wind-tousled hair.

Her sister was locked in the Tower of Teeth, and Rylo had refused to see her for the last two days. Anxiety had spurred Avery's body until she couldn't sit still any longer. After one day of letting herself sink back into guilt and despair, she forced herself to get outside with her friends. Susan, Kyla, and Rue were all up for training and they'd set up a good system for her to bury her concerns for Morgan in physical activity. This morning they hiked the craggy mountains of Nephel. She needed to explore the rocky canyon and the high alpine peaks miles from the Towers. To get away from this place and just be free in the wilderness. Her body craved the wild, rugged areas away from the opulence of Rylo's court. Only that could calm the increasing worry she had for Morgan.

To her surprise, Rylo had approved of her outings, even though he'd refused to meet with her. The only caveat was that Selene joined. Avery didn't even know how the Sage of Nephel had time to go stomping through rocky outcroppings with them, but it seemed to be made into a priority. To nobody's surprise, Selene refused to walk on the dusty trails and the dying grasses that dotted the mountains. Instead, she flew above the women, just near enough to intervene if they tried something that Rylo deemed unacceptable, which seemed limited to running away and hurting a Nepheli. Neither were something that Avery planned to do anyway.

Only hours after she got back from her hike, Edet had arrived. Apparently Rylo was willing to meet with her, but only at a formal supper. As she dressed for her first mandatory meal with Rylo since the Latians left, she wondered what Savine was doing at that moment. She'd been so scared for Morgan's safety that Savine's own well being wasn't holding its place in the forefront of her mind. She wondered if she could send some sort of communication down their bond from this distance. Why couldn't she? She could still feel that connection, even if it was faint. Mentally, she grabbed onto that bond and caressed it, feeling slightly foolish.

"What's got you looking so star-eyed, girl?" Edet asked.

Avery flinched at Edet's voice. "Oh, nothing."

"Looks to me like something. You'd be missing your soulmate, I'm sure. And not even accepting the bond yet." Edet tutted again as she shook her head. "No wonder you humans are all but eliminated here. Not much sense in your heads."

Avery didn't respond as Edet began piling her long blonde hair into some sort of up do. "Only death could separate me from my soulmate," Edet said as she shook her head again and continued wrestling Avery's hair into submission. "And even then I should have joined him. Should have never... Oh what matter is all that? I mean to say, don't be a fool about your soulmate again, girl." Edet turned Avery so she was looking up at the woman, her scratchy hand on Avery's chin. "Cherish what Althea gave you. Don't waste it away, not even on family."

Edet released her chin and Avery turned to face the mirror again. At that moment, she felt a soft caress through the bond and a warmth filled her inside and out. It was so reminiscent of that early warmth she felt when she and Savine touched for the first time, and the sensation left her with such a longing that she had to remember to breathe. She gave the bond another squeeze and mentally stroked it in return. So she could still communicate with Savine on some level from this distance. She let herself relax, thinking of good days to come, and sent all the joy and hope she could muster down their bond.

"There!" Edet croaked. "You're as presentable as I can make you. I'll leave you to your pining. Remember what I say now. Don't take your soulmate for granted again, foolish girl!" With that, Edet turned and left the room.

Avery felt a wave of Savine's response down the bond. It felt like a cool breeze in a coniferous forest, like going home. Her heart longed to feel his strong arms wrapped around her. She sat in the chair, looking at her reflection as she tugged on their bond, bringing forth the feelings she experienced when she was safe in his arms.

Things would have been different if he were here. He wouldn't have allowed Rylo to send Morgan to the Tower of Teeth. He would have stood up for her, protected her in a way that Avery couldn't possibly manage.

A soft caress went down the bond and across her spine. The heat in that caress made Avery think of Savine's lips pressed against her skin, the tingling sensation that arose when he touched her. She leaned back in her chair, closing her eyes as warm pressure built deep in her belly.

She imagined tracing Savine's roiling essence, the way he groaned as she pressed her lips and tongue to the faint lines under his skin. The bond between them, so faint compared to how it felt when they were close to each other, went still as she waited, the anticipation of how he would respond making her flush with heat.

His response rocketed into her. Needy desire pulsed through her tingling skin as she imagined his hands tracing their way along her thigh. She gasped for more as a delicate, light touch grazed her skin. Strangely, she didn't even need to touch herself, the trace of Savine through the bond was enough to have her biting her lower lip and gasping for more.

Avery imagined peeling Savine's leathers off him, exposing his beautiful, hard body and pressing her hands against his bare skin as she worked her way down to his hard length, imagining herself working around him everywhere but where she knew he'd want her hands.

She gasped as Savine's reply came quicker than she expected. Pressure built inside her core that left her eyes rolling in her head and her hips bucking. Avery imagined stroking, teasing his erection as she rode the wave of desire he'd sent her.

The waves of his desire were rising now, crashing against her like the sea against sand, breaking down her barriers as she felt herself becoming raw and exposed to the bond that was stretched between them. Finally, her climax overtook her, ripping through her as she tried to stifle the cry that broke from her parted lips. Savine's orgasm spilled down their bond, the magnitude of it taking her breath away.

Soft, gentle embraces wrapped around her and she looked at herself in the mirror. The tightness in her face had relaxed, the anxiety that had been haunting her since Morgan had been taken eased, at least for now.

Avery sent her own waves of caressing love down the bond as a gentle warmth enveloped her senses. Why hadn't they tried this earlier? This would be enough to get her through the next couple of weeks until she could be back in Savine's arms.

A knock on her door stirred her from their bond and back to reality. Selene entered the room, her posture full of stately grace, but for the tight lipped frown on her face.

"I'm to fly you to Rylo now," she said as she assessed Avery's appearance.

Avery nodded as she stood. "Do you get sick of being his messenger?"

Selene's frown deepened. "I am happy to serve my king in any matter of tasks, but I look forward to you and your sister's departure. I have more important things to do with my day than tend to your needs."

Avery grinned as they made their way to the balcony. "I can't wait to leave either. With my sister."

Selene didn't respond as she lifted Avery and flew into the skies. Her black wings beat upward and Avery couldn't resist noticing just how stunning the satin sheen of her wings looked against the sunset.

Selene unceremoniously placed her on the floor of the expansive balcony outside the banquet hall. The last time she'd been here was the evening Savine left. God, she missed him. She mentally caressed the bond between them, needing to feel that connection before she faced Rylo and begged for her sister's freedom.

The room had about a dozen winged fae, all staring at her as she followed behind Selene. She noticed her friends already seated at a long table as others made their way to their chairs. This must be an intimate supper, featuring only Rylo's closest courtiers. Avery took her seat near the head of the table, across from Selene who sat next to Kyla. On her right was a man she recognized from her kidnapping. She didn't know his name, and she felt a chill travel down her spine as she remembered his eyes on her after she stabbed Weston. The cold, cruel smirk on his face as Weston breathed his last breath.

Her heart stuttered as she tried to control the anxiety growing in her. She didn't know if she could do this. How could she convince these cruel folk to let her have her sister back? How would she even get them to listen to her, when they'd already hurt her so much?

Kyla gave her a wary glance. She wished she could ask for Kyla's help. Now that she was experiencing her own crisis, she had a better understanding of how Morgan must have felt that evening in this very room.

"Excuse me," Kyla said to Selene. "I need to speak with Avery privately."

Avery's ears were ringing as she silently slipped from the table and followed Kyla to a private alcove draped in diaphanous black curtains.

Kyla placed her hands on Avery's shoulder as Avery choked back a cry. "That man I'm by. He was there when I killed Weston. Just being by him made the memories of what I did to him rush back." Avery couldn't stop the shaking that went through her body as she continued, "It was easier when Savine was with me. It's been easier to have them avoid us. But I don't know how I'm going to convince them to release Morgan when I keep picturing Weston's blood on my hands."

Kyla made soothing circles with her hands on Avery's neck and shoulders, the tension she was carrying slowly fading. She didn't manipulate Avery's emotions, didn't even ask. "You have experienced a tremendous amount of trauma since you arrived in Aeritis, Avery, and you've faced it with such courage. You've chosen to see the positive side of your situation and you've handled yourself better than can be expected. I know from my own experiences in the war that past pains can haunt us at unexpected times. The man you're sitting by is Elio, one of Rylo's closest courtiers. Perhaps it helps to name the man and see him for what he is. His allegiance to Rylo is strong, perhaps even the closest thing a king like Rylo can have to a friend. It's your natural instinct to feel this way to him. You know you're sitting between two wolves, with Rylo on your left and Elio on your right. It was purposeful on Rylo's part. He could have easily placed Susan or Rue next to you. They aren't on the other end of the table just because of their rank."

"What should I do?" Avery asked, the trembling in her body becoming less noticeable. Kyla let her hands fall to her side.

"Take courage. Rylo wouldn't dare harm you. Not when he knows it would cause a war with Latiah if he did. Stand up for your sister, and don't let Rylo's obvious intimidation tactics get to you. Some battles are fought on the battlefield with weapons, but you'll soon learn that many more are fought at dinner parties with words. Never forget that I'm here for you."

Avery took Kyla's hand in hers, squeezing it tight. "Thanks for the pep talk." She let out a steadying breath as she said, "I know you wanted to be in Orofine with the others, but I wanted you to know how thankful I am to have you with me."

Kyla smiled and bowed her head, the tiny beads and bells in her hair clacking together.

They walked in silence back to their chairs. Rylo still had not joined the party, but everyone else was seated. When a servant offered her wine, she took the bottle and poured a glass for herself, not risking being under the control of a Nepheli, even a servant. Drum beats on the balcony had everyone turning to see Rylo flying into the room. Everyone stood, and Avery followed as the Sun King made his pompous entrance into the throne room. The orange and pink glow of the sunset seemed to be drawn into the room with him, his skin glowing in glorious radiance as he flew toward Avery and his seat at the head of the table.

Rylo looked at her, a twitch in his lips was the only thing he revealed on his indolent face as he took a seat and motioned for the table to do the same.

"Good of you to join us this evening, Avery," Rylo drolled, the same smirk on his face as a servant poured him a glass of honey colored wine. "Kyla, it's always a pleasure."

"Likewise, Your Highness," Kyla said, taking a sip of her own wine.

"I trust you have been comfortable? Has Selene provided you with your needs?"

Avery noticed Selene tip her face toward her king from whatever held her attention down the table. Her violet eyes sparkled against her dark skin.

"Yes, of course," Kyla said. "Selene was kind enough to join us on a hike through your mountains today."

Avery's hands shook as she tried to contain her growing anxiety over what Rylo would say about her sister. She couldn't imagine how Morgan must be suffering right now as she sat here, drinking a glass of wine in a room drenched in splendor. It made her sick to think about.

"Please," Avery squeaked out and she felt the fae man beside her shift his attention to her. Rylo looked at her as well.

"What was that, Avery?" Rylo asked, leaning back in his seat with wings draped neatly over the low chair.

"Please... Just let Morgan out." Her voice shook, but she forced herself to continue. "She just misses our home. It's not fair to punish her for that."

Selene raised an eyebrow. "I've personally seen to your sister's needs. She is not in any physical danger."

This made the aching dread in Avery build. Selene could do so much worse than physical danger. Savine was a personal victim of her abilities.

"That's not encouraging, and you know it! Just let her out. She's suffered enough."

Rylo's eyes became slits as he shook his head. "She will be released when she is ready. For now, you have my assurance that your sister is in no real danger. She is alone and no one is to bother her as she convalesces."

"*Convalesce?* She's going to need to convalesce from being in your torture tower!" Avery said, her voice shaking with emotion.

"Do not speak to what you don't understand," Selene said. "Your sister will come back to you stronger due to her time in the Tower of Teeth."

"I grow tired of this conversation. Due to our previous agreement, you know I cannot harm Morgan and I will release her to you in Orofine," Rylo muttered before he turned his attention to Kyla. He wasn't going to let Morgan out until it was time to leave this awful place. She'd failed her sister. Avery's shoulders slumped as Rylo spoke to Kyla. "Tell me, why did you choose to change your hairstyle? It hasn't gone without notice that you two and Morgan chose to cover your foreheads."

"It's an American style," Kyla explained. "Perhaps I was trying to help the witches with their homesickness."

Elio spoke for the first time to the group. "Or perhaps it has something to do with you disrupting our goddess. Selene shared how you dared approach her without express permission just after you altered your hair and stopped wearing headdresses."

Rylo cocked his head to Elio. "Good point, Elio. After you wore that ridiculous headdress to supper, and now you cover your forehead with hair, I must wonder if you are keeping things from me, and seeking answers from our goddess."

Avery had to lie for Kyla. She couldn't let Rylo know that Althea had marked her. "Kyla's right. Morgan and I are homesick and we convinced her to change her hairstyle with us. I was being nosy and wanted Kyla to bring the goddess down to me. I've never met a deity before. Apparently that's not a thing, is it? I'm sorry. I didn't mean to be disrespectful."

Elio chuckled as he said, "You really shouldn't indulge these humans, Kyla."

But Rylo and Selene stared at her unconvinced. Fortunately, the servants arrived with trays of meat. It appeared to be venison, but Avery was never really sure what she was eating here. Kyla rose and walked to Avery's side as she placed a generous portion on Avery's plate. Her warm smile shone with gratitude as she made her way back to her chair.

Chapter 15

Morgan

The bright sunlight burned Morgan's sensitive eyes as she clung to Selene. The air around her was cool and crisp and her scars tingled as the breeze skimmed along her exposed face. Morgan had lost all sense of time while in that cell, but came out with a clearer head than she'd expected.

Her time in the dark hadn't been the torturous experience she'd feared. Instead, she felt stronger than she'd ever felt in her life. Nobody would believe her when she admitted that she'd faced her demons in that dark solitude and triumphed. She'd found that darkness within herself and embraced that side of her, and now her shadows seemed to respond to her instinctively, like they were an extension of herself.

With that thought, a cool band of shadows nestled over her eyes, covering the sharp rays that stung her vision.

"It seems the time in the dark has done you good," Selene said. "The Tower of Teeth can break some folk, but it can also forge and strengthen."

Morgan nodded, but didn't speak to the woman. Her shadows pranced around her face, retreating as she landed on the cool shade of

Rylo's library balcony. Selene turned without another word and flew back toward the Tower of Teeth. So much for a goodbye.

As Morgan moved into the room, her shadows slithered beside her, like a faithful companion. That was what they'd become. Her companions in the dark; a beautiful, misty piece of her that was alive with power and potential.

She saw the Sun King before he saw her, sitting silently with a book in his hand. He had that casual air about him of someone who was perfectly content. His suntanned skin and amber locks were too perfect. It wasn't fair that such an arrogant man should be so gorgeous.

Finally he looked up at her, a small smirk tugged at one side of his face, exposing the slightest dimple on his cheek. "Ah, Morgan. You have returned from your stay, I see."

"Yeah, Selene just got me out. I'm sure you knew." Her voice sounded scratchy and unused as she spoke.

"Sit," Rylo commanded. "How was your time in the Tower of Teeth?" A tea set for two appeared on the table as Morgan leaned into the low back couch.

"You stuck me in the dark for days. How do you think it went?" Morgan asked, grinding her teeth as she spoke. The shadows around her began snaking closer to Rylo and he tried to kick them away.

"It was for your best interest. You needed to get the absurd notion that you can leave Aeritis out of your mind. And you needed to get command of those lovely shadows of yours. Am I correct to assume that both things occurred during your time alone?"

Morgan let the shadows twist up the couch Rylo sat on until they reached his torso and slithered up his body, caressing his neck. He pressed his back against the couch, wings tucked in tight. She tugged her shadows slightly against Rylo's throat until his golden eyes lit like bright orbs and his skin began to glimmer. Then she released the shadows, pulling them back into herself.

She reached for the tea set and poured herself a cup of piping hot, reddish tinted tea. It had a cinnamon and acorn scent and reminded her of the cool fall day outside.

"Does that answer your question?" Morgan asked with a grin.

"Do you plan to be a kingslayer twice over?" Rylo replied as he poured a cup for himself. His skin still seemed to sparkle with golden light as he took a steadying drink.

"Right now? No. But I won't guarantee that if you ever stick me back in your stinking torture tower."

Rylo's look of boredom slid away as he eyed her with distrust mingled with curiosity. "I will not coddle you like Savine has done to your sister. You are not my soulmate and make no mistake, I plan to use that great well of power in you for the coming conflict. Selene told me what she saw in your soul. What *you* saw. Your raw ambition, an analytical mind and someone who takes calculated risks. Tell me, have you found that part of yourself again?"

Morgan looked at him and considered how she should respond to such a question. She saw a lot of herself in the darkness. Parts that were ugly and parts that were beautiful. But most of all, she saw her inner strength and her need to outwit these fae. She wasn't going to let these people who'd already hurt her take away her power again. She wanted revenge, yes, but she also wanted a greater purpose in Aeritis if she was trapped here. Finally, she decided she'd be honest with this man.

"Yeah, I did."

"Good. Do you see all these books?" Morgan looked at the room as Rylo waved his hands. Floor to ceiling bookcases wrapped around the room. "They're a fraction of what I have collected over the years. Knowledge is power, and I think you can agree with that."

Morgan nodded, not sure where he was going with this statement.

"Since I first discovered humans could enter our realm through Sapphire Falls I have collected every book and ancient text on the humans I could find. The witches at The Cleaving were far more powerful than any fae, and when they worked together they were unstoppable in magical strength. Your sister accidentally tapped into this strength, but I want you to learn it properly. I want you to study their history. Practice their spells and grow that power in yourself. Nephel has long been subjected to attacks from more powerful armies and greedy nations that have stolen our land. I was able to secure just a fraction of that land back from Savine in exchange for his little mate, but I want it all back. And you are going to help me get it."

Morgan knew that Savine had initially seen her sister as some sort of gift that he could control, but this seemed to be some kind of power-hungry fae ruler trait.

"Why would I do that?" Morgan asked, crossing her arms.

"Beyond becoming the most powerful being in this realm? What is it you want, Kingslayer?"

Morgan grinned. While thinking in the dark, she knew what she wanted out of this place. She wanted to be the one in control, the one calling the shots. The shadows slithered away from her, reaching out toward Rylo again.

"I want three oaths from you, and I will speak the words of the bargain. You'll agree to them no matter what I ask for," she said, smiling up at the surprise on the man's face.

"Three oaths? You drive a hard bargain. The fae rarely agree to such things."

"Well, that's what I want. If you want to use my brain and my magic then you'll agree. Otherwise I'll just be loafing around your home until I go to Orofine."

Rylo pursed his lips. He hesitated long enough that she thought he may refuse her offer.

"Agreed. Three oaths in exchange for your mind and your magic."

They both stood, shaking on the agreement. As their hands touched, bright light, like that of the sun, wrapped around her arm and mingled with the shadows that stretched up Rylo's arm.

Their magic was in conflict against each other, and she saw his skin continue to gleam like morning light as he sat back down.

"Don't be alarmed, pet. I was testing your truthfulness with a bit of my essence. If you were lying you'd be blistered from head to toe," Rylo drawled as he took a chocolate from a box that appeared from thin air. "Now when can I expect you to follow through on your oaths?"

Morgan smiled and looked down at the darkness snaking around her legs. She liked it, this unlikely companion always at her side. "Whenever you least expect it."

Avery

"So you spent the week alone in the dark?" Avery asked, still not sure if she believed her sister hadn't been tormented, or even starved during her time in Rylo's famed torture tower.

Morgan sliced the thin pieces of meat on her plate, taking a delicate bite. "Yeah, at first I felt a growing panic, but I let it die down and just embraced the darkness."

Avery shook her head. "What did you do then?"

Morgan shrugged before sipping the wine from her goblet. She'd arrived at their shared room clean, calm, and rather pleased with herself only a few hours earlier. After she'd unexpectedly entered their shared room, Morgan asked if Avery would take a walk with her. Despite the time outside together, Avery hadn't been able to piece together what had happened to her sister during her stay in the Tower of Teeth.

"You know. What I usually do alone. I did yoga and meditated. Plus I reflected on my life before coming here and my soul, and practiced using my shadows." Morgan effortlessly let the shadows that had been circling her legs move up her body before sweeping forward to caress Avery's cheek.

The touch was cool, calming, and so Morgan that Avery wasn't at all surprised this darkness came from her sister. What Avery couldn't stop was the pang of jealousy that settled in her heart. Of course Morgan would master her magic with ease. Of course it would happen while she turned a means of torturing her into a week long yoga retreat in the dark.

"And you're fine with all this? With the way Rylo punished you for trying to leave?"

Morgan looked at her with green eyes, flecks of amber dancing amongst the jade. "I think Rylo wasn't trying to punish me as much as force me to face what I already knew. I can't go home. Not yet, not until I learn how. But I can use my strengths and talents to make my time here better."

Avery's mouth gaped so far open she could have swallowed a fly. "It just doesn't make sense that you're so calm about all this. He *locked you away* for a week!"

Morgan took another bite of her food, sighing as she said, "I think it was what I needed." The shadows built around her then glided through the room, lifting objects and setting them in new places. "I feel like I'm gaining control—not only of my magic, but of who I can become here, and even gaining some control over Rylo."

Now Avery really didn't understand what her sister meant. "Well, fortunately we'll be leaving for Orofine soon! Then we won't have to see him again."

Morgan bit her lip. For the first time during their conversation, she looked unsure. "I think I need to stay here, Ave. I don't think my time in Nephel is over yet, but you should go."

Avery jumped up, closing the distance between herself and Morgan. "Morgan, please. We need to stick together. Once we're in Orofine we can practice magic together without worrying about Rylo's motives."

The scars along Morgan's cheeks tightened as frown lines appeared on her face. "I don't think I can go there. Not yet anyway. I finally have access to Rylo's library, and being around people who look like my attacker... It's too intense. Plus, I don't doubt they'll attack me for killing their king. We have no way of knowing what's been happening there."

Avery squeezed her sister's hand. "Morgan, don't. I don't want to lose you again, please! Let's just stay together through this. We're better together. I'll make sure you're safe there."

Morgan pulled her hand back before she brought her gaze to the remaining bites of her dinner. Finally, she turned and looked at Avery. "I don't know, Ave. I have a very bad feeling about this..."

"Please, please just say you'll stay with me! I can't lose you again, Morgan, and I can't stay here. I need to see Savine again, plus Rylo is still the one who kidnapped me and has hurt Savine so much."

The tightness in Morgan's expression relaxed a bit as she said, "Yeah, you're right. We should stick together."

Chapter 16

Savine

Savine sat on the carved wooden throne. The wood was worn in places where his ancestors had rubbed the grain smooth and the bumps from the inlaid jewels hurt his ass. He was considering commissioning a new throne for himself and Avery, but perhaps that was thinking too far ahead. Avery was too disinterested with the crown, so he wouldn't push the role on her. Besides, most rulers of Latiah didn't have their spouse or soulmate rule alongside them. Perhaps it was best that he continued a long tradition of ruling on his own.

The joyous homecoming had lasted less than a day before Savine felt the magnitude of what he was stepping into as King of Latiah. A little over two weeks had passed since Savine arrived in Orofine and he wanted nothing more than a few quiet moments by himself. But try as he might, he wasn't getting that time. Perhaps it was for the best to be this busy without Avery by his side. Once she was here, he would demand some time for her alone, away from the incessant pleas and requests from noble families and city folk.

A fae from a migratory band was speaking to him now about their concern over their band's winter supplies. Under Jasper's rule, migratory groups were no longer able to travel freely and had struggled to adjust to a stationary lifestyle. It was no surprise that folk accustomed to hunting and gathering would not be able to take up growing crops. Savine felt compassion for the displaced fae. But it was like this every day, hearing the stories of how his father had harmed his own people, weakening his own nation until they were a shell of the once powerful nation.

The only bright side was that Jasper's greed was helping solve the imbalance in their society now. The former king had stockpiles of supplies—grains, dried meat, fish, fruit, extra furs, weapons, and oddly more sanitary cloth for wiping shit than any nation could ever need.

"We will support your band of fae through the winter. You may take whatever stock from our supplies here in Orofine that you will need to survive the winter, then you are free to return to your way of life. There is no longer a decree against migratory groups roaming Latiah freely."

The man bowed. His fur cape slid forward as he rose again. "You are a just and kind king."

Savine gave a small bow and motioned for his cup. Darby was there beside him with a hot cup of tea and he took it eagerly.

"How many more today?" he whispered. After this he had a meeting with his preliminary council, then was expected to oversee the preparations for the Night of Feasts.

"Three, Your Majesty," Darby said as she took the cup back from Savine.

Savine shifted in his seat before the next fae entered the room. He looked to his side to the guards beside him. He hadn't said anything to Avery because he'd never want to hurt her, but he missed Weston. Weston was not only his guard, but had been his friend for many years, even if he'd never admitted it to him. It was one of those things he knew he had to work on if he was to be a good king. Letting the people who mattered know that they did matter. These new guards, while still his rebel warriors, weren't men or women that he'd been close to.

Savine adjusted his long strands back behind his crown, then gestured for another subject to be admitted.

The woman who entered the throne room was old—older than many of the fae remaining in Orofine, with weathered skin and tattered furs. He didn't have to hear from her to know that she had been struggling when she should be nearing her rest. The fur essence under her skin was so faded that it appeared little more than scuffs.

She walked slowly, cane in hand and he stood, walking to offer his hand as support.

"A chair. Now." Immediately, one of the guards was dragging a chair over for the woman. She sank into the seat and looked up at him with milky white eyes. Either she was losing her vision, or she was a seer. He could hear murmurs from the nobles in attendance, but didn't listen if they were in respect or disdain for his actions.

"My King," she croaked with a bow. Savine bowed out of reverence for the old woman.

"Grandmother, I am honored to have you in my home. What can I help you with?" Savine said as he took his seat on the throne.

"I am the last of my family line. My sons, daughters, and granddaughter were killed by your rebels in the war across the pass. My soul yearns to enter its rest, but there is nobody to care for my body as I release my essence to Althea."

Savine breathed in deeply. This wasn't an uncommon story, and he knew there was so little he could do to bring comfort to those left behind after the conflict. The old woman continued, "My granddaughter was the last to die. It's said she died at your own hands during the final conflict. You, we have heard, used the Goddess' deep magic, ripped from the very ground by a witch and fed into you. You cut down your own people indiscriminately with a force beyond what any fae should possess."

Savine's jaw ticked, tension growing in his body and he looked to the guards beside him. Already, they had their hands on their swords. "That is true. War is a mighty and terrible thing, and I must carry the souls of those I killed in the war for the rest of my days."

The ancient woman began quietly laughing to herself as she rocked in her seat. "And you think you are better than King Jasper? You, slayer of your own blood?"

The woman transformed with such speed Savine didn't have time to react before a great mountain lion was sinking her fangs into his throat. He reached for his essence and with a snap of his hands, he pressed rigid thorns around the old cat's throat. The cat's claws sunk into his shoulder and she tightened her hold on his neck as he pressed more of his essence into her. There was no way in the Abyss that he'd let this old woman kill him. Not now that he'd finally overcome his father. His essence rocked through him and filled the woman with so many brambles and thorns that it was impossible for anything to survive in that state.

He opened his eyes and saw the guards surround them, pressing swords into the old lady's body. Her shifted form went slack against him and Savine pushed the dead mountain lion off him, standing to see his bloodied clothes and hands. A few of the courtiers gasped at his appearance as Savine walked toward the side door, Darby and his guards at his side.

"Leave me!" he shouted. "I'll be fine." Savine stalked through the residence, gasping horror from onlookers as he went to his rooms. Although he wanted to be alone, he knew guards were following close behind him.

"Savine! Wait!" Darby shouted. "Let me call a healer for you! Your neck, it's punctured."

Savine waved his hand in her direction. "I'll be in my rooms."

Once he was alone in his rooms he looked at his injuries in the mirror. Bruising was already forming under his fur cloak. He threw the garment to the ground, inspecting the puncture wounds around his neck and shoulders. The old woman had done all she could to assassinate him, risking her soul to the Abyss to do it, yet she had been far too weak and frail. While she'd attacked with what little essence her body possessed, the assault would have never killed a strong fae in the prime of his life like him. If only he could have helped her—provided her with a safe place to take her rest, then he could have saved her from her own bloody end.

He couldn't blame the woman for attacking him. She was right, he'd indiscriminately killed many loyalists that day, and perhaps he would pay for it now that he was back in the capital.

A knock at the door sounded before Darby entered, accompanied by a healer with Bayberry features. She cleaned the wound quickly before healing the damaged skin. It was, as Savine suspected, a minor injury. After Savine dismissed her, he asked Darby to stay.

"What do the folk say about my mate, Avery? Tell me everything."

Darby's face twitched and she wrung her hands as she took a deep breath. "The former loyalists see you as the true king. They respect the right of your rule, but there's been whispers, even amongst your own warriors, about the power of the two sisters in Aeritis. They say King Rylo shared a prophecy about them, and the folk are afraid and distrust these women. I even heard one of them killed King Jasper with some kind of small explosion."

Savine clenched his hands and felt the pressure in his jaw. "They see Avery and her sister as an enemy to the fae?"

Darby was quiet as she looked toward the ground. "Many do after what everyone witnessed during that final battle. There are many rumors that have circled around about the role she played in filling you with deep magic. And others fear them because of what the witch did to King Jasper."

Savine pressed his fingers to the bridge of his nose before he looked up at Darby. "My soulmate will be here in less than one week! I want no one who could cause her harm in this residence. Give a list of the fae who have started these rumors to Garnel and Raikin. Have Garnel deal with the rebels and Raikin with the others. Thank you for your help, Darby. You may go."

Darby looked at him with a sad expression, but said nothing as she made her way to the door. Savine turned and looked out the window at the city below. He wasn't going to let Avery come to harm. Not after all he'd been through to finally have a soulmate.

He searched for that connection between them. It was so faint, like a tiny piece of him that could so easily be erased if he wasn't careful with it. He mentally tugged on that bond just as Avery had done the day before. He thought of her tight curves, the swelling peaks and dips of her human body. He remembered the way she'd moaned under his touch and his tongue, then he sent all his wanting need down the bond to her.

Minutes later, he was hit with a surge of need that made him hard just feeling how badly Avery wanted him in return.

Only a few days left before she would be his.

Chapter 17

Morgan

Morgan rode on the back of the enormous eagan for the final travel day to Orofine. She still couldn't believe that she was riding on the back of an eagle—an eagle the size of a minivan. Susan and Avery joined her, while Rue and Kyla rode with one of the Nepheli warriors. Rylo was flying beside them, insisting he see them to Orofine himself. The trip wasn't exactly comfortable, especially riding all day. The wind stung her eyes and it was a chore to hang onto her seat, a contraption that was a mix of a saddle and a chair.

Then there was the issue of where she was going. Morgan had told Avery why she wanted to stay in Nephel, but she couldn't get her sister to see her side of things. Avery's plea was enough to convince her to join her in Orofine, even if her instincts were shouting at her to turn around, to flee from this unknown threat to her life.

Plus she was beginning to enjoy her quiet mornings studying in Rylo's library and afternoons practicing magic and self defense with Avery's friends. Susan had begun to join her during the mornings at the library instead of hiking through the mountains with Avery, Rue, and Kyla. She and Susan had already practiced a few spells in one of the old spell books, including one that allowed Morgan to control her shadows enough to *levitate* above the ground. It was incredible—this feeling that anything could be possible through her magic. The potential for what she could accomplish was enough to keep her up late into the night, pouring over old spells and practicing to see what she could achieve.

Now Morgan was soaring through the sky, and she could see a city down below. It was a bustling community, bigger than the population of the Towers. As they banked in lower, she saw the entire city was made of wooden structures built into tree trunks with branches void of needles or leaves.

"Oh!" Avery gasped. "The whole city is made of treehouses! How did Savine not share that with me?"

Morgan smirked as she turned to look at the excitement on her sister's face. She bit back the urge to ask how a soulmate could leave out those kinds of details when he described his family home.

"It's beautiful," Morgan said instead.

The eagans glided down to the ground, landing at the base of a huge outdoor staircase leading up to what must be Savine's treehouse palace. The building was a series of interconnected rooms linked by outdoor bridges and exterior stairs. It was amazing, like no architectural feature she'd ever seen. But it did look like it would be cold in the winter. The structure was flanked by steep, heavily forested mountains. The air was fresh and crisp with the scent of wet trees. It even smelled like the woods she explored in Montana. It was all so familiar, yet so foreign at the same time.

Around them was a growing crowd of fae. Some had that strange bark essence, like Savine and Kyla, while others looked nearly plant-like with a greenish tinge to their brown skin. Still others had the striking marks of fur under their skin. The shifters.

Morgan watched as Avery made eye contact with Savine. Her sister unstrapped from the saddle and jumped off the eagan's back in a flash. She heard her squeal with delight as she ran to Savine's arms. Soon, Kyla was doing the same to her mate and Rue was welcomed with hugs from other Latians.

Morgan stepped down from the eagan, but that's as far as she could go. She felt a growing sense of overwhelm and her shadows encircled her arms protectively. Susan put a gentle hand on Morgan's shoulder.

"Are you okay, Morgan?" Susan asked.

"I don't know if I can face all these people," she muttered, her shadows circling her and Susan.

Susan squeezed her shoulder. "Just take your time. It will be okay, and I'm here with you."

The crowd grew around the eagans. Most seemed peaceful, but there was a growing murmur as fae began pointing at Morgan by the eagan. Morgan's heartbeat was skittering so fast, she wanted to escape as soon as possible. A fae with a furred essence made eye contact with Morgan and showed his teeth, snarling at her.

Morgan shook her head. "This was a mistake. I'm better off in Nephel."

Susan looked at the sneering man as a few others approached, walking swiftly toward the eagan. The great bird shrieked as one of the men shifted into a huge grizzly bear.

Morgan's heart was pounding in her chest. She felt like she was going to die of fear as the bear bounded toward her. The crowd screamed as the flustered eagan reached down irritatedly and grabbed a woman in its enormous beak.

Something inside Morgan snapped as she lost her hold on her own panicking nerves. Before she knew what she was doing, she unleashed her writhing shadows at the bear and strode toward him. She felt herself becoming weightless, just as she had practiced. The shadows wrapped and entangled the monster, seeking to kill the threat to her. She let his strangled body fall to the ground. Yet still, she floated just overhead.

Avery was shouting something and other fae monsters were approaching, but Morgan didn't let them near her. Her shadows wove through the crowd and she whispered the words of a spell she'd read. With an explosion like a grenade, the whole area was shrouded in a cloak of darkness, dotted with falling starlight.

Suddenly, a brilliant light and a gusting wind filled the darkness and Rylo walked toward her like a glowing star. "What are you doing? Get over to your sister," he barked.

"I'm calling in an oath now. You will swear to remove me from Orofine and give me safe passage back to Nephel. I can't stay here."

Rylo looked at her through glowing eyes. "I can't do that. It's an oath that is in direct contrast to an already agreed upon bargain. It would..."

"DO IT! Now, damn it!" Morgan screamed.

Rylo looked over his shoulder to the chaos behind them. The darkness was still settled all around the crowd and the people screamed in terror. Morgan could hear Avery shouting her name, but she couldn't stay here. It was impossible. These monsters wanted her dead, and she'd known it before they'd even left Nephel.

"I will suffer the consequences," Rylo said in a cutting tone.

"Will you die?" she asked, mounting the eagan that Susan had already climbed on in stunned silence.

"No, but..."

"Then take the oath," she said, pulling her shadows back toward herself. The bird would need to be able to see to get out of here.

Rylo nodded and said the words of the oath. "I, Rylo Finnian, swear to remove you, Morgan Hollis, from Orofine and give you safe passage to Nephel immediately."

As soon as he said the words, Rylo's hands began to grow black veins across his glowing skin. He held the injured hands to his chest like a broken thing. Susan grabbed Morgan's hand like a lifeline.

"Let's go!" Susan shouted.

"If you truly value your life, you will fly," he said as he mounted the empty seat on the eagan's back. The other birds followed their lead as they took to the vast, empty sky above.

Morgan looked back at the stunned shock on Susan's face and the growing agony on Rylo's. The blackened veins were up to his elbows.

"Can I do anything for that?" Susan asked.

"Are you a healer?" Rylo grunted out.

"Well, I am from Bayberry," she said with far too much optimism in her tone. "Oh and Morgan, can you share that spell you used when we get back?"

Rylo groaned in quiet agony. "Can you heal me or not?"

"I can try, but shouldn't we land?" Susan asked. "I don't want to fall off the back of this bird."

Rylo's tone was tense. "Keep your balance, you ridiculous woman! The Latians will likely go to war over this mess. We can't safely land in the middle of their nation."

Morgan turned to see Susan wrinkle her face at the Sun King. The black veins were spreading quickly. "It's almost past his elbows now," she said.

"Not helpful, unless your plan was to become a kingslayer twice over, possibly thrice since we don't know if your sister's mate survived whatever you did with your shadows," Rylo bit out.

"It was only an observation," Morgan muttered.

She watched as Susan unstrapped from the chair and cautiously made her way forward to Rylo's seat. She touched his shoulders and began working her magic. Morgan hadn't heard of Susan's healing skills, but whatever she was saying seemed to at least be stopping the spread of blackness up Rylo's arms.

"There. That's all I can do. I'm not exactly a skilled healer, but at least the damage isn't spreading," she remarked before she crawled back to her seat.

"Will it go away?" Morgan asked. She looked at the throbbing black veins against Rylo's golden skin.

"No, it's not going away. I broke a bargain. I will be forever marked as deceitful."

Morgan grimaced. "So that's why you didn't want to take my oath?"

"No, and if you had just acted on your own accord I wouldn't have had to. Susan could have flown you to Bayberry for a month, or wherever your hearts pleased. Now I'll bear these marks for the rest of my days."

"Well, you could have said so!" Morgan protested, but Rylo just gave out a bitter laugh.

"You wouldn't let me get a word in," he argued.

"Enough!" Susan shouted in a squeaky voice. Clearly the woman wasn't used to shouting.

They all settled into an uneasy silence. Morgan wondered what had happened to Avery during that mess of a situation. She hoped she hadn't hurt her or their friends in the explosion.

Avery

Savine was pulling Avery to the safety of the palace, but she kicked at him, trying to break free as he hoisted her into his arms. "Morgan!" Avery shouted for her sister, but she couldn't see her through the impenetrable darkness.

"Shh.... Little Flower. Don't fight me," Savine whispered as he carried her up the stairs. But this was wrong. It was all wrong. Where was Morgan? One moment Avery saw her watching as she ran for Savine, and the next the world was cast into dark shadows with an explosion that sounded like a bomb going off.

"Where's Morgan? Someone needs to get her! And Susan! Where are they? Is Rue here?" Avery said as she stopped kicking.

"Rue and Kyla were already at the stairs when the darkness settled in. Ave, I think that was from your sister," Savine said gently as he set her down into a large room made of carved wood.

"You think *Morgan* did that?" Avery asked incredulously.

Savine nodded. "I saw some shifters change forms near her. I shouldn't have let anyone be there when you landed, but the eagans drew in a crowd. I'm so sorry for endangering you and Morgan."

Avery stared at him in shock. Was he trying to get rid of her sister? Surely he knew that she'd be sensitive to the shifters. Hell, even Avery would have felt panicked if she'd seen a massive bear in that courtyard.

"You did this!" she shouted at him. "You didn't want Morgan here, did you?"

"Avery, of course not!" Savine said, hurt in his eyes. But Avery didn't care.

She turned to get her sister back herself and Savine reached out to stop her. She didn't even hesitate as she struck him with a powerful green light, and Savine slumped to the ground.

She ran as fast as she could down the stairs back to where she'd last seen Morgan. Kyla and Garnel were on the stairs with some other warriors, talking in low tones as she rushed past.

"Avery! Don't go down there!" Kyla shouted, but Avery didn't look back. She just kept running until she reached the bottom of the stairs.

A crowd was gathered at the base of the stairs. Some were holding dead or wounded fae and others were shouting vitriol against Avery and Morgan.

The eagens were gone. There was no sign of Morgan as she began to try and push through the crowd. What if she was hurt, or even worse, dead on the ground? What if someone had taken her sister in the chaos?

Morgan didn't even want to come to Latiah. She'd even warned Avery that this very thing could happen if she showed up in the capital city. But Avery hadn't listened. She'd pushed past the fear that they could be in danger here, and thought only of keeping her sister close to her. But by insisting that Morgan join her in Orofine, she'd endangered her sister in a worse way than if Morgan had stayed in Nephel.

Avery noticed the crowd moving in closer to her. As she began backing up toward the stairs and back to Savine, someone's essence struck her, sending a shock of pain through her arm and down to her feet. The mob moved in closer as Avery tried to escape, but couldn't move from where she stood, rooted into the ground.

Avery sent out some of her magic, knocking a few of the fae down, but others were too quick for her. She screamed as large hands grabbed her, pulling her limbs in different directions. Suddenly, she was lifted up and thrown into the air before she dropped to the ground. She heard the crack of bone as she hit the hard wooden ground, then hands were back on her, pulling and striking her. Someone punched her face as she tried to stand, then the kicking began. Avery tried to fold herself into something small, to protect herself from the attack, but there was nothing she could do to stop the assault on her. She tried to yell for help, but her voice was a whimper as someone kicked her hard in the stomach.

Suddenly, a wave of emotions came over the crowd. Avery felt it too. Cold dread coursed through her veins and the hands and feet stopped attacking her. Then an explosion of angry thorns tangled around the crowd. The fae screamed in terror, but there was nothing they could do. They were entwined in Savine's grip and Kyla's emotional control. She felt someone lift her gently off the ground, but couldn't make out the face.

"Oh! Goddess help her," the voice murmured. Rue. It was Rue who held her.

"Give her to me," Savine growled and Avery felt her body being passed to Savine's strong, warm arms. The bond between them sprang to life and she felt the steady beat that only his presence brought her.

She tried to look at him, but could barely make out his face.

"No, my flower, just close your eyes," he said as he carried her back up the stairs. She felt his essence pulse into her and the pain leaked away as she drifted into a comforting oblivion.

Chapter 18

Savine

Savine sat in a chair next to his bed, Avery's limp hand in his. She'd been in and out of consciousness since the attack two days ago, and Savine wasn't going to leave her to wake up alone. Kyla had done what she could to set Avery's broken wrist, but there was little they could do for the cracked ribs that damaged her frail human body.

Every time Avery breathed in, she'd wheeze and she was beginning to grow unusually hot, her body its own dry furnace.

As he listened to Avery's labored breathing, Savine felt a chill of cold dread seep down his spine. Avery didn't have the long life, natural healing abilities and essence to heal her. She was only human and delicate in a way that was unheard of for the fae.

"Water," Avery muttered from her sleep. Savine picked up an earthenware cup from the side table and tipped the contents into her mouth. Her cracked lips were temporarily moistened by the liquid and she leaned back down into the pillow.

As she laid back, Savine adjusted the furs around her. Maud, the Bayberry healer who had tended his wounds after the mountain lion shifter attacked, entered the room without knocking. He'd already told her to come in without disturbing Avery.

"May I examine her?" Maud asked. Savine nodded as he watched her pull back the furs that he'd just arranged around Avery. He held his breath as the woman lifted Avery's nightgown. Across her abdomen was extensive bruising, as well as along her chest. The woman laid her hands on Avery's injuries, trying again to heal Avery with her essence. The first few tries had failed, and this seemed no different. Savine watched with clenched teeth as the woman forced her essence into Avery's body.

Finally, Maud sighed and pulled back from Avery. Savine quickly folded the blankets over Avery's still form. "I believe there was an internal injury to her midsection and her lungs, but the injuries continue to not respond to my healing essence," Maud said.

"What do we do next?" Savine asked, apprehension in his voice.

"We pray for the goddess to heal her," Maud responded before excusing herself for the bathroom to wash up.

"But—" Savine protested. "I need a second opinion. Is there anyone else?"

The woman emerged from the bathroom as she said, "I'm the only Bayberry trained healer in Orofine. Your sister has some training, I understand, and there are other Latian healers in Orofine. But nobody who uses their essence to heal."

"Your essence isn't healing her!" Savine shouted, surprising himself with the anger that ripped through him at the woman's useless comment. Maud stepped back with alarm, and Savine took a steadying breath. "There must be tinctures or salves to help. Something..."

"Your Majesty, your soulmate is a human with human frailty. There is little I am trained to do to help someone with these injuries. If she were fae, her body would already be healing itself."

From the bed, Savine heard Avery mutter something. He came close to her as she said, "Infection. Maybe pneumonia."

"She says she has an infection, and something I do not understand. Does any of this make sense to you?" Savine said, taking up his place by Avery's side.

"I'm so sorry that I can't offer more help," the healer said as she left the room.

Savine suspected that the woman was purposefully letting Avery die. Perhaps because she was, despite being a Bayberry, loyal to Jasper and the loyalists. What else would explain her presence in Orofine during the war?

Savine stood, whispering into Avery's ear, "Just a moment, Little Flower. I'll be right back."

He went to the door and saw a guard standing in the open air hallway. "I need my sister. Bring her here at once." The guard nodded and Savine returned to Avery's side. Her breathing continued to come in short, loud gasps.

After a few minutes Kyla arrived. "Is she worse than before?" Kyla asked.

"Listen," Savine said as he clutched Avery's pale hand in his. His essence hardly moved under his brown skin as he watched Avery's chest rise and fall.

Kyla pursed her lips. "It sounds like there is liquid in her lungs. What did the healer suggest?"

Savine grunted. "That healer's days are numbered."

"Is Avery's skin still hot?" Kyla asked.

"Yes, like an oven. I've never felt anything like it."

Kyla frowned, pursing her lips. "I have. Garnel felt that way and Avery gave him some human medicine. Did her backpack make it off the eagan?"

Savine shrugged. He had no idea where Avery's backpack ended up in the chaos of her arrival. He'd been a fool to let the folk gather as the eagans landed. He'd been so focused on weeding out the folk accused of speaking out against her that he hadn't seen the greater population as a threat.

"I don't know if I can heal the heat that courses through her body. But it sounds like she has fluid in her lungs. We should at the very least get her upright. Perhaps it will help her breath easier. Then I will go search for the bag and send an airborne fae to Hyacinth. I don't know if she can get here soon enough to help Avery, but we must try."

Savine agreed and they moved Avery into a sitting position. She cried out in protest and slumped back into the pillows, but her wet breathing sounded a little better.

"Antibiotics," Avery muttered.

Kyla looked at him with confusion, and Savine didn't know what Avery needed. Had he ever felt this helpless? At least when she had been taken from him, he could act. But now all there was to do was sit and pray to the Goddess that she would heal his soulmate.

Kyla reached down and pressed her hand against Avery's forehead. Savine heard the slight hiss she made as she withdrew her hand, shaking her head as she looked at him. "I'll search for her backpack and get a few tinctures and salves. Just wait here."

Savine felt helpless as Kyla left the room. Avery's eyes fluttered open before she began wheezing and coughing again, her body shaking from the effort. "Tell me how to help you. What can I do?"

Avery shook her head and turned her face toward the window. Another ragged cough hit Avery so strongly that she bowed over in pain. Savine stood and got another wet cloth from the sink in the other room. Then he poured her a fresh cup of water before sitting down beside Avery as he brought the cup to her lips.

There was nothing he could do to help her vulnerable, injured body. He was useless to her, and yet he wouldn't dare leave her.

"Hold me," Avery croaked. He placed the wet washcloth on her forehead, and settled in with her limp, hot body burning against his own.

He was drifting off to sleep, a deep weariness overcoming him after two sleepless nights by Avery's side, when he heard the door click open.

Kyla was back, Avery's backpack strapped to her own back, and she wasn't alone.

Hyacinth was by her side. Her wild, tangled hair was filled with sticks, weeds, and other plant matter and the pockets of her dress were near-bursting with supplies.

Savine stood up, gently placing Avery's head on the pillow as another wave of coughing racked through her. He'd never felt more relieved to see the old Bayberry healer.

"Stand aside, boy. I'll take it from here," Hyacinth said, pushing past Savine and to Avery's side. "Poor child! She's burning up with fever, just as Kyla said. Kyla dear, get her human medicine out of that backpack."

"How are you here?" Savine stammered out the words, but he still was in disbelief that she'd appeared when he needed her the most.

"Your remaining rebels just arrived in Orofine. Jay brought most of the rebels back, but a few chose to remain in Bayberry and the Middens permanently, including Gaelyn. I traveled with the returners. I suspected that Avery would need my assistance, although when I chose to travel here I thought it would be in an educational capacity. I can see I arrived just in time."

A wave of relief washed over Savine. If there was anyone that he could trust with Avery's health, it was Hyacinth.

"Here they are!" Kyla said, handing Hyacinth a small, bright red bag. Hyacinth quickly opened the bag, pulling out small plastic packages. Human medicine. All of it contained strange letters that none of them could discern.

"I don't want to give her the wrong thing," Hyacinth mumbled as she placed the items on Avery's lap. "Let's wake her. She's the only one who can make hide or hair out of this language."

Avery groaned as she returned to consciousness, but she quickly chose the medicine that she needed to reduce her fever. Hyacinth asked all of them about the injuries and inspected Avery's body. She listened to the story of the attack, deep concentration on her face as she examined Avery.

"Now, the work begins. That fool of a healer, Maud, couldn't get her essence to respond to Avery's illness. I'll try in a moment, but first we can give her body a boost to begin the healing process." Hyacinth stepped away from the bed and began digging through her pockets, muttering to herself and placing herbs and tinctures on the table as she went. Kyla began setting the plants into an indiscernible order as Hyacinth tossed them on the table. Savine couldn't stop himself from watching closely as Hyacinth began preparing a mixture of herbs, bark, and other plant matter. She pressed and ground the herbs with a mortar and pestle that had fit in a wide pocket near Hyacinth's waist.

"I know you are King, and have the right to do as you please, but give me some space! I cannot concentrate with you hovering about," Hyacinth barked.

"I just—I can't lose her. Do you think you can heal her?" Savine asked.

Hyacinth turned from her work and looked at Savine. Her features softened as she said, "I have healed much worse, including Susan when she was just a child. She caught some human ailment that was nearly the death of her. But sometimes cases that seem simple can have complications." She turned back to her work, continuing to pound the plants, bark, and herbs into a paste.

Kyla turned to Savine, warning him, "You may not want to be here for this." Kyla glanced back to Hyacinth who was slathering the paste on cloth strips.

"I'm not leaving Avery's side," Savine said. His tone was harsher than he intended, but his sister nodded.

"I can feel her resilience, Savine. But I know from experience, it is hard to watch a soulmate be healed."

Savine felt a sinking worry in his stomach as he looked at Avery, pale and feverish on the bed.

Hyacinth ordered, "Get someone to prepare a bath. Hot as she can tolerate." Savine got up and started the bath himself. He didn't need someone serving them at this time. All he wanted was to be by Avery's side as she recovered.

Once the water was deep enough for Hyacinth's approval, Savine carried Avery to the bath. Her fits of coughing and shallow breaths, as well as the other injuries to her body, had left her too weak to walk on her own. Savine set Avery down on a towel as he helped her take off her nightgown before he slipped her into the water.

While Savine helped Avery to the bath, Hyacinth added some plants to the water. He recognized the rabbitbrush, wooly mullein, and choke cherry bark in the water.

"I'm starting with the lungs," Hyacinth said curtly as Avery let out a shallow gasp when she hit the hot water. "This bath is similar to steeping tea. My hope is that she will be more open to receiving my essence through the water. With the help of the plants, I can work the healing in two parts."

Hyacinth pushed up her sleeves before she dipped them into the murky water. Immediately, the water began to illuminate and Avery let out a small cry. Savine moved to be closer to her, holding her lolling head in his arms. The fever coursing through her body had made her delirious, and Avery looked at him as if through a fog. The water shone with light and color as Hyacinth's essence swirled around Avery. Avery's shallow, choked breathing became more rapid, reaching a crescendo of weak, panting coughs.

"You're making her worse!" Savine gritted out.

Hyacinth didn't reply, but Savine felt Kyla's steadying hand on his shoulder. "Shh. She's responding to Hyacinth's essence, see?" The purple and blue bruising below Avery's chest was changing to a light brown hue, and the dark lines across her midsection seemed to be diminishing.

"Carry her to the bed. Quickly," Hyacinth said, and Savine immediately scooped Avery out of the bathtub, soaking his own shirt as she leaned against his chest, rasping for air.

Savine set her down on the bed and moved to pull the blankets and furs up around her, but Hyacinth stopped him. He looked over to Kyla, who carried the plant infusion on strips of cloth. Both women worked quickly, wrapping Avery's exposed flesh in the herbal cloth.

After they were finished, Hyacinth turned to Savine. "Let her rest with the plants on her for the entire night. I'll return in the morning to see if she's made progress. If she hasn't, we still have options to try."

Savine put his hand on Hyacinth's shoulder. He didn't want to consider what would have happened if Hyacinth hadn't arrived when she did. "Thank you for all your help. I owe you a debt."

"Do not start talk of debts. She hasn't recovered yet. You'd do good to take your mind off her sickness and get some fresh air. Latiah needs you to continue ruling, even with Avery ill," Hyacinth replied as she packed up her remaining tinctures and salves.

Savine couldn't do that. He knew Raikin could handle the role as he stayed beside Avery. There was nowhere more important than beside Avery.

He saw Kyla and Hyacinth to the door, closing it behind him and returning to his bed. To the bed he wanted to share with Avery not as a patient, but as his soulmate, bonded and beside him.

Morgan

Morgan woke up in a dark room. The last thing she remembered was the feeling of weightlessness as she fell asleep in the eagan's saddle. Was she back in Nephel?

A small glow came from the corner of the room and she let her eyes focus on the shape of the light. It moved suddenly, approaching her with unnatural quickness.

"You're awake." Rylo's voice came from the glow and his body seemed to become brighter, casting an eerie light around the room.

"What the hell are you doing in here?" Morgan asked.

Rylo let out a dry chuckle. "You're in my room. You were so asleep that I carried you here. I was also fatigued and didn't want to fly you down several stories to your own bed."

Morgan flinched and made a face at him. "You've been watching me sleep from the other side of the room? That's just creepy. If you were so tired, wouldn't you want your own bed?"

Rylo just smiled in the darkness, his golden eyes glowing before he turned his back on Morgan and walked to the balcony, looking out on the night sky.

Morgan shivered as she crawled out of bed. She was still wearing the same tunic and pants that she'd worn on the flight, and she quickly became aware of how dirty and stinky she was from days of travel.

"I'm going to go," Morgan said as she began walking to the door.

Rylo turned, his golden wings slightly spread. They were so beautiful. Not just golden, but interspersed with pale yellows and deep golds, almost brown. She resisted the urge to walk over to his side and touch them.

"You're going to regret what you did," he said, stepping nearer to her. "You just made an enemy of your sister's powerful soulmate."

Morgan sighed. "Avery has always chosen to follow her heart and dive head first into things. I'm not like that. I've thought about it for days, and I couldn't live in a whole nation of folk who wanted me dead. It wasn't like I didn't try to explain that to her—multiple times!"

Morgan turned back to the door, then she heard a rustling behind her and Rylo put his hand on her shoulder. "Why choose me over Latiah? Do you not fear that I'll kill you? After all, I am the one who has killed many humans."

Morgan felt the smile spread across her face as she looked up at this predatory man. She took his hands in hers, studying the black lines that now jutted out against his golden skin. They were surprisingly soft, the hands of a man used to being served. "You don't scare me. Look what you did to yourself for me."

She dropped his hands and felt her shadows dance around them. Rylo's golden eyes glowed as he stared at her.

"I wasn't going to let a necessary asset be wasted. Had you explained your plan, I could have found another way. But that isn't what you did, is it? Now I will bear a permanent reminder of your foolishness."

Morgan flicked her gaze up at the ceiling. She needed to get out of here and get some rest. "Whatever you want to call it. I know *you* aren't going to kill me, so I'm staying in Nephel."

She didn't let him get another word in as she walked out the door and headed to her room.

Chapter 19

Avery

Avery woke up feeling panicked as she looked down at the tightly woven strips of cloth covering her naked body. She looked like a mummy, wrapped and ready to be placed in a sarcophagus. Maybe they'd thought she had died, and were preparing her for burial?

She looked at the heavy arm across her wrapped body and saw Savine asleep beside her. As she stirred, he opened his eyes and looked at her with such joy she thought her heart might crack right out of these wrappings.

"Hi," she said softly. "Did you think I needed to be mummified?"

Savine cracked a half smile. "You must be feeling better if you're making what I can only imagine is a human joke."

"Got me there," she replied, lifting her wrapped arms. "But what's the deal with the wrap job?"

"Do you recall any of last night?"

Avery thought back. It all felt like a haze as she recalled Savine putting her in the bath and Hyacinth imbuing her essence into the surrounding water. "Kind of, but the details are foggy. I knew I had a fever, suspected I had broken ribs that were causing a lung infection. Maybe pneumonia? Plus the rest of me felt bruised all over."

Avery began tugging at the itchy wrapping around her arm. Under the layer of cloth was a thick coating of plant matter. It resembled crushed and rotting leaves. "What is this supposed to be?" Avery asked.

"It's Hyacinth's work. Before we unwrap you I've been instructed to draw a bath and call for Hyacinth."

"I thought Hyacinth was in Bayberry. How'd she even get here?" Avery asked as Savine made his way to the door to speak to the guard in the hallway. Avery guiltily thought about Weston. He should be the one in the hallway now. The one guarding his king. Instead, Avery had taken his life only for Rylo to prove a point.

Savine must have noticed the tension on her face as he made his way back to the bed. As he sat down, he explained all that had happened after she'd become delirious with fever.

Avery felt hot and itchy all over as she realized how she'd blamed Savine and ran into an angry mob without thinking things through. "I'm so sorry. I was an idiot for hitting you with my magic and bolting like that. And I know you weren't trying to get rid of Morgan. I just feel so bad that Rylo took her and Susan like that. I shouldn't have left them behind when I ran to you."

"You can't blame yourself for what happened, and don't blame yourself for Morgan choosing to leave with Rylo either."

"She chose to?"

"From what Raikin has extracted from certain individuals involved, yes. She attacked a Latian shifter, then killed several other Latians before fleeing with the Sun King."

A tight knot twisted in her stomach. It couldn't be true that Morgan would attack so indiscriminately. But she didn't have time to think about what happened to Morgan before Hyacinth entered the room.

"I've prayed all night that you would pull through, and look at you! I couldn't have hoped for better results," Hyacinth said as she leaned in for a hug, the branches in her hair snagging on Avery's own unkempt waves.

"Savine, I hope the bath is prepared. Let's get the cloth off the girl and give Avery a good scrub."

Avery looked at Savine, suddenly feeling slightly self conscious. He'd stayed by her side while she was sick, but now that she was feeling better, she wanted to retain some privacy as she had these festering plants scoured off her body.

"Savine, you haven't left this room in days. Why don't you go check in on your nation? I think Hyacinth and I can handle the bath."

Savine scowled as he moved protectively closer to Avery. "No. I should stay by your side."

Avery gave him a soft smile. She might never get used to having a protective, bordering on possessive man around her at all times. She never would have tolerated this kind of behavior from any human man she'd dated. While part of her loved the primal need he had to protect her, she also wanted to maintain her own autonomy in Latiah. If they were going to make this work, she'd need to still feel like she had a voice in her own choices.

"It's okay, old man. I'm just getting cleaned up. Come back later when I'm looking more human again," she said, trying to keep her tone light.

Savine sighed, looking like he wanted to refuse her gentle orders. "Very well. I'll leave you two alone."

He leaned forward and gave her a kiss on her forehead before he walked out of the room.

Avery felt a sense of relief that Savine wasn't in the room when she glanced at her naked body in the mirror. Covered in pungent plants, she looked part swamp creature, part human.

"There were showers in Bayberry. Surely they've got them here too?" Avery asked Hyacinth as she looked at the clear water in the tub. "This is just going to make a huge mess."

"You're to steep in the tub until I say so, child. I'll be using my essence on you to extract the last of the illness clinging to you."

Avery didn't argue as she slipped into the water, instantly turning the fresh water a deep tannin brown. Hyacinth submerged her hands into the water, slightly brushing against Avery's arms as she began chanting. The water and Avery's skin began to glow, but Avery just tried to lean back against the tub, relaxing as much as possible as Hyacinth worked.

As Hyacinth worked, Avery thought of Kyla's goal to find out what the Divine Five were. Maybe Hyacinth knew what that meant.

"Hyacinth, have you ever heard of the Divine Five?" Avery asked as Hyacinth's essence slipped across her skin.

Hyacinth paused, her nut brown skin losing some of its luster. "That's something I haven't thought of in a long time—but yes I have. Why do you ask?"

Avery shared the instructions Althea had given Kyla, and Hyacinth's face tightened as she talked. Finally, Hyacinth took her hands from the water.

Avery could feel the clarity in her lungs as the last congestion disappeared. Her aching bruises were gone too, and before long Avery felt like herself again. Starving, but healthy.

"Do you remember when I told you that you must never use yourself as a vessel for deep magic again? It's volatile, dangerous, and you could easily become overwhelmed by its power."

Avery nodded and stretched, feeling vitality return to her body. "Yeah, and I haven't tried it since. Why?"

"The Divine Five are five objects imbued with deep magic at the time of The Cleaving. The witches who separated the realms used them, but they were all that remained of them after The Cleaving. From what I understand, fae nations took them for themselves, but what has become of them from there is only legend."

A fucking quest.

Unbelievable. They now needed to recover some lost relics for this deity.

"Thanks for sharing. Kyla will be happy to know what they are finally."

The worry lines on Hyacinth's face faded as she assessed Avery. "Of course, dear! And I must say, that went better than I'd hoped!" Hyacinth said as she dried her hands with a towel. "You may not have remembered it, but Savine sent for the only Bayberry healer in Orofine. She had no such luck healing you, but your body responded quickly to my essence."

Hyacinth paused, her wrinkles pressed tightly together across her face as she put her hands on her hips. "I best meet with Maud. I recall her training many years ago. Perhaps there is something to Savine's suspicions of the woman." She seemed to be speaking to herself before she turned to look back at Avery, still soaking in the dirty bath water. "You can have that shower now. I'll leave you to it."

Avery found the shower behind a stone wall. Built to fit an army, the shower had a cedar bench around the edge and multiple shower heads. A shower for a king, she guessed as she washed up. Avery began feeling slightly lightheaded as she showered, needing to sit on the bench to rest between soaping her hair. Her body must still be weak, even if she was feeling better.

Savine

Savine couldn't form words for the relief he felt when he entered his bedchamber to find Avery dressed and eating a hearty bowl of forager's soup. A smile parted her lips when she looked up at him from the table.

"Thanks for letting me get cleaned up. Are you hungry? Hyacinth got enough soup for both of us."

Savine closed the space between them and knelt beside her, pulling Avery close. His lips crashed into hers, and he kissed her with an intensity that bordered on pain.

As he pulled away, he scanned Avery, making sure he hadn't hurt her too much. He hadn't meant to. Just all the fear, all the concern about her was getting to him. Savine needed Avery to be safe, and he'd kept botching that up.

Avery grinned at him, she was unharmed and looking healthy again. "Wow. That's a hello. I'm going to need you to greet me like that from now on."

Savine chuckled as he sat in the chair beside hers. "Goddess help me, I'm just so thankful that you're alright."

Avery's smile diminished. "I'm really sorry for what I did the other day. I shouldn't have gone after Morgan like that."

"The thing that matters most to me, Avery, will always be keeping you safe."

She stretched out her hand to his, squeezing it tight, and Savine felt the warmth of her touch fill him. "No more reckless decisions, I promise. You've got enough to deal with. Also, I'm sorry I ruined the first few days I was in Orofine. I'd love a tour, but is it even safe for me to go out?"

Savine thought about the executions he'd ordered over the last few days. Those directly involved in her attack had paid with their lives after Raikin had interviewed them. That had been the only time Savine left Avery's side. To serve out justice against those who tried to kill his soulmate. He wouldn't tolerate it. His people would learn to accept Avery, or would pay if they threatened her.

"You're safe now, Little Flower."

Avery wrinkled her nose at him. "Did you *kill* them?"

Savine tried to make his expression blank, but the raw rage still pumped through him.

"You did, didn't you? It's written all over your face." Avery gave him a teasing smack on the arm. "I'm never going to get used to you *killing* people to keep me safe. You know it's not normal."

Savine frowned. Was Avery lying? Did she not want him to protect her? "Harming you will never be tolerated in this nation. Not with me as king."

Avery raised an eyebrow at him. "I'm going to be honest, and don't think too much into it, but, it's kind of a turn on. I'm not backing down that it's not normal, at least not for humans, to have this insane level of protectiveness. But there's something very sexy knowing the extent you'd go to keep me safe. Moving forward, let's just try to avoid any unnecessary killings."

"There will be no more threats to you here. The rebels are back from Bayberry, and the city and the King's Residence are secure. The Night of Feasts is just two days away, and there will be a celebration in our honor." There was so much more they needed to discuss. So much that they'd left unresolved back in Nephel. Avery had shown up, just like she promised, but did that mean she wanted to be bound to him? Would she accept the role that being his soulmate would put her in? It felt better to not know than ask.

But just as if she read his mind, Avery said, "Before we have a celebration to honor both of us, maybe we can discuss where this is going?"

Savine felt his essence wriggle beneath his skin as he sat rigid in his chair. Here it came, the rejection he'd feared for weeks now.

Avery sighed and squeezed his hand. "I've had a few weeks to think about it. Between training and hanging out in Nephel, it's all I've been thinking about. You know I'm adverse to responsibility. I always have been, and had no plans on changing my lifestyle at home. It's been tough for me, seeing myself as a queen, or consort, or whatever we choose to call it. Plus you need to win your people over, and that's not going to happen if you have to keep killing them on my account."

Savine's heart rattled against his rib cage. "What are you trying to say?"

Avery laced her fingers through his, looking at him with a kind of longing that made him dread her next words.

"I can't be Latiah's queen. It's like the assassin thing again. I'm not ready for the role, and I feel like it's an insult to your folk if I take that role."

Savine pulled his hand from hers and pushed himself out of his chair. He was across the room in seconds, looking out over the city below. His hands shook as he grasped the windowsill.

Avery was rejecting him. She came back just to tell him this news in person. There was no denying that he'd worried for weeks over this, knowing that she couldn't possibly choose him.

His own heart was beating so wildly that it was all he could hear, and Avery's touch on his shoulder made him flinch. She tugged at him, turning him to face her.

"Savine, just listen. Please. I can't be queen, but I want to be with you. All I could think about when I was away from you was how alive you make me feel. How you make me feel more at home than I've ever felt in my life. Nobody is going to take that from me, because, well, I love you. I love you, Savine, and I don't want to spend another day without you. Now that I know you, now that I've met you, I can't imagine living my life without you in it." She looked up at him, and he was beyond words. Never did he think this was what she was about to confess to him.

She looked up at him, and his whole world was reduced to her wide brown eyes. "Well, say something!" she said.

Savine smiled down at her as he said, "I love you too, Avery Hollis."

She stood on tip toes and he tugged her close to him, lips pressed together as she parted eagerly for him. Savine didn't hesitate as he swept his tongue to meet hers. Avery loved him. His whole body strummed as he let her words sink into his soul.

She pulled back from his kiss, swaying on her feet as he steadied her. "Okay, woah. Can you help me back to the bed? I'm feeling dizzy." Savine scooped her into his arms, carrying her across the room to the bed.

He brought her a cup of water, feeling the need to claim her as his soulmate continuing to stir within him. Goddess damn him, she was still sick, and all he could think about was burying himself inside her.

"What are you thinking?" Avery asked, sipping the water.

"Ave, you know what I'm thinking right now," Savine smirked.

Avery let out a little laugh. It was like the twinkling of bells, so light and delicate. "You want to complete the bond? Well, considering my frail human body can't handle *kissing* I don't think that's an option right now. But as soon as I'm better, I'm yours. I want to feel that full soulmate connection with you."

"And I want that with you. How will this work though? You don't want to be my queen. What will I call you to my subjects?" Savine asked as he thought about the logistics of what she'd actually said.

"Call me your soulmate, but can we wait a while before I take the official title of queen? Maybe just let me practice magic and support you from the sidelines. Then if your folk aren't actively trying to kill me I can take a more open role. But I'm warning you, politics aren't my thing. Don't fire Raikin."

Savine laughed at that and slid into bed with her, thinking about what she was suggesting. "You'll need a title, and I'm not going to hide how I feel about you. The folk will talk about why I haven't made you queen."

Avery pulled her body closer to his, the bond between them pulling tight. "Let them talk. Nothing else matters as long as we know what we are to each other. I'm your soulmate, Savine and I'm not going anywhere. Now, I need a nap. Then I want you to give me a tour of your treehouse. By the way, how did you forget to mention that detail?"

Savine tangled his hands in her hair and pulled her head onto his chest. "It didn't seem to matter at the time. It was always just my former home."

Avery yawned.

"Rest, Little Flower, you're safe with me now," Savine whispered into her ear, more for himself than Avery's reassurance.

Chapter 20

Morgan

"Should we borrow this spell book?" Morgan asked as she picked up an ancient book bound in leather. "I think learning to communicate mind to mind could be useful, plus that spell on using a fae's essence sounded intriguing."

Susan nodded as she reached out her hand to take the text. "Are you sure Rylo won't mind us taking the books to our rooms?"

Morgan passed the book to her as she looked through the stack on the coffee table in front of them. They'd spent the day pulling every book they could find on witches and spells from Rylo's expansive library, but they still hadn't found any mention of the Divine Five. At least they'd discovered that ancient spellbook. Susan had gasped as she looked through all the spells, obviously passed down from one witch to another over time. How did Rylo acquire such a book?

Elio entered the room. Morgan hadn't figured out what Elio was to Rylo. A friend? Did he have friends? An advisor maybe? Asking what their relationship was felt too personal.

"What have you found there?" he asked, taking in the stack of books. Whatever he was, Elio was far nicer to her than Selene, who still scowled at her every time they made eye contact.

Susan gave him a friendly smile. "Would King Rylo allow us to remove one of the books from the library? It's a spellbook."

Elio crossed his arms, looking at the book in Susan's hands. "It's a spellbook for witches? Goddess knows how King Rylo got his hands on such a book! It's probably the only copy left in Aeritis, and should stay here. King Rylo said you're welcome to use any books in this room though. Although I'd caution against practicing magic in his library. This room is like a place of worship to him."

That was a gentle no. "That shouldn't be a problem. Could we have some paper? We can just write the spells down that we'd like to practice," Morgan suggested.

Elio nodded as he walked toward a cabinet in the back of the room, returning with thick parchment paper, ink, and a quill.

Morgan smiled at him, taking the paper and ink and placing it on the table near the books. "Thank you."

Elio pressed his hands together, a grin on his handsome face as he looked at Susan. "If that is all, I was instructed to show you a place King Rylo designated for you to practice magic."

Susan and Morgan didn't object as he began walking toward the balcony. Perhaps they would practice just outside the library? That would be convenient.

The fae stretched out his wings and gestured for the women to step close. His bronze eyes twinkled as he smirked at their surprise.

"Oh! We're flying there?" Susan asked.

"It will be faster that way," Elio said. "You humans are so small it should be no problem to carry you both together."

Morgan mumbled, "That's not insulting at all."

Elio cocked his head at her, confusion on his face. "Did I offend you? You, especially, are very small. I was only pointing out the convenience of flying."

Morgan shook her head, but Susan let Elio wrap his arm around her waist, a silly grin on her face. She seemed to be thrilled to be in Elio's strong embrace.

Morgan smirked as she said, "Fine. Why am I objecting to being toted around by a handsome fae man?"

As he wrapped his arm around her waist, Elio flew downward, his grey wings beating the cool fall air across Morgan's body. They only flew a few stories before he landed on a large balcony. It had couches pushed back against a far wall, giving it plenty of space for movement.

"You are only one floor above your rooms. It should be easy to find your way back. Do you need anything else?" They both shook their heads.

"Thank you for your help!" Susan said, the grin still plastered to her face.

"I'm happy to help. If you need anything else, let me know. I know Selene has grown tired of assisting with King Rylo's witch project. I'm willing to help you in your growth to become the weapon we need to reclaim our lands. I think King Rylo has an excellent vision for utilizing your strengths."

Morgan resisted the urge to roll her eyes up toward the sky. Susan still looked at him with something resembling puppy eyes.

"Okay. We'd better get to practicing magic now," Morgan said, growing impatient with this conversation.

"Of course," Elio said. "I do mean what I said though. I think both of you will be useful. King Rylo hasn't mentioned Susan much, but I saw you during that whole kidnapping business. You have resilience."

Susan blushed. "Thank you, Elio."

"Well, have a good day," Elio said as he launched skyward.

Morgan turned to look at Susan, her cheeks still rosy. "Was he trying to flirt with you while also mentioning the time he helped kidnap you?" She grimaced. There were things about the fae that she would never adjust to.

Susan shrugged. "I think it was a nice compliment. I'm often over-looked. It's nice to be noticed for once."

Morgan shook her head. "Girl, the bar is low."

"Oh, never mind all that," Susan replied, batting her hand at Morgan. "Let's practice our magic. Did you have time to memorize any of those spells?"

"The one that utilizes a fae's essence. I think it could be useful if I'm ever in a situation like Orofine again. But, I don't think I should actually practice it yet. The book said to use it only under life threatening circumstances."

"There is nothing wrong with being prepared. However, I think you're right that we shouldn't start with such a spell. I memorized one for detecting hidden dangers. Should we start there?"

Susan took a strangely defensive position that Morgan wasn't aware she could make. She must have detected Morgan's surprise as she said, "I find it helpful to ground myself a bit before I practice magic, but I don't think it's necessary."

Morgan followed her lead, listening to the words of incantation and repeating them with Susan. She let Susan try the spell on her own, listening as Susan explained how she channeled into her magic.

Susan cast the spell and her eyes widened at a corner of the balcony. She walked over and picked up a small knife, hidden amongst a pile of pillows. Morgan smiled as Susan carried the blade to her. "That area was illuminated red. You didn't seem to notice it, so I'm assuming the spell only revealed the potential danger to me. I wonder how a knife got left out here?"

"That's amazing. Can you hide it on yourself? Let's see what happens if someone is carrying a weapon."

"Of course!" Susan agreed, and Morgan turned her back, looking out to the sky. There were fae flying through the air, going from one tower to another. It was incredible how this city could be so interconnected without streets.

"Your turn," Susan said. Morgan turned around and couldn't see the knife.

"Tell me the incantation one more time," she said. Susan repeated the words again and made additional suggestions on how to call her magic to do what she willed.

So far, Morgan had managed to control her shadows with astounding accuracy. They were probably the only reason she'd survived Orofine. But expanding beyond shadow manipulation hadn't happened yet.

She let her magic build under her skin, feeling the need to release its build up inside her. Then she muttered the words of incantation, feeling the power sting out of her fingertips. Susan was illuminated in red, but the focus was at her ankle, just below the hem of her long skirt. Morgan walked over and pulled the small blade from her sock as Susan clapped with pride.

"Well done! You're a natural!"

Morgan grinned. She loved magic. It felt as if this was the thing she was meant to do all her life. Her true calling, and she knew she was damn good at it.

Chapter 21

Avery

Avery woke to light streaming into the room she shared with Savine. She didn't see him anywhere, but wasn't surprised either. He had to be busy, and returned to work after it was obvious Avery was going to be okay. She had no idea how long she'd slept either, but she felt refreshed and strong.

The wood floors were warm under her bare feet as she made her way to the door. Rue stood guard next to another guard and Avery invited her in.

"I'm relieved to see you up and moving around, Avery," Rue said as she sat down beside Avery. There were two linen chairs in the sitting room that led to Savine and Avery's bedroom, and further back, their bathroom.

"Thank you. I didn't mean to sleep so much, but I think my body needed rest. I'm feeling a lot better now."

"Do you need anything to eat? I could have something brought up."

Avery shook her head. "No, I just wanted to see you. How have you been since we got to Orofine?"

Her smile was sad. "I'm adjusting. It's a lot to take in. My folk never lived in the capital city. We were nomadic, so I've never experienced just how busy Orofine and the King's Residence are. I think I'm falling into my new role as best as I can, and I'm honored that Savine appointed me to lead your guards."

"I was wondering if he would. I'm glad he did too. There's nobody else I trust like you, Rue."

Rue's face lit up. "That means a lot to me, Avery. We went through so much together, and I trust you too."

The mention of their past made Avery think of her sister, Susan, and all the pain she'd experienced at the Towers. Being forced to kill Weston in a cave, having to live with that guilt everyday was a burden she knew would never ease. "Yeah, we have. Do you know if Weston had a family? Are they here?"

Rue shook her head, taking her time to answer. "From what I recall, he didn't have a soulmate. Not surprising, I think he's only around Kyla's age. But, he did have a family. I think a mated mother and father, and an adolescent brother. His father fought for the rebels, but I haven't seen him at the King's Residence. I know some warriors stayed behind in Bayberry. Perhaps they chose to not return to Orofine."

Avery's chest tightened. "I want to apologize to them. I never wanted to hurt anybody, and I can still feel Weston's blood on my hands. Sometimes I wonder if the sensation will ever wash away."

Rue moved to Avery's side and wrapped her arms around her, tugging Avery into a tight embrace that made Avery bury her face in her friend's shoulder. She didn't hold back the tears as she cried for Weston, letting herself mourn the man whose life she'd been forced to take.

Rue's voice shook as she said, "I don't think I can ever forgive Rylo for doing that to you and Weston. It was monstrous and it still haunts me."

Avery pulled back from Rue's embrace. Her eyes glistened with tears, springy curls framing her tear stained cheeks. "I'll never forget his sacrifice. You're here with me now because of that. I never got a chance to ask how Susan handled it."

"We helped each other through the nightmares." Rue sighed, and it seemed she was reliving her own experience. "She's so strong. I know Selene will keep an eye on her, but it hurts knowing she's not with me."

Avery felt taken aback for a moment. She couldn't imagine Selene ever doing anything to keep Susan safe. "Do you know a different Selene at the Towers, or are we talking about the same Sage?"

Rue shrugged. "You have reason to hate her. What she did to us was wrong, and how she tormented Savine is unforgivable, but there's more to her than she lets others see. She got to know us, and I even think she protected us from the chaos at Jasper's death. I kind of miss her company."

Avery tried to hide the grimace that she was forming. "I'm glad you saw another side of her."

Rue gave her a friendly push on the shoulder. "You're terrible at hiding your true thoughts, Avery. Even if you can lie. It's okay though. I understand why you don't like her."

Savine walked into the room at that moment. He carried some wrapped packages in his hand. "I knew Rue would join you as soon as you woke, so I brought enough of these honeyed cakes for both of you. A baker from Orofine brought them specifically for you, Little Flower. Word of your attack has reached the city, and you're receiving sympathy and well wishes, now that all of Latiah understands you're my soulmate."

Savine

"How did you know my love language was food? You perfect, perfect man," Avery said with a wide smile.

She was teasing him, but still his wretched heart buckled against his ribs. Nobody had ever said those words to him, and they still came as a shock to him that Avery loved him—truly loved him for who he was.

Avery and Rue both took a sweet cake from the package and bit into them, honey smearing across both women's lips. A knock brought their attention to the door, and Savine went to answer it.

"I don't mean to disturb you, My King," Darby said.

"It's no issue. In fact, Avery, I'd like you to meet Darby. Darby has been like a mother to me. We were separated during the war, but she's done an excellent job keeping things in order for my return."

Darby bowed low and Avery gave her an assessing look. "I'm honored to meet my future queen."

Avery plastered on a smile. It wasn't her genuine smile, more the polite one she gave to strangers and folk she was wary of. "I'm happy to meet you too. But, the title is a work in progress. For now, please call me Avery."

Darby turned her attention back to Savine. "King Savine, there's something of concern that I found while cleaning out the old king's possessions. I think you and Avery would like to see it when you are free."

Savine tried to keep his essence from stirring. There was something Jasper was hiding. He looked at Rue. "I'm sorry Rue, but I need you to go back to your post."

Avery looked at him, her lips tight and her eyebrows lifted.

"Of course, My King," Rue said without hesitation as she walked to the door.

Savine turned his attention to Darby. "Is it what I hope? Did you find the source of the dark magic?"

Now Avery's eyes widened as she looked between Savine and Darby.

"I believe it's about the portals to the human realm. It appears there is one near Orofine, and I have reason to believe it's been in use."

Savine nodded to Darby before he turned to Avery. "I know I promised you a tour. I never would have dreamed to start your tour in my dead father's apartment, but I would like you to see this too."

"Okay. Can I have a minute to change my clothes?" Avery asked motioning to the night dress she still wore.

Darby nodded. "Of course. I will meet you in Jasper's former apartment." Without missing a beat, she turned and left the room.

"What are you thinking?" Savine asked.

"It is a surprise. We knew humans were able to get through, but I didn't expect there to be so many of them in Aeritis."

Savine shook his head. "I have been trying to unravel my father's mess for weeks now. I blame that on why I miscalculated on allowing Latians near your eagans. I haven't been thinking straight, trying to keep track of so many problems."

Avery rested her free hand on Savine's shoulder. "It's okay to make mistakes. This is a hard transition, and you can't blame yourself for others' actions."

"It's just..." The guilt for her injury was still tearing him apart. He knew she forgave him, but how could he forgive himself for such a mistake.

Her lips twitched into a tiny smile. "I know that look. Please, Savine, forgive yourself."

He let his face sink down to her head, letting the sweet scent of her flow over him.

Pulling back from his touch, she took a bite of the honeyed cake, chewing thoughtfully. "Did you know about the portal?" she asked. "Rylo made it sound like he's seen humans come through Sapphire Falls frequently."

Savine shook his head. Most likely his grandfather had known, and it seems his father did too. "You were the first human, other than Susan, that I'd met, and I never suspected Susan was anything but a Bayberry."

Avery bit her lip, putting the honeyed cake on the table, not even bothering with a plate. "I should write to Morgan and tell her. Maybe this portal will be open to her."

The last reports Savine had from the trees made him suspect that Morgan was becoming closer with the Nepheli King, using his personal library each day, and entering his private chambers. He knew Avery wasn't ready to accept her sister's alliance to Nephel, but she needed to be selective with the information she shared with Morgan.

"I know you don't want to hear this, but use caution there. We don't need other nations learning about Latiah's secrets."

Avery's eyes flashed with hurt. "She's my sister. She— " Avery paused, pursing her lips. "No, you're right. It's just hard, not having her with me, and it stings that she chose Rylo over me."

Savine stroked her cheek, rubbing his thumb across her lower lip. "No my Little Flower, she didn't choose Rylo over you. She chose Rylo over me and my folk. And for that I'm sorry." Avery put her hand in his. "You're right. Morgan made her choice, despite how much it hurts me. I'll get changed and let's see what Jasper was hiding."

Avery

"This map shows all the known portals in Latiah and the surrounding nations," Savine speculated, tracing his finger over Quartz Mountain. They stood at a table in what must have been the former king's personal dining room. "Quartz Mountain is written in my father's hand, like it was added more recently."

Avery pressed her finger to a list of dates. "Look at this. It's a recording of humans entering Latiah." She read the list, not fully understanding the dating system, "Older male. Severely injured. Died two days after arrival. Young female. Dead on arrival. Young male. Dead on arrival." She felt her stomach sink as she read the list. Nearly every human died while crossing the portal. And the ones who did survive? Well, either they succumbed to their injuries, or they were possibly killed.

Darby held another list. "This seems to show the warriors Jasper sent through the portal. But how would he manage to do that?"

"He sent warriors into our world?" Avery asked, trying to sound surprised.

Darby nodded, handing the list to Savine. "It appears he began sending warriors through a portal near Orofine about twenty-three years ago."

Savine's face hardened. "Has anyone else seen this information?"

Darby shook her head. "No, I've been the only one going through Jasper's things, as you instructed."

"Let's keep it that way. Bring these documents to our rooms. I want to look at them more closely," Savine said as he traced his finger to the lake near Bayberry. He looked at Avery with a knowing expression. She noticed what was missing right away.

The portal Susan entered Bayberry through was still unmarked. She truly had stayed unknown her whole life.

Were there others like Susan? Those who entered Aeritis as children, only to be raised in secret?

"I'll see to it," Darby said. She began collecting the papers and maps. "While I have both of you here, I was wondering if you wanted to share some opinions on what should be done with this place. I know you've chosen to forgo the king's apartment, instead choosing your own rooms. But there is this suite of rooms and your mother's apartment as well."

Savine looked around, the hardness on his face increasing. The rooms were spacious—much larger than the smaller set of rooms they currently shared. These rooms felt more like a home, with a living room and two bedrooms off to one side.

"Can I look around?" Avery asked. Savine nodded and pointed toward the master bedroom.

Savine pointed to two rooms off the living room. "These bedrooms connect. Many kings and queens used them as shared connecting rooms with their soulmates or spouses, but my mother and father chose to live in separate apartments."

Through the king's bedroom was a large and lavish bathroom. The enormous carved bathtub could fit at least two, and Avery grew weak in the knees at the truly magnificent shower. Granite tiles lined the space and multiple shower heads pointed to the floor. Farther into the bathroom was a private closet, still filled with Jasper's clothing.

Darby gave a small smile as Avery admired the space. "There's a kitchen off the dining room too. King Jasper preferred to take his meals here when he could, inviting only his inner circle to dine with him. He had his favorite cook serve him in the private kitchen."

Avery walked into the living room before going back to the dining room. A view of the city spanned in front of her as she walked to the curved, wooden windowsill. It was shaped to blend seamlessly with the mighty trunks that formed the building. She walked past the dining room and into the kitchen, where she gazed at the huge stove and ample counter space. All that was missing were modern appliances, and this would feel like a well-appointed American kitchen.

Avery eyed Savine. His face softened as he looked at her. "You like this better than our current rooms, don't you?"

"It's very beautiful. The view's amazing, and it would give us a lot more privacy. I could even cook for us sometimes. But I don't want to make you move in here if it makes you uncomfortable."

Savine sighed. His essence seemed to swirl with unease. She hadn't seen him look so lost in his own pain in over a month, and this was already bringing those harsh memories back to him.

"Darby, can you give us some privacy?" Savine asked.

"Of course, My King. I'll just bring these papers down to your rooms."

She left the room on silent feet, leaving Savine and Avery alone in his father's old home.

Savine tilted his head to the closed door near the bedroom door. "There is my father's private study and office. He turned what was supposed to be his soulmate's bedroom into a room that holds so many of my painful memories. If I did something wrong as a child, I'd be sent there to wait for my punishment. Darby was often the one who had to bring me back to my rooms, which is why I think she brought the documents to the dining room."

Avery closed the distance between them, wrapping herself in his arms and feeling the warm tug of their bond between them. "Oh Savine, I'd never ask you to live in a place that brings up such terrible memories for you."

"I'm trying to be stronger than my past, but sometimes the past has a way of sneaking up on me in this place. I think staying busy and focusing on all that needs to be accomplished is the only thing keeping me from giving in to the desire to burn this whole place to the ground." His ragged breath escaped out of him as he spoke. "I hope it's okay with you, but I offered Kyla and Garnel my mother's old apartments. I felt it was only appropriate to give them their privacy after all they've done for me."

She let her head rest against his chest, feeling the quick pace of his heart. This man. This beautiful, wonderful man had so much love to give her, and yet he still doubted himself. His past was something they'd work through together, one day at a time, and she knew she'd do all she could to make Savine feel the love he'd been denied for so long. "That's fine with me. I'm happy to just be with you."

"I know many monarchs don't share a room with their soulmates or spouses, but I hoped we could be different. I've waited so long for you—so long that I can't bear—"

Avery stopped him, pressing her finger to his lips. "Of course we're sharing a room. I don't want to be away from you either, Savine."

Savine gave a tiny nod. "I'm sorry I can't give you this." He gestured to the beautiful room. " I just—there's too much of him in here."

"You don't have to apologize. I'd never want to make you live somewhere that makes you uncomfortable. Maybe at some point we can remodel. We could expand our rooms and make them more of a private home. I don't think I'd be comfortable with our future kids sleeping in a whole different area of the King's Residence anyway, so eventually we'll need more private rooms."

"Kids?" Savine asked, eyes sparkling.

Avery gave him a playful shove. "Don't be getting any ideas! I'm not talking now. But someday."

Savine laced his broad fingers with hers and bent down, kissing her with tenderness that filled Avery's soul. "I would be honored to have children with you someday," Savine whispered against her lips.

"Like far into the future. Now, let's get back to our tour of this crazy treehouse."

Avery felt Savine's smile on her lips. "That sounds like an excellent idea."

Chapter 22

Morgan

Morgan and Susan were both settled into the low-back couches in Rylo's library. They'd been undisturbed for two days as they poured over ancient texts, looking for any clues about the ancient witches and the Divine Five. It was remarkable that Morgan could even read this strange language with its foreign alphabet, but it was like her mind instantly translated what she was reading. Another one of those Goddess gifts that she felt a mix of gratitude and disgust for.

Yes, she was being used for some purpose that she still didn't even understand, and that absolutely disturbed her on a daily basis. But there was also this part of her that reveled in the power and control she was building with her magic. How each day she'd practice spells in ancient books until she was exhausted from the effort and she'd collapse into a dreamless sleep in the bed she once shared with her sister. Or how those incredible shadows seemed to do her will more and more each day.

"Tea, please," Susan muttered to the room. Immediately, a tea set appeared, steam wafted out of the spout of the teapot. Susan poured a cup for Morgan and a cup for herself.

"We could use a snack too," Morgan said. It took a bit longer, as if the enchanted library was considering what Morgan needed most at the moment, but then a plate appeared with fruits and nuts. Morgan gave a tight smile. She was getting used to life here. Whether she wanted to stay in Aeritis or not, her day was beginning to have a comfortable rhythm to it.

"Morgan, are you concerned about Avery? Do you think she's worried about you?" Susan asked as she set her tea cup down.

"My sister can take care of herself. She's always been independent, and despite living in the same town and seeing each other pretty frequently, we were both wrapped up in our own lives. In some ways, it feels the same here. But, I did send a letter to her the other day. I asked Selene to send it."

"Do you think she did?" Susan asked.

Morgan shrugged. "We'll see. It's not like I've heard from her either."

Susan tapped her fingers on her thigh, a nervous tick Morgan had noticed Susan do a few times. "I don't mean any offense, but I would have expected the two of you to be closer. Perhaps I'm wrong in my observations."

Morgan sighed. "We're close in our own way. We've always checked in with each other, but I'm more private than she is. Avery's always ready to share what's going on in her life, and isn't afraid to ask for help. I've just—I've always been a bit in the shadows compared to my sister. In school she always had a big group of friends that I was on the outskirts of. I've always been more studious. I like yoga and meditating. I chose a job that paid well and challenged me. She chose jobs with zero benefits, but they're her passion," Morgan said, holding up an ancient tome. "It's probably why I like sitting in this dusty library. I think she's used to assuming that what she wants is what I want too, but here, where my life is on the line, isn't the place for me to let that happen. I'm sure she's fine in Orofine with Savine."

"I can see that. Avery, from what I've noticed, seems to wear her emotions openly for all to see. I think she wants what is best for you, but perhaps what is best for her isn't what's right for you."

Morgan took a handful of huckleberries and popped them into her mouth. The sweet tang reminded her of home, picking huckleberries with her family in the late summer.

"Yeah, I also think we're better off using our talents here, looking for answers to what Althea is searching for."

Susan nodded as she picked up the book that she'd been reading earlier. They both went back to silently studying and the quiet of the room felt peaceful in its own way. As Morgan scanned a book titled *The Fae After the Cleaving,* she found a sentence that stopped her in her tracks. "Oh! Here! I think I might be onto something about the Divine Five. It says, 'the five formed by the witches were scattered amongst the nations of Aeritis, never to be bound again. The divine gift of Gaia never to be forged for ill use again.' Well, that's vague, but it's the closest I've come to finding the words five and divine together. What do you think it means?"

"I think it tells us that the witches were responsible for whatever the Divine Five are, so we can at least narrow our search to the same place. The five witches responsible for The Cleaving, and the years shortly before and after that event."

Susan turned back to her book. Morgan tried to concentrate on the text in front of her, but her mind and body felt restless. She needed to get up and stretch, maybe go through a few sun salutations.

"That's a start, at least. I wonder if Rylo has any other texts in his other book collections? I'll go see if I can find him and ask. I think we've pulled every book on witches and humans from this library."

Susan looked up at her, concern in her eyes. "Do you think that's a good idea? Regardless of him letting us stay here, I don't think he should be disturbed."

"All I'm doing is asking him for a book. I'd hardly consider it disturbing him when I'm using him as a glorified librarian," Morgan huffed as she headed to the door.

She walked into the dark, stone hallway, buried somewhere deep within the tower. Morgan had learned to navigate the halls easily, even in the low-lit space. She walked quickly through the passage she'd had to take the night she'd returned from Orofine. The night that Rylo had put her in his bed. His reasons still didn't make sense, but she hadn't seen him for long enough since their return to question him further. As she walked through the dark hall, she heard voices coming from inside the rock wall.

She recognized Rylo's honey-smooth voice immediately, the lazy arrogance in it giving him away anywhere. Two other voices rose through the rock, as if amplified for her to hear.

"My king, do not take Morgan with you on this journey. Goldoth has never sworn an alliance with us, and taking her could jeopardize utilizing her as a weapon. What if they have her killed for her role as a kingslayer?" Elio asked, and Morgan felt chilled overhearing a private conversation concerning herself.

Selene's voice spoke next, her velvety tone didn't match her harsh words. "Do you think the king is a fool? The thinly veiled threat by Goldoth's king makes it clear that if she is not presented we risk war."

Rylo's blase voice replied, "You both are overestimating Goldoth's interests in us. There's a new king on the Latian throne. A man all other nations know I have seen as an enemy, and yet, I welcomed him to my home. As our southern neighbor, Goldoth wants to know where our allegiance lies. The witch is but a party trick. Now that we and Latiah have these Goddess-touched humans, Goldoth is bound to be curious. I have no plans of making an enemy out of Maglar and Mara. Only a fool would go up against the strength of the ore nation, and I am no fool. Further, I will need a strong ally if Latiah attacks in retribution for Morgan's actions."

The other man spoke, "If you must meet with Goldoth, have them come here. You shouldn't travel to another nation, and the witch should be kept here. If they wish to see her shadows, bring them to us."

"I am no coward. We'll travel to the south, and Morgan will come with me. Selene, you'll of course stay here to run things in my stead. But Elio, I'll have you at my side. There are many reasons why I wish to visit our neighbors to the south. Write back to say that we'll arrive two weeks after the Night of Feasts."

Morgan could hear shuffling from within the wall. She backed up, bumping into a faelight sconce on the wall. She reached up to try and straighten the light, but it was too late. The orb clattered to the ground, plunging the hall into darkness.

"Who's out there?" Selene asked, and Morgan tried to sneak away into the shadows. The wall dissolved before her and she met Selene's gaze. "Just the witch we were speaking of," Selene said as she pulled Morgan into the room.

Morgan didn't bother putting up a fight as she was tossed to the floor. The room was illuminated with soft light from the wide balcony overlooking a cloud-covered sky. A spacious sitting area meant to accommodate wings and a table laid with tea met her.

"Who do we have here?" Elio asked. His wry smile showed just a hint of arrogance.

Morgan didn't dare speak as she lifted herself off the ground and looked at Rylo. His eyes seemed to gleam like two golden orbs, and Morgan didn't know if it was in delight or displeasure.

"Selene and Elio, you are dismissed," Rylo said with a wave of his hand. Both left without question.

"Morgan, don't you know it's rude to listen in on private conversations?" Rylo asked as he took his seat on the couch. "Tea?"

Morgan shook her head.

"Well don't just stand there, take a seat. If you're going to listen in, at least own it and don't loiter about like an unwanted pet," Rylo said, pouring himself a cup of tea.

She sat down across from Rylo, and couldn't help but notice how his long, lean muscles seemed to flex just by raising a cup of tea to his supple lips. He quirked a tiny grin at her as he set his teacup down.

"So, what did you overhear?" Rylo asked.

"Just that we'll be traveling to Goldoth to meet the king there."

Rylo let out a shrewd laugh. "Just that! And what do you think of traveling to another nation in Aeritis? Your last travel plans went so poorly, wouldn't you agree?" He lifted his hands up, exposing the black lines that snaked up to his elbows as he moved around the table and sat down next to Morgan.

"Do you actually want my opinion?" Morgan asked, meaning it.

"Your opinion will not make a difference, but I like to hear a person's reply when I know they aren't satisfied with the outcome."

"Then why ask at all? You already know I didn't want to go to Orofine, but I still went. Do you think this will be any different?"

"Of course there will be a difference. You aren't Goldoth's kingslayer. You'll be treated as an honored guest and will be at my side. You'd like that, wouldn't you? To be on the arm of a king?" Rylo said, reaching his blackened hand to her chin. He caressed her jawline, and Morgan felt a tingle down her spine from his touch.

Morgan batted his hand away. "I'd be happiest staying here. You've been generous enough to open your library to me and I want to continue to utilize my time there. Actually, that's why I came here. I was looking for you to ask about some other texts you may have," Morgan replied, keeping her voice cool and calm.

"I'm sorry, that is not going to be possible. I'll need you with me. *You* could very well be the cause of war in my lands, thanks to that move you made in Orofine, and I find myself in need of an alliance. If bringing you with me gets that alliance, then so be it."

Morgan knew he had a point. If Avery's lover was offended enough to declare war against Nephel it would be all Morgan's fault. She was the one who'd screwed up the plans— and probably left a few bodies behind in her wake. But she didn't need him knowing she felt guilty over it.

"And if I refuse to go with you?" Morgan added, "If I used one of your oaths to stay here?"

"It would be a waste of an oath, Kingslayer. I have need for you yet, and will see no harm come to you in Goldoth. We go to Goldoth for reasons beyond the diplomatic."

Morgan knew Avery didn't trust Rylo. He'd kidnapped her, after all, but he'd never shown her any reason to distrust him. Despite the time in the Tower of Teeth, Morgan had come out stronger, more resilient. She didn't even fault him for putting her there after she'd done exactly what he'd told her not to do. In some ways, she wondered if he knew that she would come out stronger, yet there was still the nagging point that Avery had emphatically declared Rylo to be insane.

"You know my sister thinks you're crazy, right?" Morgan said, changing the subject. "She told me how you locked Savine away for *years* in the Tower of Teeth. Why should I trust you after what you did to her and Savine?"

Rylo leaned in closer to her, a sharp smile on his face. "I showed your sister the side of me she most wanted to see. The mad king, as Latiah believes me to be. Do my people treat me as if I am mad? Would they allow me to rule if I were?"

Morgan leaned closer to Rylo. Close enough for her to smell his sweet and spicy scent. "So it was all an act? I thought you couldn't lie?"

"Perhaps there is some truth to my actions. Often where truth and lie meet is not a clear line. More to the point, why would I want them to believe anything other than what they already think of me? To see me as mad, as frivolous and cruel."

Morgan reached out and traced her finger along the black line at Rylo's fingertip. A dark mist grew around their feet, dancing up their legs. "So you admit you are those things. You had my sister kill an innocent man and locked Savine away because you're cruel."

Rylo caught her wrist in his hand, bringing it up to his lips as a featherlight touch from his mouth moved along each of her fingertips. Her heart thudded in her chest at his touch.

"I am cruel, and you best not forget that, kingslayer," he said, licking her wrist before he released her hand. Her shadows writhed up around them before she pulled them back into her.

Morgan felt a little off balance with this beautiful, strange man admitting to being cruel while also flirting with her. This was flirting, right? But she wasn't going to let him know that he'd frazzled her. "Tell me, cruel king, what do you know about the Divine Five?"

Rylo let out a wry laugh. "Oh you have been a studious girl in my library if you've found any knowledge of the Divine Five! Please, tell me what you know first."

Morgan pursed her lips, she wouldn't reveal what Kyla was instructed to do. "Only that it must have something to do with the ancient witches. Maybe it could reveal something about what Avery and I were called here to do."

Rylo's feathers spread out, golden in the low light. "You are curious, aren't you? Well perhaps you'd be interested to know that I have one of the Divine Five. In fact, I placed it around your sister's pretty neck just to see how it would react to her magic the night you arrived. It was a disappointment to see she didn't seem to wield it to the extent that your ancestors did. But perhaps we can try with you instead."

Morgan poured herself a cup of tea, refusing to let him see the nervous flutter in her belly. She was finally getting somewhere and making progress on what could be keeping her trapped here. Whatever task it was that she needed to finish, the Divine Five most likely were involved. "The necklace? I remember seeing the yellow stone on her."

"Created by the witches that caused the Cleaving, that necklace contains deep magic. It's a vessel for the deep magic that only a powerful witch could access. During the battle in which I captured Avery, she managed to access that magic and siphoned it into Savine, making herself a vessel. Yet, when she wore the very necklace that held deep magic at Jasper's death, she was powerless." Rylo looked down at the shadows that once again snaked around them. "I have no doubt that you will answer the call to the deep magic and use it when it's necessary."

Rylo's gold-flecked eyes seemed to take on a deeper shine, as did his flesh. It was as if that piece of the sun that was part of him shone brighter, mingling with her darkness.

Morgan's heart was pulsing in her chest. She was finally making a breakthrough in the mystery, but her voice was steady as she spoke. "I'll willingly go to Goldoth with you, but I want you to give me and

Susan every source you have on the Divine Five," Morgan said between sips of tea.

Rylo's wings wrapped around him, close enough for Morgan to reach out and touch. "Not that you have a choice to go with me to Goldoth or not, but I will provide the texts. Only because I want to see what your beautiful mind discovers about the witches of the past, and what you will do with that information."

Morgan smirked and finally gave into the urge to touch one of his magnificent feathers. Rylo shuddered, but didn't pull his wings back. The feather was so soft, and Morgan couldn't help but wonder what it would feel like to have those feathers touch her naked body. "Fine, but I want my gun back before we go to Goldoth."

Morgan continued to stroke the king's feathers. Rylo let out a gasp as he said, "I would never deny my Kingslayer her weapon."

She smiled as she watched his face look on the verge of being fully undone by her touch.

Chapter 23

Avery

It felt good to be in the fresh air, hiking with Savine into the forests surrounding Orofine. Spending the morning working on her magic with Hyacinth had left her restless, rather than fatigued, like if she didn't get out of the King's Residence, she'd lose her mind. The spellwork she practiced for healing salves had been mentally exhausting, but her inactivity over the last few days had her itching to move her body. When Savine searched her out in the healers rooms, she'd been more than happy to slip away and join him outside.

Avery knew Savine was taking shorter strides to let her set the pace, and it made her smile, knowing that he'd even adjust his gait to keep her comfortable. She was dressed in her fleece jacket over Latian pants and a beaded shirt, plus her hiking boots. It was a funny mishmash of an outfit, but she still felt thankful to have her jacket. The late autumn air was crisp with the promise of frost on the horizon, and Avery wondered what it would be like when this mountainous canyon was covered in feet of snow. Already most of the underbrush had shed their fall colors.

"So, where are we headed?" she asked.

"To an ancient grove of cedars up the mountain. I'm going to speak with the trees about Nephel. I want to ensure your sister is safe. Also, I'd like to find out if the rumors of an alliance with Goldoth to the south are true."

After finding out how Morgan had taken out several fae and fled back to Nephel, Avery wasn't really sure Savine should worry about her sister. Clearly she could take care of herself, and despite Avery's attempts to help her, Morgan seemed set on choosing her own path.

"Why do you visit this specific group of trees to talk to?" Avery asked. They were passing through a forest dense with trees—why not choose some closer to Orofine?

"Other than spending a few precious moments with my Little Flower in a day filled with tedium?" Savine looked back at her and winked. Avery's heart fluttered at the small gesture. "The trees have their own sense of hierarchy, just as the fae do, and these cedars are often willing to speak candidly when I seek them out. It's where I was going the night of the prophecy. But to be more specific, younger trees are wilder, less willing to speak to the fae. These cedars are well informed and will give me the information I seek."

Avery looked ahead up the trail and saw steam rising through the forest.

"Makes sense. Is that a hot spring up ahead?"

Savine quirked a grin in her direction. "It is. Would you like to get in?"

"Of course, I love hot springs! But do you have time to soak? Don't you need to get back to the tree talk and boring meetings?"

Savine hesitated, a flicker of uncertainty before his face turned resolute and he reached for her hand. "Ave, you're alive and back with me. Fuck all the meetings. If you want to get in the hot springs, I'm getting in with you."

Avery leaned against Savine, feeling the hard planes of his muscles against her body. His rain-drenched forest scent surrounded her.

"You weren't planning this, were you? Using speaking to the forest as an excuse for us to sneak away from the treehouse so we could seal our bond in the hot springs?"

Savine's smile was so big, he seemed lighter, so unlike the hard, bitter man he was when she first met him. "I'd actually planned for this to happen tomorrow night in our bedroom. But, I like the idea of sneaking away from the burdens in the residence to bond with you better."

Savine wrapped his arms around her, cupping her ass as he leaned in to kiss her. He pulled back and Avery thought she could get lost in his soft blue eyes and the rippling motion of his essence; the way his wind tousled hair fell effortlessly around the crown on his head.

She was his, completely, fully and he was hers.

She'd never had someone to call her own. It was comforting and terrifying all at once, knowing that agreeing to this was a lifetime commitment.

Avery had always shirked commitment, yet here she was, jumping head first into this commitment without a doubt in her mind about her decision. It made her heart race and her body feel grounded all at the same time.

"You are everything I ever dreamed or hoped for. I'm yours, Savine. I never knew I was waiting my whole life for you, but I was, and now that I have you I'm never letting you go," Avery said.

Savine's eyes dilated, and with an infinitesimal nod of his head he was scooping her into his arms, carrying her to the water's edge. He held her tight enough that she thought she might bruise where his hands dug possessively into her flesh. The bond between them bucked and writhed, and Avery relished in the feeling of his desire for her down their bond. Heat pooled between her legs and her own desire pulsed down their bond.

Savine let out a deep groan as he placed her feet on the ground.

"You can feel how bad I want you, can't you?" Avery asked as she began stripping off her jacket, then her shirt. The crisp air stung her exposed flesh, cooling her heated skin.

"I can feel it. I can smell it. Abyss damn me, Avery, I want to be buried in your need for me," Savine growled.

His eyes took in her exposed body as she dropped her pants, standing before him in only her underwear. When he reached for her, she gently pushed him back and slid out of the last remaining garments, exposing all of herself to him. She stepped back, letting her feet hit the cool flat rock of the hot spring's edge.

"I told you to come and get me at the lake. Well, Savine. Come and get me now, and never let go." She stepped from the flat rock ledge and into the hot water, letting the steam surround her. The pool was deeper than she'd expected, up to her breasts, but it was lined with a stone bench for sitting and resting, or in their case, having sex. She slid away from the bench, feeling the granite sand bottom beneath her feet.

Savine stood on the edge, his erection straining at his leather pants, but he didn't move as he watched her in the water. The last green ferns of the season covered Savine's boots and moss covered rocks glistened in the steam from the springs.

"Just look at you. You're beautiful," Savine said, his voice husky. "I never let myself hope for this—but here you are. And you are *mine*." The essence under his skin swirled as he tugged off his clothing. In quick, steady movements, he was bared to her. *He* was the beautiful one. So unlike any human man she'd ever been with. His body was a work of art, muscles stacked on muscles and accentuated by that pulsing, shifting essence. In one stride, Savine entered the pool while also letting his crown sink away.

He submerged himself under the water, swimming across the bottom of the pool toward her. Through the clear water, Avery saw Savine reach out and grab her ankle, pulling her toward him. She couldn't help but laugh and scream as he pulled her down into his arms and under the hot water. She found his face and kissed him hard. The feel of his body surrounding her, with the warm, soothing water was pure bliss.

When they surfaced, Avery gasped for a breath and clung to Savine, her arms wrapped around his neck. All the hard edges of his fae features were softened into a silly grin. She let out a squeal of laughter at the smile on his face.

He laughed with her. "Goddess above, Avery, I never knew loving a person could be so... so fun. But you bring that out in me. This part of me that I didn't even know I had. Is it a human thing?"

Avery wrapped her legs around Savine's waist, feeling the hard length of his erection between them, as she traced his essence while he held her close in his strong arms. "It's an us thing, old man."

Savine knelt deeper into the water. Its heat drifted around them as he slowly brought them across the pool and set Avery down on the bench at the water's edge. Savine worked his hands down her side, squeezing and teasing her flesh as he explored her. Avery's nipples pebbled, and she knew it wasn't from the chill in the autumn air. She felt the connection between them tighten, like their bond was this living thing, demanding they unite their bodies and souls. She thought about all the love, all the need she had for him, and sent it down that mysterious connection between them.

Savine let out a moan as he locked his eyes on hers. "Avery. Goddess damn me, your arousal is consuming me."

With a slosh of the water, Savine caged his arms around her and pressed his mouth against hers. She tilted her head back and opened her mouth to him, tongues crashing together. Avery kissed him and touched the invisible scars on his back, touching each one in tandem to her deepening kisses to erase the years of pain, of trauma, that he'd experienced. She kissed him for the new beginnings for both of them. He didn't say it, but between them, she could feel the barriers he'd built up around himself over the years begin to crumble.

Savine's hand swept up to Avery's peaked breast, his warm hands heating her cooled skin and Avery couldn't stop herself from arching into his touch. He squeezed and teased her sensitive skin. Damn, she wanted to melt into him right now and he hadn't even touched between her thighs.

She grabbed Savine's wrist and guided his hand down to her heated center. Savine growled as he dipped a finger into her.

"Fuck, Ave, I can feel how slick you are for me, even in the water."

Before she could reply, Savine grabbed her by the ass and set her on the cool, flat stone surrounding the pool. She shuddered at the sting of it on her hot, aching body, but she didn't protest, didn't fight the chilly embrace against her heat. Savine knelt before her on the bench as he reverently spread her thighs. The adoration mingled with lust in his eyes was the most beautiful thing she'd ever seen. She'd never known love like this.

Avery leaned back on her elbows, her arms sinking into the soft fronds of a fern, and spread her thighs farther, letting him take in all of her. She could *feel* his low hum vibrate off the stones as he tightened his grip on her thighs.

"Don't make me beg. I've waited long enough for you," Avery moaned.

Savine's hands roamed up to the apex of her thighs, stroking her clit in a way that made her shake. "No Ave, I want to feel you come for me first."

He slid one finger inside her, stroking and touching her as she squirmed against his hold. Finally, he added another finger into her center and pumped into her slowly at first, but increasing his pace with each heartbeat, each pulse of their bond. She was already feeling the pressure of her orgasm building at the base of her spine, but when Savine stroked her clit with his thumb, her body responded like he'd hit her with a jolt of lightning. Coiling tension threatened to burst out of her.

"Savine," she shouted, like a thunderclap, Avery plummeted into her orgasm.

"Ave, you're mine." Savine's voice was raspy and his essence bucked across his skin. Even as she was lost in her own release, she knew Savine was experiencing it with her through their bond.

His mouth was on hers, and Avery bit and sucked down on his bottom lip, drawing blood as her body crested with wave after wave of bliss, Savine still gently caressing her inner walls.

When Avery opened her eyes, she saw her soulmate staring at her with such tenderness that it made a knot form in her throat.

Savine slipped his arms around Avery and guided her into the heat of the pool, positioning her on his lap, legs straddling either side of him. Avery could feel his hard cock pressing between them. She reached her hand down, guiding his length forward and pumped his cock, causing a moan to escape his lips.

His voice was rough as he said, "You are the best thing to happen to me, Avery Hollis. I am still broken and will undoubtedly make mistakes, but I want nothing more than to have you at my side, as my partner and mate."

Avery smiled, twining her free hand into his hair. "I see you, Savine. I see all of you and there's nothing I don't want. You are this lost piece of myself that I didn't even know I was missing, but now that it's here I don't think I could survive without it."

With that, Avery guided Savine's cock to her center and slowly slid down, stretching around him as she took in every inch of him. For a moment, they just looked at each other, and Avery could have stayed in that moment forever. Then the tension between them built, the insatiable need to ride him caught up to her. Avery rolled her hips and Savine responded, meeting her movements beat for beat. She leaned down and kissed the swirling essence along his neck.

As they moved together, the bond between them tugged and writhed, pulling and sweeping them closer until Avery thought she could die from the need to meld herself into Savine's body.

More.

She needed more of him, all of him.

Body and soul.

As if he knew it too, Savine arched up, gripping her in his strong arms as he turned them, laying Avery down on the cool stone and bed of moss behind them. He brought his hard, firm body down to her, putting just enough of his weight on her that she felt herself become fully consumed in him.

"Ave, I never thought..." Savine said, emotion on his face. Before he could finish his sentence, he kissed her. All of his need for her, all of her own desire to share this life with him reached a crescendo as Savine's thrusts built into a frenzy of desire.

She was so close to the edge when the taut bond that had been tugging for weeks burst open between them. Avery crested over the edge and came with Savine's name on her lips. He followed, burying his face into her neck as her inner muscles pulsed around his pumping cock.

Then, the bond fell loose. Brilliant colors filled Avery's vision as she and Savine were transformed into light and brilliance. She clung to Savine as the final spasms of their release flowed through them. They were both glowing in a soft green light. She touched Savine's chest and the light softened, sinking into his skin and revealing his essence below.

"That was... That was life changing," Avery panted.

Savine nodded, stroking her cheek and she could actually *feel* the strange glowing light soak into her face.

"Look at you. Glowing with our bond." His thumb stroked her lips before he took her in a soft, gentle kiss.

He pulled out of her, but kept her close to him as he gently lowered them both back into the hot springs. The water stung her cooled flesh and she leaned into his warmth as she began looking at the forest around them.

"Savine! Look what we created."

All around them, the forest was no longer fading with the end of fall colors. Instead, it was teeming with vines creeping up tall pines and firs, flowers of all colors were interspersed across the forest floor, and the ferns had grown to be the size of small cars.

"We've made something beautiful together," Avery said with a smile.

Savine slid her into his lap. "Don't slide away from me yet, Little Flower."

He plucked a few stray flowers on the edge of the pool and tucked them behind her ear. "Our magic made that. But you're the most beautiful flower in all the forest. And I get to spend the rest of my days with you as my soulmate."

With a tenderness that made her throat catch, Savine cupped Avery's breast, rubbing the glowing light into her skin. She reached over and began exploring Savine's skin, rubbing the afterglow of their bond into his skin.

Savine kissed her neck, sweeping his mouth across the hollow at her collar bone.

She was getting turned on again, and fast, but she also was curious about the bond. "Do mates usually glow from their bond?"

Savine worked his lips up to Avery's ear and gave it a nibble. "I don't know, Ave, but I want every last part of our bond to be a part of you, and I want you to do the same to me. Just let me love you," he said, gently tugging her hair back.

She didn't need to respond with words. She leaned back on the cooled stones and let him explore all of her, letting that light become a piece of her.

Slowly, all the light from their bond settled into her skin and she began doing the same for him. She traced every ridge of hard muscle and every invisible scar, brushing the gleaming glow into his essence.

After the light became a part of him, Avery sat beside him, letting her head rest on his shoulders as the warm steam settled against their slick skin. "I never want to leave this place," Avery whispered.

Savine wrapped his arms around her. "Mm. Neither do I, Ave. Let's stay a while longer."

"That sounds perfect." She leaned into his warmth and closed her eyes. The bond between them seemed to open new senses between them. She could feel his emotions more sharply, including his sated contentment.

Avery gasped as a sudden searing pain shot through her head. She gripped her head as another wave of agony pierced through her skull. Savine pulled her away, inspecting her for injury.

"What's the matter, Avery?" She couldn't respond as her skull began ripping apart, shredding her from the inside out. She covered her eyes as tears began streaming down her face.

"Goddess above," Savine whispered.

She reached up to her head once more and felt a sharp gilded crown resting on her head. She looked at Savine, his face was just as shocked as she felt. Trickles of blood streamed down her face as the unrelenting pain continued.

Savine sucked in a breath as his crown emerged from his head, and it wasn't just the boughs and antlers, but tiny flowers threaded through the gilded crown.

"What in the hell just happened?" Avery asked, nausea twisting through the pain.

Savine beamed at her with pride. "You have your own crown of boughs, antlers and small flowers."

Avery scowled. "Is this normal for the mate of a king?"

He pulled her close into a hug and pressed a kiss on her head where the crown met her scalp. She winced from the raw pain lancing through her skull. "No, this is not normal. But it's alright. We'll navigate this together."

"What do you think it means?" she asked, leaning into his strength. Her head was pounding and she felt dizzy.

"It means you're the Queen of Latiah."

Avery's heart sank. She'd wanted to be Savine's soulmate. She'd never felt so sure about anything in her life as she did about accepting the bond between them. But, she wanted it on her terms, and somehow those terms had just been very physically taken from her.

Chapter 24

Avery

Avery's head was still pounding as she and Savine made their way toward a side door of the treehouses. She couldn't help but feel like the moment she and Savine had chosen to bond their souls together was forever overshadowed by the heavy crown on her head. This physical sign that she'd have to step up to the role of queen, whether she was willing or not.

Avery went to open the door, but Savine placed his hand on hers. She turned back and looked at him, a softness on his hard face. Her stomach sunk as she saw the pure love in his eyes. "Ave, let me go in first. I'll distract anyone who might see us so you can make your way up to our rooms."

There was nothing she wanted more than to escape to their rooms. But, the crown already weighed heavy on her brow. Everyone would know by the Night of Feasts that she was the True Queen of Latiah.

"No, Savine. I need to face this by your side." Her mouth was dry and her heart hammered in her chest. "We're a team now."

"Together then." He opened the heavy, carved door and held it open for Avery.

The room she entered was quiet, an open window letting in the crisp autumn breeze. But she could hear movement just outside the door. Folk were running along one of the many open halls connecting this tiny segment of the treehouse to the rest.

Avery turned back to see Savine silently latch the door behind them. He held out his arms, ready to embrace her. Before he could speak, she let her face sink into his hard chest, his arms wrapping around her and holding her tight.

"It feels like a lifetime ago that I was flinching from your touch," Savine said, stroking Avery's hair. "I was so lost in my own hurt that I physically couldn't accept a hug. And somehow, you worked your way into my heart and soul to the point where I crave your touch. It brings me life. Ave, you helped me find myself again, and I'm not going to let you lose yourself now."

He touched the cool metal of the crown jutting from her head. Just that brief contact made Avery wince. "This changes nothing about what I promised you. If you don't want to be queen in practice, then I support that. If you change your mind, I'll be ready to share the nation with you."

Tears welled in Avery's eyes. She wasn't ready for this, and hearing Savine give her the choice to not be thrust into her role as queen was the only thing keeping her from splintering.

"Are you sure?"

Savine stroked her cheek, brushing his thumb across her lips. "It's your decision. You just gave me the most precious gift you could give me, and I'm not about to pressure you into something you don't want."

Avery sucked in a breath, "Thank you, Savine." Slowly, she pulled away from his strong, comforting embrace. "Alright. Let's do this!"

Savine cocked his head and lifted his brow as he placed his hand on the doorknob.

Avery fidgeted with her hands as she waited for him to open the door. "Don't make me second guess my decision to face everyone! Let's just do it quickly, like ripping off a band aid."

Savine smirked at her. "Band aid? Is this another strange human word?"

Avery nodded and put her hand on his, forcing him to turn the doorknob.

The fae lights of the hall were already glowing, and Avery realized just how long it had been since she and Savine sneaked out of the treehouse and into the forest. A guard running through the hall immediately caught sight of Avery as she strode down the long, wooden hall. He was a few floors above her, but as he saw her, he shouted, "I've found Avery!"

"Avery!" a loud call rang out through the halls. It was Rue. Of course she was searching with the others for her and Savine.

"Rue!" Avery shouted back, her head pounding from her own voice.

Savine laid a hand on Avery's shoulder and whispered in her ear, "Let's make our way down to the Throne Room. I have a feeling we'll find many concerned folk."

Avery turned to Savine as she tsked and teased, "You take one afternoon for yourself and the whole place goes to shit."

"Such are the responsibilities of the crown." Savine traced his own crown with his fingers. "How does your head feel?"

"Terrible," she replied, lacing her fingers in his as they began descending the stairs to the lower level of the treehouse.

Savine was right; the throne room was full of busybodies milling about. No doubt wondering where their devoted king could have run off to on a late fall afternoon.

"My King!" Raikin said as he stepped forward with a deep bow. His eyes became nothing more than slits as he studied the crown on Avery's head. Murmuring began behind him as the courtiers and servants assessed Avery. Raikin turned from Avery to Savine with a knowing gaze. "You are bonded?"

Avery's cheeks began to burn, knowing the room of fae were about to know what she and Savine did this afternoon.

Savine opened his mouth to speak, but before the words were out, Jay swept in with a bow. "My Queen!" he shouted and brought his large frame into a low kneel that brought his head below Avery's.

Avery couldn't stop the smile that formed on her face as Jay looked up at her with a mischievous grin. "I know what you did this afternoon," he muttered for only her ears.

Raikin followed Jay's lead and bowed before Avery. Then Kyla and Garnel knelt down. Soon, the whole room knelt before her one by one, calling her "My Queen."

Avery's heart pounded. She didn't know if she wanted to run from the room or accept the reverence from all these Latian Fae. As they slowly stood up, towering above Avery once again, Avery glanced at Savine.

He looked at her with an odd mix of possession and pride, his essence swirling and his features set, ready to take on anyone who doubted her role as his queen and mate.

"Avery is my bound soulmate and the Goddess herself has blessed her with the crown of Latiah. She is the True Queen of Latiah. We are not to be disturbed for the remainder of the evening," Savine announced as he stepped closer to her side.

Kyla and Garnel began approaching, but he brushed them off in a way that commanded respect; a practiced, authoritative wave as he ushered her from the room and up the stairs.

Savine wrapped his arm around her shoulder as they walked side by side. She could feel his love pulsing through their connection. If being queen was part of having Savine, then maybe it was worth the trade off after all.

Morgan

Morgan and Susan walked quickly behind Selene as she led them into a private library Morgan hadn't seen yet. She knew, from the night Rylo had put her in his bed, that this library was in the same area of the Towers as Rylo's bedroom. How many libraries did this man have?

Selene stopped in front of a red stone wall, devoid of any markings to identify that there was actually a room here. She pressed her hand against the stone and it groaned in response before dissolving before their eyes.

"Quickly," Selene muttered as she slipped into the room. Morgan and Susan didn't hesitate to follow into the library. Morgan couldn't contain her gasp as she looked at the room in front of her. A cozy den seemed to be carved directly into the stone with room enough for only the three of them. Soft pillows lined a bench and two leather chairs were squeezed into the corner. It was so tight that even with her wings tucked, Selene's feathers brushed against the bench. The walls were chiseled into shelves, and on them were stacks and stacks of books up to a ceiling that had to be at least twelve feet high. Tiny fae lights twinkled, casting the room in a warm glow.

But the most remarkable thing was the floor to ceiling window with a direct view of Sapphire Falls. From this point, Morgan could see the mist drifting into the air from the plummeting water.

Jumping off the falls had been useless, and Morgan hadn't given the falls much thought since she'd gone to the Tower of Teeth. But seeing it now sent a shock of yearning through her chest. Home was on the other side of that barrier, and yet she couldn't get there, no matter how hard she tried. Morgan sighed and turned away from the window.

"King Rylo offered a few books that you may find interesting here," Selene said, pointing to a pile of brittle old books on the table. "They are some of the oldest remaining manuscripts in Aeritis, so do be careful with them. Despite the aging spells some long-dead king placed on them, I wouldn't doubt you two could ruin them. Why Rylo indulges you is beyond me."

Morgan tried not to roll her eyes at Selene's little speech. She had no plans of destroying a precious artifact.

"We'll be careful not to mess them up," Susan said, sliding her hand on the top book.

Selene gave a perfunctory nod and moved toward the invisible door. As she opened the door she turned back to them. "Oh, once I leave this room you will be stuck in here until King Rylo or I come to fetch you. We're the only ones able to enter this room. Use your time here wisely. I won't have time to usher you about tomorrow, with the feast preparations."

The door dissolved and Selene was gone in a breath.

"She's not very nice, is she?" Morgan asked Susan.

Susan shrugged. "I don't know. She is the Sage of Nephel. It seems she's plenty accommodating for how busy she must be."

Maybe Susan was right. She couldn't help but judge these folk based on one bad, very traumatic experience. But there still was something unnerving about them, even the Nepheli who didn't have the under the skin tattoos and the jarring resemblance to her attacker.

She didn't even know what horrors Goldoth could hold.

"You're probably right. Anyway, why don't you take the top book and I'll take the next one," Morgan said, settling into one of the leather chairs.

"Fine by me. Do you think Rylo knows the information we're looking for but is making us find it ourselves? You said he knew about the Divine Five," Susan asked, sliding into the chair beside Morgan. The sunlight from the large window shimmered on Susan's red hair and freckled nose.

"Oh, I have no doubts he already knows the answers we're looking for. He seems to take pleasure in withholding information and probably likes knowing that we're having to work for the answers he could just tell us."

"That's what I thought too," Susan mumbled, cracking open the old tome in her lap.

They both fell into a comfortable silence that had become so routine now. Both of them reading and searching for the information they needed.

"Oh, oh no, Morgan," Susan groaned as she lifted her head from her book.

Morgan jumped in her seat, startled from Susan's voice in the silence. "What?"

"The Divine Five are five relics from the witches that separated the two realms during the Cleaving, which is what we already knew. But this says that one artifact was given to the King of the Cavern. The King of Goldoth is known as the King of the Cavern. Do you think Rylo is bringing you there to steal Goldoth's relic?"

Morgan's stomach flipped. There was no way Rylo didn't know that Goldoth had one of the Divine Five. "Obviously he knows. These are his books."

"Oh of course," Susan said in a quiet voice. Morgan didn't mean to come across as harsh.

"Sorry, I didn't mean to snap at you. But yeah, he knows. He was way too eager to go to Goldoth."

Morgan heard a whooshing sound and Rylo stood in the doorway. His skin glowed in unnatural beauty and his mouth was curled into a devious smile. "Of course I know. Why else would I be so willing to bring you along, pet?"

Morgan snorted. "Pet? Stop calling me that. I am not some animal."

Rylo's tall, lithe body filled the space, his wings relaxed from their tight position when he stopped in front of Morgan's chair.

"Oh yes, you'll be playing the part of my pet in Goldoth, all the while looking for a lost relic that calls only to the witch bloodline."

He was so close she could smell his spicy scent, his knee brushing hers. "You could have shared this with me the other day."

"But where's the fun in that?"

Morgan glanced over at Susan who looked very uncomfortable, either being in Rylo's presence or with the conversation.

Rylo looked at Susan and smiled, making a dimple show on his left cheek. "Dear girl, you have worked so hard finding this information. Why don't you retire for the afternoon?"

Susan's eyes grew round as she looked at Morgan like she was seeking permission to flee the room.

"Go, I'll be fine. Let's practice that spell we found on revealing when someone is withholding information tonight," Morgan said, shifting her eyes to Rylo and pointing her chin up in defiance.

"Yes, that should be... um... helpful," Susan said in a high-pitched voice, seeped in discomfort as she fled the room. As soon as she walked out, the door disappeared and Morgan was left alone with the Nepheli King.

He continued to look at her, that mischievous smile still on his face making the dimple on his cheek pop just enough to drive Morgan wild. But, she had no reason to let on that his presence was affecting her.

"So what's up?"

"What's up? Is that how you greet a king?" Rylo asked, sliding into the leather seat next to her. The back slipped apart, making room for his wings to be draped through a hole and he leaned his head back, closing his eyes.

At that moment, he looked so normal. Like any tired man after a long day of work, just wanting to relax.

Not bothering to open his eyes and look at her, he said, "I'll never cease to be amazed at the dishonor you and your sister show to your superiors."

"Because we're human?" Morgan asked. She knew he was talking about his title as king, but if he was going to constantly try riling her, she'd have to dish it out in return. And after the way she'd seen him react to her touching his wings, she knew he wasn't referring to her species.

"For you to even say that tells me you know what I mean. You will be the most powerful being in this world, apart from Mother Althea and some of her daughters. It's more about the principle of respecting a title."

"Yeah, I've never cared too much for titles." Morgan set the book in her lap down and leaned back into her own chair. "See, I've always given respect to people who earn it. Who worked for it. Not somebody who was given a title."

Rylo moved so quickly, Morgan didn't even have time to react before his arms were caged around her, his wings spread so wide that they bumped the book shelves on either side of the room.

"You know nothing of what I have worked for. I was never meant to be king. It was always supposed to be my sister, Lilith, who ruled. To be thrust into this role, believe me *pet*, I have scraped and fought for every bit of respect I have in this nation."

Fear mingled with desire as Morgan took in Rylo's perfect features, scowling in an anger she'd never seen on him before. Not even when she'd nearly killed them while plummeting down to the ground had he looked so enraged. So why was she kind of turned on by it?

She reached her hand out and traced the hard line of his jaw. "Okay, I believe you. You're a big, tough king who earned his respect."

Rylo grabbed her chin between his long fingers. He stroked the jagged scar tissue on her right cheek before he wordlessly let go and sat back down.

Shame slammed into her from that touch. She looked in the mirror so infrequently here that it was easy to forget she was so damaged. But she wasn't going to admit that vulnerability to him. Not after she knew he'd touched her scar to put her in her place.

"Why should we collect the Divine Five? No more withholding information. What do you want to do with them?"

Rylo winked and waggled his finger at her. "No more withholding information? Now where's the fun in that?"

"You're insufferable," Morgan said, picking up her book.

"Do you still wish to return home?" Rylo asked and Morgan's eyes shot to him. What was he getting at here?

"Of course. If I had the choice I'd leave."

"And give up that power you're mastering? All that practice well into the night on that balcony of yours would be wasted in your realm. Do you really think you'd just go back to your dull, human life and not regret knowing what you could learn, what you could control?"

Morgan scowled, but didn't give him an answer. Learning about magic and mastering her own skills had ignited something in her that her desk job never offered her. He was right. How could she just go back to normal life after this?

"If you find the Divine Five, if you control them, you would have the power to open portals, and close them permanently from any stray shifters who may wander into your realm."

"What's in it for you?"

Rylo's skin took on that incandescent glow again. "What, indeed. Of course, you would need to use the Divine Five to help my nation first. Then you'd be free to go. I want *all* our former lands back. For far too long, Latiah and Goldoth stole what was once ours. Help me restore the Nephel nation utilizing the power in that deep magic and you can leave."

"Didn't Savine return your lands in exchange for Avery?"

"A fraction of what was once ours. I want it all back, but we do not have the military strength of our neighbors to defeat both nations and win back our land. You will be my weapon."

Morgan pursed her lips. She didn't want to be a weapon. "No. I don't think so."

"We have an agreement, pet," Rylo sneered. "You have little choice in the matter. Especially after what I did for you in Latiah." Rylo lifted his hands up, showing the black streaks across his faintly glowing skin.

"Me helping you in exchange for the three oaths. Yeah, I know. But if I get these five relics, what's going to stop me from going home and sealing your realm off permanently?"

Rylo's eyes sparked into a blazing fury. He moved once again, caging her against the chair with his wings and his arms.

"Because, kingslayer, I will stop at nothing to prevent you from betraying me. If you try to betray me, I will make you suffer."

Morgan discreetly reached for her shoes. The same ones she'd worn over the waterfall. That one little piece of home that wouldn't last long. She drew out a sheathed knife Avery had given her and pressed the blade to Rylo's throat.

"Don't fucking threaten me. *You* do not control me. *I* am not your possession to control, and I never will be."

Shadows mingled with golden light as the darkness crept up, like a dark mist coating Rylo's wings and body, holding him in place. His heart was beating so quickly, Morgan thought she could hear the drumming.

"My pretty little kingslayer. How wicked you can be," Rylo murmured. She could feel him twist under the restraint her shadows placed on his immobilized arms.

She nicked his neck, enough for a tiny drop of blood to well up. Her finger swept through it while her shadows released their hold on him. Rylo pushed forward and pressed his lips to hers.

The kiss was hard and cruel, and she welcomed it. She opened her mouth to him and his tongue swept in. Morgan met his tongue with hers, tangling in a passionate battle that she'd never experienced before. Damn, this man had lit a flame in her that would never be quelled. The kiss didn't ease up as she tugged on his shirt, pulling him closer to her. He sucked her lower lip into his mouth and nipped it, drawing blood as he pulled back from her.

He was glowing in the evening light. The light shining through him seemed to dance along his perfect skin. *Shit.* She was so out of her league here, but she wasn't about to let him know that. Morgan panted as she pressed her hand to his chest, pushing him back, "I'm not yours. Learn that now because the next time you say I am yours will be your last."

Rylo let out a cold, harsh laugh. "Oh, that will not be the game we play in Goldoth. Get used to it. You are *mine.*"

Chapter 25

Savine

The streets of Orofine were adorned with the harvest. Piles of winter squash, dried beans and grains in barrels, and apples spilled into the streets. It was tradition to display and share the rewards of a long, hard growing season with the whole community, and Savine made sure the tradition was being returned when Latiah needed it most.

The overstocked food that Jasper had been keeping for himself was being redistributed to the folk who were left with nothing after this war, and Bayberry had generously provided the rebel army's winter supply to them before Jay brought the warriors home.

Avery leaned back on Savine's chest as Jari navigated the busy streets. Savine could feel the softness of the fur coat she wore rubbed against his chest. Her bold, red gown was draped over Jari's sides.

The day was unusually cold for autumn, with an icy rain slashing down on them as they made their way through the crowd, and Savine savored the heat of Avery's body against his, his essence keeping them dry together. She pointed to a crowd of children playing a common game with a stick and a hoop, laughing as the children took turns pushing the hoop along Jari's side.

Despite his doubts, Avery had accepted him as her soulmate. They were forever connected at a soul level and that bond between them had been as soul-shattering as their shared orgasm. Abyss damn him, he'd felt the tattered and torn pieces of his soul mend as the bond filled him, stitching him back together.

Savine knew the crown atop Avery's head was a heavy burden that she didn't want. He'd tried to teach her how to pull the dainty band back into her skull, saying she didn't need to reveal it if she wasn't comfortable, but it wouldn't work. He didn't know if it was because she didn't have any essence running through her, or if they hadn't found the solution yet, but her crown was stuck on display for all to see. Even with the crown on her head, Avery looked happy, and that made Savine incandescent with joy. He didn't know how he could live with such lightness in his heart after so many years of pain.

Jay and Raikin rode side by side in front of Savine and Avery. Kyla and Garnel were behind them as other courtiers and warriors followed behind them, parading through the city, a tradition that led them to the temple to receive a blessing from Orofine's city goddess. It was a blessing to have the Goddess of the Harvest in his city, especially on the most important holiday of the year.

Jay turned back to them, smiling with a wide grin. "What do you think, My Queen?"

"That sounds good coming from you! Maybe I'll get used to being called queen!" Avery shouted above the crowds, making Savine's ears ring. He supposed his human soulmate would never learn volume control.

"Being queen is very becoming on you. Be proud of your title," Jay replied.

Savine could barely overhear Raikin's chastising tone, "Please save this conversation for a more appropriate time."

Jay turned and winked at Avery. Savine's heart tightened as Avery laughed in reply. She turned to him, a mischievous smile on her face. "I don't know anything about queenly behavior. You know that, right?"

"You can be as queenly as you please, my flower. Create the role you want, but wear the crown proudly. It brings you the security I've so desperately wanted for you."

She waved to the crowd as they bowed before her. Savine eyed the crowd for any threat against Avery, but the faces he met were not angry or frightened. The mood was celebratory, and Avery was close enough to be safe in his arms. There was a distinct reason he'd turned down Jay's suggestion to let her ride Dandelion beside Jari. Savine had no intention of letting Avery out of his arms, especially after the attack on her during her arrival in Orofine.

He had no doubt in his mind that there were still folk who wished to do her harm. Yet, with the crown on her head, she had the same protection he bore as the True King of Latiah. She was the True Queen, and he couldn't help but praise Althea that Avery carried this added protection. Only a desperate Latian would consider forfeiting their soul to the Abyss to kill Avery now.

Avery leaned her head back against Savine's shoulder, wrapping her arm up and around the back of his head as she pressed delicate kisses to his neck. The crowd let out another cheer. Jari snorted in disapproval, but Savine allowed all of it to soak in. He closed his eyes, sinking deeper into her touch as his cock twitched.

He could not be getting an erection in the middle of a fucking parade. "Avery," he hissed.

Jari tripped, jolting them to the side and a scream of agony cut through the crowd.

Savine looked down to see a young boy, no older than eight, between Jari's front and back legs.

Instinctively, Jari stopped as the child's toy rolled to the other side of the street.

"We hit him!" Avery whispered. "We just hit a kid." Her voice shook with emotion, but Savine didn't let it get to him.

He dismounted Jari and helped Avery down. Immediately, she knelt at the boy's side as Jay hopped down to move Jari away from the injured child. Savine crouched beside Avery. The boy's arm appeared to be broken, crushed under Jari's weight.

"We need a healer!" someone yelled from the crowd. Hyacinth had to be somewhere nearby, but Savine felt helpless as he scanned the folk pushing in close.

"Kyla! We need you!" She was at Avery's side immediately, assessing the child's injuries.

The guards pushed the growing throng back, with Garnel barking orders to the citizens to give them space.

"I can do this," Avery said in a small voice. "I can heal him here." Kyla nodded and Savine stood, giving Avery room to work.

She sat beside the boy and pressed her hands to the young child's arm just as a woman ran frantically from the crowd. "That's my boy!" she shouted. Savine let the woman pass as she looked at Savine with a shocked expression. "What does your witch do to him?"

"Do not fear," Savine replied as he held the woman back from her child. "She's a powerful healer."

As he spoke, green light poured from Avery's hands, encircling the crying boy's arm. She continued to pour her light into the child. He could hear her singing softly, whether to call her magic forth or to comfort the child, he wasn't sure. The language was in her native tongue and had a soft, soothing melody. Slowly, the boy's cries became a quiet sniffle.

Avery slumped back, rocking with effort, and Savine let go of the mother, grabbing Avery's arm to steady her as he helped her sit down. "I guess I'm still a little weak," Avery said.

The boy jumped into his mother's arms. Savine heard the two crying and laughing together. The woman turned, still holding her son tight in her arms. "Thank you, My Queen." She bowed low, stooping so low she was below Avery seated on the ground, low enough that her dress became wet from the ground.

All around them, the citizens of Orofine followed the mother's lead, bowing low enough to bring themselves below Avery's tiny frame. Kyla and Garnel, Jay and Raikin, and all the procession with them prostrated themselves with the city before their human queen.

Savine joined his people as they bowed before his queen, the only person he'd ever bow for. Avery's eyes brimmed with tears as she stood up, taking in the crowd around her.

The small boy rushed from his mother's side and tugged on Avery's dress. Avery stooped down, getting face to face with the little one. Savine couldn't hear what the boy whispered in Avery's ear, but he saw the kiss the boy planted on her cheek and the big grin on Avery's face.

Avery turned to Savine, pulling him up beside her. "How do I get them to stand up?" she whispered.

Savine motioned with his hand, releasing the people from their low kneel. He helped Avery up on Jari before he mounted behind her. The delicious warmth of her body sunk between his legs as she moved back to avoid Jari's impressive antlers.

An adolescent shifter shouted, "A kiss! Kiss your queen!"

Who was Savine to deny his folk and his queen? Savine pulled Avery close as she turned her face to meet his. For the briefest moment, Avery looked at Savine. Her deep brown eyes danced with playfulness and there was a rosy glow to her cheeks. She looked at him with such undeserved adoration it burned his chest. Then her lips met his in a tender kiss that left the crowd around them cheering.

This jubilant procession was so familiar to his homecoming. The overwhelming pride from the folk around him, the acceptance of not only Savine as king, but Avery as his queen. It felt too good to be true. He knew the next street over there would be an angry mob, seeking revenge on Jasper's death.

And yet it never came. Street after street, revelers cheered and bowed as Savine and Avery made their way through the streets with the other people who mattered most in his life.

"I'm feeling a bit jealous of that boy who gave you a kiss," Savine whispered into the curved shell of Avery's ear. He felt the goosebumps raise on her neck and she leaned her head back on his chest.

"Maybe you should be a bit jealous. He was a little charmer."

"What did he say to you?"

Avery smiled with such happy contentment. "He said, 'Thank you for taking away my owie.' I did that though, I helped him. Savine, I want to do that each day. Is that okay? As a queen?"

"Ave, I told you in Nephel that you choose how you spend your time here. Crown or not, I hold no expectations for you."

Avery nodded and pressed her lips to the bit of Savine's exposed neck. "Have I told you how much I love you?"

Kyla

Kyla had felt the confidence in Avery's emotions when she chose to heal the young boy's broken arm on her own. Her talents as a witch were slowly building each day, and Kyla beamed with pride at Avery's skillful techniques used to heal the boy's arm.

The display of support for Avery as the crowd bowed before their queen was something Kyla never expected to witness. From what she remembered in Orofine, there had always been a distinct separation between the king and his residence, and the citizens of Orofine. However, Savine and Avery were already breaking down that barrier between themselves and the city folk.

It only made sense that her brother wanted to break that tradition. He'd never kept himself from his folk during the war, always being there to hear their needs and find a solution to help them. Yet he'd been so unwilling to let anyone do the same for him. Now that he had Avery, Kyla had no doubt that he'd found that emotional support he'd been denying himself for far too long.

She could even feel it in the connection between them. The emotional part of their bond was strong now that it was sealed, and while she tried not to notice, she sensed the deepening bond between them.

Kyla smiled at her own soulmate as they approached the temple. Garnel looked back at her, light shining in his hazel eyes. "Have I told you how much I like your bangs?" he asked. "Such an interesting human word, too. Bangs. They frame your sweet face in a way that I cannot resist admiring, my perfect woman."

"I think you have told me at least twenty times since I arrived back to you. But don't stop. I like you showering me with compliments."

The temple was in view now, on the far side of the city, nearly outside of the wall of enchanted trees that guarded Orofine from danger. She wasn't sure if Althea's daughter would notice the mark on her forehead under the glamour that she'd placed on herself. She prayed that the Goddess of the Harvest would not react as negatively as her sister in Nephel had reacted.

"Kyla, what is worrying your beautiful mind?" Garnel asked, pulling their war elk closer together. She envied Savine and Avery's closeness as they rode Jari together. But that would be impossible for her and Garnel. He was nearly too large for his mount as it was, and she was far too tall to sit between Garnel and his elk's antlers.

"You know what I hide. What if I anger the goddess?"

Garnel shook his head at her. "No need to worry. You're not seeking information. You're only celebrating the Night of Feasts."

Kyla nodded, but she couldn't let go of the nervous energy that twisted through her.

Soon she watched as Jay and Raikin dismounted in front of the temple. Avery and Savine followed, and citizens rushed to provide them with the produce to be offered to the Goddess of the Harvest.

This was always her favorite day as a child. Watching as the goddess accepted their offering, receiving a blessing before she would return home to prepare for the evening festivities. Then she'd sneak down to watch her mother and father entertain diplomats and guests. Savine would always notice her and bring treats to her hiding place behind the large trunk pillars.

But as she grew older, the day had lost its magic. Her father's wrath had warped their family, and she understood the pain he inflicted on Savine. Her mother did nothing to help, too afraid of the retribution she faced to protect her own children. The celebrations and false smiles felt nothing more than another jagged wound to their family.

As Kyla walked toward the temple, her heart pounded. She could see the Goddess of the Harvest, welcoming Savine and Avery to the temple. Avery bowed and received a blessing, her goddess mark clearly visible below the crown peeking out of her hairline.

Garnel took her hand in his and squeezed it. The look of concern on his face made a lump form in her throat. She shouldn't be letting her concerns get in the way of this new beginning. What happened in Nephel wouldn't happen here.

Despite now knowing what the Divine Five were, she had no clue where to begin searching for them, and the fear that she'd upset the Premier Goddess in some way weighed heavy on her.

Kyla approached the goddess, head bowed in respect. At some point, someone had handed her a basket of dried huckleberries to present to the goddess.

The goddess' ethereal light shone in hues of orange and red, her face a mask of indifference as she looked Kyla over from head to toe. "Your gift is accepted," she remarked in an uninterested tone.

The goddess' head snapped up and she looked at Kyla with wide eyes. "A blessing for you, my dear."

The goddess placed her hand on Kyla's forehead. A scorching burn bit through her head as a voice laced with power and iron filled Kyla's mind. *Do not hide what the Goddess has gifted you. Find what my mother seeks and guide the witches to the Divine Five. Do not delay.*

Kyla stumbled and Garnel reached to catch her before she found her footing. A chill had seeped through her flesh, and she shivered in Garnel's arms.

"What is it, love?" Garnel whispered into her ear.

Kyla looked up to see the goddess had moved on, blessing some citizens. Her face was once again soft and welcoming.

"She threatened me in my mind when she touched me. Let's go home. Tell Savine I'm feeling unwell."

Garnel gave a quick nod before he turned to speak to Savine. Kyla didn't wait before she walked to her elk and climbed on. As she walked, she could feel Garnel's emotions rising in anger. Their bond felt flooded with his need to defend her from this threat.

When Garnel was beside her, she showed him her forehead.

"I can see it. It's glowing, as though she branded you with her touch." He swept his finger over the mark, and Kyla could feel the hot welts on her skin. Anger seared down their bond. Garnel's voice was sharp and he touched his dagger on his belt. "Stay right here. I'll be back."

"Garnel! No!" Kyla hissed, but he was gone. She jumped off her elk, working through the crowd, but as Garnel used his large body to press through the throng, Kyla struggled to squeeze through the gaps.

She touched a woman, sending her urgency and the woman leaped out of her way. The next folk received the same emotion, and she worked her way through the crowd to her soulmate. Even among the Latian folk, Garnel towered above everyone. She tugged on the bond, trying to slow his purposeful gait. Garnel pressed back against the bond, sending his rage to her.

There was no stopping him.

Garnel was towering over the goddess in an instant. Before Kyla could stop him, Garnel plunged the blade into the Goddess of the Harvest's heart. A piercing scream filled the temple square as light and blood flowed from the wound.

"No one touches my mate!" Garnel shouted. Then he let out an agonizing cry that made Kyla's essence stand still. His body began shifting involuntarily into his bear form, changing partly then shifting back.

The goddess was in a heap on the ground, light and blood drenching the stones below her. Avery ran to the goddess' side, pressing her magic into the woman and Kyla watched as the wound began cinching itself together. The woman's formerly rosy complexion was so ashen, Kyla didn't know if she was alive or dead, but it didn't matter to her as Garnel cried out in pain.

Kyla sent comfort into him, yet nothing was working to calm him as his body continued to shift. Savine pressed his essence into Garnel, wrapping him in a tangle of vines. The vines coiled and wound around Garnel's writhing body, but Kyla didn't stop her brother. He had to know how to stop this. The pressure of the vines seemed to stop the shifting, and Garnel collapsed on the ground. Kyla pressed herself to Garnel's side, letting her face fall to his chest.

"It's gone," Garnel rasped, his eyes an empty void.

"What's gone, my love?" Kyla asked, her palms pressed to his cheek.

"My bear form. She took it from me."

Kyla looked at the goddess being lifted and carried back to the temple. A weakened voice forced its way into her mind, *Find the Divine Five or your mate will lose his shifting essence permanently.*

Kyla turned to Avery. "We have to find those relics."

Chapter 26

Rylo

An entire day had passed, yet Rylo could still taste the lingering sweetness of Morgan's mouth on his, the tang of her blood on his tongue. He hadn't meant to kiss her, yet the way the flecks of gold in her green eyes had illuminated when she held that blade to his throat had made it impossible *not* to kiss her.

The shock on her face when he nipped her lip between his teeth was another thing he wouldn't soon forget. Or how he'd felt her tug him closer to her. Damn him, he'd no intention of forming anything beyond a working relationship with the witch, yet each time he was around her, she'd surprise him with her wit, her spark, and her rebellious nature.

She was something he was beginning to crave, like a sweetened cup of afternoon tea and a good book by the fire. While he'd never go without that afternoon indulgence, he needed to find a way to stop his obsession with the dark haired human.

Rylo looked to his servant as he helped him dress for the evening. The Night of Feasts had always held a bit of magic that made Rylo look forward to the holiday. It wasn't lost on him that he'd need to avoid that pretty human all evening if he was going to drop his obsession with her. Just thinking of her in the decadent dress that he'd had commissioned for her made his chest tighten.

A brisk knock on the door interrupted Rylo's thoughts, and he nodded to the servant to let Selene in.

It could only be Selene or Elio, but on a night like this, it would be Selene. Elio would be too busy preparing for his entrance.

He often wondered what he would do with this nation if it wasn't for Selene. She saw to the day-to-day nonsense of unhappy citizens and minor threats. She even carried out his more ludicrous ideas, like stealing Avery from Savine during the battle with the Latian royalists.

Yes, they were an excellent team. He had the idea and she would see it to formation.

She walked in wearing a deep purple dress with sharply pointed shoulders and a sweetheart neckline. He'd chosen the color specifically to match the violet in her eyes, and as he suspected, the result was stunning. The gemstones adorning the bodice glittered in the fae light. The wide skirts drew attention to Selene's graceful and stately countenance.

"Perfect as usual, Selene," Rylo said as he twirled her at the tip of his finger. "Did you see to it that Morgan received her dress? Oh, and the friend. Susan, of course."

"I brought both of them the dresses, but it seemed a waste to offer the finer gown to so scarred a woman. Susan would have carried it better. At least she has some of the elegance taught to her from her folk."

Rylo raised an eyebrow as he looked at Selene. "You, who has willfully been the one to cause scars on folk for years, don't seem to appreciate the beauty hidden in those scars. Have you not learned that the most powerful of us are the ones who are not broken by our scars, but find strength in them?"

Selene's lips tipped downward in a scowl. "I was only making a statement that I believe Susan deserved to wear the finer gown. Although she does look lovely in the teal."

"And I want to make a display of Morgan's beauty. Her scarred face is nothing but a reminder of her tenacity to survive and her presence of mind in challenging situations."

"As you say, My King. Is there anything else you need before we go to the celebration?"

"Just an answer to a question. Are you longing for the fox tonight?"

Selene's face was a mask of indifference. "I am not given to such baser emotions as longing, My King."

"Good. Now, see to it that everything goes smoothly this evening. Our last major event resulted in the death of a monarch," Rylo said as he chuckled at his own joke.

"Of course, Sir."

Selene left the room without another word and the servant returned to preparing Rylo for the revelry.

Avery

Avery sat in the bedroom she shared with Savine. He was busy dealing with the fallout from Garnel stabbing the goddess to prepare for the Night of Feasts with her. However, he'd left her a gorgeous dress and she couldn't wait to see his face when he saw her in it. The dress was a blood red gown with gauzy skirts and a cropped top. The top was embellished with beads the color of fall leaves. It was the kind of gown that made her feel like a queen, even if she never thought she'd want the role. Her hair was piled in a loose bun, allowing the natural wave to show through. The delicate crown sat daintily amongst her curls. On her neck she wore a few simple gold chains.

She looked pretty and felt that way too. After saving the boy and healing the goddess, Avery started thinking she could create a place for herself as queen. No, she didn't want to get involved with politics. She'd leave that to Raikin and Savine. Any future conflicts could be dealt with by Savine and Garnel too. But she could happily take on the role of caring and nurturing the folk of Latiah.

After all those years of hurt and conflict, maybe she could help bring peace to this place. She'd heal the sick, listen to complaints, and try to come up with modern solutions that didn't cause folk to lose their heads, their livelihood, or their sanity. Obviously, Savine wanted what was best for his citizens, but after seeing how little so many residents of Orofine had, Avery knew that wasn't how Jasper handled things.

She wasn't delusional to believe that there weren't folk here who resented her, who still wanted to hurt her. But, Savine was right. The crown gave her the protection they both desperately needed her to have.

A knock on Avery's door made her jolt. Rue entered the chamber. Her curly black hair was pulled back into a neat bun with a leaf shaped pin holding it in place. She wore a flowing silvery grey satin gown with a dramatic cut that went nearly to her navel, exposing her brown skin. Small silver leaves held the dress together at her chest.

"I love that dress, Rue! What a statement!" Avery remarked, looking at her beautiful friend.

"Yes, I wanted to thank you for it. It arrived in my room after we returned from the Goddess of the Harvest. What's to be done about Garnel?"

"I wish I could take credit for that dress, but it's not from me. Was there a note on it?"

"No note, just the hairpiece and the gown. I apologize for assuming you sent it."

Avery smiled. "No need for that. But whoever sent it to you has amazing taste. As far as Garnel goes, Savine's ordered him to not attend the party tonight. It seems like a minor punishment, considering he tried to off a goddess on her own holiday."

Rue pursed her lips. "That was unusual. The goddess did something to Kyla, that much I could tell, but I couldn't understand what it was."

Avery had talked with Kyla when they returned to the residence. She'd filled her in on the demand from the goddess to find these Divine Five. She didn't like it—none of it. She found herself as some kind of pawn to a religion she didn't understand or trust.

But if these goddesses were threatening her friends? Well, she'd play nice until she could get away with no longer being the sweet human girl, forced to give in to their games.

Another knock sounded at her door, and Rue opened it. Avery couldn't hear the exchange, but the fae who knocked was gone without entering her room.

"Here's a letter for you," Rue said.

Avery recognized Morgan's handwriting immediately and she tore into the letter. The letter was written in English. Morgan apologized for leaving in such an abrupt way, and said she was safe and happy in

Nephel. She begged Avery not to let Savine retaliate for her actions, saying she needed to do what was best and she couldn't get Avery to listen to reason when she'd tried to talk her into letting her stay.

Avery's stomach flipped. She wasn't a good enough sister for Morgan. Time and time again, she'd overshadowed and overpowered Morgan's voice, and this time it had nearly cost both of them their lives.

"Avery? Is everything alright with Morgan?" Rue asked, a slight hitch in her voice.

"Yeah, she's okay."

"And you? Are you okay?"

Avery nodded. "I just could have prevented all the drama from happening if I had just listened to Morgan. I knew she was worried about coming here, and wanted to stay in Nephel. I shouldn't have pushed her."

"Mistakes happen, and I don't think you could have prevented that attack. They were after both of you."

Avery shrugged and turned back to the rest of the letter. "Susan is doing well. She and Morgan have been spending most of their time in the library. At least they have each other."

"Yes, they do. Have they read anything about the Divine Five or the ancient witches?"

Avery began reading the letter aloud, sharing what Morgan learned about the Divine Five being relics, just as Hyacinth had shared. The letter ended with Morgan informing Avery that she would be traveling to Goldoth with Rylo after the Night of Feasts.

"I don't want her going to another fae nation. What if she's hurt? It's bad enough she's with that asshole Rylo," Avery said as she threw the letter down on the side table. "I probably can't get a response to her before she leaves, can I? How'd this letter even get here?"

"Bird I suspect," Rue replied, taking a seat in a high backed chair.

"If they're leaving right after Night of the Feasts then I don't have time."

Avery slumped into the chair next to Rue's. "My Queen, I don't mean to disagree with you, but you did just say you needed to listen to Morgan."

Avery interrupted her friend, "Don't start calling me 'My Queen'—I've been queen for a day."

Rue gave a subtle bow. "Of course, Avery. But I must remind you that your sister is a smart woman and fearless even without combat training. Her magic seems to instinctively work to protect her from danger in a way that I've never witnessed before. She will be fine."

"It's just hard because I've always been more outgoing and outspoken, so I've stood up for her. And now that she's in this realm I'm still freaking out about the risks she's facing."

"Well, she did face the Tower of Teeth and came back stronger from it. She can handle herself, and I don't think King Rylo will let something happen to her."

"You realize he's part of the problem, right?"

Rue smirked. "But without his schemes, you wouldn't be queen."

Avery let out an exasperated sigh. "I didn't even want to be queen. And I'm still not forgiving Rylo for the shit he put us through."

"You don't have to forgive him, but he has other motives for keeping your sister safe. Regardless of what he did to us. He's selfish and conceited and thinks Morgan can give him the kingdom he wants. He's not going to let anything get in the way of that."

Avery let a long silence build between them as she thought about what was really troubling her. She tugged at the bodice of her dress as she said, "Plus, I feel terrible for how I've treated Morgan. It's not the first time I've ignored her when she's tried to tell me something that matters to her. I don't know why I do it, but I just tend to try and take control for both of us."

Rue gave her a slow nod. "I mean this with kindness, but I saw that between the two of you. You have to trust Morgan to make her own path. She's a capable witch."

Avery bit her bottom lip. "You're right. I just wish I could tell her in person how sorry I am."

Rue didn't hesitate to say, "I can tell she loves you. She's already forgiven you."

Avery stood up, rubbing her stinging eyes. "Now I'm getting upset, and we have this big party to go celebrate. I need something to drink."

"Let's get you a drink, My Queen," Rue said as she tugged Avery toward the door.

The throne room had been transformed into a lavish ballroom. The wood shined with polish and the Latians, dressed in their best, walked the room, drinks in hand. Musicians were taking their seats to the side as Avery looked around for Savine, but didn't see him in the room yet.

Maybe they were supposed to come in together, announced as king and queen? She still wasn't sure what the protocol on being royalty entailed. Regardless, she needed a drink. Rue handed Avery a bright green cider, and Avery instantly recognized it as the same drink she'd once had with Savine in his tent the night before he had burgers prepared for her.

Avery looked across the crowded room to Jay and Raikin. "Let's go join the guys over there. Maybe they know where Savine is."

"The guys?" Rue asked, looking confused.

"Jay and Raikin," Avery said, continuing across the room without missing a beat.

Jay smiled his broad, mischievous smile. "My Queen," he said, bowing deeply.

Avery teasingly slapped his shoulder. "You're embarrassing me, Jay."

"Well it seemed you made an impression on the city today. You'll have all the folk bowing before you if you continue saving small children and helping injured goddesses."

Raikin pursed his lips. "You did well. We need to do that sort of engagement with the city each day. As folk get to know you they'll learn to respect you."

"Always the strategist, aren't you Raikin?" Rue asked.

"Someone must be. Which is why we are making an example of Garnel's foolish behavior tonight. Savine will be entering the throne room soon and will go directly to his throne. Kyla and Garnel will follow shortly after. Savine is going to publicly punish Garnel. He's being stripped of his duties and under house arrest for a month. We have guards prepared to escort him to his rooms."

Avery frowned. "Does Garnel know about this? I thought he was just going to miss out on the party."

"We met privately with Garnel. I explained to the King and general the importance of making a public punishment. Garnel stabbed the Goddess of the Harvest on her own holiday. If it were anyone else, Savine wouldn't hesitate to impart a more severe punishment. Although, I now understand better why he reacted the way he did."

"Because of Kyla?" Rue asked.

"Exactly. It's no excuse, but seeing a mate in danger can do things to a fae."

Avery nodded. Savine was already possessive and aggressive. She didn't need to see how he'd react now that they'd accepted the soulmate bond. "Do you need me to play any part tonight?"

Raikin shook his head. "I want you to socialize. Get to know the courtiers and the major members of the city. We need the folk to learn to accept you as queen, and the first step will be building trust. Savine needs to make a show of strength, but you need to convince the Latian citizens not to distrust you. Especially after the two events with your sister."

"That makes sense. I'm sure accepting a human as queen is going to be tough for a lot of fae."

"Unbelievable is more accurate," Jay piped in.

"Jay is right," Raikin said. "There will be more folk who don't believe this is possible. There have been so few monarchs to rule jointly, but the ones who have were both powerful fae before uniting."

"Enough talk of politics!" Rue said. "My Queen wants to dance and be merry tonight."

Avery let out a sarcastic laugh. "That might be tough, with Savine punishing his best friend in front of everyone. The mood won't exactly be fun."

"That is when you'll need to lift the spirits of the room," Jay replied.

Avery lifted an eyebrow. "Easier said than done."

Raikin squinted his eyes toward the large wooden doors. A guard gave a slight signal and Raikin lifted a finger in response. "Savine should be entering the throne room momentarily. Avery, stand near the throne where he can see you. Rue, you stand guard for her, of course."

The two women made their way to the front of the room. Savine entered, wearing a buttoned shirt in a matching shade of blood red.

His fur jacket looked hot and uncomfortable, but the tight black leather pants he wore made Avery's mind drift to exploring him after this evening was over.

Savine's harsh expression softened when he looked at her, and a wash of warmth pulsed through the connection between them. His lips quirked into a subtle smile as he sat down on his throne.

"Tonight should be a night of celebration. To our unity as a nation, to our new queen, Avery Hollis, and a celebration to the Goddess of the Harvest. That all shall come. But first, we must witness the trial of Garnel Ursus for his attack on the Goddess of the Harvest."

Some members of the assembly sucked in a gasp. She didn't know how that rumor hadn't reached everyone's ears by now, but some folk seemed shocked to hear what Garnel had done.

Garnel entered the room, and stunned silence followed. He was in manacles, wearing a torn shirt. Deep gashes on his skin showed through. He'd been whipped. Did Savine order his closest friend to be tortured like this?

Avery's eyes widened and she tried to make eye contact with Savine. His face was stony as he watched his friend walk forward. Kyla was nowhere to be seen.

Avery looked to Raikin, who now stood at her side. "Who whipped him?"

Raikin's eyes darkened. "He did it to himself. We tried to stop him, but he demanded that he carry the marks to the throne room."

Avery's stomach churned. This was the kind of shit that she wanted to stop. There was no reason for the fae to continue this tradition of senseless violence.

She shook her head in disgust, turning her face to the polished floor.

"Don't look down. They are all watching for weakness," Raikin murmured.

Avery held her chin high, hoping this macabre scene would be over soon. She couldn't even focus on the words that Savine spoke as he doled out Garnel's punishment. All she caught was that he'd be stripped of his title as general and sentenced to house arrest for one month.

"Who's going to be the general?" Avery asked incredulously. There wasn't anyone who could fill that role for Savine as well as Garnel did.

"Shh... Garnel of course. He'll be stripped of the role for a month and reinstated shortly after his house arrest after a grand gesture to put him back in the King's good graces."

This was exactly why she didn't want any part in politics.

Garnel was escorted out of the throne room by guards, men and women who were loyal to him until a few minutes ago.

"Where's Kyla? We talked when we got back, and I thought she'd be here."

Raikin looked at her like she should know. "We can't have Kyla celebrating the Night of Feasts with her soulmate sentenced to house arrest. She agreed to skip the evening's festivities."

Music began playing and a low roar of conversation began around the room. Raikin said, "Now is your time to get to know your subjects."

Avery sighed. This evening was going to be terrible.

Chapter 27

Morgan

Morgan was back in the throne room where she'd shot Jasper. Despite the attempts to clear the room of evidence, Morgan had found the spot where a bullet wedged itself into the floor, leaving a small nick on the polished stone where someone had pried it out. She slipped off her heels and rubbed the spot with her bare foot, reminding herself that it actually happened. She'd actually shot a man in this very room.

The strange thing was that she still didn't regret it. She thought she'd have some feelings other than satisfaction and relief, but she didn't. Those feelings never came, and she suspected they never would.

Avery was alive and getting the fairy tale ending to her story.

Morgan pressed her foot back into the tall heels and looked around the crowded room. Susan left to get them both drinks, but Morgan had hesitated, wanting to give herself this reminder of what she'd done here.

When she thought about it, she knew she was living her own sort of fairy tale story too. She was dressed in the finest gown she'd ever seen, ready to join a royal ball. The silver hue was cast in starlight, shimmering and illuminating slightly as she moved. The full skirt and corseted waist made her feel elegant.

But despite the kiss she shared with Rylo, Morgan didn't want a prince charming to sweep her off her feet. She wanted control, knowledge, and she could gain those things right here in Nephel.

Even today as she and Susan got dressed together, Morgan practiced a spell she'd read in an ancient text. The spell was a way the old witches communicated mind to mind, and Susan had managed to speak directly into Morgan's mind. Eventually, Morgan could do it back.

Morgan wondered how far she could communicate with Susan when one of them was practicing that incantation. She muttered the incantation under her breath and her mind opened up, like it was creating a pathway between herself and Susan. She searched the crowd and directed her thoughts to her friend's mind.

Does this work from across a room? Morgan asked as she pressed into Susan's mind.

She couldn't make out Susan's thoughts. Rather, when she pressed into Susan's mind, Morgan could *feel* her friend's presence, like they were touching. They'd already tried sending images or emotions across the connected minds, but nothing else seemed to work.

I can hear you clearly. Would you prefer a Bayberry cider or red wine from Nephel?

Morgan couldn't help but smile at the voice echoing in her mind. It was like having a walkie talkie in her brain. Magic like this definitely beat out any human technology she was missing.

I better try the Bayberry cider.

Morgan saw Susan gliding across the room, carrying two glasses in her hand. All around her, tall winged fae mingled and drank, a giddy energy filled the room.

Good choice. Where are you?

Still by the bullet hole, which is totally morbid. I'll meet you by that pillar with the sun on it.

Susan smiled at her as they found one another and she passed Morgan her cup. The liquid was bright green, unlike any cider she'd ever seen. She took a sip and she never thought her taste buds could actually dance until now.

"So that was a fun experiment. Can I just take a minute to geek out on how cool learning magic is?"

Susan paused momentarily, like she was contemplating asking what Morgan meant before she said, "I haven't had this much fun learning magic since I was young. In a way, I'm happy we're both here, with the library and our shared interest in experimenting with our magic."

Morgan took another drink of her cider and giggled. "What's in this stuff? It's delicious!"

Susan took another sip of her own cider. "It's made from a rare tree that only grows in Bayberry. It's quite strong." Susan giggled at her own statement.

Morgan's stomach growled and her next drink of cider seemed to go straight to her head. "You know, for being a night celebrating feasting, there's a serious lack of food around here."

There were a few servants walking the room with trays of dainty hors d'oeuvres. Morgan grabbed a bite of crusty bread topped with some cured meats and a spicy sauce. Could one of the fae servants trick her into spilling her secrets if she ate something off this tray? She didn't know how far those rules went.

"In Bayberry, the celebration begins at midnight and we eat, drink, and dance for two nights straight. There's a large bonfire and folk will dance around the fire until they collapse in exhaustion. It's all vegetarian food too. I miss not needing to check if the food I'm about to consume contains meat."

"Do you wish you were home?" Morgan asked, wiping crumbs from the corner of her lips and feeling a bit guilty about snarfing down some meat in front of Susan.

"I miss home, but in a way, no. I was never allowed to leave. There was too much danger in someone discovering that I'm a human. But now that everyone knows, I have freedom that I've never known before."

Morgan knew what Susan meant. She missed her parents fiercely, and was worried about what they were experiencing with the loss of both their daughters. But, being in Aeritis had awakened something in Morgan that she would have never known if she remained on Earth.

Trumpets blared, echoing off the high ceiling that danced with starlight. Morgan turned to where the sound came from. Fae were moving close around the balcony and the two witches walked together to join the group.

Elio landed on the arm of a gorgeous fae woman. Her cascading blonde hair reached her pristinely white wings. Morgan looked at Susan. Despite the placid smile, her eyes gleamed with jealousy. Behind them, Rylo landed, Selene at his side. She wore a violet gown, encrusted in jewels. The damn thing probably had tens of thousands of dollars worth of gems on it.

But it was Rylo who made her breath escape her in a gasp. His graceful golden wings were out on full view, a magnificent glow to his presence, and his clothing was a brilliant gold, perfectly matching the subtle hues of his wings. His crown seemed to be kissed with sunlight. It was all too much, looking at this perfect man that had kissed her with such unrelenting passion only a day ago.

She turned her face down to the effervescent green drink in her hand, hearing the servants announce King Rylo's arrival. As he walked past, she couldn't help but look up at him. His face was the perfect picture of indifferent royalty, but for a moment he met her eyes and gave her the faintest hint of a smile, his dimple making a quick appearance. Her stupid heart deceived her as it clambered in her chest. She wasn't actually interested in this king, and why would he want her? He could, and probably had been with any of these super model beauties in the room. Hell, he probably had something with Selene. She was always at his side, after all.

Rylo took a seat on his throne, a drink in his hand, as music began. Fae all around her began partnering up to dance. Elio approached them, taking a long gulp of the green Bayberry cider in his glass.

"How are the witches this evening?" he asked, his charming smile obviously for Susan only.

"We are well," Susan said, a blush on her cheeks as she took another sip of her own drink.

"Susan, would you like to dance with me?" he asked.

She frowned. "What about the woman you flew in with?"

Elio wrinkled his nose. "That's my cousin. She's distantly related to Rylo too. She's my link to royalty."

"Oh! Your cousin!" Susan said, beaming.

Elio smiled back at her, and Morgan felt a pang of jealousy at the way he looked at Susan. His desire for Susan was earnest, without games or tricks. "Yes, my cousin, Susan. I enter the feast with her every year. Now, would you do me the honors of dancing with me?"

Susan looked at her with a pleading expression.

"Go, I'll be fine," Morgan insisted.

"Thank you, Morgan!"

Susan gave a cheerful wave and walked toward the growing throng of dancing fae. It was fine that she was alone. She didn't need to dance or laugh, or feel wanted and beautiful. Really, hanging out alone by the pillar was perfectly fine.

Morgan watched as the room began to spin with twirling couples. Some took to the air, dancing to the music above the rest of the crowd, delicate feathered wings spread out like fans. The dancing couples' wings pushed a warm breeze around the room, cooling Morgan's perspiring face.

"This may be the only time I wish I had Nepheli wings," a deep voice said from beside Morgan. Her attention was snapped away from the enthralling movement overhead to a man she'd never seen before. His skin was so white it appeared pale blue. He had bright blue eyes and a smile of sharp teeth. The man's hair was the color of purple seaweed Morgan once saw while on vacation along the Oregon coast. A faint scaly pattern dotted the man's skin. Despite his strange, and obviously inhuman features, the man had this striking air about him that caught Morgan's breath.

She wasn't scared. She wasn't even nervous standing in front of this man. Instead she felt *intrigued.* Like she wanted him to whisper all his secrets to her, and she'd happily listen.

"They make me wish I could fly too," Morgan said with a quick grin.

He smirked with shark-like teeth, saying, "I'm Kai. You are?"

Morgan stuck out her hand, offering to shake his, but he didn't take it. "Morgan. You're not from Nephel, are you?"

Kai shook his head, "What gave it away? Are my gills showing again?"

The cider must be working overtime on her, because Morgan laughed like he was cracking the funniest joke she'd ever heard. "What are you, a mermaid?"

The man leaned in close, his chest was near enough to press against hers, and Morgan felt her back bump into the pillar behind her. "Do I look like a maid to you?" His voice was so deep, it rumbled.

Morgan gulped in a breath of air. She knew better than to start something with one of these fae, but damn, that voice alone made her toes curl.

"Merman then?"

"Sea fae. The ambassador." His mouth turned up in a flirty smile as he said, "And you, curious little creature, must be the witch I've heard so much about, the kingslayer. I've been wanting to lay my eyes on you, but King Rylo has done a thorough job keeping you sequestered from the rest of the court. Now that I have, I do not think I'd like to stop looking." Kai's hair fell in an effortlessly handsome way across his face. "Can I get you a drink?"

Morgan wasn't so entranced that she was going to accept a drink from a man she had no reason to trust, even if she did feel like she was under a bit of a spell being around him. "I can get my own. Want to join me?"

Kai winked at her as he pressed his hand to the small of Morgan's back, leading her across the room to the side tables with glasses.

"Of course."

Morgan looked around to the couples pairing off around the room. Some were just dancing to the rhythmic beat of the music. A couple was clearly making out on the dance floor, limbs entwined together as they held glasses of plum red wine in their free hands. Other couples were moving to the dark corners of the room. There were black gossamer curtains running along alcoves of the room and to the balcony. Their midnight dark fabric seemed to glow slightly, like it was sprinkled with stardust. She could make out figures behind the alcoves through the diaphanous fabric. Some were obviously stripped of their elegant ball gowns.

Was this party becoming an orgy? Already? They'd hardly even eaten anything and these dignified and snobby Nepheli were going straight to public sex. Maybe she'd been mistaken about what the fae meant by *feasts*.

And yeah, that was definitely the direction this party was headed as she made out the outline of wings brushing against spread thighs behind the thin curtain.

As they walked toward the wine table, Kai kept his hand on Morgan's lower back, making small circles with his thumb. Morgan wasn't opposed to hooking up with a random sea fae. Actually, the thought excited her. She hadn't had sex in months, and even though he had inhuman features, she found Kai attractive in a way she would have scoffed at two months ago. Plus, he hadn't seemed disgusted by the thick scars tracing her face and neck. It would be better if there were no attachments the first time she hooked up with someone after her body was scarred.

Back at home, she'd like to go to Missoula to have a one night stand every once in a while. It gave her just the tiniest taste of letting go of the pressures and expectations that she placed on herself. Letting herself be free every once in a while was always her little reward when she got through a particularly stressful project at work.

Kai pointed to the deep, plum colored wine. "Have you heard of the Bayberry wine that heightens pleasure?"

Morgan quirked her mouth into a half smile. "So that's what all these fae are drinking? I was wondering why this place was turning into an orgy."

"Yes, it seems this vintage is quite potent, and it was distributed before the actual feasting."

Morgan slid her arm across Kai's torso toward the empty wine glasses. Damn, she could *feel* how hard his muscles were from just that small touch. She reached for a glass and lifted the deep purple wine. "And you'd like to share this wine with me?"

Kai leaned down until his lips pressed against Morgan's ear. "If you agree to enjoy it with me, of course."

Butterflies fluttered through Morgan's stomach and she poured the glass of wine for herself, swishing it in the glass. The heady scent of fermented fruit filled her nose. "Before I drink this, do you have protection? Because I'd like nothing more than to hook up with you."

Hard lines formed above the ridge of his nose, confusion in his eyes. "Protection from what?"

"You know, like a condom? So I don't get some fae venereal disease."

He looked like he was swallowing down a laugh. "There's no such thing as a venereal disease, thank the Goddess. You're funny, Morgan."

Morgan just rolled her eyes. "Of course there isn't. I've got an IUD so you don't have to worry about me getting pregnant."

Kai brushed his hand across Morgan's cheek and she had to stop herself from wincing as he touched her scars. "You think of everything, don't you?" He pressed his lips to her temple and began working his way down her face. His lips were cool and she could smell a faintly salty scent on his skin, sweet and cool, like an ocean breeze. Yeah, this was exactly what she needed. A man who *wasn't* Rylo. Who didn't look at her with those amber hued eyes and leave her body craving more and more from him, while her mind knew he was trouble.

She wanted uncomplicated passion without any of the issues that would come with fucking the king who controlled her entire life.

Morgan brought the lust potion to her mouth, draining the cup before she could second guess her decision. The sticky sweet flavor danced across her tongue as she poured more into the glass. Kai's lips were on her neck, making her skin raise in goosebumps, pleasure rippling through his touch. Everything felt enhanced, like she could immediately *feel* more. Heat began to build under her skin, and the heavy, embroidered dress suddenly felt far too constraining.

She pulled back enough to look at him, sparkling blue eyes met hers and she lifted the cup to his mouth. He drank greedily and without hesitation.

A voice echoed through her mind. *Are you okay? Did you just drink the Bayberry wine?*

Susan.

Of course she was keeping an eye on her.

Morgan looked across the room, meeting Susan's gaze. She held a glass of Bayberry wine and Elio stood behind her, his arms wrapped tightly around her.

I'm fine. I knew what I was drinking and chose to share it with Kai here. Are you okay?

I think I may be so happy I don't think this is actually my life. Check in if you need me. Susan's presence faded from her mind, and Morgan turned her attention back to Kai.

"You're so unexpected," he said, taking her hand in his and pulling her toward the dancers.

Her limbs felt needy with desire to tangle her body around Kai's strong frame. Morgan began to feel an ache between her legs. She needed friction against her aching core, and soon.

A glimmering flash of wings crossed in front of her, severing her connection to Kai's hand. Morgan gasped at the rigid silky plumage that had slammed against her hand.

"If you wish to keep your meager life a few moments longer, I suggest you remove your hand from what is mine." Rylo smirked at Kai before he turned his attention to her, and she didn't know if the look on his face was disgust or desire. All she knew was that she'd never seen someone so gorgeous in all her life. His skin was aglow, his hard body so enticing beneath the finery of his clothing. She had to pry her eyes over to Kai to keep from gawking at the King. Kai, who was being blocked by Rylo's fully spread wings.

How big were those wings anyway? His wingspan was *enormous*.

Her shadows that had been easily kept at bay all evening danced up and around his legs, like puppies who missed their master. She tried to draw them back in, but they bucked, frantic to not lose contact with the Sun King.

"How many times do I have to say you are mine, pet?" Rylo purred. How dare he hit her with the possessive bullshit right now?

Her nipples hardened into tight peaks, rubbing the silky fabric of her dress. It was all she could do to not fall into his arms. Damn, her stupid body was betraying her in the worst possible way. If she'd known Rylo would go all domineering asshole like this, she would have avoided the lust potion.

"I'm not your anything!" Morgan seethed, her breath came out in a pant as images of Rylo's hard and naked body over hers came into her mind.

Rylo turned to Kai, and Morgan couldn't see what look he gave the sea fae, or what he might have murmured. But whatever it was, Kai momentarily cowered. Oh fuck, he was going to leave her with Rylo, wasn't he?

"I apologize for intruding, King Rylo. Morgan, thank you for sharing a drink with me," Kai said as he turned and walked into the crowd of onlookers.

"Wait! You don't have to leave. I wanted to share this night with you, Kai!" But Kai didn't even bother to look back at her.

Rylo leaned in closer. His spicy scent filled her senses. "It seems all you will be sharing with the sea fae is the wine."

"Thanks for cock blocking me, asshole!" Morgan shouted over the throng of onlookers talking as the music that continued its evocative beat.

"I'm not having my pet embarrass me at my own feast. Now, come on." Rylo reached his arms around Morgan before she could protest, picking her up like she weighed nothing at all. His long, lean arms pressed her close to his chest and he lifted them both into the air, flying over the guests.

Morgan had no intention of leaving the party, especially forcibly in Rylo's arms. She hit his chest, making her small hands into fists. She kicked at his grasp around her legs and wriggled.

"Put me down! Let me go!" she shouted, but Rylo looked at her with pure smugness as he beat his powerful wings toward the balcony. Servants pulled the gauzy curtains back, exposing the room to the night air and the couples seeking privacy on the balcony.

The chilled breeze hit Morgan and she sucked in a deep breath. Her skin was still so heated from that lust potion that the coolness of the night came as a shock. She continued to wriggle in Rylo's arms, but the reason behind her struggle began to shift. She couldn't help it. The friction between their bodies felt so good against her touch-starved skin.

Rylo tightened his grip on Morgan's thigh as he flew higher into the dark sky. The moan she let out should have embarrassed her, but she couldn't think about that. She couldn't even remember why she'd been mad at him for interfering with Kai. *Why would she choose Kai when Rylo wanted her and she wanted him?*

His hand stroked her thigh, slow and methodically. Her blood was going to heat to a boiling point if he kept touching her that way.

"Ah, damn Rylo, your touch feels *so* good."

Rylo smiled down at her, landing in a familiar space that Morgan quickly realized was his private rooms. His bedroom.

"That's the wine talking, pet. You shouldn't have drank that Bayberry concoction," Rylo said, walking past her as he slid the golden jacket off, leaving him in only a thin white linen shirt.

She could see every outline of his sculpted chest and abs through the dim light; his skin giving off a faint glow that accentuated every crest and ridge of his body.

No, there wasn't anyone she wanted to be with tonight but the Sun King. Denying that had been a lie.

She moved close enough to grasp the hem of his soft shirt between the tips of her fingers, pulling him toward her. Standing in heels, she was almost tall enough to line her face to his chin.

Heat intensified through Morgan, and she thought she couldn't survive another minute without Rylo's hands on her. Touching her inflamed skin, pressing his lips to hers, stroking and exploring every inch of her over sensitive body.

She pressed herself against him, feeling the hardness of his cock through the thick layers of her dress.

"You want me. You want me and you haven't even had a drop of that sex wine." Morgan's voice was laced with desire. So much desire that she should feel embarrassed by her blatant lust for Rylo.

She wrapped her arms around Rylo's neck, crashing her lips against his in a searing kiss. She kissed him like her life depended on his mouth against hers, and to her delight, he kissed her back eagerly. Her core was throbbing and needy. If she didn't get some relief soon she might just implode.

Rylo tore his mouth from hers, tugging his shirt from her hands as he backed away. She watched as he poured himself a glass of wine and sat down in a chair. The same chair he'd been in when she woke and saw him watching her sleep.

"Sorry, pet. I can't do this."

Morgan's aching, burning body seemed to throb more with the challenge.

"What do you mean? You took me away, made that huge gesture in front of everyone, and now you're not going to fuck me?"

The slightest dimple popped on his cheek as he smirked at her. "I don't fuck women who are under the influence of that wine."

"So now you're an altruistic asshole? You literally kidnapped my sister."

Rylo shrugged, stroking his chin with his long fingers. How she wanted those fingers inside her. "But I never harmed her, and look how it worked out for her. She's queen now, according to my spies."

Morgan's skin prickled with the need to be touched. She was going to die from arousal. Spontaneous combustion.

"Then bring me back to Kai. *Please.*" She wasn't above begging at this point.

She *had* to get out of this dress. Breathe. Calm down. Or at least get herself off if he wasn't going to do it.

Morgan tugged on the corseted back, finally loosening the stays and letting the heavy gown drop to the floor. She stepped out, wearing only some lacy undergarments and her heels.

The look on Rylo's face was pure torture. Gone was the smug, bored king. The man who never let his true emotions show, always looking indifferent. No, now he looked like a man completely undone. Like one more moment and he would lose complete control over whatever was keeping him in that seat.

Morgan traced her fingers down her throat to the swell of her breasts.

"Goddess help me, you're beautiful, pet. And I bet you're burning from all that wine you drank. I can smell your arousal. You're so needy for my cock, aren't you?"

Morgan cupped and squeezed her breasts, feeling the tension in her rise. She let out a harsh laugh. "You've made it clear you're not offering up your dick to me tonight. I'll take care of my needs myself."

Rylo let out a low hum, leaning back in his chair, wings tightly tucked behind him. She watched him lift the wineglass to his lips. A small drop rested on his lower lip and never had Morgan ever wanted to be a droplet of wine so badly as she did in this moment as Rylo's tongue sucked it back into his mouth.

Her throbbing core needed relief now.

She walked backwards to the bed, letting her hands explore her own body as she went, then positioned herself where she'd make sure Rylo knew just what he was missing out on.

Her hands roamed her flesh, enjoying the texture of the lace against her skin. Rylo watched with those intensely glowing eyes as she spread herself before him, and began to circle her clit. She was already on the edge of climax from the wine alone, and it wouldn't take long before she found her pleasure. She slid two fingers into herself, making sure Rylo could see everything.

Tension coiled deep inside her, building quickly as she set a rhythm that had her ready to scream. When she fell over the edge, she closed her eyes, letting her body ride the waves of her release. As the waves of her orgasm slowed, she opened her eyes and saw Rylo hovering just above her, wings spread.

She searched her mind for a way to connect to his. She didn't know why she was trying, maybe because she liked shocking him. He, who never seemed shocked by anything.

There. His mind was like a fluorescent light, beaming and active with connectivity. Linking her mind to his felt easier than connecting with Susan, more natural as she slid in.

Don't you wish you'd been the one to give me that orgasm? She said into his mind.

His eyes widened and he stepped back.

"How did you?" he stammered.

Kiss me like I'm yours.

Rylo pressed his body to hers, then swept her up in a searing kiss that made her see stars.

Chapter 28

Savine

"Good morning," Avery whispered, her fingers running through Savine's loose hair. Mid morning light streamed into their room. Avery looked at him with slightly puffy eyes from the late night and festivities.

Savine pressed his lips to hers, kissing her slowly, languidly, like they had all the time in the world to enjoy each other.

"Good morning, Little Flower," he murmured into her ear. "How are you feeling?"

"Like I was hit by a train." She flopped onto her back. "How much of that fairy wine did I drink last night?"

Savine chuckled. "Enough to inebriate a creature much larger than you, I'm afraid."

"Did I really try to play music over my phone?"

Savine pulled Avery tight against his chest, her eyes closed as she rested there. He could feel her discomfort down their bond—a pounding headache and queasy stomach. He didn't know if she was aware that she was sending it down, but he accepted it nonetheless.

"You did play music through your phone. You said many human words that made little sense, like 'I had one last charge on my external battery,' and 'I have the perfect music downloaded.' Everyone who witnessed the strange music coming from your phone seemed to believe it was magic. And the dancing you led? It was brilliant."

Avery brought her hands to her face. "Ugh, then I cried when my phone died, didn't I? That was it though. It's not going to work again."

"You did make a nice recovery when the musicians began mimicking your human music."

Avery let out a snort. "So much for queenly behavior. Sorry about that, Savine. You're probably mortified."

Savine stroked the edge of her crown. "No, Ave. You brought life to the festivities. I don't think anyone has had that much fun in the King's Residence before."

"Well, it is a treehouse. Treehouses are made for fun. You old folk needed to lighten up a bit. I'm just sorry that Garnel and Kyla had to miss the party."

Savine sighed. He was too, but now that he knew what set Garnel off so intensely, he wasn't surprised by his actions. It still hurt him to see what his friend chose to do to himself as punishment.

"I want you to know I didn't order Garnel to be whipped. I could never do that to him."

Avery traced the lines of Savine's essence with her fingertip. "I know. Raikin told me. But can we begin moving away from that kind of policy in general? Maybe less corporal punishment."

She was right, and he knew it. What was the purpose in using harm for punishment? "And this is why you'll make a great queen. You and your human ideas are going to revolutionize how Latiah is run."

She snorted again. "Don't get too carried away here. I'm not a politician. But I do want to get out in the city each day, get to know the folk and help where I can. Plus keep training with Rue, Kyla, and Hyacinth."

"That sounds like a good plan."

"So we've slept in without anybody disturbing us, which seems like a feat in itself. Do we get to spend the whole day in bed together?"

Savine pressed a kiss to her forehead. "I made sure our schedule was clear for the day. But, I'd like to go back to the woods at some point. I never did speak with the trees. Would you like to join me?"

"Later—I need to get over this hangover first, then I'd like to do more of what we did last night when we got back here. But first I need something greasy to eat and whatever you use to help a headache."

Savine stood up and slid a pair of soft, linen pants on. They hung low on his hips, and Avery looked at him like she wanted to devour him.

"It's unfair how beautiful you are. Damn, you're like a statue."

Savine just laughed and walked to the door. Two former rebels stood outside his door, guarding the entrance. Since most of the rebel forces had returned, he'd increased the number of warriors who were his personal guards to ensure everyone had ample time for leave, as well as covering both himself and Avery. Rue, of course, was the head of Avery's personal guards. After what she did to stay by Avery's side, Savine could never deny her that. His own head guard was an older man who'd been loyal to Savine through the whole of the civil war. Both had the morning off after the late night festivities.

"Please have the kitchens bring up a tray of breakfast. Tea, bison sausage, and eggs. Send for something for Avery's headache from Hyacinth as well," Savine said. The young guard bowed and went to deliver the message.

Savine crawled back into bed. Avery was lying on her back with her eyes shut tight.

"Let me help you," he said.

Avery gave the faintest nod, keeping her eyes shut tight. "Do fae not get hangovers? Of course they don't." Savine went to the bathroom, warming a hand towel under the tap and folding it to fit across Avery's forehead and eyes. He placed it across her face, and she let out an audible groan.

He began gently rubbing her temples, feeling her relief through the bond as he worked his way across her scalp, careful of where the crown chafed her scalp. He wished they could figure out how to get the crown to recede like his own did, at the least to give her some respite from the burden.

"Oh Savine, what did I ever do to deserve you?" Avery moaned.

Savine felt the old tension coil in his chest at her praise. With every day they spent together, Savine was learning to let go of the recoiling doubt that pushed forward when Avery praised him. He didn't know if he could ever grow accustomed to it.

Savine rolled Avery onto her stomach. He straddled his legs across the small of her back, making sure not to press his weight against her, and began massaging the muscles where her head and neck met. He worked his way down her neck to her shoulders, taking care to gently release the tightness in her muscles. As he soothed and kneaded, he felt the tension in her slip away. Down the bond, the discomfort started to disappear.

He began kneading lower down Avery's spine and she let out a muffled moan as he worked his hands downward.

A knock came to the door and Savine called them in without hesitation. Avery needed to eat and take some healing tincture for her head. Only then would he be able to enjoy his quiet morning.

Brisk footsteps entered the room as Darby came in with the trays of food leaving them on the table in the sitting room. Savine quickly climbed off Avery's lower back and leaned against the headboard.

"Thank you, Darby!" Avery called out from the pillows.

Savine looked at her lying face down as he said in a low voice, "How did you know it was her?"

"Who else would be walking with that kind of energy after last night?" Avery retorted with a muffled laugh.

Avery rolled onto her side as Darby peeked into their bedroom, a serene smile on her face. "You're welcome, dear. Is there anything else you'll be needing this morning?"

"You shouldn't even be out of bed after all the work you've done for the Night of Feasts. Go get some rest. We're quite comfortable here," Savine said.

Darby leaned against the doorframe, laugh lines brimming her face. "It gives me joy to serve you, Savine. You know that." She crossed her arms and seemed to be thinking of a different time altogether. "I just wish your mother had been here to see you. She would have been so proud of you! King of Latiah and with a soulmate wearing the boughs and the antlers."

"I'm just grateful Savine has you, Darby. You've been a lifesaver for both of us as we adjust to Orofine," Avery said, leaning against Savine's upper arm.

Darby nodded, "If that's all, I need to see to the cleanup from last night. Then perhaps I will take a rest." She left the room, her brisk steps tapping on the wooden floor and out the door.

Savine went to the table and brought the two breakfast trays to their bed.

"It smells delicious!" Avery said, taking her tray. There was a small vial next to her teacup, something for the headache no doubt. She lifted it up and picked up the paper folded on the tray. "Hyacinth suggests I take the tincture with food then says we should get some fresh air to ensure I don't have my symptoms return. That's funny. The first time I got drunk my mom had no sympathy for how hungover Morgan and I were. She made us go outside with her, even though we were miserable."

She tipped the contents of the vial into her mouth and grimaced as she struggled to swallow it down. "That's disgusting!" Avery grimaced.

Savine took the vial from Avery, tasting the remnants from the bottle. The flavor was sharp and bitter, burning his taste buds. "Pine needles and bitterroot, I'd suspect. Hopefully it helps with the pain. If your healer is ordering us outdoors, where would you like to go?"

"Can we actually go talk with the trees? I would love to know if Morgan is okay."

Savine pressed the palm of his hand to her cheek. "Of course, Little Flower."

Avery

The chill of the fall air had already killed the plants that Avery and Savine had grown when they accepted their soulmate bond. In fact, the biting wind made tears stream down Avery's face as they quickly walked past the hot springs.

"I knew they wouldn't last, but it still makes me sad to see what we created dead, you know?" Avery said as she led Savine deeper into the forest.

"It was inevitable, but I agree." As he spoke, he sent a passionate wave of emotions down the bond. "But I'll admit, I was thinking of something else."

Avery turned and lifted an eyebrow at him. "Savine!" she teased, "We're never going to make it to the cedar grove if you keep doing that!"

Savine grinned, and Avery thought his smile when he was actually content was the most sincerely beautiful thing she'd ever seen. "Little Flower, you have ruined me. I'll never be able to get anything done when I have the memories of those hot springs in my mind. Goddess above! I can't even walk into the woods without being distracted."

Avery giggled and kept walking. "Don't blame me!"

Savine slapped her on the ass and she let out a surprised shriek. "The blame is all yours, Ave."

God, she loved it when she could draw out this side in him. It was so unexpected— this grumpy, old-ass fae man teasing her and laughing with her like this. She'd never believed it was possible a few months ago.

The trail grew steeper, the wind whipping through the limbs overhead, causing branches to sway and bend. "How far do we have to go? This wind is brutal! We should have never left our bed."

"I had no intention of leaving our bed, but remember Hyacinth insisted you get some fresh air. The cedars are getting close. Look to the left and you can see the first one." Savine pointed ahead, and Avery could make out the cedar boughs rustling in the breeze.

Pushing through the wind, they made it to the copse of trees. The cedars were so large, even Savine was dwarfed by their massive girth.

He approached quietly and Avery stood back, letting him connect with the trees through mycillious, the language of the trees. The cedar's trunk began quivering and Avery gasped at the way its branches stooped and shook low in the wind.

She could hear Savine speaking in a strange, whispery language, and the sound of it soothed her. Like it was a comfort to hear him speak in that mysterious language. Finally, he drew back, his face hardened with the weight of his duty again. Gone was her playful soulmate, and before her was the king with the weight of a nation on his shoulders.

"What is it?" Avery couldn't stop from asking.

He shook his head. "Your sister really will be traveling with King Rylo to Onyx Caverns in a few days' time."

Avery felt a tightening in her chest. Would Rylo take Morgan somewhere and abandon her if it fit his needs? "That's what her letter said, but what does that mean? Why?"

"If I had to guess, he most likely seeks an alliance, although I do not know why he brings Morgan with him. Goldoths are fae who draw their essence from rocks and minerals. Their military might and wealth are profound."

Avery chewed on her lower lip. "Why would Rylo ally with them? Does he want to go to war with Latiah? We did what he asked!"

Savine took her hand in his. His large hand was so much warmer than hers, like he was hardly affected by the driving wind. "He may think Latiah views his broken oath with you as an act of war."

Avery's eyes widened. "We can't go to war against my sister!"

Savine shook his head. "I have no intention of fighting another war. I've fought for nearly twenty-six years and have no desire to return to battle. There's far too much reconstruction here that I would never dare to engage in another conflict."

Relief stemmed down Avery's spine. "Do you think Morgan will be safe with Rylo?"

Savine shrugged. "There are rumors she's been in his private rooms. She's most likely as safe with him as anywhere in Nephel. Perhaps more safe, considering his interest in keeping her close to him."

Avery sighed. "Okay. She'll be fine. She knows what she's doing."

Chapter 29

Morgan

Morgan couldn't get comfortable on the floor of the cavern. The dripping water and the scent of rot reminded her too much of the abandoned mine shaft. Around her, winged fae were trying to get comfortable too. Some seemed to be sleeping, but others were quietly lying on the cold, hard ground.

She caught Rylo's gaze across the cavern, studying her. He sat against the stone walls, resting his head. His wings were splayed out in an awkward angle. They seemed like a huge inconvenience most of the time. Morgan stood and walked across the cavern, sitting beside the Sun King. She leaned her head against the wall, looking into his golden eyes.

"Can't sleep?" she asked.

"I could ask the same of you." Rylo reached out his hand and traced Morgan's collarbone. His fingers were cool and made her skin prickle.

"We'd all be sleeping better if we could have flown to a hotel. You may want to consider investing in real estate. Maybe get better accommodations on all these flights. Who's ever heard of a king sleeping in a cave?" She batted his hand away from her.

"A king who likes to travel quickly and without fuss," Rylo said, flexing his fingers like he could still feel her touch on them.

Not much had happened between them since he brought her to his room on the Night of Feasts. They'd kissed and the flame from that damn fairy wine had burned brighter. When Rylo noticed her increasing arousal, he stopped kissing her, built what amounted to a pillow barricade between them, and told her to get some sleep. It was easier said than done as she struggled through her need for his touch.

Eventually, she was almost to the point of tears when he reached his arm across the pillows and began slow, gentle strokes across her back and shoulders. He'd sung her a slow, soft melodic tune that seemed filled with longing and remorse. The tension she couldn't shake slowly began to dissipate with his caress until she drifted off to a deep, dreamless sleep.

But nothing between them happened the next morning, or the days that followed. She worked for hours in both libraries each day, running into Rylo occasionally. They made plans for their journey to Goldoth, but it seemed like there wasn't much to the attraction he'd shown her that night.

Morgan accepted her unwanted feelings she was developing for him weren't actually reciprocated.

"When will we arrive in Goldoth?" Morgan asked.

"Technically we crossed into Goldoth today. We made it across the Wastewater several hours ago. Tomorrow we will enter the Onyx Caverns and meet the King Maglar."

Morgan scraped her hands across her forehead. She was trying to let go of her nerves that kept her feeling worried about meeting another king.

"When can I have my gun back?" Morgan asked. Rylo hadn't given it to her before they took flight on the eagan, and she doubted he would give it back.

"Why not now?" Rylo said, smirking. He reached into the bag at his side and pulled out Morgan's handgun.

Morgan pulled the clip out of the gun. She'd used three or four bullets when she shot Jasper. Too many, she knew now, but she'd had such a rush of adrenaline that she couldn't help it. To her horror, there were no bullets left.

"What the hell, Rylo? You shot the rest of my ammo!"

Rylo cocked his head to the side, giving her a confused look. "I've no idea what you are saying."

"The gun! You shot all my bullets. There should have been ten or eleven left in this clip, and they're all gone!" She could feel guards moving in close. Rylo lifted a hand for the guards to stand down, unconcerned by the tone coming from the kingslayer.

"I still don't understand what you are accusing me of doing. Yes, I tried your weapon. It worked perfectly fine when I used it. I told Selene to continue tests. She said you may need to imbue it with your magic before it fires again, but that shouldn't be a problem for you."

"The gun doesn't work without bullets. They aren't something I can just create out of my shadows or any magic! They're human made, and now I don't have any if I need them."

She shrieked and her shadows began streaking out of her, filling the cavern with inky darkness, extinguishing the fire in the center of the room. The fae in the room cried out, but Morgan ignored them. "What if I need to use it to stay alive?"

Rylo scoffed and took the gun out of Morgan's hand. He let a bit of his essence shine out of him, bringing light to her darkness. Slowly her shadows began gathering back into her, prancing around Rylo as they skittered out of sight. "I do apologize. I didn't understand it had a finite number of uses. But you don't *need this* to keep you alive. You have yourself. All those spells you've been memorizing, and these dancing shadows."

Rylo raised a shining hand up to her remaining shadows and they extinguished the light coming out of his black veined hand.

"Honestly pet, you have all you need to protect yourself right here." Rylo brought his hand up, pressing it to her forehead.

Morgan nodded. She looked across the cavern at the others. They seemed to be busying themselves with making a new fire and avoiding her and Rylo's interaction. Which was just fine. Ever since he scooped her up and flew her out of the party, everyone had treated her like some sort of pariah. Even Susan assumed Morgan was lying when she said she only shared a bed with the Sun King.

She didn't like it, everyone assumed that she was sleeping with Rylo to get some sort of special treatment. They'd already assumed the same about her sister, so why not think Morgan was doing the same thing? She wanted these folk to see her for what she was. A woman who had her own strength and power without needing to sleep with a king to get recognition.

Maybe she should call in one of her favors and make him share that there was nothing happening between them. No, that would be a stupid use of her favor. She wanted to use it for something that would make a difference. In the end, it didn't make a difference what his citizens thought of her.

"Care to share what is racing through your beautiful mind?" Rylo asked, a bright dimple showing on his cheek.

Morgan murmured the enchantment and sifted through the void, looking for a way into his mind. There it was, bright and bold. She slid into his mind like sliding into a comfortable sweater.

Want to know the truth or should I tell you a lie?

The corner of Rylo's mouth twitched. "Tell me what I want to hear."

Morgan raised her eyebrow. *I was thinking of that kiss we shared the other night.*

Rylo leaned in, his lips caressing the curve of her ear. "Lies, pet. I can smell when you are aroused, and you are not thinking about something that arouses you."

Morgan wrinkled her nose, pulling back from those perfect lips of his. "That is disgusting and invasive. And fine, I was thinking about how I'll make you the next deceased king on my list. As you pointed out, I don't need a gun to do it."

Rylo let out a loud, long laugh. "Oh pet, I love how lies slip off your tongue so effortlessly. Do try them on the King of Goldoth. I have one more thing for you before we arrive at Onyx Caverns tomorrow."

Rylo pulled out a sparkling necklace set with yellow stones on gold. She spoke into his mind, not daring to say what she realized. *One of the Divine Five?*

Rylo gave a tiny nod. He lifted the gems, gesturing to Morgan's neck, and she nodded in agreement to let him place the jewels on her.

He reached around her throat, moving her long, dark hair to one side as he let his fingers linger in the silky strands, then he clasped the necklace around her throat, letting it rest against her chest. Slowly, he traced the path the necklace took down her neck, across her shoulder, and to the divot between her breasts before he traced the jewels up and around her neck again. Rylo moved Morgan's hair back into place and looked at her with sparkling eyes.

The jewels felt heavy on Morgan's chest. She'd read in a book that deep magic carried a heavy burden, but Morgan didn't think the book meant it in a literal sense.

"Does it call to you? Can you feel its power?" Rylo asked.

It has a heaviness that goes beyond its weight. I'm not sure how I'll draw the deep magic out of it, but I'll experiment with it.

Rylo's voice was low, like he wanted the information for Morgan's ears only. "It can mask your goddess mark, but you should let it show. I want to show off what a prize you are."

Morgan rolled her eyes. "I'm not a prize or a possession."

"Not to me you aren't," Rylo said, stroking his long finger across her cheek.

I'm thinking about how I'd like to slice into your soft throat again.

"No, I don't think you are," Rylo said, leaning back on the ground, wings flattened under him. "Get some sleep, Kingslayer."

Kyla

Kyla had never seen Garnel so despondent. Although they had moved into her mother's former apartments and had ample space, Garnel hardly left their bed. The house arrest, while a light punishment for stabbing a goddess, was eating at Garnel's soul.

She couldn't get him to work past the guilt he had for threatening his own life with his senseless attack. Kyla understood that he was incensed when he realized what the goddess had done to her, but it wasn't like the goddess had actually harmed her. It was all instinct, and one that could have been avoided.

Garnel was on his side in bed as Kyla prepared to leave their apartment. His shirtless back revealed the healing scars from his self flagellation. Although she tried to heal them with salves, Garnel had been insistent to see through his punishment for his reckless behavior. She gave him a quick peck on his forehead, but he didn't respond. Down their bond Kyla felt how he struggled with self-loathing and doubt.

"I love you, Garnel. Only two more weeks and you will be free."

He blinked at her, but didn't bother speaking. For days it had been like this. It had gone on so long, that she thought she'd have to share the only thing that may wake him from his despondency before she was ready. Maybe if he knew her secret suspicions, his mood would brighten and he would return to her.

Kyla walked to the outdoor hallway, connecting one tree to another as she passed her father's former apartments and went down a spiraling stairway to Avery and Savine's small suite. It was odd to have a king and queen occupy such modest accommodations, but they didn't seem to mind.

Avery was waiting for her in the hallway, Rue beside her, as they had done the last several days.

"I've been thinking. We need to get serious about finding the Divine Five," Avery said as a greeting. The thought had already been haunting her. If Garnel was going to be reunited with his bear form, they would need to make finding the Divine Five a priority."

"I agree, and now that we know what they are, we need to start looking for clues. I'll write to Susan and ask if she's found any descriptions of the relics."

Avery nodded. "Savine was trying to keep it quiet, but Darby found documents that show your father was able to open a portal outside of Orofine. He sent fae through it. That, plus the dark magic that was used at the final battle in the Middens makes us think he might have had access to one of the Divine Five, and he learned how to use it. Have you ever seen him with a bone shard?"

Kyla racked her mind for a memory of a bone her father might have kept close. "No, I never saw anything like that. Does Savine remember one?"

Avery shook her head. "Nothing."

Kyla could sense Avery's honesty in the answer. Since she and Savine had accepted the soulmate's bond, Kyla had noticed a lightness between the two of them that made Kyla feel at ease about her brother and his well-being. He'd always had so much hurt buried within him, but had masked it around others. Kyla was the only one who could sense the cataclysmic pain that her brother carried within him. It was still there, that sort of thing would never fully heal, but it felt more manageable.

"We'll figure it out. What's the plan for today?" Avery asked, turning to Rue and Kyla as they stepped outside the comfort of the warmed King's Residence and into the icy morning air. With the city behind them and the forest stretched in front of them, Kyla noticed the frost lacing dead leaves on the forest floor.

Kyla had learned to appreciate this time with Avery. Her eagerness to continue to learn combat surprised Kyla, but it was the growth in her magic, especially as a healer, that made Kyla look forward to their daily training sessions together.

Rue smiled, her breath puffed out from between her teeth. "I think we need some more of the cardio you humans enjoy, then let's practice with your battle axe."

Avery nodded as she pulled her fleece jacket tightly to her. "After that I'd like to go into the city and check on a girl I healed yesterday. Kyla, would you join me?"

"Of course. I'd be happy to."

The run up the mountain wore on Kyla more than she expected. She didn't know if she could possibly feel this tired. She leaned against an aspen and slid down to the ground, letting her head hang between her knees.

A wave of nausea hit her, and Kyla asked for a sip out of Avery's human water bottle. The durable material made it an excellent choice for their daily hikes and runs through the woods, and Avery was always happy to share.

"Are you okay, Kyla?" Avery asked, sitting down beside her.

Despite the chill in the air, Kyla could feel the perspiration clinging to her forehead.

"I think so. Just tired and a bit queasy."

Rue asked, "Would you like a bit of food? I have some here."

Kyla wrinkled her nose at the thought of food. "No thank you. I think I just need some rest and a bit of water."

But Avery looked at Kyla with slit eyes, brows wrinkled. "Can I assess you? I just want to make sure you're safe to go down the mountain on your own."

"If it makes you feel better," Kyla said. Avery's question was honest, curiosity and concern coursed through her touch as she gently placed her hands on Kyla's shoulders. Avery closed her eyes, concentrating, and Kyla felt the stirring of her magic across her shoulders.

Kyla's essence shuddered under her skin as Avery's magic wrapped around her. Green strands of light danced across her skin, working their way down to her abdomen.

Avery's eyes snapped open and Kyla nearly jumped up in fear from the expression on her face.

"Holy shit! Did you feel that?" Avery asked

Kyla shook her head, suspecting that Avery noticed what she had hoped for.

"There's a second heartbeat inside you. Kyla, I think you're pregnant!" Avery wrapped her in a tight hug, and Kyla could feel her excitement skim off her. "I'm going to be Auntie Avery!"

Rue joined in, hugging Kyla from the other direction. "Congratulations! Your child is a blessing from the Mother Goddess!"

Kyla shivered at the name of the Premier Goddess. She had been experiencing some sort of crisis in her faith in the deity over the last few months, and she didn't want to mention the Goddess when speaking about her unborn child. What if it drew attention to her child, making them a target just like her soulmate had become? The loss of Garnel's ability to shift was crushing him, and she still couldn't reach him to bring him back to her. She wouldn't allow the Goddess to harm her child. She'd protect this precious gift to the Abyss and back if Althea dared come after her child.

"Thank you," Kyla said demurely. "I thought I might be pregnant, but the child is too small for me to fully sense them with my essence. I was hoping it was true." She pressed her palm to her abdomen, and even though she couldn't feel anything there yet, she knew deep within her was a spark of life, a piece of herself and Garnel.

"We should bring you to Hyacinth. She'll be able to tell if you are pregnant and can help strengthen you with whatever tinctures and herbs she's got," Avery said.

The walk down the mountain was steady, enjoyable even, as the women worked their way down the trail single file. Kyla shared her concerns about Garnel, and how he was struggling with the loss of his bear self, and the weight of his actions.

Avery assured Kyla that Savine didn't hold any ill will against Garnel, but Kyla already knew that. Savine had been visiting them both, checking in to see if Garnel was doing better. But he was always the same. Always lost to her.

Savine had set aside rooms for Hyacinth in the northern wing of the King's Residence. It was nearest to the forest, and included a door carved into an ancient cedar tree. Avery pressed on the bark, opening the passage and revealing the spiral staircase within the trunk. The three women took the steps quickly until they entered the warm and welcoming rooms of Hyacinth's private clinic. The room smelled of herbs, stewing greens, and oils.

"Welcome dears! Avery, I wasn't expecting you until this afternoon. Was there trouble with the girl in the city?" Hyacinth said, taking Avery's hands in hers. Her dark hair was tangled with twigs and herbs, and her nutty skin showed the slightest signs of middle age.

"Actually, we want you to examine Kyla," Avery said before Kyla could even get a word in to the older woman.

"Kyla?" Hyacinth asked and gave her an assessing gaze. "May I touch you?"

"Yes, please," Kyla said.

"Oh! Yes! Very faint essence. Maybe no more than four or five weeks along. Oh, Kyla, dear! Come, come. Let's have a look at you."

Hyacinth immediately helped Kyla lean back on a comfortable bed. Kyla gave her permission to examine her as the other two women made themselves scarce in the adjoining room.

"How long, dear, have you been trying for a pregnancy? It's not always easy to release your fertility."

"Actually, we decided shortly after Savine took the crown. We have been waiting for an end to the civil war and didn't want to hesitate. I wasn't sure if I had released my fertility, but it must have worked."

Hyacinth pressed her herb-stained hands against Kyla's abdomen. "You must have used a large amount of your essence to induce fertility so quickly. That is not often capable for folk, but I dare say you wanted this. Often women hesitate and don't use enough of their essence to become fertile, which is why they don't become pregnant quickly."

Kyla let out a small laugh. "I very much wanted a child."

Hyacinth took Kyla's hands in hers. "Your pregnancy is early, but there's a strong essence already rooted in place. Perhaps this one will be a bit like you."

"What can I do to take care of us now?" Kyla asked.

"It's simple really. Rest when you are tired, eat when you are hungry. Men often turn into clucking mother hens over their mates, but I daresay Garnel has always been that way with you. The most important thing is to listen to your body. You'll know what you can do, but I think you'll find that you can continue most of your activities. Perhaps no battles, but I've prayed to Althea every night that the time of war is past. If you don't mind, let's bring in the other girls. I've got another matter to discuss with the three of you."

"Of course," Kyla replied.

Hyacinth called the other women in and began preparing tea for everyone. Once they were all comfortably assembled in the room, and tea was made, Hyacinth began speaking.

"I've been thinking, and I want to know how your search for the Divine Five is going."

Avery shrugged. "We've found some information about Jasper possibly having access to a relic that sounds like one of the Divine Five. I've been wondering if he could have used it on the forest during the last battle. Savine said it seemed there was darker magic used on the trees."

"Possibly, although it is challenging for fae to access deep magic. He would have had to part with a great amount of essence to do so. It would have cut into his lifespan, but if he were desperate enough, he could have decided to take those risks," Hyacinth said. She took a sip of her tea, and Kyla wondered what she gave herself to drink. Everyone seemed to have a different blend of herbs and spices to meet their needs. Kyla could feel her tea restoring her strength and reducing the nausea in her.

"Avery said the relic could resemble a carved bone. Do you know any rumors of one?" Rue asked.

"The only Divine Five relic that I know with certainty is in Nephel. The Nepheli kings and queens have often worn it. It's a necklace made of gold and citrine jewels."

Avery's eyes grew wide and Kyla could sense her anxiety rising. "I wore that! The night I was supposed to assassinate Jasper. Rylo said it would mask my goddess mark."

Hyacinth pursed her lips. "Could you sense the deep magic within it?"

Avery shook her head. In all the chaos that followed, Kyla hadn't noticed Avery's necklace. It mattered little now. The necklace was out of their grasp.

"I didn't notice anything unusual except for a heaviness," Avery replied.

"You should write to Morgan and see if she can get her hands on it," Rue said.

"What if I just tapped into the deep magic again and formed my own relics? I accessed it before and I was fine."

Kyla felt the nervous energy from Rue and Hyacinth as Hyacinth said, "No, that is far too dangerous. Promise me, Avery, that you won't be so reckless again. You'll need other witches with you to safely extract the deep magic. You could have killed yourself doing what you did. Also, we don't know what Althea wants with the Divine Five. It's best to collect them first and see what her purpose is."

Kyla felt the discomfort inside her build. "Unless she wants to use them in a way that would harm us."

Rue looked at Kyla with incredulity. "Why would Mother Althea want to harm her creation?"

Kyla looked at Avery, felt her sense of doubt rising as Avery said, "Why would a goddess force this task on witches if she couldn't achieve her goals herself? She wants the Divine Five for something, and I don't think it's just to collect these old relics."

"When she took me, I felt her divine power, but nothing of her emotions. Either she was shielding them, or she is void of emotions. She has a purpose that she's not disclosing. But if I don't complete this task, she could punish Garnel. Perhaps even my unborn child."

Avery shook where she was sitting, the rage building within her palpable. "I'm not going to be some tool that bitch uses to harm anyone. If the coven that separated the realms during The Cleaving could trick her, then we'll figure it out too."

Hyacinth let out a tsking sound on her tongue as she said, "Child, you do not know what you speak of. The Cleaving was no trick against Althea or Gaia. It was for the freedom of the human race."

"Althea doesn't want to harm you, Avery. Surely not," Rue agreed with Hyacinth and Kyla felt a stirring of unease inside her. She didn't agree, but feared voicing her thoughts. Anytime she'd meddled with the Premier Goddess' task she'd faced disaster.

Finally she said, "Regardless of the reason, we must find those relics."

"We're going to need to get back to Susan and Morgan eventually," Rue said. "They have more access to the information we need."

Avery nodded. "Savine's going to flip when I tell him I'm going back to Nephel. But we don't need to worry about that yet. First, we've gotta find that other relic here." Avery turned to Kyla. "Where would your father keep something he didn't want found?"

Kyla pressed her fingertips to her abdomen, reminding herself of what was at risk if she failed to find the Divine Five. "I haven't the slightest idea of where to begin our search."

Kyla couldn't wait to return to her apartment. She hoped her good news would cheer Garnel up. At the very least, she hoped he would speak to her and get out of bed. She rushed from the other women after her tea was finished and made her way over to her own rooms. As she entered the apartment, she knew immediately that Garnel hadn't left their bed.

"I'm back, my love," she said softly, walking to his side of the bed where he lay staring at the wall. He didn't move or remark as she sat down, her back brushing against his thigh. A few weeks ago this touch alone would send him grasping to pull her closer to him, but now he didn't react.

She rubbed her hand across his arm, feeling his emotions. It was still the same despondency and self-loathing he'd experienced previously.

"Can I help you feel better?" she asked, gently. He'd only let her do that twice since he'd lost his ability to shift to his bear form. As she ran her fingers across his arm, she noticed how his essence had faded ever so slightly.

"I don't know, love. I feel like I've lost a part of myself. I'm not like Savine with an essence with many abilities. I have one. Shifting into my bear form is the only thing I have, and that's now gone. I can feel my essence fading." He looked at her with such pain in his eyes. "I may have ruined our lives, Kyla."

Kyla stroked his arm and his essence moved slowly under his skin. "We're going to fix this, Garnel. You'll get your bear back and your essence will stop fading. I'll damn the whole Abyss before I let you fade from me."

He cracked a weak smile at her threat. "You would, wouldn't you? I'm sorry I haven't been myself. It's bad enough being under house arrest, but..." He shook his head, and Kyla felt the despair in his tone. "But to lose who I am is the worst punishment of all. To know if I don't get my bear back I'll likely die, and I never was able to give you what you wanted."

Kyla climbed into bed next to him, her nose touching his as she wrapped her arms around his solid body. "I'm not losing you, and you have given me what I most wanted."

Garnel pulled back and looked at her, his mouth and eyes wide. "Do you mean you're pregnant?"

Kyla couldn't stop the tears that rolled from her eyes or the smile on her face. "I am! Avery noticed first this morning and Hyacinth confirmed it."

Garnel tugged her against him, his body shaking with laughter and tears. "It's what we've always dreamed of." He sat up, keeping his arms tangled around hers as he lifted her up too.

"My love, it is what we've dreamed of," Kyla said, pressing her lips to his. For the first time in weeks, he responded, nibbling and teasing her own lips as she opened for him, welcoming his touch, desperate for it.

He abruptly pulled back, and she felt shame down their connection. "I've ruined this for us. What if you can't find the Divine Five?"

She shook her head, not letting that fear build within her. "We are going to figure this out. We're getting those relics and you'll be restored to your full power before our child is born."

He brought his hands down to her abdomen, pressing his large palm against her. "You're right. We will have the family we always wanted. Nobody, not even the Premier Goddess herself, will take away our happiness."

Chapter 30

Rylo

Onyx Caverns were just as Rylo remembered them from his first visit, so many years ago. The palace underground was lit in low fae lights, casting dark shadows across the rock hewn walls in the towering cavern entrance.

Maglar met them with an entourage of Goldoths beside him. His skin was white with faint silvery lines. Even his bald head was etched with the lines, like a vein of metal in solid stone. His grey eyes reflected the light, causing them to shine like orbs. Eyes made for seeing underground, for stalking prey through this labyrinth of tunnels and mines.

Rylo looked at Morgan. She wore a blank expression, except for the tiny shake in her hands, nobody would know that she was uncomfortable. But he saw her discomfort. This place, these people would bring up her experience in the tunnel in her realm. The Goldoths' essence sketched across their skin was similar to the Latian shifters. She looked back at him, green eyes wide with doubt.

He knew she'd react this way, and yet he'd still brought her here to this place of nightmares. She was the only one who would be able to locate the lost relic, and he needed that relic if he was going to access the power that would come with combining the Divine Five together once again.

Maglar sneered at Morgan before bringing his attention back to Rylo. "King Rylo. Good of you to join us. Welcome to Onyx Caverns. And for bringing your prize with you. Is she truly marked by the Goddess?"

Rylo gave Morgan a harsh tug into his arms and lifted her hair up, revealing the five stars of Althea. "As you can see, she is."

"And the necklace she wears? You decorate your slaves as you would a queen," Maglar replied, showing a sharp-toothed grin. His soulmate, Mara entered the towering cavern through an arched doorway at the back of the expansive space. She slipped in beside him, past their guards. Like Maglar, she was bald, and her essence seemed to sparkle like a cut diamond against her pale skin. Her silvery dress looked as if it were dipped in glimmering diamonds, blending almost seamlessly with her essence.

"King Rylo, welcome to Goldoth."

"It is my pleasure, Your Majesty," Rylo replied with a bow.

"The necklace, Rylo. Why does your human wear such fine jewelry?"

Rylo grinned and rubbed his fingers across the necklace on Morgan's throat. "I assure you, it is nothing more than a means of control."

"You control her through the gems? Rumors have already spread of her dark magic. You're right to put a stopper on it."

Rylo traced his black veined hands across Morgan's collarbone. How he loved the delicate details of her bones. Like a fragile bird, he had to resist the temptation to feel them snap between his hands.

"Something like that. If she wanted, Morgan could be the most powerful force in Aeritis, after the Goddess, of course," Rylo said. Not a lie. None of this was a lie.

"In that case, we'd prefer to take our own precautions. We do not like to leave our slaves without chains in Onyx Caverns." Mara stepped forward, holding a finely crafted collar with a leash of the same material stretching out.

A guard took the collar and leash into his hands and carried it to Rylo. Rylo took it in his hands, feeling the biting cold of the metal. Just as he'd put a stopper on Avery's magic, the Goldoths were within their rights to demand this and Rylo expected as much.

"A wise choice, Mara," Rylo said as he lifted the collar to Morgan's throat.

Rylo felt Morgan's presence slip into his mind. Cool, dark, and comforting. Like staying in bed on a rainy day.

Don't you even think about putting that thing on me. I'll ki—

The connection between their minds came down like a wall dividing them, leaving him with a cold sense of longing. Her eyes widened, and he felt her shaking with betrayal as he clicked the collar in place and took the leash in his hand.

"I won't be turning my witch over to your care. I need the key and the leash for myself."

Mara grinned. "We would never take your property from you, but I shall hold the key. It hasn't escaped me that you carry a mark of your own on your once gleaming hands."

Maglar's expression turned cold. "Yes, Rylo, please explain how you broke a vow and now carry the consequences."

Rylo brushed off the menace in Maglar's voice, letting his own tone sound bored with the conversation. "I was put in a position where I had to accept Savine's mate's oath. She expected me to leave Morgan in Latiah after one month in Nephel. I did no such thing, and carry the mark to prove it. As I said, I refuse to turn my witch over to you, just as I did not give her to the King of Latiah."

"That is reasonable. She should have respected your ownership of the witch," Maglar said without question. Fool. How could such an idiot have control over such a powerful nation and military? It made Rylo want to rage at the insult of it all.

"We'll have guards show you to your rooms so you can refresh before supper," Mara said as she led them toward the arched doorway leading deeper into the tunnels of Onyx Caverns. Darkness settled over them in the halls. Of course, Goldoths could see clearly in such dark conditions and had little use for faelights. Their senses were adapted to such living conditions.

"Your hospitality is appreciated," Rylo said as he tugged the leash that connected him to Morgan. She tugged back, trying to knock Rylo off balance in the darkened tunnel. A tingle went down his spine, anticipating how much fun Morgan would be when they were alone and he could hear her rage at him.

It was going to be delicious, seeing her angry and at the end of his chain. Perhaps he *should* be thanking Mara for the collar.

***

Morgan

Morgan wasn't going to hesitate this time. She was going to turn herself into a kingslayer twice over, starting with Rylo. She'd never felt so humiliated as she did, stumbling through the black tunnel at the end of Rylo's leash. Morgan tugged on the leash, trying to topple him off balance, but it didn't happen. He didn't even seem phased by her pulls on the chain.

Finally, the queen, Mara, stopped in the dark chamber. "Here you are, King Rylo. We were not sure if you wanted to keep your witch in your quarters, but we have provided accommodations for her in your room. If you would prefer her housed in the slave quarters, we can do that as well."

A chill went down Morgan's spine. No. He wouldn't dare make her stay in *slave quarters*. She couldn't even imagine what that would be like here, in this damp and cool cavern. She pulled on the leash, bringing herself closer to Rylo. Not because she wasn't already seething at him, but because he was all she had here. If he abandoned her—she couldn't even comprehend what it would be like to be utterly alone in this strange and cruel land.

Then she realized that's exactly what Avery faced. When she arrived in Aeritis, she was completely alone. She had no one and no understanding of the world she'd fallen into. No wonder she was so adamant that they stay together. It was always about protecting her, keeping her from the frightening danger of being left utterly alone.

"That won't be necessary. I prefer keeping my pet beside me," Rylo said, tugging Morgan toward the open door. The stone from the hallway had disappeared, similar to what happened in Rylo's library. He whispered something to Elio, but she didn't bother trying to listen. Her ears were ringing with her rage anyway. Eavesdropping was futile.

She stepped into the room, but only for the distance that the leash allowed. She was still in disbelief that he'd actually put her in chains like this.

The room was carved from black stone, cold, so cold Morgan thought she might be able to see her breath. The bed was large and covered in a black blanket. On the floor was a small pallet containing a thin blanket. *This* was what the Goldoths provided for her to sleep on? Not even Morgan could fit comfortably on the small bed, even though she was small. It looked built for a spaniel or some other medium sized dog. She shook her head with disgust.

The door closed behind Rylo and Morgan felt some slack around her neck. She turned to him, seeing him looking at her with that damn fake expression and she punched him, square in the nose.

Rylo raised his hands to his face, dropping the leash. "Why the fuck did you do that? I think you just broke my nose!" A small trickle of blood flowed down his nostril, hitting his upper lip. It probably wasn't broken. She hadn't hit him *that* hard.

"How dare you!" Morgan seethed before she turned her back on him, keeping her voice low enough to keep the entourage in the hall from hearing them.

Rylo grabbed the chain and pulled Morgan close. She coughed from the sudden jerk at her throat, the cold metal burning her skin. "How dare I, what, Kingslayer? Keep you alive and beside me? Put on an act to get us what we both came here for?"

Morgan turned, the pressure on the chain moving to the back of her neck as she pushed against his chest, giving herself space. "These fae are monsters! They actually think I am your *property!* And you let them believe that. You let them think that I'm nothing but a—"

Rylo filled the gap between them, putting his hands on her shoulders and she tried to wriggle from his grip. "Look at me, pet." Morgan twisted, trying to get released and as she did, the chain snaked tighter between them, twisting around Rylo's arms and Morgan's body, bringing them even closer. "Morgan, *look at me.*"

Morgan stopped struggling.

She looked up at the fire in his eyes as he held her tight, relentlessly close. She could feel his pulse drumming in a steady beat.

"I said what I needed to say to keep both of us alive. I'm not sorry for that."

"And you like having me on a chain. Something to show off to your royal friends."

A gleam in his eyes caught her by surprise. Damn. He did like seeing her chained to him.

"I'm not going to deny that your anger had me… intrigued to see how you would react when we were alone. You caught me off guard with your punch, a mistake on my part."

"Well, I *am* mad at you. I thought you were going to abandon me," Morgan said, casting her eyes away from his intense gaze.

"Never, pet. You are *mine.* I'll not abandon you for anything." Rylo untangled their chains and dropped his end down, sweeping his blackened hands up to her cheeks.

Unease mingled with need stirred in her stomach. "But why? What do you mean when you say I'm yours?"

"I mean I'm not letting another nation take you from me," Rylo said, as his mouth slipped into a sly smirk, his dimple showing. "Was there anything else you thought I meant by that statement?"

Rylo leaned in, and if Morgan had her shadows they'd be shifting around them in a frantic dance. She could feel how close his lips were to her ear and felt him sniff her. Okay, that was a little weird, but she also kind of liked it.

This tension between them was so confusing. If she were in the human world and he was an authority figure, she wouldn't act on her desires with him. They were too strong and felt too complicated.

But the rules were different here. The lines between what was right and what was wrong were blurred, and she hadn't felt this way about someone in—honestly, ever. Her need for him felt like a wildfire burning under her skin, even when she was furious with him for collaring and leashing her like a dog.

Then her more level-headed, practical side would kick in and remind her that she knew *nothing* about this man. He hadn't given her any information about his past, about how old he was, what he liked for fun, or if he even had any real friends. Why get entangled with someone who hadn't offered to disclose *anything* about his life, oh, and he also kidnapped Avery and held her soulmate in prison for years.

"Morgan," Rylo said, stroking the icy skin under the cuff of the collar. "Was there anything else you thought I meant by that statement?"

Morgan closed her eyes, the warmth of his touch soaking into the burning cold of her skin. She breathed deeply, smelling his spicy scent.

Her eyes popped open and she looked at him, staring intently at her, so close their lips were nearly touching. "I think I have Stockholm Syndrome or something."

Rylo's brow furrowed. "Explain."

"It's where you start having empathy for your captor. Developing complex emotional feelings for them, even though rationally, it makes no sense."

Rylo stepped back, and for a moment, she thought she saw something like hurt in his eyes.

"I'm not your captor. I was ready to let you stay with your sister. I've never held you against your will."

Sure, she chose to stay with him, but she hadn't had the choice to stay with him in the first place. He'd forced that on her, making her nothing less than a captive.

"You forced me and my sister to stay with you! You just demanded that I am yours, not only a few minutes ago, but also in front of your whole nation!" Morgan said, pulling back from him.

"There's a difference. You chose to be with me. You chose this," He said, tight lines creased his forehead.

"God, I can't believe I'm even having to lay this out there. The night I arrived, you gave me no choice. None! It doesn't matter that I chose you a month later. You are still my captor."

Rylo's heart was beating so quickly, Morgan thought she could hear it. His breathing seemed quickened, and the look on his face was anything but the bored mask he usually wore. He looked as if her words had stung him.

He turned his back to her, and she watched him press his arms against the stone wall, face turned away from her.

She climbed onto the foot of the bed, suddenly exhausted from the arrival in Onyx Caverns and the argument they were having. The leash clinked against the floor as she got as comfortable as she could.

Rylo turned, his swollen nose looked painful from this angle. "I chose you. I chose you because you are clever and talented. I saw it the moment you entered the Towers. I don't regret that, and I will not let someone take you from me. I've had too much taken from me to lose someone else. But, Morgan, if you feel I am keeping you captive against your will, I'll let you return to your sister. You can train with her and we can still work out an arrangement where you help me achieve my goals as I help you meet yours."

Morgan shook her head. She stood up, walking slowly toward him. "I—I don't want to go to Avery. Everything you say is a half truth, and I don't know how much more I can stand. I just wish you'd say what you really mean and be straight forward with me. Especially in a place like this where you're the only one I can trust."

Rylo brushed his fingers along her cheeks, touching the cord of scars. "I'll not let them harm you, pet. That I swear. I can't help that I never say what I fully mean or that I keep information back from others. It's how I've survived for decades, but I will try. I'll try strategizing with you."

Morgan sighed, placing her hands on top of his, tilting her head up to look into his amber eyes. "I'm not asking you to share all your darkest secrets. I'd just like to know before you make choices that affect my autonomy. Even if I am working for you, even if I'm choosing to be with you, I'm not something you can just use and discard. I have my own needs and opinions, and I just want you to respect them."

Rylo closed his eyes, holding in his breath before he released it slowly and opened his eyes to look at her. "I'm a sovereign, pet. What you're asking of me goes against everything I've done as king. But I will try to share information with you before it's sprung on you, if that makes you feel less like my property."

Morgan nodded. Rylo was making a compromise. She couldn't even believe it. Letting go of his hands, Morgan pointed to the bundle on the ground. "Just to be clear, I'm not sleeping there. You are going to have to get your pillow barrier back up again or you can squeeze on the dog bed."

Rylo let out a quick, hard laugh. "We'll share the bed, pet. It's the least I can do after collaring you."

"What's the deal with Goldoth treating people like dogs? It's gross."

"I think we've only seen the beginning of this. Don't be surprised if I'm feeding you table scraps at supper tonight."

Morgan shook her head and closed her eyes, hoping that the nightmare situation she found herself stuck in would disappear.

Chapter 31

Savine

Savine sighed, bored from his seat on the throne. He'd left his life of action, of always being outdoors and near the forest, for a mundane life atop a chair. The day to day inner workings of government were dull, duller than Savine expected. Thank the Goddess the war was over and he'd come out victorious, but Goddess damn him, what he wouldn't give for an excuse to charge through the Middens on Jari or use his essence to defend his people.

At least he had Avery, and she'd jumped into life as his soulmate and queen better than he could have dreamed. She'd found her rhythm, knitting together a close group of women for support as she navigated her new world and new roles. She didn't even seem too upset about her sister not being at her side. He couldn't wait to show her the shared throne he had commissioned for them. A throne wide enough for two, with supple leather comfortable enough to sit in for hours side by side.

Savine motioned for a drink, and Darby was there beside him, carrying a cup of wine. The next citizen would be escorted in soon, under heavy guard after the mountain lion shifter tried to take his life.

A Latian with the woodsy essence similar to Savine's entered the room. With guards on both sides, Savine understood why the court gasped when they saw the man. He was bruised and sliced open on his arms and neck. His leathers were tattered, nearly disintegrating on him. Unlike most fae, who naturally smelled like their essence, his scent was something dirty and rotting.

Those in the throne room made way for the man, leaving a clear path to the throne. When the fae saw Savine, he started shrieking with laughter; like a man lost in the madness of his own mind.

The guards on all sides of him drew their weapons, ready to end the wretch before he got too close to their king.

Savine felt Raikin's quick, fluid steps toward him. He'd been hiding in the shadows, observing, as he often did when Savine held court. "This man was found wandering the forest north of here, rambling something about carriages without moose pulling them."

Savine frowned at Raikin. "Was he alone? Did he say where he came from?"

Raikin slowly nodded his head. "I was informed there was a body with him. He was decomposing in a way that shouldn't happen to a young fae with so much essence left in his body. The trauma to his head suggested a weapon made of iron."

Savine's eyes widened. "Carriages without moose?" Raikin nodded.

"See that Darby prepares a private meeting space."

"A wise choice, My King." Raikin slipped away, speaking to the guards who turned with the filthy prisoner and led him out of the throne room.

Savine dismissed his court, leaving through a side door as he followed Darby into an outdoor hallway that led to another segment of the King's Residence. Try as he might, he always thought of it in that way now, with the playfulness Avery brought to the word.

"The guards are making the man more presentable for you and they'll meet you in the city view room. Is there anything you need?" Darby asked.

"Bring something hearty for the man. Raikin has reason to believe that he came through the portal. He'll most likely be hungry. Avery has suggested that most of the area on my father's map would be wilderness in her world. If so, the man may be starved."

Darby pursed her lips. "We should assume he went through on the old king's orders. If so, he is your enemy." She took Savine's hands in her small, pale green hands. "Please, Savine, be careful meeting with such a man. We know now that your father was dabbling in powers that aren't meant for a fae. Who knows what he's done to these folk to be able to send them through a portal and back like that."

Savine shook his head, trying not to dismiss her worries, but there was no reason to fear this fae. "Don't fear. Just bring the food up once the man joins me."

Darby bowed low, leaving Savine alone in the hall. The cool breeze brushed past him and he inhaled the faint scent of the forest. What he wouldn't give for some time alone with Avery in the forest instead of dealing with constant disasters like this.

He felt down the bond. There she was. Running, he thought. She felt light, happy, and free. Mentally, he stroked that bond, sending his love down it. It was easier now, always feeling her close, even when she wasn't near him. Always being able to connect to her, to be reassured that she was safe, she was happy. Thinking back, he wasn't sure how he survived those two separations without this deep connection to her.

She responded down the bond and it felt as though she were dancing in his soul. Goddess alive, he didn't know how he'd survived so long without *her*. Without this better half of himself.

Savine took one last long, deep breath, scenting the moisture on the cedar boughs and went back inside. He made his way to the city view room. It was empty, which was what he hoped. He looked out the paned windows that provided a view of Orofine below. The city was bustling with folk, even though the weather was turning brisk.

So far, the city had seen a steady stream of nomadic groups enter the city, seeking help or looking for reassurance that Jasper was actually gone. Many of the folk he'd met were in poor health, desperately in need of food after being forced into a lifestyle that they weren't accustomed to. He could see one such group, making their way to the gates of the city, loaded with supplies that Savine prayed would last through the harsh winter. This group, like so many, wanted to return to the nomadic lives that they'd been denied under Jasper's regime, and Savine hoped that many of them would find solace in the free and open plains of the Middens next summer.

A knock on the door caught his attention, and Savine called for the folk to enter. Raikin led the way into the room, a few guards and the cuffed man behind him. The man was bathed, hair still damp, and his clothing was fresh.

He looked at Savine with hatred in his eyes as he spat at Savine's boots.

"You don't deserve the crown atop your head," the man hissed.

Savine felt nothing but cool distaste as he looked at the emaciated man. The man despised him, had served his father loyally, yet what had it gotten him in the end? His essence was so faded that the whorls on his skin were but a ghost of what they should be.

There was something familiar about the man. No doubt, Savine would have seen him around Orofine if he'd served Jasper in any close capacity.

That was it. He was a former guard for his father. "Kinlon, isn't it?" Savine said, his tone soft.

The man sneered, tugging at the chains that held him back. "You betrayed your father and your folk! How dare you wear the boughs and antlers."

Savine quirked his lip into a half-smile. "The Goddess and the folk of Latiah seem to think otherwise. Despite your treasonous words, no harm will come to you in this room." Savine directed the guards to let the man sit. Raikin called for Darby, and she brought in a tantalizing stew. The scent of it made Savine want some for himself, despite having recently eaten.

He didn't give in to the temptation as he watched the man dig into the dish. Kinlon moaned and slurped, shaking as if he couldn't survive another moment without sustenance. The chain between his handcuffs was just enough length that he was able to feed himself, but not enough to cause harm to himself or Savine and Raikin.

The sight of the man eating with no dignity made all thoughts of eating disappear. He looked at Raikin, who wore a revolted look on his own face. Wordlessly, he watched the man finish his meal.

When Kinlon was finished, he turned his attention back to Savine. His face had splatters of stew meat caught in his beard, and his eyes had a spark of disgust. "I suppose I'll soon die from poison. In any case, I hope you rot in the depths of the Abyss. That you will feel no relief for what you have done to Latiah."

The guards moved in closer, weapons drawn, but Savine waved them back. If this man did take Savine's life, he would be joining him in the depths of the Abyss. There was no lesser consequence for killing one's sovereign. And that was what Savine had become. He had absolute power over this nation, over his folk. Including this nobody who detested him so palpably.

"You best watch your words. You won't be the first to find the trees will act out my punishment for me," Savine said through gritted teeth. "Raikin, will you see the guards out? I believe we should have a private conversation with Kinlon."

Raikin stood and ushered the guards out of the room, latching the door behind them. "My King?" The question in Raikin's tone was heavy with meaning. He knew what Raikin was capable of doing to draw answers from this man.

"Not yet, Raikin. Feel free to ask questions, though."

Raikin nodded.

Savine sat across from Kinlon, Raikin standing behind him. "Tell me, Kinlon. I haven't seen you on the battlefield in at least a decade. Where did my father send you?"

The man scowled at Savine before he kicked the bowl from the low table between them, launching the mess of stew and earthenware bowl toward Savine.

Savine pressed his hand up, releasing some of his essence as a wall of foliage came between them, stopping the bowl before it clattered to the hard wooden floors. Did he need to use his essence to stop a bowl? No, of course not, but he did want Kinlon to remember *who* he was and what essence flowed through his veins.

Savine sent vines forth, binding the man's legs. The man pursed his lips, eyes alight with frustration and rage.

"Your participation will make this go much more smoothly," Raikin said.

The man leered, "I haven't forgotten your betrayal, Raikin Aspinen."

Raikin raised an eyebrow to Kinlon. "You were nothing when I chose my allegiance to King Savine. *Nothing*. You best not forget why I've been so valuable to kings."

Savine pressed his thumb and forefinger to the bridge of his nose. He needed to be here for this, but he was beginning to think that he'd rather be anywhere but here.

"I grow tired of your spewing dissonance. Tell me, how long were you in Montana and how did you return?"

This took Kinlon by surprise. His eyes snapped to Savine's and he showed a mouth of rotting teeth. Teeth that couldn't rot like that in a fae with a healthy essence coursing through his body. "You know of the other realm then? The realm made of humans."

There was no reason that he would tell this scum about Avery. No reason to share all that he knew. "I have found Jasper's documents on his progress in sending Latian warriors through the portal."

There was a spark of interest in the man's dull features. "Then how would *you* know the name of the realm when King Jasper didn't? The humans we found couldn't speak our language. No fae that I knew of returned to Aeritis."

Savine didn't allow himself to reveal anything to this man.

Raikin said, "Perhaps you were not privy to such information."

Kinlon let out a harsh laugh. "You have no idea what information was provided to The Hunters. None. What training and experimentations we underwent to prepare for our journey. I underwent *thirteen years* of training to prepare for my journey through the portal."

"How do you know you are the only one to return?" Savine asked.

"All of us had the ability to return. It was successfully tested and we had our orders to not return until our task was complete. Only things did not work out as we planned."

Savine felt Raikin lean in, close enough for his essence to stir from the nearness of his body. "You are saying Jasper had the capacity to slip between portals?"

"Of course he did. We all had the power to return after our mission was complete. Our king would never abandon us to the fate of being trapped in a *human realm*." Kinlon spat at the ground, his faded essence swirled slowly.

"It was a human and a human weapon that ended Jasper," Savine replied, his tone neutral.

Kinlon's face twisted with disgust. "A *human* killed my king? Was it the two born of one womb? Tell me, is it true that they are here?" He began to look frantic, trying to jump up, but the bindings on his legs were too tight and he fell to the ground. Kinlon thrashed on the ground, knocking the table forward.

Savine looked at Raikin and they both picked up the man. Savine bound him tighter with vines and set the man back into his seat.

This man somehow knew about the prophecy. He knew that twin women would return to Aeritis. How was it possible that so many knew for so long without him hearing word of it? How could his soulmate, his Avery, have transformed the political landscape so thoroughly?

"They cannot be allowed to live! They will destroy our nations and expose us to the evils in their realm. The fae will fade if they are allowed to live. They will fade and diminish just as I have." Kinlon lifted his chained hands up to his face. "This is what their world does to us. It eats away at our essence. They have already taken some of our kind for their experiments. Distant places, untraceable and unreachable. Those that are not caught are forced to roam like animals as we searched for the two from one womb. I found the corpse of one of the Hunters, killed by the sisters!"

"Enough!" Savine growled. Kinlon fell silent to the power in Savine's voice.

A soft knock rapped against the door. The guards would still be outside the door, so anyone knocking would have gotten past the guards.

Raikin went to the door and opened it, letting Avery in.

Kinlon's eyes widened in shock as he took in Avery's distinctly human body and the delicate crown atop her head.

"NO! No! She *cannot* be queen!" he shouted as he scrambled to move toward Avery.

Avery gasped at Kinlon's quick movements.

The man released his essence in a violent eruption of binding weeds and thorns. Savine shielded Avery from the blast with his own essence, but it was Raikin who was finished with this conversation.

Kinlon writhed on the ground, a sticky sap covering his face.

Savine moved across the room, wrapping Avery's arms around him. Protect her. He must keep her safe from harm. The mantra chanted through his brain as he pulled her closer.

Avery tucked her face into Savine's chest. She let out a gasp as she buried her face from the scene before them. Savine didn't want this man to die, not yet. He still needed more information out of him. He signaled to Raikin that it was enough. Raikin began pulling back his essence, controlling the sap as it slid off Kinlon and onto the wood floor.

"Can we get out of here?" Avery asked. Savine nodded.

"I'm finished with him today. Bring him to the prison and see what information you can gain from him," Savine said as he took Avery's hand and led her toward the door.

"Of course, My King," Raikin replied.

The fresh breeze off the mountains met them and Savine breathed in deeply. He could feel the bond bucking between them, his need to get Avery to safety becoming too much for him to stand.

"Please explain what that was about," she muttered as they walked through the hallway. She was leading them up, either to his father's or mother's former chambers. He followed blindly while the need to protect her, to consume her, coursed through him. Savine needed to get her back to their rooms and make her his again. The bond demanded it, forced him to claim her.

Always his desire to fill her, bury himself in her wasn't far away. But this? When that threat happened, he felt himself become obsessed with the need to claim her as his own true mate again and again. He hadn't expected this from the soulmate bond. Nobody had warned him, but then again, he'd spent so long avoiding any conversation about soulmates that maybe he only had himself to blame.

His voice came out low and rough as he said, "That man, Kinlon, has been through the portal to your world and back."

Avery stopped walking and looked up at Savine. "He has a way to return?"

Savine closed the space between them, pressing himself into her, needing to feel her, to taste her. "Yes, but I don't know what it is yet. That's why I cannot let Raikin kill him at this point. We need more information. But for now, it's enough."

He looked down at her, the bond between them growing taut as he sent his desire down the connection. "You know what seeing someone threaten you does to me," he said, voice full of suppressed desire.

Avery smiled. "You know I like it when you get possessive and obsessive. I was bringing you up to Kyla and Garnel's rooms, but we could make a quick stop in our rooms first."

"Quick? I have no intention of being quick," Savine said with a half grin.

"Quick is a relative term." Avery pressed her hand to his hardening cock. He let out a gasp as the heel of her hand rubbed against him, applying just the right amount of pressure. Sweet goddess, he needed Avery's touch. Avery continued to rub her hand against the leather of his pants, making the bulge of his erection push uncomfortably against the ties.

"Avery, not here," he rasped. She looked up at him with a hint of mischief. Cruel, torturous witch. He wasn't about to spend his seed in his leathers in the middle of the outdoor hall.

Chapter 32

Savine

A stifled cough behind them brought Savine's attention to someone approaching. Dear Goddess, no. It was Darby. The woman was practically a mother to him.

"My King, My Queen," she said with a grin as she passed.

Avery let out a giggle as Savine grabbed her by the waist, hauling her over his shoulders. She shrieked and laughed with surprise as he began carrying her back toward their rooms.

"Scream all you'd like, Ave. I'm happy to have *everyone* know not to interrupt us."

"We should make as much noise as all those mates you had to listen to for decades."

"A bit of payback does seem to be in order," Savine said as he carried his mate through the interconnecting halls and stairs, his erection tenting his pants for all who passed to see.

Savine pushed their door open and latched it behind them. He brought Avery over to the fur-lined bed and set her down. Her long golden hair was tied back with a bit of leather and her body had that glow to it that she always had after she finished running with Kyla and

Rue. Fuck, she was beautiful. She looked up at him with a hunger that threatened to devour him.

Reaching down to her old hiking boots, Savine undid the laces, tossing them to the floor.

"Take my shirt off," she demanded. She raised her hands up and Savine pulled the shirt off her. The binding around her breasts was next as he lifted the tight fabric up over her head, releasing her small, firm breasts.

"Abyss damn me, you're perfect," Savine muttered, more to himself than her.

Her voice was like chimes as she said, "I never get tired of hearing you say that."

Savine tugged his own boots off as he moved closer to his soulmate. His essence swirled and shook under his skin as he took both her breasts in his hands, kneading them and feeling their weight. Her nipples formed hard peaks between him and he couldn't resist tasting them. The sweet saltiness of her skin alone could undo him. He licked and lapped at her like a man starved for contact.

Had a breast ever been as fine? He couldn't remember there being one as perfect as Avery's, and he worshiped them as he memorized every curve of her soft flesh, every groove of her hard nipples.

"Oh, Savine," she groaned when he nipped at her pebbled curves.

Avery squirmed under his contact and he knew she wanted more, always craving more of his touch and it made him want her all the stronger as he felt how quickly she responded to his ministrations.

"You greedy thing. How wet are you for me?" Savine asked. His lips found hers as he began undoing her pants.

She pulled back and lifted herself up to let him shimmy her tight leather pants off. "Soaked. Drenched already for you. I was wet for you the moment you blocked that guy's essence for me."

Avery spread her thighs wide for him, letting him take in the sight of her glistening entrance. Savine growled and dipped his fingers along the edge of her core. She *was* already so wet for him. He stroked her in a slow, teasing rhythm that had Avery panting in frustration. How he liked to draw out her pleasure, to see her react to his every touch. Finally, Savine pressed his finger into Avery, feeling her inner walls already throbbing, already so close to finding her release.

His own need to be inside her was almost too much for him to wait. He didn't know if he could last another moment without burying his cock inside her to the hilt.

"Savine, I need you. All of you in me," Avery whimpered as she rode his hand. "I want to come on your dick."

"Thank fuck."

Savine slid his fingers out of Avery. He watched as she shivered from the loss of contact. He didn't want to leave her feeling empty, but he had to get out of these damn leather pants. They were probably doing permanent damage to his aching cock by now.

The Abyss damned leathers seemed to be stuck to his overheated skin, and he attempted to wriggle out of them, but couldn't get them off without looking like a fool, tugging and working on his pants. Avery giggled.

"Are you stuck?" she asked, a smug expression on her face.

"Abyss damn me. This is humiliating."

She slid off the bed and knelt before him. Suddenly, even his essence went still as Avery looked up at him, naked and gorgeous.

"Let me help," she said and her tone made his heart skip a beat. It was deep and heady, like the only place she wanted to be was kneeling before him.

Slowly, tenderly, she slid her hands up his legs to where the tight leather pants were tangled at his thighs, his cock poking out of the top like a forgotten pet, trying to pry through a hole in the gate.

"God, how did you get into these things?" Avery asked as she slowly peeled the material back. His cock sprung out of the top of his leathers and Avery let out a little snicker.

"Fuck, are you still laughing at me?" The indignity of it all was almost too much for him to bear. What did she see in him that made her want him so much?

Finally she tugged down his pants to his ankles and helped him step out of them. "No, Savine, I'm not laughing *at you*. I'm laughing because your dick just popped out of your pants like it was saying 'Hi! Nice to fuck you!'"

Savine grunted, "Well, at least the pants are off." His essence writhed with the humiliation of the whole scene. He closed his eyes, trying to remember how good she'd felt only moments ago.

She gripped his cock with both hands, working it in steady pumps. Now he was groaning in pleasure. She released him, letting her nails scrape against his length in a perfect mix of pleasure and pain.

Avery stood up, pulling him toward the bed and crawled on top of the furs. All Savine could do was follow as the need to fill her consumed him with the beat of their bond.

His body framed hers as he reached down and kissed her. The kiss was rushed and messy, his desperation to be inside her stronger than his desire to slow things down.

"Savine," Avery rasped as she reached down and took his cock in her hand, guiding it to her entrance. She rubbed herself against him, coating his cock with her slick heat. His tip pressed against her, and he pushed inside Avery in one hard stroke, leaving him seeing stars.

Avery gasped and they both didn't move as he let her adjust to his size. She gazed into his eyes, her dark pools ensorcelling him.

"Oh God, Savine!" Avery cried out as she writhed under him.

"Did I hurt you?" he asked. He never wanted to cause her pain, but he knew that he'd left her sore after their first time together and had been concerned he could cause her pain ever since.

She shook her head, closing her eyes as he began to tentatively move inside her, her inner muscles already so tight around his cock.

"No, Savine, no, you're perfect for me," Avery said, her voice deeper, more husky than normal as she met him stroke for stroke, finding a rhythm that had them both building toward release.

He could feel her pleasure building quickly as his own orgasm threatened to rip through him, and then he felt the deep flutters of her inner walls around his cock, sending him cascading into his own orgasm as he shouted her name for all his nation to hear.

After they were both sated and limp in each other's arms, Savine slid from the bed and brought Avery a warm washcloth. He pressed it to her thighs, wiping their fluids from her. Once he was done, he slipped both of them under the furs, enfolding his body around hers as he stared down at her.

The contented smile on her face warmed him in a way he'd never experienced with any other lover. He'd never realized he could find as much pleasure in what happened after sex as he did in the act itself. But it was different with Avery—more intimate in a way that he didn't even know was possible. He thought of the hard, cold man he'd been before he found her. That man wasn't even capable of imagining that he could love and be loved in return, and yet here he was, with Avery at his side.

She was the most precious gift he'd ever been given. His soulmate, willing to love him, despite all his flaws, all his brokenness. Avery loved and accepted him in a way that felt so good it hurt.

Chapter 33

Rylo

Rylo sat at a long granite slab of a table next to the Goldoth queen. Her brilliant diamond skin glittered in the small fae lights that illuminated the dark expanse of the dining room cavern. Morgan was right behind him, standing. She wore the same silvery gown he'd provided to her on the Night of Feasts, and as before, he had a hard time taking his eyes off her beauty.

As he suspected, and despite her finery, he would be feeding her table scraps from his own plate. She'd wrinkled her nose at the proclamation from Maglar, but didn't comment or complain. That was one of the things he was drawn to about Morgan. She had an uncanny sense to know when to hold her tongue and when to speak up and voice her opinion, unlike her sister who would have probably already asked where Goldoth keeps its relic.

The growing attraction he held for her was something he hadn't anticipated, yet he saw no reason not to explore the allure she had over him. It was the sort of relationship he welcomed with the women near him. As long as they remembered he had no interest in anything other than a physical relationship, he saw no issue. Morgan would be the kind of woman who understood his motivations and his reason for keeping their relationship strictly physical.

He'd need to address it in a straightforward manner, rather than in his typical games of the heart. After all, that was all she'd asked of him. To no longer say half truths and use trickery.

He felt the leash between them tug tight and turned to see her adjusting where she stood. She shot him a scowl, and he could have sworn that he felt her attempting to burrow into his mind. The tiniest scratching on the surface of his thoughts, yet it was impossible. She was shackled by Goldoth's magical chains.

Grimils wearing iron collars brought plates of food and set them before each member of the dinner party. Rylo didn't bother to hide his disgust in being fed by a dark fae designed for battle. How could Maglar and Mara force such beings into subservience?

"Is something not to your standards, King Rylo?" Maglar asked in a harsh voice.

"No, this looks perfectly acceptable. Is it your famed broiled cave fish?" Rylo asked, keeping up a blase tone. He poked the fish with his fork, nearly translucent scales peeling back to reveal a soft white flesh traced in flecks of grey and brown.

Maglar grunted his response. "Caught locally in Onyx River, deep underground."

"Downstream of your mine tailings, I presume?" He heard Morgan let out a tiny snicker.

"Yes, the tailings do go into the river, but they are perfectly fine. We have been using that river for our water and food source for centuries with no ill effect. Try some, I insist."

"Well, if you are insisting, then I mustn't refuse such hospitality," Rylo drolled.

Morgan let out a small snort.

Mara took delicate bites beside him. He was going to have to try these folks' toxic fish. He took a bite and found it just as horrid as he expected. He *hated* fish, even after his sister married that horrible troll from Goldoth and he demanded imported and preserved cave fish at meals, Rylo would always find some excuse to make himself scarce.

At least this was freshly caught muddy-flavored fish.

He took a generous gulp of his wine. Another strange flavor struck his tongue. Goldoth imported their wine from nations to the south that Nephel had little dealings with.

"King Rylo, offer some to your witch. She looks famished," Mara said with an unsettling grin.

He turned to Morgan and saw the pinched look on her face that accentuated the ridge of scars across her cheeks.

"Care to taste the national dish?" Rylo asked.

"Thank you for offering, but I'm not very hungry."

Rylo nodded and turned back to his wine, trying to get the dirty flavor out of his mouth.

Mara's smile was nearly a grimace as she said, "Rylo, I really must insist. She must try some cave fish."

"If she is not hungry, I'll not force her to eat."

"It is rather bad manners, isn't it? She must have a taste." Mara turned and looked at Morgan. "Try some of mine. It's perfectly safe, but you have never tasted the likes of it."

Rylo had to stop himself from rolling his eyes. Morgan didn't need to taste the likes of her foul fish.

He could see Morgan didn't want to eat something that he fed her. Smart girl. He could have her spilling her secrets, including her thoughts on the taste of this disgusting fish. Her intense stare at him made him feel like she was weighing and measuring him, deciding if she truly could trust him with her secrets.

He wished he could get into her mind, tell her that she didn't need to fear. They were a team, they had the same goals, and he wouldn't jeopardize her secrets for these folk. Instead, he tried to reassure her with his face, letting it soften from his typical bored expression.

"Okay. I'll try a bit," Morgan said, looking at him in a way that told him that she was trusting him. When had someone outside of possibly Selene or Elio even truly trusted him on a personal level?

Rylo tugged on the leash, pulling Morgan close. She was close enough for him to smell. Her scent of crisp winter air and oranges dulled the scent of murky fish from his senses. He took a small portion of the fish on his fork and lifted it up to her rosy lips. She opened for him, and he slid the food into her mouth.

Her eyes widened as he watched her swallow. Was she going to keep it down?

"Can I have a drink, please?" Morgan asked and he didn't hesitate to lift his goblet to her mouth, letting her drink deeply.

Mara's crystalline eyes sparkled and Maglar pressed the flat of his palms together in a slow rhythm. "Now," Maglar broke the silence that had descended on the room. "How did you travel to our realm?"

Maglar looked at Morgan with hard, dark eyes, but she stared back at his unrelenting gaze. A sense of pride welled in Rylo's cold, black heart.

"I don't know how I got here. It's not something I planned," Morgan replied.

Mara frowned. "Do you have information on your side of the portal that led you to King Rylo specifically?"

"No, of course not."

Mara's lips pursed. "Rylo, give your little witch another sip of that wine, please."

"Of course, Queen Mara," Rylo said, holding the cup to Morgan's lips.

"Now, what does the Goddess want with you? Why would she choose *you* to be branded with her stars?"

Morgan frowned, but didn't back down from Mara's words. "I don't know. I'm held against my will by King Rylo. He's locked me in his torture tower and has now forced me to join him here."

Rylo kept his face a cold mask, but inside he was laughing. How he loved hearing her lies mingled with truth slide off her tongue, watching her play the King and Queen of Goldoth for fools. These two actually thought they could force the truth out of her just with a bit of food and drink. How did they not know that only the one who shared the meal could draw the truth out of a human?

"If you are kept against your will, why would he dress you in such finery?" Maglar asked, tipping his chin to her dress.

Morgan looked down, the picture of a demure slave. "He does it to shame me. He says that he likes seeing something so scarred and ugly dressed as she shouldn't be. It's a game for him." She paused and her voice shook as she said, "He likes to call me Scar when we're alone."

Rylo nearly spit out his wine as Maglar let out a cackle. "Rylo, we'll do well together. Now, I have something I'd like to share with you. Can one of your folk bring your witch back to your rooms? I'd suggest she not be present."

Rylo could hardly hear Maglar's words over the ringing in his ears from what Morgan said. Did she believe what she said, or was it another one of her lies? He didn't consider her *ugly* and hadn't cared that her face was damaged. There was such loveliness to her intelligent green eyes, her full lips, and pale skin against her black hair.

"Yes, of course. Elio can see her securely back to my chambers. I don't trust her with another."

Elio stood, their eyes met, and Rylo felt assured that he knew what his task would be as he walked away with Morgan's leash in his hands.

When they were out of the room, Mara turned to him and said, "I was wondering why you chose to keep her scars in place. She's difficult to look at. Such a waste, I'm sure she was once a true beauty. Now I understand your choice."

Rylo gave a quick nod and took another drink of his wine. Goddess alive, he wanted this supper to be over soon.

He noticed Maglar call a slave over and whisper something into his ear. The slave turned and quickly left the room. Other slaves came forward and cleared the table of the cave fish. Shortly after, a runny pudding dessert was brought in. Topped with flakes of gold, Rylo took a tenuous bite. To his surprise, the flavor was better than he expected.

He was beginning to wonder why they'd called Morgan out of the room, when he heard a bone chilling wail in the corridor. Rylo looked to Maglar, who once again rubbed his hands together. Mara's face was unreadable as she continued eating her dessert.

"Are you unconcerned about that sound?" Rylo asked with genuine curiosity.

"Oh! You *are* in for a treat! Yes, we haven't shared our little secret with anyone, but..." Maglar shook with anticipation. "We believe you are of a like mind in our hopes for this realm. There are forces at work that could destroy our very way of life, and we see you are prepared to accept the natural balance of things before those events can manifest."

Rylo felt a sense of unease grow in his stomach, and it had nothing to do with the fish and wine combination. He truly didn't understand what the man was talking about. He wasn't used to being the surprised one. He was used to being the one revealing secrets when the time was right.

"Yes, of course." His agreement with Maglar's statement felt sticky on his tongue. Too close to a lie.

The shrill cries filled the space as two small slaves entered the room, chained at their wrists, feet, and wearing the same collar Morgan wore. It was hard to tell if they were male or female in the low faelights, but based on the filthy sacks they wore and the long, stringy black hair, Rylo suspected they were women. The grimils who held their leash dragged the two folk, tugging them across the cold stone floor of the cavern. One of the women was the source of the frantic screams. The other didn't seem conscious until Rylo saw the slight lift of their head.

"Here they are! My prized possessions," Maglar beamed as he stood and took the chain leashes in his hand.

Rylo could see more clearly that they were both female. Tiny, emaciated women, they made Morgan look large in comparison. Rylo covered his disgust as Maglar gave the leashes a hard tug, jerking the women closer to him. The screaming one let out a painful gagging sound as her collar dug into her exposed throat. Rylo took in the marks on their bodies, the various bruises, scrapes, and cuts.

"Stand!" Maglar commanded, and both women stood on spindly legs, weak as a newborn colt.

Beyond their filthy conditions, something was very wrong with these folk. There was no visible essence. The two women looked up at Rylo with far too large of eyes. Unnaturally huge globes stared back at him in a filmy shade of grey. Their skin was so white it seemed almost translucent, just like the cave fish at supper. The two women were mirror images of each other. Twins.

"Show him your ears," Mara said harshly.

The sister who'd been screaming let out a harsh shriek, yanking and jerking on her chains.

"They are not used to seeing others," Maglar mumbled. "We keep them under close watch. Their powers—they could destroy these caverns in their entirety."

Slowly, the quiet sister pulled back her ears, revealing what Rylo had begun to guess. Curved ears, human ears.

A sick, twisting sensation wrapped through him. "And your forehead?"

The girl moved the mass of slick, blackhair, revealing the five stars of Althea.

"Goddess alive," Rylo gasped. The prophecy flashed through his mind. He turned to Maglar. "Do you know their age?"

"Nearly twenty-six. I was called in after their birth. The mother, of course, didn't survive, but the mark was there upon both their foreheads. Just before I was called in, I witnessed a fascinating prophecy. When I saw them, I knew I held the future of our realm in my hands."

Rylo's face didn't display any of the emotions that were boiling inside him. What did this mean for Morgan? Was she even the one spoken of in the prophecy, or was that just a coincidence?

Another shrill scream filled the cavern as the more violent sister charged Maglar. Drawing up his essence, Maglar created a barrier of stone. The girl hit the rocks with a crunch, tumbling to the ground. Her collar tightened around her neck as she let out a strangled choke for the second time. The other sister dropped to the ground, crawling to her sister as she scooped her into her frail arms and whispered something that seemed to sooth the woman.

"Calamity and Tyranny are their names. Their powers as witches manifested slowly, but by the age of six they were able to do brilliant and terrible things with their magic. We've had witches before, but nothing of this magnitude."

Rylo did frown at this statement. "You make it sound as though humans and witches are commonplace."

Maglar grinned with pride. "Yes, they are. We are very selective with whom we let visit Onyx Caverns, as you know. This is, after all, your second visit. The last must have been when we sent our cousin to marry your sister. A pity how all that turned out. Have you ever wondered who works our mines? Who completes all that labor? Sure, we Goldoths are known for our fine crafts and mineral extraction, but those who do the hard work are our human slaves."

"How? How can that be possible and why would you share that secret with me?" Rylo asked. This was worse than anything he'd imagined. He never dreamed that Goldoth held witches in captivity.

"When I heard how you stole the young rebel's human soulmate, and you orchestrated the murder of Jasper, my interest in you was piqued. When I heard how you tore the sister of Savine's soulmate from her at the gates of his home, I knew I'd found my ally. Humans are fragile, even witches can only survive forty to fifty years. These two are middle-age, and I need to utilize their power before they are no longer serviceable."

Rylo didn't mention that he had another human in his own realm who was already beyond those years, yet hadn't aged. He would need to write to the leaders of Bayberry, Riggins and Po, to hear how they tethered their daughter's life to their longevity. He'd take no chances of losing Morgan.

"I am flattered my reputation has reached you down here deep underground, yet you still haven't explained how you came to have such a labor force."

Rylo looked down at the sisters, holding each other close. The injured one shook in her sister's embrace.

Mara chimed in, her dazzling eyes sparkled in the low light. "Goldoth has always utilized humans as their labor force; even before The Cleaving, humans were the ones to work our mines. We have moved deeper into the earth since then, but they have remained. Not even the witches cleaving our two realms apart could take our slaves from us. Our ancestors made adjustments. We no longer kept human villages above ground. They were emptied anyway. These humans have changed over the millenia, adapted to life in the dark. Our slaves live their entire lives underground, knowing nothing of sunlight, of the changing of seasons. This is to ensure their safety and keep our secret."

A chill ran down Rylo's back and he had to suppress his own sun glow from releasing, his essence stirring restlessly under his skin.

"And now you seek an alliance to defeat the other nations of Aeritis. You, with your strong armies of fae and endless resources, wish to ally with my much smaller, weaker nation. What is the advantage in that?"

The quieter sister let out a long, sorrowful moan.

"Take them away. See that Tyranny is healed. She needs her strength in the coming months," Mara said. Maglar scowled at his soulmate, but didn't object to her command. She turned her attention back to Rylo. "Both women have been headstrong since they were girls, but especially Tyranny. We've had to break her over the years to get her to the state she's in now. If only she were more placid like your witch. Alas, we make due as we must with what the Goddess has generously gifted us."

"They seem little more than animals to me," Rylo replied.

Maglar beamed with pride. "Not at all! Wait until you see their powers, and you will better understand why we exercise such caution. Tyranny is a necromancer. She has the power to raise the dead. With the short mortality rates of our humans, it came as quite a shock when *that* magic stirred in a seven year old." He laughed as if it was the funniest joke he'd ever said. Bile stung Rylo's throat as he let out a false laugh. "We were battling walking corpses in the dark mining tunnels for months. Calamity can draw the earth into itself, like an implosion. Which, of course, is very destructive in a cave. Then, there's the spell work to a lesser extent. Due to their dangerous natures, we haven't had the ability to train them as we would have liked."

Rylo held his empty cup up, and a grimil came forward, refilling it. He took another long draw from the glass before he continued. "You still haven't answered my question. Why seek an alliance with me? You could easily defeat my nation on your way to overpowering others."

Maglar's striped essence writhed under his skin, his dark eyes seemed even blacker. "You would be our buffer against the Latians. We would prefer to strike to the south first before overtaking the north. Warring in the Latian winters is not possible, even their own civil war was stalled by the coming snow each year. We'd need our ally to hold the front until we were ready to make a move against the elk folk."

This was *exactly* why Rylo needed to secure his own borders. His nation was but a small speck between two giants. Over the centuries, these two nations had whittled his borders down to nothing more than a strip of river canyon. Yes, he commanded the skies, but what did it matter if he lost the ground his folk called home?

"Yes, of course." Rylo's essence pushed against his skin. The need to release the growing tension under his skin itched and burned at him. He kept his wings tight against his shoulders, trying to prevent his twitching wings from displaying his discomfort. His sun glow ached to show these two who had true strength here.

"We have no desire to host a two-front war. Not yet. You are free to engage if you must, but I would prefer we hold the Latian border until we have a shared attack. We will not be able to aid you this winter, you understand. You would be free to keep our alliance between us, and we expect our secrets will not leave your lips," Mara said. Maglar responded by drinking deep from his cup.

"And if I do not keep your secret? If I don't choose this alliance?" Rylo asked. He had no doubt that this alliance wasn't truly up for discussion on his part. It was certainly more of a tow the line or face the consequence sort of moment.

Mara reached out a finger, touching the blackened skin on his hand. He shuddered involuntarily and a bit of his essence glowed against his skin, making him the brightest thing in the room.

"It's odd that you survived this, oath breaker. There's something you are not telling us, but we'll let you keep your secrets. We will have this alliance, and there will be an oath involved. We've disclosed too much to allow you to leave here without protecting ourselves. If you choose not to ally with us then we will make a slight adjustment to our plans. Once Calamity is unleashed, it won't be difficult for her to topple your towers and the folk who reside there."

Maglar grinned at his wife. "Since the death of Jasper, we deliberated together and knew you would make an excellent ally. We've heard of the power your witch contains. The shadows that dance for her and can cause such destruction. Don't disappoint us now King Rylo, or you and your witch won't escape these caverns."

Rylo's heart pounded. He'd assured Morgan that he'd not allow any folk to harm her. He couldn't let that happen. Rylo had to do what he could to protect her, and if this alliance gave his people the security they needed to weather a storm to the south, then so be it. He had no allegiance or loyalty to Savine or Avery.

He drew in a deep breath. He was cornered and—a shadow, cool and sweet stirred in the outer reaches of his mind.

Rylo.

Morgan. Relief stirred in him. She'd been released from the collar that tampered her magic.

Rylo, if you can hear me, distract the king and queen. I'm going for the relic.

Clever, beautiful mind.

"There's no need for confrontations. I'll agree to an alliance with Goldoth, but I have my own conditions to consider. Let's discuss this further without threats. If you truly want an alliance, then it needs to be an alliance, not a threat."

"An understandable request. Come, let us retire to more comfortable accommodations to develop a better understanding," Mara said as she stood.

Shadows, dark and comforting, spilled against his mind again.

Do your worst to those assholes.

Chapter 34

Morgan

Elio pulled Morgan along through the dark tunnels deep under Aeritis. She'd lost sense of what time of day or night it was hours ago, but she suspected it was late into the night. They were led by two Goldoth guards, one shimmering with flakes of mica, the other resembling the same sandstone red as Edet.

Morgan hadn't given much thought to what Edet was, but now it seemed evident that she was a Goldoth. She wondered if she missed the cool darkness of her folk's caverns, or if she preferred the sunlight and changing of seasons. She wasn't even sure if all of Goldoth lived underground. She knew it was a larger nation, there could be whole cities above ground.

Left to herself, Morgan knew it would be impossible for her to make it out of this place alive, especially with the collar putting a damper on her magic. If only that idiot hadn't used all her bullets in his blood lust experiments.

Maglar had given her the creeps, and Mara was right there with them. Cold, cunning, and cruel, she knew they wouldn't hesitate to collect her as another slave. But she wouldn't have hesitated to become a kingslayer, and add the name Queenslayer to her repertoire.

It wasn't normal how easily she'd slid into this world; how she craved the challenge of life here and the need to gain knowledge of her unexpected powers. Day by day, she'd slipped away from the person she'd once been, and yet she hadn't. Graduating top of her class, securing a lucrative position in tech right out of college thanks to years of coding and proving herself on her own, wanting to climb the corporate ladder to make a name for herself.

This was what she continued to do, but in another realm. The stakes were higher here, but the rewards were sweeter. Now, if she could survive this place, she could get back to growing in her power. Most likely to help Rylo defeat these assholes.

Elio tugged hard on her leash as the Goldoth guards unlocked her door. Without a word, he pushed her into the black room. The fae lights turned on with a lazy glow as she walked toward the darkly blanketed bed. She kicked the dog bed for good measure, one tiny fuck you to the folk who believed they could own someone.

She let herself flop back on the bed, closing her eyes in exhaustion. She wasn't surprised when the Goldoth king and queen tried to extract information from her. She was just happy they bought her lies, but it was puzzling that they believed they could control her truths when they hadn't been the ones to offer her food or drink. There'd been a moment where she was worried that Rylo would make her spill her secrets, it being the first time she'd had to eat or drink something he offered her. She'd made it a point to use extreme caution with where her food or drink came from, and had so far avoided the unpleasantness of spilling her secrets to any fae who gave her a bite to eat.

The tight bodice of her gown squeezed her waist and chest. Morgan needed relief from the corset before she could let herself drift into sleep. She stood, tugging on the laces before she slipped out of her stays and let the heavily ornamented dress spill to the floor.

Wearing only the slip under her gown, she took a deep breath, the first she'd had in hours. Crawling back into bed, she tucked herself under the covers and tried to let her exhaustion overtake her. The fae lights dimmed and darkness consumed her. Not even the light of the moon or stars infiltrated this windowless room. But she couldn't relax to fall asleep, even though her body felt exhausted. The collar around her neck itched and the heaviness of the relic tugged at her chest.

Or was that the twitchy itchies? That sense of foreboding that she and Avery had all their life seemed to be at a constant simmer under her skin in Aeritis, and she learned to live with the reality that her untimely doom could happen at any moment here. But now her chest felt tight, and even the relief of taking off the gown hadn't taken away the unrest in her heart, the sickness stirring in her stomach. It was obvious to her that this was a dangerous place, it was no surprise that she couldn't let her body calm down enough to find proper rest.

As she tossed and turned in the bed, Morgan heard the click of the lock and the crack of the door. No light pooled from the tunnels outside, but she sensed someone stepping into her room.

She could only hope that it was Rylo, but the unease in her stomach told her otherwise.

"Rylo?" Her voice shook as she said his name.

"It's not Rylo." A dull amber glow cascaded off Elio's skin.

"What the hell are you doing here?" Morgan asked. The fae lights gleamed to life, illuminating the bronzed skin and grey wings of Elio.

He didn't answer, only moved forward to the bed, pulling the blankets off her and tugging her by the arm. Morgan twisted and writhed, escaping his grasp. She leapt to the other side of the bed, putting space between them.

"Don't touch me!" she shouted. She saw him flinch from her loud tone. Right, sensitive fae hearing. It was probably her only weapon against such a powerful man. "I'll scream if you come any closer."

"Don't be a fool. I have no intention of hurting you and shaming my king. We have work to do." He dangled a key over the bed. "Let me get that collar off you. Do you think your shadows can disguise us?"

"*What?*"

Elio's face looked like carved bronze, so inhumanely beautiful it didn't seem real. "The relic. The reason we are here."

Morgan stepped around the bed, tilting her neck for Elio as he clicked the collar off. The icy metal fell to the floor with a clank and Morgan rubbed where the collar had stung. She'd only worn it for less than a day, and already it had chilled her skin to the touch.

Her shadows poured out of her, dancing at her feet as she stepped back from Elio's grasp.

"Thanks for that. How did you get that key?"

"I have my ways of getting what I need," Elio responded as he moved toward the door.

"Fair enough. Where do we go from here?" Morgan reveled in the power that returned to her fingertips, the misty darkness that called to her. She grabbed a wool dress and slid it over her head before putting on slippers.

"According to Rylo, you have the answer to that." Elio pointed to the necklace. "We don't have much time. Rylo is only going to be able to distract the Goldoth monarchs for so long before he's dismissed for the evening, or before word gets to them of your escape."

Morgan closed her eyes and let her mind settle. She focused on the necklace pressed against her throat, the heavy sensation wrapping around her. Then she felt it. A tug, a calling that she hadn't noticed before. She pulled her magic toward the necklace, feeling her shadows wrap around her throat. Morgan's ears began to ring, a sharp shrill sound that she'd only heard twice before. The sound she heard when she and Avery went through the portals. Yet there was no pressure change, nothing yanking her back to her realm.

She took another deep, calming breath, letting her mind become clearer, more focused. The necklace seemed to sing to her now, calling her to follow its path. Before she followed that tug, she reached out for Rylo's bright, bold mind. She wasn't even sure if she could reach him from this distance, but she did, following the connection she'd established between them. He needed to know that she had her magic back and she was going after the relic. After all, the sooner she completed that task, the sooner they could go home.

Her voice was otherworldly and full of power, as she said, "I can feel it calling to the other relic," and she stepped into the tunnel. The tugging led her deeper underground through passageways that became rawer, less refined as she and Elio walked in silence into the belly of Aeritis.

Avery

The musty scent of dirt and old lumber filled Avery's nose as she held Savine's hand tight, the warmth and the pulse of their shared touch giving her a sense of calm in the silent darkness. Kyla stood on her other side, and Avery's shoulder grazed Kyla's arm. It felt as though she had a phalanx of support as they made their way down the dark and damp tunnel to Kinlon's cell. Garnel and Jay were following behind them. It was the first time Garnel had left his room in nearly a month, but Savine had demanded he be present to interview Kinlon.

So this was Orofine's own prison. The raw gloom of it was unnerving, with tangling roots of trees exposed around the roughly hewn passages. Muddy cells dug out of the earth and secured with some kind of bones made Avery's skin prickle.

"What kinds of bones are those?" Avery muttered.

Savine squeezed Avery's hand. "The bones of an ancient line of elk rulers. They gave up their freedom in alliance with the fae, to protect this nation from its enemies."

Avery let silence descend on them again as they walked deeper into the prison. There were a few stirrings from the cells, but it was strangely, eerily quiet.

"Are there prisoners in here?" Avery finally asked, her curiosity getting the better of her.

"Yes, Avery, we do keep our prisoners here," Savine replied, a hint of sarcasm in his tone.

Avery tried to make out someone in the cell that passed, but the light was too low for her to see what the cell held. "Why are they so quiet?"

Kyla gave her arm a squeeze. "There are others like Raikin. One is the warden of the prison and he keeps the prisoners' mouths bound with his essence."

A chill went down her spine. Avery knew Savine was ruthless, knew he had a side to him that would stop at nothing to secure his folks' well being and safety, but there was something unnerving about knowing that she'd bound herself to a man who continued to let folk live in these conditions.

There was a part of her that wondered if she needed to take on a bigger role in ruling the nation just to allow folk more rights. She'd never seen an American prison, and knew there were problems with her own country, but this seemed crueler than anything she could imagine.

Finally, they stopped at a cell where Raikin stood, waiting. Savine placed his hand on the white bars, and they opened immediately to his touch.

"I've prepared the prisoner for you, My King," Raikin said. Jay moved around them to stand at Raikin's side. Even in this dreary place, Jay smiled and winked at his soulmate. How had he gotten to that point? To overlook Raikin's faults and only see the good in him?

They entered the cell and Avery gasped at the state Kinlon was in. He was bound to a table, sap dripping from his face and arms, burn marks slowly healing across his skin from the scalding substance.

His eyes were closed and he only wore pants. She could now see just how emaciated the man was. His ribs jutted out and where Savine and the other men in this room were stacked with muscles, Kinlon's skin clung to his skeletal frame.

She heard Kyla let out a strangled gasp at the sight before her. "Savine, this man is wasted away. His essence is drained and he has nothing left."

"Then he'll give the last of himself in service to his king and queen," Savine said, his voice a cold growl. Addressing Kinlon, he said, "Open your eyes. One last thing and your soul may rot in the Abyss for eternity."

Kinlon groaned on the table as he cracked an eye open. "You will never be my king, and I'd rather spend eternity in the Abyss than help a human scum sent to destroy my realm."

Raikin spoke up. "He was ready to share all his secrets yesterday. Perhaps we need to…"

Avery interrupted. It was one thing to try and talk to this man, but it was another to watch Raikin torture him. "No, we're not going to force his answers out while under duress."

"If you insist, My Queen," Raikin replied.

Avery stepped closer and she felt the bond between her and Savine tug at her. "Kyla? Can you help in a gentler way?"

Kyla stepped forward and pressed her hand against the man's arm. She felt Garnel move up with her, keeping close to his mate.

The man's face relaxed for the first time and his breathing steadied. He closed his eyes before he opened them again. "The best I've felt in—You've manipulated my emotions. Such relief."

Avery moved closer to the table, standing side by side with Kyla. "How long were you in the human realm?"

Kyla continued to hold the man's arm, her essence stirring restlessly under her skin. "A little over a decade. We've been searching for you all these years."

"How did you know where to find me? How would you have recognized me?" Avery asked, her voice shaking with the knowledge that she'd been hunted in her own world, yet miraculously never caught. Maybe that was the cause of all those twitchy itchy moments between herself and Morgan. Instinctively, she'd known that she was in danger.

"We sought twins marked by the Goddess. We searched where we could without being caught, but your kind have found us out. Took us if we were caught." His eyes locked on Avery and his face hardened. Kinlon's body shook on the table, trying to free himself of Kyla's grasp. "Ah! Damn you, traitorous bitch! Get your filthy essence out of me!"

Kyla didn't speak as she continued to push her essence into him, once against sedating him into complacency. He sighed deeply again and his eyes looked glazed. "Your kind took some of us. I don't know where they were sent, but the ones who were caught were never seen again. After several years of being hunted, I realized they were some sort of secret spies for your nation."

Avery wanted to laugh at how ludicrous this sounded. "The FBI? Are you trying to tell me the US Government has captured fae?"

"Believe it. I've been hunted for years. They drew me off your trail and I was forced to take refuge in the forest. My essence didn't work properly there so I've survived through my wit."

Avery frowned. "You said you were looking for a human marked by the Goddess, but I never had the mark until I came here."

The man shook his head. "Untrue. It was always there, just not visible in your realm. You have no magic there, so such things couldn't be seen by your kind. That mark was on you at birth, as all marked by the Goddess are."

Avery didn't dare look at Kyla and her freshly trimmed bangs covering her glamoured forehead.

"How would you even know that?" Avery asked. "I never saw a fae until I got here."

"I saw you myself once in the forest. You were working on a trail, using that large axe of yours against the roots of *living trees*. You, the queen of Latiah, once injured trees for a job." Kinlon said with a bitter laugh. "Your sweat-soaked hair was tied back and you took off your hat to wipe your brow. I saw it then." A chill ran down Avery's spine. She'd been stalked by fae warriors before she ever reached Aeritis?

"But why didn't you, um, finish the job?"

The man thrashed and screamed, tearing his arm from Kyla's tight grip. He grimaced and said through gritted teeth, "I made a mistake once in letting you get away, but I'll not do it again!"

The binding holding him to the table snapped, and Kinlon gripped Avery by the throat. Despite his weakened state, he squeezed so tight that Avery's vision began to blur. Her ears were ringing as she reached for the iron blade at her waist. But Savine was quicker. He pushed his essence forth, impaling Kinlon through the eye with a sharp, spinning branch. The man fell back on the table, shaking as his essence drained before Avery's eyes, leaving him looking like a husk of a man.

Avery's heart was pounding as Savine drew her closer, pressing a brutal kiss to her lips.

"Well, Avery, Kyla, the wardens should call on your services more often," Jay said.

Raikin nodded in agreement. "He hadn't revealed that information to me. But I did find out how he found the fae your sister killed. Over the years, the Hunters had adjusted to your world and began using a human device to communicate with one another. A satellite phone, I believe he said. I recognized the word phone from your language. Kinlon got an alert from the other fae that he'd caught Morgan, and he shared his location. When Kinlon arrived, he found the fae and the iron used to kill him."

Savine huffed out a breath, still gripping Avery close to his chest. "Savine, I'm okay," Avery whispered and his grip loosened on her, but the need to be consumed by Savine was building. This desire to jump his bones right here in a prison cell was already building. She was a freaking beast. Wanting to have sex in a prison just because her life was threatened. What was even wrong with her?

"Excuse me. I'm still adjusting to the bond," Savine said in a rasping voice to his friends.

Garnel gave him a sympathetic look. "It will never go away. You'll always have that need to protect your soulmate."

Jay and Raikin nodded in agreement. "It's a natural response," Jay said. "None of us would fault you for the reaction it brings out in you afterwards either."

He looked at Avery with a knowing smile. "In both of you."

Avery could feel Savine's heart hammering in his chest. "Let's get out of here," she murmured.

Chapter 35

Rylo

Rylo left the other Nepheli at the table as he and the Goldoth monarchs moved into a private room. He sat on the hard, stone bench as Maglar called for more refreshments. Rylo hid his grimace. He didn't think he could stand another one of Goldoth's refreshments.

"King Rylo, we need to continue discussing the terms of our alliance," Mara said with a smirk as she slid onto the bench next to him. Her glimmering skin sparkled in the fae lights and her dress dipped low enough that as she leaned in, Rylo could see her breasts. He had no doubt this was all part of her strategy, but it disgusted him nonetheless.

"And what are your terms?" Rylo asked, scooting away from Mara's leering face.

Maglar took a seat on Rylo's other side. His large frame shifted the stones as Rylo found himself wedged between the two monarchs. Goddess above. He hoped Morgan could find that relic quickly so he could make an escape. Now that she was free of the collar, there was no reason to linger in this putrid tunnel.

"As we said, you will secure the northern border. Once we have finished our campaign to the south we will bypass your territory. In exchange, we will save your folk from a bloody war that you could never win, but you will become a vassal to Goldoth."

Rylo couldn't believe what he was hearing. They expected him to give up his nation, his folks' freedom, in exchange for the privilege of being bypassed in their war? He couldn't stand being near them for another moment. He stood, walking away from the two sneering fae.

"I'll never agree to such terms," Rylo snarled.

Mara let out a cold, cruel laugh. "Then perhaps we should demonstrate what you are refusing to agree to." She motioned to a guard in the doorway. "Send for Tyranny and Calamity. I believe a demonstration is in order."

Maglar looked at Rylo with such vitriol that he could feel the King of the Cavern's essence seeking him out. "You need to think carefully about what you are denying your nation by refusing our alliance. They will not survive this war if we do not get what we want. That will be on you, Sun King."

Once again, Rylo heard the terrifying shriek of the witches as they were dragged into the room. The cowering sister flinched at Maglar and the other hissed in their direction.

"I didn't want to have to do this. I thought you would share our enthusiasm for the direction we want to take this realm, but I believe Mara is right. A demonstration must be in order," Marglar said, shaking his head at Rylo.

Rylo walked near the wall, giving himself space from the twin witches. "There's no need. I'll return to my rooms and we can continue this discussion tomorrow. Surely we can come to a true alliance."

Mara stood, taking the witches' chains from the guard. "Stand against the wall," she said to the guard. He let out a stifled cry, but didn't resist the order. Maglar stood and walked over to the guard. The silver traces of his essence coiled under his skin as he struck the guard, turning his body stiff.

"Thank you, dear," Mara said as she turned to Rylo. "Tyranny is much easier to manage when we've incapacitated her victim, you see?" Mara unlocked the wilder sister's collar. The girl lunged from Mara in a snap and jumped on the guard against the wall. With a piercing scream, she slashed at the man and sunk her teeth into his neck. The guard fell to the floor and Tyranny moved over him, clawing and biting the man until his blood poured out across the stone floor.

Rylo stood, shocked against the wall, unsure whether he should flee or try to keep a sense of calm. Inside, he wanted to run from the room and warn his folk before going after Morgan and Elio. But how would they complete their task if he failed them now? He needed to keep up a sense of composure, even as the woman tore into the flesh of the guard.

The other sister, Calamity, let out small shrieks as she watched her sister claw into the dead guard.

"King Rylo, you are looking a bit pale. Would you like to sit down?" Mara chided.

Rylo shook his head. "Not at all. However, I do not see the purpose of your little display. Is this supposed to convince me to hand over my nation to you?"

Maglar let out a cold laugh. "Go ahead, Tyranny."

The tiny woman stood up, blood dripping from her chin. She seemed calmer than she was when she entered the room, more at ease, and that realization chilled Rylo's blood. The woman looked at Rylo before she rolled her eyes back in her head, exposing only the whites. She lifted her arms up over her head and began to mutter something Rylo couldn't understand.

The corpse on the floor convulsed then jerkily began to stand, turning toward him in a shaky gait.

"What is this thing?" Rylo muttered as he moved across the room to stand nearer to Maglar and Mara. Surely their close proximity would keep this act of dark magic away from attacking him.

"I told you Tyranny was a necromancer. She is quite capable of raising an army of the dead," Maglar replied.

Rylo shook his head, not able to comprehend the horror he was witnessing.

"Now, if you do not agree to the terms, you have had a taste of what your folk will face," Mara said with a saccharine smile.

The creature moved closer to Rylo. So close, he could see the insides of the former warrior.

"I won't do it," Rylo said, letting his essence gleam under his skin.

Mara shook her head. "Then you leave us no choice. At this moment, a group of warriors are on their way to confiscate your witch. We will be happy to add her to our collection of slaves."

Rylo couldn't let them get Morgan. She was his and his alone, and he'd damn all of Onyx Cavern to the Abyss before he allowed them to touch her. His essence pooled inside of him, a molten well of sunlight and heat until it burst forth, striking the King and Queen of Goldoth and incinerating the jerking corpse of the guard.

Morgan

The acrid scent in the tunnel was building. It was so terrible that it was beginning to burn Morgan's nose. Although she couldn't see Elio as they blindly followed the pull of the necklace, she felt his strong presence close behind her. It was a little unnerving to be alone with a fae other than Rylo. In all her time here, her contact with other fae had been so limited that she still felt like she didn't really know much about them, other than what she'd read in the library.

"I think the smell is getting worse," Morgan whispered.

Elio didn't respond and Morgan let her mind try to connect to Rylo. It was fuzzy from this distance, his mind a blur of light. *We're going into the mines. Be safe.*

She didn't know why she added that last part. Between the two of them, he was much more likely to be able to handle his present situation. Morgan wished he could reply, but that seemed to be a witch's power that he lacked as a fae.

Morgan focused her mind back on the necklace, its strength fading while she connected to Rylo's mind. The heavy pull that she experienced toppled her forward, but Morgan didn't hit the ground. She let out a shriek as she plunged into the air. Her body was falling so quickly, she would never survive the impact from the crash. Her shadows plunged with her, and she tried to make herself float, to control the fall in some way, but her efforts weren't working. The necklace strained at her, increasing her speed as she plummeted into an abyss.

Bright bronze light filled the mine shaft and Elio's strong arms wrapped around her. "I have you," Elio said, tugging her close. Morgan shook against his chest, thankful for this strong fae and his unwavering loyalty to Rylo.

They landed with a graceful swoop and Elio helped Morgan steady herself back on the ground. The rotten smell consumed them both and Morgan watched Elio heave up his supper as she followed. The sting of her vomit burned her throat and she tried to clean herself up as much as possible.

"Let me fly us out of here. We need to leave," Elio said through dry heaves.

Morgan could only shake her head and point at the necklace. The heavy draw of it was stronger than ever, penetrating her mind as she struggled to walk forward. "What is that smell?" Morgan asked.

"It's—No offense, but it's faintly like you," Elio said through gags.

Morgan flipped herself around and looked into Elio's eyes as best as she could in the darkness. "*Excuse me?* I do not smell like that!"

"No, not really. You're more scented with orange, but under that there's this earthy, salty scent to you that fae don't have."

Morgan just shook her head. "It's because I'm human. I stink, that's what you're saying. Humans sweat and smell bad. Are you trying to say that you think this is a human scent?"

"That's what I suspect. This place is dark and these fae are hiding something."

As he spoke, Morgan felt cold, clammy hands cover her face and tug her back. Elio let out a strangled shout. The tunnel was blasted with his essence, illuminating the corridor with light and heat. Morgan sent her shadows forth, wrapping around her attacker. With a snap, she felt the attacker's hands release her, the body made a heavy thump on the ground.

"Can you light this space up with your essence?" Morgan asked.

Elio didn't answer, but his skin illuminated in warm, coppery light. On the ground lay half a dozen creatures. Morgan crouched down to get a better look at the things on the ground. They were small, ranging in size from Morgan's height to around five foot six inches. Their closed eyes were unusually huge, taking up most of the upper half of their face. But it was their ears that caught Morgan off guard.

They were rounded, just like hers. Their skin was so pale she thought she could see the veins and organs underneath. Morgan shivered in revulsion as she stepped away from the humanoid creatures.

"Are they human? They smell like the stories of human scent."

Morgan grimaced again at his accusation of humans being stinky. She certainly didn't smell like this.

"Their ears are rounded, but that's the extent of the similarities to my species," Morgan replied. "Come on, we need to get the relic and get out of here."

"No more noise. With those eyes, they'll see us through the darkness before we see them. Wrap us tightly in your shadows."

Morgan wordlessly followed his directions and returned to following the call of the relic.

They walked for what felt like hours, and her exhausted feet ached. Every muscle was tired from the long day she'd had, but she didn't suggest a break or a stop. At last she heard harsh, cruel voices and a scream of pain pierce the air. Morgan paused, grabbing Elio's arm.

"What was that?" she whispered.

Elio's eyes looked like saucers, the source of the sound was ahead of them. Her shadows wrapped tighter around them and she continued walking.

The tunnel took a sharp turn and Morgan found herself in a well-lit, open cavern. They didn't step out of the shadows, hugging close to the mouth of the tunnel. Morgan's stomach churned at the sight before her. Hundreds, maybe even thousands of those creatures, dressed in rags and covered in filth, were working to extract a shimmering, glowing ore. That was the source of the light in the vast cavern, filling the space in luminescence.

Muscled fae stood by, whips in hand. Morgan heard a curse across the cavern and the crack of a whip. She watched in disbelief as an elderly woman was struck repeatedly. None of the other workers reacted as they continued digging the ore and loading it into carts. The woman fell to the ground in a breathy cry, but still nobody reached out to help her.

Morgan's eyes stung and she turned away from the scene. She couldn't do anything to help the woman. If she did, she'd only get herself killed. As she turned, she bumped into Elio's chest.

"The relic," he hissed, reminding her of the purpose of this little adventure. Morgan nodded as she let herself connect back to the call of the necklace. To her horror, the tug was leading her deeper into the illuminated cavern.

She shook her head, trying to pull Elio back. She needed to retreat. Going in there would get her killed. Elio pointed into the open space before them. Morgan's eyes could hardly make out what it was that Elio saw.

"There, on the spire. That must be it," Elio said in a voice so quiet Morgan could hardly hear what he said over the ringing in her ears. She squinted, wishing she had the superior fae vision Elio seemed to have. She saw it too. A jewel-encrusted scepter was on top of a spire, nearly forty feet into the air.

Morgan tried connecting to Elio's mind, searching for him in the darkness, but she couldn't reach him. She couldn't find that connection that she could slide so easily into with Rylo, not even the clunky connection with Susan was there. Maybe she couldn't speak to him mind to mind since she didn't know him as well as Rylo and Susan.

This wasn't the time to experiment with her magic. She needed to convince this man that going into that cavern would be suicide.

"We can't go in there. They'll kill us," Morgan protested.

Elio let out a harsh huff. "I saw you kill one of the most powerful fae in all Aeritis. You took out at least twenty Latians according to Rylo when you chose to flee Orofine. If anyone can do this, it's you."

Morgan pursed her lips and observed the happenings in the cavern. There were at least fifty Goldoth guards, overseeing hundreds of creatures mining the ore. The creatures were small, weak, and didn't show any indication of having an essence or magic. She looked up the cavern and saw a small tunnel cut out of the stone near the ceiling of the massive cave.

"You can fly me over?" Morgan whispered.

Elio nodded. "You grab the scepter and I'll fly us up to the tunnel near the top."

So he noticed it too. Observant man.

"What about the fae down there?" Morgan asked.

"On appearance, they don't look like they'd be as powerful as myself or you. Use those shadows for the ones behind us, and I'll use my essence against the attackers ahead of us. Is there a spell you can use?"

Morgan thought through the spells she'd read about. She'd use the spell to enhance his essence. "There's one, but I haven't tried it. I may not get the words correct. It uses your essence. Is that okay?"

"How so?" Elio whispered, trepidation in his voice.

"I'm not sure. It sounded like I could enhance your essence in an attack. I don't know if it will harm you though. I don't have to do it if you don't want me to."

He nodded. "I trust you. Try it."

Elio didn't give her time to respond before he scooped her into his arms and they were exposed to the creatures in the cavern. Morgan heard the surprised outcry around them. She closed her eyes and said the words of the incantation she'd memorized, just in case. Despite her eyes being closed, she could make out the explosion of bright light bursting out of Elio. Screams of pain filled the room as Elio's essence ripped through the room, blinding everyone in their wake.

Elio didn't even pause his flight as he shouted, "Morgan, open your eyes, now!" Morgan did as he commanded and saw the scepter just in front of them. She reached her hand out, grabbing it just as Elio banked to the right and rose up the tunnel.

Below them, the creatures cried out in stunned panic. She didn't know if she'd permanently blinded an entire cave of workers, or if it was only temporary, but their cries made her feel horrible. She'd done this to these folk, just to get some stupid relic.

They landed with a thud as Elio hit the ground. His breath came out in a heavy rasp.

She crawled out from under him, rolling him onto his side as well as she could.

"Elio! What can I do to help you?" The words came out louder than she meant, but it probably made no difference with the screams of the cavern.

"You... You drained me," he panted. "That was all I had."

"What do you mean?" Morgan asked. She had to shout over the wails of the folk below in the tunnels.

Elio's tan skin began to fade to a pallid ashen shade. "My essence is gone. I'm not getting out of here. Get to Rylo before they realize what we've done. Save my king."

"No!" Morgan cried out.

"Tell Susan she is my bright star." His words faded to a gasp as hot tears stung her eyes.

His breathing slowed, and Morgan pressed a hand to his chest. Elio's heart beat faded and ceased under her hand.

She'd killed him, killed a man that was trying to help her, killed whom she thought might be Rylo's only friend. She wanted to lay down and cry, to take back the spell she'd so carelessly cast. Instead, she picked herself up off the ground, lifted the scepter, and let out a piercing scream. If she was going to survive this cavern she'd need to flee now.

The scepter responded like it was made for her, singing in her ear. Something within that contact snapped and magic flooded into her body. She started shaking uncontrollably as pure, deep magic flooded her system.

She let the magic flow through her, glowing across her skin. Her vision was clearer, even in the dark, and she could make out details she hadn't seen before. She leaned down and pressed a kiss to Elio's forehead.

"Thank you for helping me," she said as she began running down the tunnel on swift feet, her shadows pushing her gait faster as she soared through the darkness.

If she couldn't bring Elio back, then she had to get Rylo and the other Nepheli out of here. She reached her mind out and felt his presence immediately, clear and bright, as if he'd been connected to her this whole time.

Rylo! You have to get out of here. We have to leave now. Elio's dead and I have the relic. Meet me outside Onyx Caverns.

A force pushed on her mind that she hadn't experienced before, unrestrained and powerful, and she welcomed its presence, because she knew who that power belonged to. Knew who was on the other side, demanding entrance into her mind. She let the power push back her own swirling, deep magic as brightness filled her mind. Still, her feet kept to the path, her shadows helping as her mind succumbed to the intrusion.

What did you do? Rylo. He was speaking into her mind. His typically bored tone held a panic that she'd never heard from him before.

I did what I needed to do. Are you safe? Where are you?

Possession seeped into his tone and it echoed through her bones. *Waiting for you. I'm not leaving you. Hurry.*

She let the deep magic pulse through her veins as the ground shifted above her, releasing her magic against Aeritis itself, the deep magic shot up, cutting through the thin rock layer above. Her shadows circled around her, protectively cocooning her from the falling rocks and dirt. The shadows twisted and lifted her up, up, up, through the depths of the earth and out of the rubble. Her eyes burned as she adjusted to the watery light of dawn.

She wanted to scream, to rage, and to cry. She wanted to burst out of her skin from the magic burning through her veins. Before she could do anything, sweet golden light descended in front of her and Rylo tugged her into a tight embrace, his wings sweeping around them, brushing against her shoulders and the back of her head. With the scepter in one hand, she wrapped her free arm around his neck and tugged him to her.

His lips pressed against hers with an urgency that made her heart pound in her chest. She responded and succumbed to her own need to feel him, taste him, and know he was okay. Slowly, their kiss changed from urgent and demanding to soft and tender as Rylo stroked her mouth and she returned with her own tongue making deep, languishing kisses.

He lifted her up without even breaking their kiss and took flight.

At last he pulled back and his lips brushed the tears that had leaked out of her eyes. "I thought I'd lost you in there," he said, his voice shaking with emotion.

Chapter 36

Avery

Avery woke with the worst case of the twitchy itchies since the morning she and Morgan faced the bear at Quartz Mountain. She couldn't get past this feeling that something bad had happened to her sister, that she was in danger and too far for her to reach.

Her stirring woke Savine and he pulled her close into his embrace. The hard ridge of his muscular stomach pressed against her own body, and she relished in his warmth and comfort as she shared her concerns about Morgan.

"At some point we are going to have to address this situation," Savine spoke up. "If you think she wants to return home, we need to get her to Latiah. Raikin said Kinlon told him the key to returning is having a piece of the land from the other side of the portal. It will work as a key to get the traveler back."

Avery's eyes widened and she hopped out of bed, running to her backpack stashed away in the closet. She dug through the top pocket of her bag, finding the chunk of quartz that Morgan gave her.

"I've had the key all this time," Avery whispered.

Savine looked at her with a pained expression as she slipped back into bed and under the fur covers. Avery gave him a teasing tap on his bicep.

"Don't look so worried. I don't want to leave you," she said, nuzzling against the scratch of his beard.

"I still won't stop you, if that's what you want. I only want you to be happy. I can survive anything, knowing you're happy."

Avery shook her head and smiled. "It's crazy to think that if I hadn't thrown this rock against the tent I was staying in at the encampment, I'd have gone back to Montana that day you brought me up Quartz Mountain. I'm happy it didn't happen, Savine. I don't want to live my life without you."

Savine pressed a kiss to her forehead. "But we could use this to help Morgan return home. It would be a challenging journey to get to Quartz Mountain this time of year. It may not even be possible, with the snow in the high country."

"We need to get her back. I think she'd tolerate a few months in Orofine if she knew she was going home. I'm worried about her, this morning in particular. It feels like something is very, very wrong."

Savine stroked Avery's hair. "We'll get her back, Little Flower. I'll do anything to help you."

Avery wrapped her leg between Savine's, pressing cold toes to his bare skin. He let out a hiss, but didn't fight her as she pressed her lips to his.

Savine pulled back, looking down at her. "Would you return if you could do it safely? If you could go back and forth freely? It doesn't seem like it is impossible now."

Avery's answer came quickly. "If I could freely go back and forth between the two realms I'd do it. I want my parents to know I'm okay, and I would want them to meet you. If this was a reality, I'd want to bring you home for our holidays. We could celebrate Thanksgiving with the Hollis Family, and take you skiing on Christmas Day."

"I don't know what these things are, but I think I'd like that," Savine said. "I want to learn your world as much as you're learning mine. Starting with your language. I want you to teach it to me."

Avery smiled at him and responded in English, "I love you."

A knock interrupted their conversation. Avery knew Rue was on guard so she shouted for her to come in. At this point, she was becoming used to folk walking in on her naked under a fur blanket.

Rue came in, carrying a piece of paper. "Avery, I was taking my morning break and went to my room for a moment and found this on my bed. I think you need to see it right away."

She handed the paper to Avery who sat up in bed, keeping the furs close to her chest. For a moment she hoped it was from Morgan, but it wasn't. She scanned the letter.

"Do you know who this is from?" Avery asked as she handed the letter to Savine. Hope sprung to life in her. If this letter was real...

Rue shook her head. "It could be a trap."

Savine looked at the letter; his face hardened. "The handwriting is familiar. We intercepted correspondence with a similar style during the war. It's most certainly a trap. Nobody is going around telling us the location of the relics. And why would it be in a home in Orofine?"

"But maybe this person knows about its location. We can't just ignore this."

Savine shook his head. "Avery, it's an obvious trap. Whoever this is wants to lure you away from me and most likely harm you. It's not worth the risk."

"Look, I get you're on high alert when it comes to my safety, but we have to find those relics. If we don't, who knows how long Garnel can handle not having a connection to his bear side of himself. What if his essence becomes faded like the Hunters?"

Rue shook her head. "I don't know how he's withstood the weeks without his bear already. It's unimaginable."

Savine pressed his fingers to the bridge of his nose.

"I know that look," Avery teased. "You're getting annoyed with us. You're free to join us, but I'm not going to let this opportunity pass us by." She stepped out of bed, bringing a fur along with her as she padded into the bathroom.

"Rue, could you go get Kyla? We shouldn't wait," Avery said.

"I'll be back in a few minutes!" Rue called. Avery watched her grab the paper from the bed and take quick strides out of the room.

"Ave!" Savine called as she closed the bathroom door. "We shouldn't do this."

—

An hour later, Avery was snugly situated between Jari's antlers and Savine's hard, warm thighs. Kyla, Rue, and Garnel joined them on their own elk, as well as a few other guards. Now that this was an official outing, Savine had called for more guards than Avery thought were necessary. She was wrapped in a thick wolf pelt, cutting out the chill of the bitter snow that drove against the furs. She also wore a truly ridiculous rabbit skin hat and thick fur mittens.

If she had the ability to safely and comfortably hop between realms, Avery wouldn't hesitate to bring back loads of stuff from her old home. High-performance winter gear would be at the top of the list. Plus her skis. And her bike. And leggings. She was missing American clothes at this point. Oh, and tampons. She really needed tampons. And coffee. If she was honest with herself, she'd return to her realm just to get a bag of coffee beans.

The idea that this could be a possibility made her feel excited. She wanted to share her world with Savine. She wanted him to experience a *good* burger and a beer. She even wanted to see the look of shock on his face when she drove him on the interstate. It would be a delicious torture. But then they'd return home to Latiah after a day of exploring and make love slowly under the furs.

She leaned against him, soaking in his strength. His lips met her ear and he kissed the rounded shell. It was cute, how much he loved her little human ears. She'd never thought there was such a thing as an ear guy, but Savine seemed to be one.

The city streets were quiet as they rode through Orofine. The first significant snowfall brought a hush throughout the valley as folk chose to spend the day at home.

"I still don't like this, Avery," he murmured.

"I know. But we have a plan. It's not me going in there. It's you, and I'm worried about you too."

He tightened his grip on her waist, pulling her as close as she could go against him, her ass brushing against his cock.

"Don't ever worry about me, Ave."

She couldn't help but wriggle against his hardening length.

"Ave," Savine growled, pushing her forward to give them some distance.

"Sorry! I can't stop myself! You're just so hot when you get all worked up." She wiggled against him again, the axe at her side bumping against their legs.

Savine let out a gravely laugh. She would never get tired of that laugh. A laugh from Savine was like a little reward. After so many years closing himself off to everyone, only working to better his folk, she could see the layers peeling back each day. He called her his Little

Flower, but he was the bud. Every day, opening up a little more, revealing another petal that only she got to enjoy.

"I'm going to have to start riding Dandelion, aren't I?"

"Never!" Savine growled. "I like you right here. Just don't do *that* right now."

Jari let out an indignant huff of agreement and they both laughed.

They reached the outskirts of Orofine, just outside the city gates. The homes were small, simple cottages. Most were neat, tidy homes, sparkling with a fresh layer of snow. But the one they stopped in front of was farther back, hidden by a thick copse of trees. The roof was caved in, and a side of the home seemed to be falling into the structure.

The elk all seemed nervous, snorting and panting. A guard's elk even let out a long bugle and began running back toward the King's Residence when he dismounted. The guard ran after him, but the elk was gone into the winter white streets of Orofine.

Savine hopped off Jari in one beautiful, fluid motion before he helped Avery down.

"Stay by Rue," he said, drawing his sword at his side. Avery instinctively touched the axe at her side. He didn't cross the snow up to the house, instead he paused near the trees, having a conversation in mycillious.

Savine frowned, looking back at Avery before he turned to walk over to Garnel and a group of guards.

The twitchy itchies were back, and worse than before. This wasn't right. Something about this place was very, very wrong.

"I don't like this, Rue."

Rue looked at her, frowning. "I know. It's too quiet. No birds chirping or squirrels rustling. I should be the one to go in. The letter was addressed to me."

Before Avery could object, Rue shifted into her fox form. She didn't do it often in front of Avery, but when she did, it always took her by surprise. Rue scampered toward the cottage.

Just then, a fae male stepped out of the cottage. One of the Hunters. It had to be, because they would be the only ones capable of acquiring a stick of dynamite. It was like something from a movie, the man held a match and lit the fuse on the explosive before he dropped it on the ramshackle porch and fled into the woods.

A screeching roar of panic built up in Avery. "Rue! Don't! SAVINE!"

Avery began running toward Rue, but it was too late. An explosion erupted through the house, blasting wood and debris toward the group. Avery tugged on her magic, saying the words she'd memorized, forming a protective bubble around the folk she loved. She pushed and stretched it, but she couldn't get Rue into the circle.

To her horror, she watched the small fox's body blast backward, hitting a tree. Dust and debris fell to the ground. Avery's ears rang, her head was spinning, but she seemed okay. Savine was moving so quickly, she didn't know how it was possible for someone to fly without wings like that.

"AVERY!" he bellowed as he reached her, tugging her close. Tears streaked down her cheeks and she buried her face against his chest.

She pulled her face away, and saw Kyla beside Rue, her body still in its fox form. Kyla looked unharmed, but Garnel still pulled her close, cupping her lower abdomen. Avery could see Kyla was reassuring Garnel before she pushed herself from his grasp.

Garnel let go of her, ordering the guards into the woods to apprehend the Hunter.

"Avery, she's still alive, but she's injured in her shifted form!"

Her friend was bleeding and looked injured beyond anything Avery could repair. She sobbed out, "I don't know how to fix her."

Kyla didn't hesitate to make her way to her elk with Rue's limp body in her hands. "Don't worry, I'll ride with her to Hyacinth!"

All Avery could do was nod as the tears continued to stream down her face, her choked sobs finally spilling out of her. Savine crushed her against him.

"He brought dynamite to Aeritis!" Avery cried, wrapping her arms tight around Savine's waist. "Dynamite!"

"Is that—that explosion. Is it something humans use often?"

Avery shook her head, trying to control her tone. "Not really. I use it for avalanche mitigation on ski patrol, but normally people don't have dynamite." Avery's voice shook as she spoke. "I was so stupid, so reckless to suggest we go here!"

"My love, you saved us. We're alright. It's my fault for not coming to you. The trees knew, but the description didn't make sense. They had no words for what that fae had. I should have known it was a human instrument. There will be more of the Hunters returning. We need to be on our guard. But, the relic is here too."

"Really? Where?"

Savine nodded and took her hand. He brought her to an ancient cedar along the back of the building. Savine slid the mittens from his hands, then did the same to hers. He pressed their palms into the tree, and Avery could hear the whispery speech rolling off his tongue, like branches swaying in the breeze.

The cedar opened to him, revealing a carved wooden bowl. Avery reached into the cavity and took the bowl in her hands. It buzzed to her touch and she let out a startled gasp. Magic rippled under her skin, filling her with vibrant energy. She felt the ends of her hair lift up and her vision sharpened. She was this power and it was her. There was no end nor beginning to what she could be capable of with this deep magic welling inside her.

Avery felt herself slipping away, letting the deep magic fill her, course through her.

Her voice didn't seem her own as she said, "This is it."

The painfully handsome man beside her tried to touch her, but it was too intense. Too much. She pulled away.

"Ave, what do you need?" His voice was distant, like she was hearing him through a tunnel.

She looked at him and struggled to remember who he was. He was so familiar, so handsome, and when she looked at him she felt love so strongly it made her heart ache.

Savine

Her soulmate.

"My Savine," she replied, then she remembered the attack on them. The Hunter who tried to take her mate from her. She would make him suffer for all he did today. She turned from Savine and began running into the woods.

She could feel her enemy, sense it as the magic pumped into her. For the first time, she heard the whispers of the trees guiding her forward, pushing her toward the Hunter.

She'd destroy him. The magic that flowed through her demanded it. Demanded justice for Rue's broken body and for the fear that nearly overtook her when she thought of losing Savine.

Avery ran faster than her feet should have been able to go, but she kept pushing forward, *smelling* that she was closing in on the enemy. She briefly looked behind her and saw a trail of tiny white flowers were sprouting behind her footsteps where snow once covered the ground. Far behind her, Savine ran after her, trying to keep up with the deep magic that pushed her to incredible heights.

A twig snapped, and she turned, making eye contact with the Hunter. Bitter rage tore through Avery. *Never* would she allow someone to threaten Savine's life like that again.

The iron axe attached to her belt slid smoothly through the leather holster. She took the axe in both hands. The weight of it felt so right. Months now of practicing using it as a weapon had made her stronger, more competent in her burgeoning skills.

Avery lifted the axe above her head. The man was frozen in place, blood dripping into the snow from where splinters of shrapnel had embedded into his flesh.

"Mercy!" the man shouted. A killer and a coward.

Avery didn't hesitate as she let the axe fly through the air, striking the Hunter true in the skull.

The man let out a stilted groan as he crumpled into the blanket of snow. Black, tainted blood oozed and bubbled from his wound.

The guard sent to capture the man came running up to Avery, circling her in a protective stance until they saw the deceased fae lying in the snow.

The magic that had coursed through her veins drained as her adrenaline rush descended. She dropped to her knees in front of the man that she'd just slain. Her breath came in fast, desperate gasps. The man's dark eyes glazed open at her and she knew she was going to be sick. She'd mercilessly butchered a man without hesitation.

She tried to clean herself up as best as she could in the snow. Savine knelt beside her, pulling her against his chest and she let out a long, mournful wail.

"I just killed him! The magic consumed me and I wanted him dead. I didn't even hesitate. He nearly killed you and I couldn't let him live doing that to you."

Garnel rode up the flower-strewn path holding Jari's reins. The elk threw his head up at being so close to another powerful bull elk, but Garnel's grip was strong.

Savine took Jari's reins and tugged Avery up before climbing behind her. He whispered soft soothing words in her ear as they began their ride back to the King's Residence.

Eventually, he spoke. "What you did is natural, to strike back against someone who threatens your soulmate. It's not something you need to be ashamed of—that Hunter wanted all of us dead. I'll have the known portals watched night and day. There will be no more getting through. If they do, their life is forfeit. They are an enemy of the queen, and will not be allowed to live."

"I don't think I should touch the relic again. Not until we understand what the Goddess wants with it. Also, I thought the relic was supposed to be a bone, not a bowl."

Avery felt Savine press his hand against the shape of a bowl in his coat pocket. "Perhaps there is more than one in Latiah."

Chapter 37

Kyla

Kyla raced back to Orofine. The heartbeat of Rue's fox form grew weaker with the beat of her elk's hooves through the snow. While she could practice healing using tinctures, salves, and care, she couldn't save someone through her essence. Sticky blood turned her white fur coat crimson. Rue had splinters embedded throughout her thick coat, but from what Kyla could tell, only a few of the wood shards punctured her flesh. It was bad enough for her to lose blood, but Kyla prayed that it wasn't going to kill her.

Her prayers to the Goddess hadn't come naturally off her tongue lately. She found herself daily praying to Mother Althea less and less as she watched her soulmate mourn the loss of his bear, and the shame of his house arrest. Yet now, she prayed with a fervency that she hadn't experienced since Garnel was near death.

She couldn't lose this young friend who'd become so dear to her over the course of a few short months. Rue brought laughter and light to her day that she hadn't experienced many times in her life.

When she reached the hidden door to Hyacinth's private rooms, she slid off her elk, telling her to find Jay as she carried the weakening bundle in her arms. Up the stairs she ran until she pounded on Hyacinth's door.

Hyacinth opened it immediately, and Kyla walked into her cozy healing room to see the other Bayberry healer, Maud, joining Hyacinth for tea. In all that had happened over the weeks, Kyla had completely forgotten about the woman, and whether she'd been punished by Savine for not healing Avery properly.

Perhaps she, like many others from Jasper's regime, had been quietly dismissed. She was proud of how her brother was handling the transition to power. Trusting Darby's judgment on who was staunchly loyal to Jasper and who could be swayed into serving Savine. The interviews that Garnel and Raikin had conducted in the first month while Kyla was in Nephel seemed to attest to what Darby had said.

Hyacinth hurried to Kyla's side, taking the small bundle into her arms. Her little friend hardly felt like she was still with her.

"It's Rue. There was an attack on the King and Queen, and Rue got between the blast."

Hyacinth jumped. "Oh dear! Maud, I'll need your help when the other injuries arrive. Prepare the side rooms for patients."

Kyla shook her head. "Rue was the only injury. Avery formed that barrier again to protect us and it shielded the others from harm. I think Rue was too far ahead to be protected from the blast."

"Would you like my assistance?" Maud asked.

Hyacinth shook her head, hurrying the fox to the bed.

"I will leave you to your patient then. Again, thank you for your time, Hyacinth."

Hyacinth gave a quick shake of her arm, waving the woman off. "You'll do well to return to our folk. It's been too long."

She turned to Kyla as the door clicked shut behind Maud. "I'll try to heal her in her fox form. If she shifts with these injuries she could cause serious damage."

Kyla knew a thing or two about injured shifter fae, after fighting side by side with them for twenty-five years. They had to heal in the form they were injured in, or shifting could lead to dire consequences. It was hard enough on a shifter's essence to switch forms, but when their body was healing it could be a death sentence.

Kyla watched, always in awe of how the Bayberry healers worked. How they deftly handled tinctures and essence seamlessly at one time, bringing swift healing to an injured fae. She realized she was holding her breath as she waited for a sign that Rue was healing.

"There," said Hyacinth in a confident tone. "She's healing as she should. Her wounds were hard on the small body of her fox form. A few broken ribs, a broken hind leg, and a deep puncture on the same leg, but her body was very receptive to healing."

"So she'll make a full recovery?" Kyla asked, a wave of relief washing over her.

"Yes. She'll be good as new soon. Should be able to shift after she rests. I did feel something... unexpected. Did you know Rue has met her soulmate?"

Kyla shook her head. Rue hadn't said anything to her about meeting her mate yet. "There's a bond and I felt a tug on it. I don't think it's been completed, but the soulmate on the other side must have felt Rue's pain through the bond."

Kyla thought about the folk she'd seen Rue interact with. She couldn't think who this soulmate could be, not unless they weren't Latian. A Nepheli?

"Whoever it is, I hope that they can feel her stabilizing. Even before the bond is accepted, it's a cruel thing to know that one's soulmate is in distress," Kyla said.

Hyacinth shrugged. "I'm nearly four-hundred and fifty years old and I've yet to feel the bond."

It happened, Kyla knew, but she couldn't help but feel pity for Hyacinth. She wasn't like her father, who would have never deserved to have a soulmate. Or her mother, who seemed accepting of her lot in life as the queen to a cruel king. But why should Hyacinth be denied the one to whom her soul calls?

"Do you ever wonder if your soulmate is on the other side of the portal?" Kyla prevented herself from saying "was" but the words almost slipped off her tongue. Human lives were so short. What if her soulmate had died three hundred years ago, never making it to her realm as Avery had? What if countless fae without mates were mateless because their human soulmate was on the wrong side of the portal?

Hyacinth let out a harsh chuckle. "That would be my fate. Denied my human soulmate."

The click of the door brought Kyla and Hyacinth's attention to the other side of the room. Avery stepped into the space, black blood splatter on her face and furs. Kyla moved to her, taking Avery's hands in hers. She couldn't sense an injury, but Avery was distraught.

"Are you hurt? Was there another attack?"

Avery's face was ashen as she spoke in low tones. "No, I'm not hurt. I killed the Hunter. I just feel a bit shocked from it, I think. How is Rue?"

"She's resting, but will recover," Kyla replied.

Hyacinth moved closer, taking one of Avery's hands as both women guided her to a chair. Kyla stepped back as Hyacinth gave Avery a quick assessment.

"Deep magic. Did you draw it from the ground yourself?" Hyacinth asked as she put a kettle on the stove and took out three mugs. Kyla took a seat, her aching feet needed the rest awhile ago. Other than some nausea, she'd felt few changes as her body adjusted to pregnancy.

"Savine and I found a relic. I don't know if the Hunter knew it was there, or if it was a coincidence. When I touched the relic I was filled with deep magic." She shook her head. "I couldn't stop it from happening. It was like a drug when it hit my blood." Kyla could feel the disgust in Avery's emotions. She was disappointed in herself for something, but Kyla couldn't understand what it was.

"Can you describe the relic?" Hyacinth asked, and Avery described the small wooden bowl hidden in the heart of a tree.

Hyacinth sorted herbs into the different cups, choosing what each woman needed before she poured piping hot water over the herbs. "Long ago, long before Rylo sat on the throne of Nephel, I spent years studying the ancient magic and medicine of the witches at the Nepheli libraries. I read once that deep magic will take on the qualities of the object it uses and can respond more strongly to those whose magic naturally aligns with it. Perhaps the wooden bowl called to you in a way that you did not anticipate."

Kyla thought about the necklace Avery wore the night of her father's death. How Avery had felt nothing from that necklace, yet she'd been able to access deep magic through the roots of an aspen tree. "Remember the necklace? The deep magic wouldn't call to you. We'll need to work on your control so you are not always overcome when you touch a relic."

Avery nodded. "Yeah, I think you're right. But for now I'd like to practice my control without using deep magic. It was intense, and to feel that after Savine's life was threatened... Something in me snapped. I couldn't let that man live, not after he tried to hurt Savine."

Hyacinth strained the herbs from the tea cups and handed Avery and Kyla their cups of tea.

Kyla knew what Avery meant. She too had taken lives when someone threatened Garnel. "It may sound strange to you, but it's natural for soulmates to react so intensely."

"Avery, here's a draught to calm your nerves and remove the excess magic. Kyla, a fortifying blend for yourself and the babe," Hyacinth said, then she took a long drink from her own tea cup.

Avery stared down into her cup. "It may be normal for fae to act that way, but it's not typical human behavior. Acting that way in my world would get me life in prison."

Hyacinth startled in her seat, and Kyla couldn't keep her own surprise from her face. "Could you imagine how many mates would be imprisoned if they were locked away for acting on their instincts!" Hyacinth snorted. "How strange it must be in your world, Avery!"

Avery shook her head. "There's no reason for people to go around killing others because nobody is threatening anyone. At least not normally."

Kyla couldn't imagine it, this peaceful land. "That is not how the Hunter, Kinlon, made your realm sound."

Avery shrugged, changing the subject. "What I really don't understand is how I found a relic that wasn't even the one we were looking for. Do you think there's actually a bone relic too?"

Kyla took a long draught of her tea. "If so, that would give us three if we could find the bone."

A small shrieking sound came from the table and Kyla looked to see Rue stirring. She let out a foxish bark as she continued to slumber, kicking her small legs in her sleep.

Avery cooed at the sight of Rue running in her sleep. "When she's in this form it's so easy for me to forget that she's a fae and not a fluffy, friendly little fox. But seriously, look how cute she is kicking her paws like that!"

Hyacinth let out a hard laugh. "Never tell a shifter that, Avery, if you value your tongue! They may very well cut it out for such an offensive statement."

A bang came from the door before it swung open, surprise and fear bubbling forth in Avery and Hyacinth. Kyla leaped up from her seat, toppling her tea cup to the floor where it smashed into pieces.

Dark clouds, like a stormy night's sky filled the room. Avery screamed and Kyla saw her lift her arms to protect them. Before she could cast a protective barrier around them, Kyla saw who stood in the doorway. A dark winged fae with feathers the color of ravens and skin like ebony. Her black dress flowed around her as the clouds spun in an unnatural wind.

"Where is she? Where is my mate?" and Kyla recognized the voice, clear and raging with anger.

Selene.

Chapter 38

Morgan

Rylo cradled Morgan in his arms like she was the most precious cargo he'd ever carried as they flew low through the swampy lands of the Wastewater. Despite the eagans flying ahead, Rylo refused to let Morgan down. Wouldn't even hear her protests when she said she could ride on an eagan with him, even though he had to be as exhausted as she was.

They hadn't slept in over a day, and the fatigue from the whole experience in Goldoth was wearing on her.

Rylo didn't speak a word as they flew. No witty retorts for Morgan's attempted conversation. No wry smiles. His typically expressionless face was set in hard lines, like he was ready to burn the world like the Sun incarnate that he was.

What if it had been Rylo?

What if Morgan had used that spell to burn through *Rylo's* essence? He would have been the one dying in her arms, not Elio. He would be lying in a tunnel somewhere deep under the earth. And it could have easily happened that way. Morgan had no idea that the spell she wielded would be that powerful, that she wouldn't only utilize Elio's essence, but have the capacity to drain it.

His death was on her hands. He was dead because she acted without thinking through the repercussions, something she would never do before falling off Sapphire Falls. Unlike the other lives she'd taken, Elio was innocent, as were those creatures in the cavern. She didn't even know if they had survived her spell. She'd fled the caves before she had a moment to find out if the blinding light had mortally wounded hundreds. Morgan may have just committed egregious crimes, just so she could retrieve a relic. The thought made bile rise in her throat.

"I think I'm going to be sick," Morgan spat out as she began gagging.

Rylo wordlessly flew her to what little solid ground he could find, setting Morgan on a stump that was jutting out of the marshy ground.

Morgan let herself expel all the horror, all the pain she'd caused those folk, into the murky grey water at her feet.

"Whatever you do, do not touch that water," Rylo growled. He was lying across the broken log, wings dipping to mere inches above the water's surface.

Morgan frowned as she tried to clean herself up the best she could before she collapsed at his side, bone-weary from the experiences of the last day. Her head was spinning and she didn't know how she could stay awake much longer.

"I guess you don't need to follow your own advice?" she asked, leaning her head close enough to inhale the spicy scent of him, envious of that scent, knowing that she probably smelled like those horrible tunnels. Her eyes drifted shut and she didn't hear his response.

Morgan could sense that they were inside, but she didn't have the strength to open her eyes. All she could do was lay still and feel the heat of the fire and hear the crackling of kindling. She smelled something warm and hearty cooking over the fire. Yet, she couldn't seem to open her eyes. They felt like lead weights against her face as she felt a heated touch graze her bare arm and a fur blanket press against her.

She drifted into another restless sleep, but the warmth and comfort remained near her.

Rylo.

He was at her side, always his hot and comforting presence so close that she knew if she had the strength, she could reach up and touch him, feel the heat of his skin against the cool of her own.

Muffled voices, deep in conversation, continued around her, but she was too lost in her own exhaustion to be able to make out what they were saying.

Eventually she stirred, her eyelids opening to a ramshackle hovel with a hot fire crackling in the river stone hearth.

A gasp of horror escaped her lips as she looked at a creature that would haunt her nightmares for the rest of her life. Greenish-brown skin was exposed and only a loincloth covered its lower half. A broad pot belly stuck out of the creature's midsection. Membranous bat-like wings were tucked in close to the creature's back as it stirred a large pot over the hearth.

She turned her face to the heated touch at her hand. Rylo. He was there beside her after all.

One dimple popped in his cheek as he gave her a nearly unnotice-able smile.

"You are most likely still very tired and weak," Rylo muttered. "You're experiencing burnout."

Her throat felt so dry it hurt to speak. "Where are we?"

She gave a tentative glance to the creature at the soup pot.

"In the home of Serieff. He's a Hylax that has loyally served me for many, many years. You're safe here, Morgan."

As she looked around she noticed there were no other Nepheli present. "Where are the others?"

Rylo shrugged. "Flying with all haste to Nephel. Preparing our folk for the conflict to come."

It hurt to continue speaking, but she struggled out the word, "Water."

Rylo's thumb began making tiny circles on Morgan's palm. The Hylax near the pot must have heard her request for water. He brought her a wooden cup filled with a thick murky mixture before he returned to stirring, not looking at Morgan's face during the whole exchange.

She scrunched her nose, but Rylo took the cup in his empty hand. "Drink it, Morgan, it's safe. It will restore you."

Morgan trusted him. She didn't understand how she'd become so trusting of him, but she did. Rylo brought the cup to her lips and she welcomed the tangy, nutty drink, gulping it down in long draws. Immediately, her parched throat found relief and the swelling in her tongue went down.

"Why aren't we back too?"

"You were too weak to continue flying. I wasn't going to risk you harming yourself further. Serieff is an old friend and he welcomed us to his home. His wife has made a stew, but is with their babe at the moment. Rest. When your sister experienced burnout she slept for days."

A chill ran down Morgan's spine. There was only one way that Rylo would know that. It had to have been when he captured Avery. What the hell was wrong with her, to be so trusting of the man who kidnapped her own sister?

Yet, he looked at her with shining golden eyes, and she thought he might fracture if anything bad happened to her. He pulled her hand up to his lips with a tenderness that made her heart thud with a tumultuous beat in her chest. All the while, his eyes stayed on her, like he was afraid she may slip away. That her being here and awake and *alive* was so impossible that he couldn't even blink, lest she disappear.

A squalling infant from the small room in the back of the cabin disturbed the moment and Morgan withdrew her hand from his.

Serieff spoke to Morgan for the first time since she'd awakened. His voice was rough, almost guttural, and she couldn't control the shiver across her skin as he spoke. "The babe does not sleep well without my mate beside her. Even after the child has drifted to sleep, if she tries to slip away, the babe will cry out, reaching for her and will not stop until she returns the babe to her breast."

Morgan didn't know a thing about babies, but this seemed unusual. Movies always made it seem like human babies drifted to sleep in their cribs, little mobiles singing sweet lullabies as the mom and dad looked on from the door.

Serieff brought Morgan and Rylo rough-carved bowls ladled with the rich, hearty stew. Rylo helped Morgan sit up, propping a pillow behind her back. The ancient couch, with its threadbare leather and frayed corners, had a low back, designed to accommodate wings, and the additional pillow gave Morgan's exhausted body the extra support she needed.

"That will pass soon enough once the babe is weaned," Rylo replied. "It's only natural that the babe should seek her mother while sleeping."

Morgan wasn't sure if she knew the man seated next to her as he dug into the stew with an appetite that was void of all his typical mannerly eating. She tasted her stew and found it to be delicious and filling, each bite seeming to restore her aching muscles and her heavy limbs. It didn't take away her need for more sleep, but at least she didn't feel like she'd been hit by a semi anymore.

Serieff's mate stepped out of the back room, closing the squeaky door with a trepidation that made Morgan pity her. Trapped in the dark, alone as she walked on eggshells to escape her daughter's needy touch. The woman wore a dingy dress that hung on her like a sack. Her hair was pulled back, revealing a face with a deep scar across her right cheek.

When Serieff saw his mate, he jumped from the wooden stool where he ate his meal and offered her the seat. Moving back to the pot, he ladled more stew into his own bowl and gave it to her.

"This is my mate, Aniel," Serieff said as he took a seat on the floor, his broad wings draping against Aniel's own wings. Claws at the tips of the wings moved, seeking contact from the other, like they couldn't help but be entangled.

"It's nice to meet you. I'm Morgan."

Aniel bowed her head. "King Rylo has told us of you and your power. He also shared the importance of an alliance between the Hylax of the Wastewater, Nephel, and Latiah against the growing power in Goldoth. But tell me, what will stop you from growing in power until *you* cannot be contained?"

Serieff reached out a hand and took his soulmate's in his, squeezing it tight.

Obviously, Morgan had heard about soulmates from Avery, and had seen the devotion that Kyla shared with Garnel. But, it was unexpected seeing it coming from two creatures who resembled something from a nightmare. Despite their terrifying appearance, they'd welcomed Morgan into their home, showing her more hospitality than she'd received from anyone in Aeritis. Even still, with Aniel's question, Morgan didn't feel unwelcome here. Just wanting to better understand what was at stake after their encounter in Goldoth.

"I'm not interested in taking over your world. I'd like to return home after I help King Rylo." Morgan tilted her head toward Rylo and caught a moment of hurt in his expression.

Why did he have to look at her like that? Like her words meant something to him? Like *she* meant something to him?

Aniel gave a nod and didn't press her further. She ate in desperate spoonfuls, sharp teeth sinking into the bits of meat. A squealing cry came from the other room as Aniel began eating faster. Serieff went to the room, shushing the babe and speaking sweetly in his guttural voice. The baby continued to cry, only growing louder as Serieff tried to appease her. Finally, Aniel stood up, placing her bowl on the stool. "She's cutting her first teeth. She can't sleep without me beside her due to the pain. Poor Serieff has tried to comfort her, but to no avail. Be well tonight."

Morgan and Rylo were left alone on the old couch, silence filling the house as the baby settled down with Aniel. Morgan thought Serieff would return, but as time passed, it became evident that he was staying in their room.

She tried to stand to bring their dishes to the earthenware sink in the corner, but her head spun as she lifted herself up.

"Let me," Rylo said, taking her bowl, as well as Serieff and Aniel's bowl. After tidying up the bowls, he removed the pot from above the embers of the fire and threw a few more logs to light. He placed a kettle over the flames and worked to gather tea from a shelf. Only after he poured both of them a cup did he sit down.

Rylo gave her the cup and she didn't hesitate to take it from him. He sipped from his own mug, a broad grin stretching across his face after his drink. Leaning his head back, Rylo said, "I thought I may not survive much longer without a cup of tea."

Morgan let out a dry laugh, but still didn't feel capable of much conversation. Of course Rylo would be desperate for a cup of tea after the day they had.

The furs were draped around Morgan and she untucked them, placing the blanket over Rylo's lap too. She leaned close enough to feel the heat of his body warm her cool skin.

He rubbed his eyes and let out a groan. "How did he die?" Rylo asked.

Morgan closed her eyes, picturing Elio's lifeless body on the tunnel floor. "It's very hard for me to tell you the truth," she said, her full teacup still in her hand. Her voice shook as she said, "I'm so tired. Can we do this later?"

She was a coward. She didn't want to tell this man, who she'd grown to care for, or at least rely on, that she'd been the reason Elio was dead.

Rylo didn't look at her, just shook his head. "I need to know. Elio was... He was my friend."

"You say that like it's a hard thing to admit," Morgan replied.

Rylo closed his eyes again, exhaustion obvious in his body. "You would not understand. It's my duty to be held at a higher standard than common folk."

Morgan's lips pursed. This tiny piece of information was more than Rylo had revealed about himself than any other interaction they'd had.

"I don't understand why a king would deny himself friendship and relationships," Morgan finally said. It was a risk, being this honest with him, but she took it. She couldn't help it as her desire to better understand Rylo took over.

She listened to Rylo exhale, but he remained silent for long enough to begin to unnerve her. At last, he said, "It is difficult to form friendships or relationships when you are held at a different expectation than others, but most of all, it's because those who have been closest to me have been taken from me. Yes, I didn't show my friendship with Elio openly for all the court to discuss, for there to be an attack on him because of his friendship with me. It's the same reason I keep you away from the eyes of my folk."

Rylo placed his empty teacup on the hard-packed dirt floor and took Morgan's hand in his, making slow, steady circles across her knuckles.

Morgan felt even worse for being the person who took Elio from him. She wanted to hide and never tell him the truth, to keep how she used then discarded Elio a secret forever from Rylo.

"You're important to me, and for more reasons than that you could restore my nation's borders. You challenge me in a way that nobody else has challenged me, and it's been remarkable to see you discover your powers. When you entered my mind, I was already afraid of what Goldoth was going to do to you. They'd just shown me something beyond what magic should be capable of doing. Then they admitted to me that they were sending guards to take you away from me."

He paused and looked at her, stroking her hand as he studied her face. His skin glowed slightly, his essence slipping out and it felt like being warmed on a summer day.

"In that moment, I knew I would destroy Maglar and Mara if they so much as touched you." He shook his head. "I did something that will cost my nation everything. I released my essence on the king and queen and took flight. Then you were there in my mind, I could feel the fear in your speech as you warned me to escape. Morgan, I was about to break that cavern to rubble for *you.*"

He shook his head, as if he couldn't believe it himself that he was capable of such strong emotions.

Morgan did the only thing she could do. She placed her hands on Rylo's cheeks, pulling his face to hers, and she kissed him, letting her arms reach around his hard, strong back as she worked his shirt up and up, revealing glistening sun-kissed skin over rigid muscles.

"You're the most beautiful man I've ever seen," Morgan murmured, regretting her foolish confession immediately, but he looked at her like she'd just given him a precious gift.

She shouldn't be doing this. She should be confessing that she was the reason Elio was dead, not making out with Rylo on this old couch.

But she didn't. Morgan couldn't confess that she was the cause of Elio's death. Not now, and maybe not ever.

She pressed her hand to the hard ridges of muscles along Rylo's stomach and she felt him suck in a breath at her cool touch. His skin was scorching hot, like the midday sun. The glow of it cast a brilliance against her own pale skin.

He stared at her, watching her every move as she explored all the dips and curves of his chest, his stomach, his back.

Morgan whispered into his ear, "I want you to know that what I felt that night I drank the Bayberry wine has never gone away. If anything, this need for you has just gotten stronger."

"I've wanted to explore you, to taste you and touch you since I first laid eyes on you," Rylo said in a husky voice that had lost all its sweet, honeyed cadence.

Morgan shook her head. "That's not true. You didn't even bother to learn my name!"

Rylo pressed his body into hers, trapping her under his weight as he began to kiss her neck. "It doesn't change that I desired your body."

Morgan suddenly felt very self conscious. She'd once been attractive, desirable to men, but how did Rylo find her attractive with the scars on her face and body?

As if he knew what she was thinking, his kisses worked their way up to her face. He kissed her scars, caressed the raised skin with his fingers, his lips, and tongue.

She tried to hold them back, but the sting of tears began streaking down her face. How many times had she avoided a mirror since being here? Tried to not touch her face or look at the damage that made her no longer feel like herself?

"Your scars make you more attractive to me, Morgan. They tell the story of your strength and resilience." He pulled back, looking into her tear-stained eyes. With his thumb, he brushed the tears from her damaged cheeks.

His gaze was so intense that Morgan felt raw and exposed before him, like he could see all of her, all the ugly pieces and broken bits, but he didn't back down from them. He was truly seeing her for who she was in a way that nobody had seen.

Finally, she couldn't take it anymore and she looked down at her hands, still pressed against his chest.

"What are you thinking?" she asked.

"I am thinking about all the things I want to do to you; none of them are going to be appropriate with the Hylax family on the other side of these very thin walls."

Morgan huffed out a sigh. "This is the second time you've cock blocked me."

Rylo let out a dry laugh. "I plan to remedy that very soon. There's just a lot about to happen. I'll explain what I saw in Goldoth tomorrow after you've had time to recover."

She felt the heat that was building in her wash away. "Can you at least hold me tonight? The last few days have been a lot."

Rylo lifted her up, scooting the furs off her. He draped one on the floor and removed another from behind the worn couch. Morgan took the pillow that had been behind her head and brought it to the floor, letting the heavy wool dress she'd fled Goldoth in fall to the floor. Rylo's eyes darkened as he looked at Morgan in her thin slip.

"Are you changing your mind about these thin walls?" Morgan asked, lying down on the fur Rylo had placed on the ground.

"Ah, I wish I were. But you've experienced burnout today, and I haven't slept in almost two days. I can be a patient man. You are worth waiting so I do not fuck you for the first time on a dirt floor."

He draped the other fur over her before he slid out of his pants and under the covers. The heat of him was intense, and she craved his warmth like a moth to the flame.

Morgan wriggled close enough to touch him, but she held back. This moment felt as fragile as an eggshell. She understood what he was saying, but to finally have him admit that he desired her was too much for her to resist the need to connect to him.

He draped an arm across her waist, tugging her close. His spicy sweet scent wrapped around her.

He said, "Thank you. For risking so much to get that relic. I should have said that to you sooner." A whisper-soft kiss pressed against her forehead and she felt a heaviness enter his limbs as his breathing became rhythmic and steady with sleep.

Chapter 39

Savine

Guards had alerted Savine to the presence of a black-winged Nepheli woman seen landing near Hyacinth's tower. When he heard the words his whole body seemed to react at once. He was running toward Hyacinth's rooms, his heart hammering in his throat as he feared the worst, before the guards could utter another word.

She *couldn't* take Avery from him again. He'd tear her limb from limb before he let her leave with his mate. As he ran up the spiral, wooden staircase to Hyacinth's rooms, his essence began writhing under his skin. Savine drew his sword at the top of the stairs, kicking the door open. The door splintered at its hinges from the impact and fell to the ground with a thud.

Avery screamed, and he was finally able to take a deeper breath. She was here, she hadn't been taken from him again.

But Selene was there. The woman who'd tortured him, who'd convinced him that he could never experience the love between soulmates. She was standing close to Avery. *Too close.*

Savine unleashed a stream of vines, twisting and wrapping around Selene with speed that caught even her off guard. Her wings were bound tightly to her body, immobilizing her.

"What are you doing here?" Savine growled. His essence was whirring and he felt as though he couldn't think straight, seeing Avery so close to the woman that he hated more than anyone else.

Selene gave him a searing look with her violet eyes, but she didn't fight against her restraints. "I'll admit my presence is unexpected here and you're angry to see an old friend. It's best to let Avery explain."

Avery walked to Savine and pressed her hand against his chest, giving him a comforting smile that reminded him that she was safe and he was hers. "It's okay, Savine. Selene is here to see Rue."

For the first time since entering the room, Savine noticed the other women in the room. Hyacinth had been busy brewing a cup of tea, presumably, for Selene. Kyla sat on the couch, hand resting on her abdomen. On the table, Rue slept in her fox form.

"I still don't understand why the Sage of Nephel is in my healer's tower."

Kyla shook her head. "She is here for Rue. She sensed Rue's injuries and flew swiftly to her side."

Savine frowned, puzzled by what Kyla was suggesting. "Rue is your mate, Selene?"

The bound woman gave a curt nod. "If she knows, she hasn't acknowledged it."

Avery spoke up, "Rue hasn't said anything to me, but Selene was just sharing that she's known since we were held captive in the cave."

"Ah, holding a folk captive is not an opportune moment to share that you are their mate," Savine said dryly. "Did you realize it while you infiltrated her soul?"

Selene scowled at him, but didn't reply.

"You did, didn't you?" He shook his head with disgust at the woman before him.

"Savine, don't," Avery protested. "She was scared that Rue was going to die. She's been flying since before the attack because Rue inadvertently sent her images somehow of the paper she found in her room. Selene feared it was a trap. By the way, did you know she can fly that quickly? She must be like a jet plane!"

Savine's eyes grew wider. "Your bond shares images?" He shook his head in disbelief, ignoring Avery's other question. Of course Selene could travel at high speeds. All the Nepheli fae could if they were traveling light and not burdened with cargo. Selene was known to be one of the fastest flying Nepheli alive today. Of course she could travel to Orofine in a day if she was determined to reach her mate. "My soulmate's hand chosen guard could be sending images of secret Latian information to the Nepheli Sage without even realizing it?"

Selene looked down at the wooden floor. Did she realize the danger she was in, admitting to having that sort of access to private Latian information? To be in Latiah and knowingly share that information was nothing less than allowing Savine to take her life. If the roles were reversed, Rylo wouldn't hesitate to kill Raikin for being a spy.

"It hasn't happened before, I swear to the Goddess," Selene said. She could tell no lie, Savine knew, but his heart still hammered in his chest at the threat that this bond could cause to his nation, to his love. *Selene* had captured Avery, stole her from him when he left her vulnerable in battle. He hadn't forgiven himself for leaving her, and he would never forgive Rylo or Selene for stealing her away just to use both of them as pawns.

Selene's body became preternaturally still against the binds that cut into her exposed flesh. "When it did happen, I knew that whatever Rue showed me was making her worried. I couldn't rest, knowing that she could be in danger. I was already on my way when she sent the image of the attack. What could do that sort of damage?"

Avery spoke up, "It was dy—"

Savine interrupted her before she could spill any incriminating information about the Hunters. "It doesn't matter what it was. Rue has been well cared for, as you can see. You, however, are a known enemy of myself, my queen, and this nation."

"I deserve to know what happened to my soulmate. It's my right to take revenge on her attacker!" Selene hissed. She struggled against the vines holding her fast. Savine placed his hand on the pommel of his sword.

With a burst of strength that she shouldn't be able to possess, Selene broke through her bindings, raven black wings spread across the room, nearly knocking down Avery and Hyacinth in their path. Savine growled at Selene, drawing his sword. He could feel her dark starlight essence building. That power that had once nearly destroyed him. He'd once expected to die from it, and he wouldn't tolerate it anywhere near his mate or threatening his own nation.

He moved quickly, ready to strike Selene's exposed neck when he was hit by a sharp pain on his calf, cutting straight through his leather pants.

Avery screamed and Savine looked down to see the small fox sinking her sharp teeth into his leg. Rue was awake, and attacking her own king. She let go swiftly, snarling and growling as she limped backwards to Selene's side.

Avery rushed to Savine, wrapping her arm around his side and helping him to a seat. The small shifter's teeth were sharp, but it was the toxin that some shifters contained in their bite that worried Savine more than anything. Hyacinth cursed under her breath as she rolled his pants up and began examining the bite mark.

"There's no evidence of venom, My King, but I'll make you a poultice just to be sure." Hyacinth busied herself opening drawers and pulling out varying fragrant herbs.

Savine looked to the two women, one still in her shifted form, the other with her dark wings tucked tightly around her. Selene held Rue in her arms, a look of tenderness that was so foreign to the woman's face, it made Savine turn his head.

"Savine, before you came in we were just talking to Selene, trying to get her story straight. I think she's here only for the reasons she said. Her emotions are difficult to read," Kyla said in a quiet voice at his side.

"Of course her emotions are difficult to read. She has no emotions."

Avery sat on his other side, sliding her hand into her lap. Her expression was tense. He could see her working her jaw, the tension visible. "Little Flower, look at me." She turned, those soft brown eyes meeting his as he said, "I'm alright. I'm not happy about this revelation, or Selene's presence, but don't do something you'll regret."

Avery gave him a curt nod. "I just never saw it, and it was right in front of me. All the excuses Selene made to be around us, to be close to Rue." She shook her head.

Selene brought Rue back to the table, setting her down with such care it made Savine recoil. His mind just couldn't accept what he was seeing, this woman who'd treated him so cruelly to be displaying emotions he'd thought her incapable of having.

Hyacinth knelt at Savine's side and began her healing ministrations. The sharp pain from Rue's teeth faded to a dull ache.

Selene looked down at the fox as she said, "Rue still needs rest. I think she's not ready to shift back to her fae form. I'd like to stay with her, but could we have our privacy?"

"You have got to be fucking kidding me!" Avery exploded. "You came here, uninvited, and now expect us to leave you alone with one of my best friends? Hell no!"

"I recall Rylo showed you the same level of dignity when Savine arrived in Nephel."

Savine tried to hide a smile as Avery's eyes went wide with rage. "No way are you comparing this to our experience! You *kidnapped me!* You invaded my soul and forced truths from my mouth. We don't even know what Rue has to say about this!"

Rue let out a hiss in Avery's direction.

Avery let out a harsh laugh and said to the fox, "Don't even start with me. If you knew and kept this a secret from me, I'll never forgive you!"

Hyacinth nodded and spoke for the first time since Savine entered the room. "Enough! All of you out! Rue won't be getting any rest with you bickering!"

Savine wasn't taking any chances on Selene escaping. He let his essence rise, binding Selene in thorny vines. "Kyla," Savine said with a nod toward his sister.

Kyla pressed her hand to the winged fae, and Selene relaxed against her grip. Kyla began leading Selene toward the door. From the other side of the room, Rue became increasingly agitated. Her yips filled the room and Savine watched tentatively as Avery turned back to Rue. Tension coiled in his stomach at the possible threat to his mate, and he heard Selene give a low growl in warning.

Rue stopped yipping and sat still, gazing at Avery as she approached.

"I might be mad at Selene, but I won't let anything happen to her. I promise. Feel better soon, Rue."

The fox bowed her head gracefully before she curled herself in a tight ball, trusting Avery completely at her word that Selene would be protected.

Savine fisted his hands, feeling the pent up energy coursing through his veins. Abyss damn him, he wanted to exact years of revenge on Selene, wanted to hear her cry out in agony for all she'd done to him. But, he'd never do something to jeopardize Avery's relationship with Rue. Never intentionally hurt one of Avery's closest friends, and a loyal guard.

Savine followed his sister as she led Selene down the staircase and toward the main buildings of the King's Residence.

"Where would you like her?" Kyla asked. Avery caught up to them, her small hand slipping into his.

"Bring her to the City View Room. I'd like to have Raikin and Garnel there, but I sent them to investigate the explosion with some of our warriors. I'll have Darby get Jay. He can stand in for Raikin."

Selene turned in Kyla's grip. "Savine, you disappoint me. I expected to be visiting that fetid hole you call a prison."

Avery spoke up before he had a chance. "I made a promise to Rue to not let anything happen to you, Selene. Savine understands that and will respect my word."

His heart warmed and he smiled down at her. She wasn't even looking at him, instead, had her gaze fixed on Selene, her typically soft features hardened. Just a few hours ago they'd faced an attack on both of them. She'd *killed* one of the Hunters for him, and now she wasn't accepting any nonsense Selene may be putting on him. Day by day, he was learning to accept that her love for him, her support, was real and was forged in iron that would eviscerate their enemies.

Selene's face went back to a serene blank stare. He knew that look, and knew Kyla must have manipulated Selene's emotions again. They walked the rest of the way to the City View Room in silence.

Selene's exposed skin showed tiny rivulets of blood where the thorns of her bindings cut into her skin. Savine let the bindings fall as he shut the door to the room behind him. Avery and Kyla moved to the couch, but Selene continued to stand in the entrance to the room, docile as a lamb.

"What did you do to her?" Savine asked Kyla.

"I may have gone a bit too hard on manipulating her emotions. I wanted her subdued, but she's a powerful fae. I could feel her essence wanting to escape as we walked. She was fighting my essence so hard, I didn't know how much more I should apply to her. After she said that comment to you, I pressed more of my essence into her, and it was the tipping point. I should have stopped then, but I was angry, knowing how she goaded you."

Selene stared blankly at them, lacking recognition. "How long should this last?" Avery asked.

"Selene is one of the strongest fae I've met. She should be back to herself in no more than a few hours."

It was like Savine finally had a chance to breathe after the day he'd had. He let himself sink into the couch, leaning against Avery and taking in her sweet honeysuckle and mint scent. Avery reached up and gently stroked his cheek, playing with his cropped beard.

Kyla stood and took Selene by the hand, guiding her to a chair. She helped her sit, making her wings as comfortable as she could.

He'd never change them, but both his sister and soulmate had too much kindness in them for their own good.

Suddenly, Selene's eyes widened. The deep purple of her iris seemed to expand and her wings flared, knocking Kyla to the ground. Avery let out a gasp, but whispered something under her breath, knocking Selene to the ground in a plume of brilliant green light.

She continued to hold Selene back and Savine released his essence, once again wrapping Selene in a crushing tangle of vines.

"I told Rue I wouldn't let anything happen to you, but I'll be damned if I let you hurt Savine or Kyla," Avery gritted out.

Savine let out a bitter laugh. "Perhaps we should arrange to bring you to our fetid prison after all."

Selene bared her teeth at them, but her eyes were focused solely on Savine. "Now that you have me, what do you plan to do to me, Savine? All these years you've waited for your revenge. I could see it in your face this summer when you saw me near your little human."

Savine felt the rage building inside of him. He thought back to the day Selene dragged him to the Tower of Teeth. How she ripped into his soul, blaming him for Lilith's death. The dread, the terror cut through him like a fresh wound.

Avery laid a hand on Savine's arm and he took in a gasping breath.

"You harmed me once, and you tried to do it again by taking Avery from me. There are many, many things I've dreamed of doing to you over the years. But I don't need to now. I have a soulmate. You were wrong about me and I won't waste another moment of my life on you. But what I will do, what I have the right to do as king, is ensure you *will not* be united with your mate until I say."

Selene's eyes seemed to glow in luminous violet. "You have no right. Soulmate bonds transcend nations. No king or queen can stop what the Goddess ordained."

Savine twisted his mouth into a smile. "And yet, that is just what you did to me when you took Avery from me. You knew she was my soulmate, and yet you took her."

Selene hissed, "You never deserved to have love again, not after what you did to Lilith."

Savine drew his hands into a fist. This woman was trying to get him to lose his temper, trying to force Avery into breaking her promise to Rue. His breathing was coming in harsh spurts.

Avery's touch once again brought him back to himself. He let his heart rate settle, let himself come back to reality. He never caused Lilith's death. He was a victim as much as she was, and Avery wasn't harmed at Selene's hand. She was alive as well.

"We're not talking about you and Savine anymore," Avery said. She spoke in a tone that commanded attention, like the queen she was. "If you try to say anything to him again, I'll personally break that promise I gave to Rue. Understand?"

Selene nodded, her face hiding how she felt about Avery's command. "Understood. Can you let me out of these bindings?"

"Absolutely not. You've already proven you can't be trusted, so get comfy. You're staying in those vines until we decide what we're going to do with you. Now I have some questions for you, and you're going to answer them."

"Why would I do a thing like that?"

"If you actually want to be united with Rue, you'll start talking. Look, Savine is capable of keeping you two apart. But, if you do want to see her again you'll be working extra hard to get on my good side. I control that old man over there." Avery said the last sentence in a whisper, like she was letting Selene in on a secret. As always, her whispers were hardly quiet, and Savine heard every last word.

He wouldn't deny there was truth in what she said.

"Very well. What is it you'd like to know?"

"What's going on with my sister? Is she safe?"

Selene let out a bitter laugh. "She is the darling of our king."

"What do you mean?"

"He made quite a demonstration of his devotion at the Night of Feasts. And now they travel together to Goldoth."

Savine watched as Avery's lip twitched. "Is he forcing her to do these things?"

"She seems happy to serve the King of Nephel, and appears to enjoy his attention."

Bitter disgust masked Avery's face. Savine knew she hated Rylo as much as he did. Knew how much it hurt Avery for Morgan to choose to live in Nephel over Latiah.

"What about Susan?" Avery asked.

"She is well cared for and has found romance of her own in Elio. She remained behind in Nephel as King Rylo traveled to Goldoth."

Savine couldn't resist asking, "If you are here, and Rylo is in Goldoth, then who is currently watching over Nephel?"

Selene's brow furrowed and she pursed her lips. "I did not plan on traveling to Orofine, and now that I know Rue is safe, I should return. It was impulsive of me to come here. I see now that I shouldn't have done it."

Savine folded his hands as he said, "No leadership is in the Towers at the moment? Interesting."

"I'll not return here. Rue knows about the bond now. Once she is well she can come to me. Give me my leave so I can return to the Towers."

Savine sneered at Selene.

"No, I don't think I will."

Chapter 40

Rylo

A thick lock of dark hair stuck to Rylo's neck. Peeling it off of him, Rylo looked down at Morgan's sleeping body tucked in close to his own. His arms held her close enough that he could feel her soft breath on his face. Her skin still hadn't lost its coolness, despite being wrapped in his heat. He closed his eyes, wishing to slide back into his dreamless sleep with this woman wrapped tight in his arms.

Rylo was glad he didn't give in to the temptation to have sex with her. Yes, he wanted to bed her. The restraint he'd used the Night of Feasts was gone. Especially now that he was sure she wanted him without the aid of Bayberry wine. But that would have to wait. He wasn't about to take her on a dingy fur atop a dirt floor with one of his oldest allies. No, he had the patience to wait. Wait until they were back at the Towers. Wrapped in sheets of silk, her cool body pressed against his heat. The moon to his sun.

But before that could happen, he needed to explain to her what he saw in those caverns. The horrors that those witches were capable of inflicting on his folk needed to be stopped in their tracks, and that was why he knew Morgan wasn't going to be happy with what he was going to suggest. It didn't matter. Yes, he wanted her for his lover, but he also needed her to hold up her bargain to do all she could for Nephel first.

Morgan stirred in his arms. He let his grip on her loosen, and she sat up, giving him a sleepy smile.

"Good morning," she said, brushing a curl from his forehead.

"How did you sleep?" Rylo asked.

"For being under a dead animal on the dirt, surprisingly good."

Rylo let out a dry laugh. "We are in agreement there. If all goes well, we should be back in the Towers tonight."

"And what happens next?" Morgan twirled her hair between her fingers.

"Next? I'm afraid after what we saw and did, war. It's been Goldoth's plan for years and I don't think there will be a way to stop them now that we've stolen their relic. But before that, I need you to understand what we will be facing. It's not as I expected."

Rylo told Morgan everything he'd seen after she left dinner with the Goldoth royalty. He shared about seeing the strange humanoid twins, and how when they reentered the room, the twins displayed their magic. He shared how the Goldoths had been breeding humans to work their tunnels since the Cleaving, and how they no longer even resembled Morgan, Avery, or Susan.

Morgan listened without interruption, seeming to absorb all that he told her.

Her face was twisted in disgust, but he didn't know if it was for the actions of the Goldoth fae or their witches.

Finally, he shared how he escaped the caverns just as the sister, Tyranny, seemed ready to strike a dead fae on him.

The silence between them stretched on for far too long. What was going on in that mind of hers?

"I saw the mines and the human slaves. I thought they were some kind of fae. That's where I—that's where Elio is."

The way Morgan said those words, Rylo knew she was keeping something from him. The truth of how Elio died. His stomach twisted in anticipation. How had Morgan escaped when Elio was so much stronger, so much more experienced in battle?

"Tell me what happened to him."

She chewed on her bottom lip, breathing in deep.

"I didn't mean—"

A squalling cry came from the other room, cutting her words short. *I didn't mean* what? Rylo wanted to shout at her. But he kept it in as Serieff and Aniel walked into the room, carrying the crying baby.

"I hope you slept well, Rylo." Serieff's voice was deep and scratchy, so typical of the Hylax. "I've considered what we discussed yesterday, and I am willing to bring your request to our folk. If what you say is true, the threat does not seem to be coming from this woman in our room and the one to the north. It's to the south we must turn our attention."

Rylo gave a quick nod in agreement, but his mind was still desperate to know what happened to his dearest friend. He reached out for that strange connection that Morgan had made between them. The scars of the connection hadn't faded since she first entered his mind. Following the path, mind to mind, he stretched and pushed through the cool calm recesses of her mind. It was so much easier when they were closer like this.

He watched Morgan shudder with recognition, looking at him with eyes the color of fresh ferns.

You didn't mean what, Morgan?

Morgan turned her head, not making eye contact as shadows began circling between them. Shadows entered the connection between their minds, fading everything to a deep black.

I deserve to know. Rylo practically shouted it down the connection, but his hold on her mind had already dissolved.

A hand reached out to him. He flinched, looking at Aniel grasping him. "Are you alright, My King?"

"Yes, just a bit over set I believe. Right, Morgan?"

Morgan looked at him, her shadows still circling around both of them. "You'd know best if you're not feeling like yourself."

A bang on the door interrupted the tension and the door was forced open. He immediately recognized the captain of his guards. Behind him were several guards and eagans meant for carrying supplies and large amounts of folk.

If he were here, something would have gone terribly wrong in Nephel. It was impossible that Maglar could have rallied his forces this quickly. But... Was Rylo already too late? Had he left Selene and his folk unprotected while his enemy skirted the Wastewater without his notice while he slept on the dirt floor with this human?

"Did the others from our envoy arrive at the Towers yesterday?"

"Yes, the eagan and fae are resting today. That is not the matter I needed to address with you. It's Selene."

Rylo felt his essence stir, but he kept his outward demeanor calm. He couldn't lose Elio and Selene on the same day. He relied too heavily on both of them, for more than just the running of his nation.

"She fled north. She left a message with the human witch, Susan. She said her soulmate was in grave danger." The man looked uncomfortable delivering the news. To abandon one's post would lead to a sentence in the Tower of Teeth, or worse. For him to be delivering the news that the Sage of Nephel had done just that, well, the consequences would be grim.

"*Her mate?*" Rylo spat out the word with such loathing that he could feel Morgan scoot back from him. "It's that Latian shifter girl. It has to be. I suspected as much, but she wouldn't reveal anything."

He had to get back to his folk immediately. Selene had left them unprotected in the most dangerous time possible.

"Come, Morgan." Rylo reached out and grabbed her wrist, harder than he anticipated.

She looked at him with trepidation, but didn't say anything.

As they made their way to the door, Rylo turned back to the Hylaxes who opened their home for him. "You will be rewarded for your hospitality, as always Serieff. I'll send an envoy to hear what your council decides."

The man bowed to Rylo and as they walked out the door, the baby began another loud, shrill cry.

A fresh eagan was waiting for them outside. Rylo climbed into the saddle as Morgan followed after, taking a seat behind him. Moments later, they were airborne, climbing above the marshy lands of the Wastewater.

Morgan

Morgan's heart was thumping so loud that she thought it might jump out of her chest. Rylo hadn't said a word to her since she shut him out of her mind, closing the connection that he'd figured out how to infiltrate. Even throughout the whole flight to the Towers, Rylo refused to say a word to her. When she asked him if he was worried, he just ignored her question.

Finally, she tried to let the silence settle over her, embracing the wind in her face and the soft feathers that brushed against her bare legs. The breeze had a bite to it, especially as they continued farther north. So much so that she was wishing she had a warm jacket. But, she refused to complain. If Rylo wanted silence, she'd give him silence.

He had a right to be mad, but she had a right to keep her secrets. She knew that if Rylo heard how Elio died, he'd be devastated. She couldn't do that to him. Sometimes the truth was better not known.

As they landed at the top of the Tower of the Moon, Rylo motioned her to follow him. Chaos ensued as soon as they were off the eagan. Fae she didn't know were running up to Rylo, filling him in on what was going on, and asking what they should do. For his part, Rylo kept that neutral calm about him as everyone around them was in a panic.

"Find Susan and meet me in the library," Rylo ordered Morgan, his golden eyes swimming with something she didn't understand. They were the first words he'd spoken to her since they left the small cabin in the Wastewater.

Morgan nodded, but didn't say anything in reply. Turning, she walked out of the room. Finding Susan didn't take long. She must have already been alerted that they were back, because Morgan turned a corner toward Susan's room and there she was. When she saw Morgan, she began running, wrapping Morgan in a tight hug that made her feel twitchy.

"You're back, and you're okay! I was so concerned when I heard the rumors of your escape. Did you get the other relic?"

Morgan's throat felt so dry, it hurt to speak. "Yeah, I got it. Rylo's got it now."

"But you still have the necklace?" Susan asked, pointing to the brilliant yellow stones around her neck.

She gave a half-hearted nod. "We're supposed to meet him in the library."

When they entered the library, Rylo was already waiting for them. He'd somehow had time to change and comb his blonde hair into neat waves. He was wearing a black linen shirt and black leather pants, the combination making the gold of his skin and wings more brilliant.

With a cup of tea in hand, he almost looked back to his typical casual ease. Almost, but for the imperceptible tension in his neck and shoulders. Morgan swore only she would be able to catch that tightness in his countenance.

"Sit. Pour yourselves a cup of tea if you'd like. Would you like anything to eat?"

Morgan shook her head. Although she'd hardly eaten since the stew in Serieff's cottage, she had too many nerves dancing through her stomach to try and keep food down.

Susan poured herself a cup of tea, but Morgan couldn't even do that. She couldn't stop looking at Rylo, hoping he'd acknowledge her in some way.

"Can you pour me a cup?" Morgan asked. She wanted him to know that she trusted him, that even if she wasn't able to admit what happened to Elio, he was still important to her.

"Best not. Pour your own if you're in need of a drink," Rylo said, turning from her gaze and out toward the open air view of the canyon and tunnels below.

Rylo waited for Morgan to pour her own cup, and when she didn't bother, he began telling Susan about the two witches and the secret cavern under the Goldoth borders. Morgan listened again, a chill running down her spine as he shared about the girl who reanimated a corpse after slaughtering him in front of Rylo.

"Reports from my spies have already reached The Towers that Goldoth is amassing a vast army. One that will decimate my folk. We don't have the warriors to face this force. I need the two of you to go to Orofine today and do all you can to ensure an alliance with Latiah. Selene is already there. Explain what has happened and she will work with you to convince King Savine that his support is imperative to securing his own borders."

Morgan's stomach did a flip. Returning to that place with the folk who resembled her attacker had been the last thing she wanted to do. But she'd do it. If it proved her loyalty to Rylo, if it helped protect this place and Avery.

"Why aren't you going?" Morgan asked.

"I'm needed here." His amber eyes seemed to glow as he spoke. "Prepare to leave immediately. I've already arranged an eagan for your journey."

Rylo walked toward the balcony and jumped into the air, leaving Morgan and Susan alone in the library.

Susan raised an eyebrow. "Do you want to talk about it, or should I just stay quiet?"

Morgan shook her head, trying to keep the sadness from her expression. She'd have to tell Susan what happened to Elio too. The two people she'd learned to care about most in Aeritis were the ones she'd hurt the most by killing Elio.

Once they were safely in the cave for the night, Morgan was finally able to tell Susan about Elio. It broke her to share the news, but Susan needed to know. Just like Rylo deserved to know.

"I'm sure you noticed Elio didn't return," she said, sitting down beside Susan near the warmth of the fire she just built.

Susan's chin shook. "I was told he didn't make it out of Onyx Caverns."

Morgan took a deep breath and started sharing what happened to them during their search for the relic. It was hard to even say what happened, but she had to get the words out for her friend. "I was with him when he died. We were in a cave filled with human slaves and fae. I told him about the spell that enhanced his essence, and explained I didn't know what would happen. But he trusted me." Her voice began shaking as the tears slid down her face. Susan's eyes were filled with hurt as she held Morgan's hand. "He trusted me and the spell killed him. It depleted his essence before my eyes. I'm so, so sorry, Susan."

Susan was shaking with sobs as she clutched Morgan's hand. "He wanted me to tell you that you are his bright star."

Susan let out a stifled cry as she turned and walked toward the eagan perched outside the cave. Morgan let her be, knowing that she probably hated her for what she'd done to Elio.

Finally, Susan came back to the fire, sitting down next to Morgan. "I'm just relieved he wasn't alone when he died. You didn't know that spell would be so deadly."

"I don't know how to tell Rylo," Morgan admitted.

Susan looked at her, grief in her eyes. "You have to tell him the truth, Morgan. He deserves to hear it from you."

Chapter 41

Avery

"Avery?" A voice from the doorway made Avery look up from the letter she'd been writing to Morgan. "May I come in?" Darby stood in the doorway, carrying a letter in her hand.

"Of course! What can I do for you?" Avery stood and met the pale green woman near the door, closing it behind them.

"I've received a letter from the guards near the portal north of Orofine. They've intercepted another one of the Hunters. I'd like to take you there to meet with the guards and question the Hunter."

Avery reached for the letter and read the scribbled note about the Hunter who was caught. "Savine would want to meet him too. He's speaking with the trees right now. Why don't you send a message to bring the Hunter here?"

Darby rang her hands together. She looked toward the closed door. "We don't have much time. We should travel there on our own and send a message for Savine to join us."

She wasn't making any sense. Avery didn't know Darby like Savine did, but something seemed off. "Why do we have to go now?"

Darby didn't hesitate to answer. "Everyone has heard about the human weapon used against you and the king. I've heard the guards sent to the portal were uncomfortable with being attacked without your protection to stop the human powered weapon. They want their queen there to ensure they aren't harmed by another attack."

The fae couldn't lie, but she'd witnessed plenty of them twist truths. However, Darby did have a point. She knew that many of the fae thought she'd been able to protect them from an explosion, not because of her magic, but because she was a human.

Since the attack, there'd been a growing fear of the Hunters. Savine was even in the woods, talking with the trees to find out if more had made it through undetected. Rumors of fae with an essence wasted away were flying through the city, along with rumors of strange explosives found in the forests.

Maybe if she went with Darby, she could calm the concerns of the guards, and she could interview the Hunter without giving Savine another thing to worry about.

"Okay. Let's go." Avery wrote a quick note for Savine to find, letting him know where she was going, before she put on her boots. Instead of reaching for her own jacket, she grabbed the one Savine wore the day of the explosion. Her jacket hadn't been returned to her from cleaning after the blood splatter stained it, and she'd borrowed his. It was far too big on her, but she liked being wrapped in something belonging to Savine. Under the jacket, strapped to her hip, was her axe. Darby pursed her lips as Avery attached the weapon to her hip, but didn't object.

Outside, a heavy layer of fresh snow had fallen on the deep snowpack. She trudged through the snow, working hard to keep up with Darby's light, nimble steps. Everything was easier for the fae, including walking in deep snow apparently. Each step up the steep, mountainous trail was becoming more challenging as she post holed through the snow, sinking up to her calf and pulling herself up and out of the hole only to do it again. Darby slowed her pace as she walked above the snow, not even sinking as she stepped.

"Can you not use magic to walk above the snow?" Darby asked. She looked around them like she was waiting for someone to come and help Avery make it up the mountain.

"I doubt it," Avery grunted as she took a few more steps up the steep slope. She paused to talk, not able to push through the snow and ask her question at the same time. "Where is the portal anyway? I saw it on the map, but didn't think the trail was this steep."

"Over the ridge and down the next draw. It's a great distance, and you can see why I wanted us to get there as quickly as possible. Come! They'll be waiting."

Avery hesitated. Despite the fresh snowfall from the previous night, there should be tracks from the messenger. Either Darby wasn't leading her to the portal site, or there had been no urgent messenger this morning. Her intuition was telling her that this was a trap. Darby had something planned for her. But if she was wrong—if Darby's intentions were innocent, Avery didn't want to attack first and ask questions later.

She didn't want Darby to do something drastic either, so she followed behind Darby, tunneling into her magic as she walked. She reached deep into herself and drew her magic until it itched under her skin. Down the bond, she sent Savine her concerns and fears, hoping he could follow the bond to their location.

How powerful was Darby? There was so little Avery knew about the fae she followed deeper into the wintry woods. Darby was like a second mother to Savine, and she'd stayed behind in Orofine to put

Savine's mother's body to rest. But, if she was so loyal to Savine, why didn't she flee Orofine and join him in the Middens?

At the top of the ridge, Avery felt the palpable change in the energy around her. The forest was dense just below the ridge, but from where she stood, a rocky outcropping cut across the spine of the mountains. She'd never wished to have Savine's power of communicating with the trees until now. Avery could plan her next move if only she could ask them what lies ahead.

"Not far now," Darby murmured as she began her trek down the trail. There still weren't other tracks, but Darby left faint tracks of her own. Maybe Avery was worrying about nothing? Perhaps the messenger's tracks did get covered that quickly. Regardless, she gripped onto her axe and continued to channel her magic until it was burning under her skin to be released.

Avery followed Darby into a thick ring of pines. As soon as she stepped into the circle, she heard the familiar ring that had once transported her to Quartz Mountain. Her eyes widened and she lifted her axe to defend herself against a potential attack. Something from behind her made her jump and Avery swung around, releasing a powerful jet of green energy from her fingertips.

Avery gasped.

On the snow laid four guards, their throats slit as if they didn't have time to draw their weapons. The crimson splatters were dark against the white snow. The Hunters had murdered the guards.

"Now!" Darby growled. Out of the woods emerged half a dozen fae. Their tattered clothes and faded essence immediately gave them away.

The Hunters.

Avery let her magic roil out of her, green power knocking down two of the fae. But there were too many of them. Even with their weakened essence, they attacked with a strength that she couldn't go up against.

"Please, don't let them do this!" Avery shouted.

A burning sensation hit Avery in her lower back. Pain seared through her skin, making her feel like her flesh was doused in acid. Avery fell to the cold, deep snow hard. Her knees snapped against the push of the snow and she rolled back, seeking relief from the stinging burn that ripped across her back. Hands were on her, binding her arms behind her back and her legs just above her worn hiking boots.

The all too familiar feeling of her magic being stifled hit her as the magical manacles suppressed her power within. Even the mate bond seemed to trickle to an ember within her.

"Let me go!" Avery shouted. The piercing buzz of the portal seemed to grow louder. Were they going to kill her and toss her through the portal?

Darby squatted near Avery in the snow. "In due time, *My Queen*." Her voice dripped with sarcasm, her face was screwed into a sneer.

"Savine trusted you!" Avery cried out. Her back was burning so badly she thought she would blackout from the pain coursing down her spine.

"I would never betray the True King. All I've done was for Savine. But *you*! I know better than to trust you! Humans, with their lies twisting the truth so thoroughly, they can deceive even the smartest fae. I know you have tricked Savine into believing you are his soulmate and our queen. But I see you. I know you're working to bring destruction to our realm. You and your sister are the ones foretold so long ago!"

"You've got to be fucking kidding me!"

This was about that damn prophecy again. Avery was so tired of the fae expecting her to bring about some sort of cataclysmic change thanks to some arbitrary nonsense muttered to a select few folk.

"Even now you lie with that wicked tongue. You'll bring the ruin of our nations if we allow you to stay. The Hunters have worked tirelessly to stop you from entering Aeritis, and yet you beguiled them in your realm. We will have no more of your lies and tricks."

Avery tugged against the bindings on her wrists. There was no way in hell that she was going to sit here and be killed by these fae. These fae who have spent the last decade working to end her life. Well, they've failed so far, they weren't going to get the satisfaction of killing her off now.

As she fidgeted against the bindings, she felt something in Savine's coat pocket. Something hard and round.

The relic.

She needed to work the magical bowl out of the pocket and within her grasp. She began working on her gloves, trying to slide the bindings off the cuff of her leather gloves so she could free her hand.

But she also couldn't let Darby know what she had. She had to continue to keep them all distracted. The Hunters had formed a semi-circle around them, desperate and hungry looks glowered at Avery.

"So what? You're going to kill me?" Avery asked as she tugged a finger out of the glove.

"I would never risk that. You wear a crown, probably a false crown, atop your head, but I won't risk my soul, or the souls of the Hunters in killing you. You aren't worth the risk."

"Then what? Toss me through the portal and hope for the best?"

A few fae around her chuckled. Darby parted her teeth in a sharp smile. "You'll be convinced to take your own life on the other side of this portal."

Avery's heart thudded in her chest. She needed to buy herself some time until she could get the relic in her hand and draw up its power.

She tugged one glove off. The cool snow buried her fingertips. "So you've known all along about the Hunters?"

Darby's eyes glowed with malice. "Of course I have. Kings have known of this portal for centuries and I suggested the idea to King Jasper."

"But how would you know that I'd go through the portal? Did you hear the prophecy too?" Damn, this prophecy seemed less of a secret and more like a well-known statement at this point.

"Jasper trusted me enough to tell me the prophecy, and after he thought about the humans who crossed through the portal, he began to realize the prophecy pointed to twin witches. I assumed the Goddess would mark them out as a warning, and I was correct in my predictions. Once I shared this knowledge, he trained the Hunters to seek you out."

Avery's mind was rattling. How could Darby have deceived them so thoroughly? How was she even capable of such lies?

"I thought you were loyal to Savine? You've betrayed him by working for Jasper all these years!" Her frustration mounted, but she didn't stop working on her bigger purpose: getting herself free. She twisted her arms and shifted enough for the heavy fur coat to fall to the side. The pocket was almost in line with her hand.

"I *am* loyal to King Savine. I never wanted anything more than to see his mother happy and free. She never had that privilege, and now supporting her son as king is my gift back to her. Jasper was a terrible, cruel ruler. But, once Savine fled, I never let Jasper doubt my loyalty to him. I knew my job was to secure a place for Savine to return to. That included keeping it safe from *any* threat, even a disastrous match with a human like you. Now it's time to be rid of you forever."

Before Avery could respond, Darby motioned to the Hunters behind her. Their grasp on Avery was tight as she twisted and tried to get loose, but there was no way she could get out of this.

The portal's high-pitched hum grew louder. Avery gulped the last few breaths of air in Aeritis, trying as she could to wriggle enough to knock the relic out of the coat pocket.

Just as she was ready to give up hope, the wooden bowl fell to the blanket of snow below.

Chapter 42

Morgan

Morgan's eagan banked to the right and began its descent into Orofine. Its golden-brown wings tipped so far that she worried she could roll out of her saddle. But she held tight, even as her heart thudded against her chest and her stomach churned with worry. She knew Rylo needed help, and she was willing to seek it for him. After all, it was the least she could do for him. She also wanted to see Avery. Knowing Avery was here, Avery was *Queen,* that was the only thing keeping her from panicking as she flew into the land where she was only known for murdering their former monarch.

As they flew lower, Morgan noticed guards on the expansive treehouse, drawing bows and arrows toward their eagans. The archers didn't hesitate as they released their arrows into the sky.

"Susan!" Morgan shouted. Morgan let her magic build up into her fingertips as she released her shadows out into the early morning sky. Darkness roiled out of her as Susan let out a wall of water, crashing against the arrows.

The eagan Morgan rode let out a piercing scream as it made its descent to the ground below. Guards were gathered at the same place she landed during the last time she came to Orofine.

Suddenly, Susan's voice boomed out as if she were using a microphone. So she had been practicing new spells without Morgan.

"We come seeking peace as emissaries of King Rylo. We are here to see Queen Avery on urgent business. Do not attack us and we will have no reason to harm you."

Morgan gritted her teeth. Her eagan landed with a graceful swoop. She looked up, expecting to be surrounded by guards, but they all hung back as they made way for one man she'd recognize anywhere to make his way through his warriors.

Savine walked with a confidence that made Morgan roll her eyes. He was wearing a thick fur coat and leather pants. His leather boots barely sank into the fresh snow that covered the flat expanse in front of the treehouse palace.

"Morgan and Susan, what a surprise." His tone was as cold as the frosty wind on her face.

"Did you miss us?" Morgan said in a tone that she thought Rylo would be proud of.

"Have you finally escaped from Rylo? Came seeking my goodwill?"

Morgan arched an eyebrow, ready to give a biting reply, when Susan answered instead.

"King Rylo sent us on urgent matters. We need your help." Susan said as she slid off her eagan and approached Savine. She gave a small curtsy, which he brushed off with a wave of his hand.

"None of that for you, Susan. Does this concern Selene? If so, he will need to send someone other than two witches to get her back."

"Is Selene really here?" Morgan asked. She didn't think it could be possible that Selene would flee her post when Nephel was so vulnerable.

Savine nodded. "Your answer tells me there is some other reason for your impromptu visit. Come, let's find Avery. I was coming back from the forest when you arrived."

The guards parted for them, nobody making a move to attack Morgan as they walked up the sprawling wooden steps to a large, high ceiling room with wooden walls. Intricate carvings into the wood seemed to tell a story, and Morgan was captivated by the scene of an elk laying down its life for a fae king. At the front of the room was a large wooden throne, encrusted in jewels.

Morgan couldn't imagine her sister on that throne, ruling a fae nation. She always saw her sister the same way. A little messy, a little rumpled, and with a big grin on her face.

Even though she had her own trepidations with coming to Orofine, Morgan looked forward to seeing Avery. She wanted to share all the crazy things she'd experienced, and tell her about the growth of her powers and the relic she'd discovered.

Savine took a seat on his throne, leaving Morgan and Susan standing with the gathering fae around the room. A knot began forming in her stomach as she looked at the fae with the fur patterns showing from under their winter clothing. She took a deep, steadying breath, trying to not let their presence rattle her.

Savine addressed someone from the sides. A guard, Morgan guessed. The man retreated into an alcove near the front of the room.

"Do you think he shares his throne with Avery?" Susan whispered. Morgan gave a quick nod.

Shortly after he left the room, the guard returned, a look of concern on his face. He whispered something to Savine, and Morgan watched his whole body tense. He rose and left the room without looking back at Morgan or Susan.

Nearly an hour went by as Morgan and Susan loitered around the throne room. Finally, the guard returned, walking directly toward Morgan and Susan.

Savine followed behind him, as well as a large group of people Morgan didn't recognize. Savine's face had hardened and grew flush with anger, and Morgan suspected possibly a bit of fear. He motioned for Morgan and Susan to come forward. That gnawing, itching feeling that something was very wrong began to grow under Morgan's skin.

"Avery is missing." Peeking out from his neckline, Morgan could see the geographic lines of his essence whirl under his skin. "I've felt something strange down the bond in the last few moments. I suspect she's been taken."

What the hell? Morgan knew Savine couldn't lie to her, but it seemed too weird that immediately after her arrival, Avery disappeared.

"Who could have taken her?" Susan asked.

Savine's face was like stone, but his dusty blue eyes looked like they were about to spill with rage. "Tell me what the fuck you did with her! Was this Rylo's doing?"

Morgan felt the sting of brambles coiling around her before she realized what was happening. Despite the layers of her winter coat, the thorns dug into the fabric of her clothing as she gasped. Thorns tightened around her throat, drawing drops of crimson blood. Tight enough to hurt, but not to choke. A warning and a threat.

Savine thought she would do this to Avery?

Savine

"It wasn't me!" Morgan shouted in a shrill voice so high it made Savine wince.

"You spin lies from your tongue. Rylo took Avery in exchange for Selene. Tell me where in the Abyss he took her to!"

"I swear it wasn't me or Rylo! We didn't even come here for Selene!" Morgan gasped. The thorns twined around Morgan's exposed neck. Savine wanted so badly to let those thorns sink into her sensitive flesh, to cut out the truth from her lying tongue.

"It wasn't us, Savine!" Susan shouted, her own brambles coiling around her throat.

"Give us food! I can prove it!" Morgan choked out, blood dripping down her white skin and dripping onto her fur coat.

Savine eyed her with suspicion. He didn't trust Rylo or Morgan. Even though Morgan was Avery's sister, she'd chosen an allegiance with Rylo over her own sister. What kind of sister would do that? Despite all they'd faced in life, Savine and Kyla had always been fiercely loyal to each other. They'd *never* choose to abandon the other. Having faced this very scenario, Savine knew it was because of Kyla that he made it out of the Tower of Teeth, and Rylo's years of torture.

And yet, this was Avery's sister. Avery wouldn't want Savine to harm her. She'd send him straight to the Abyss for even damaging her sister's throat, despite her own lack of loyalty.

He had no choice. He needed to give her a chance to share what she knew.

"Very well."

Savine waved over a guard, who rushed to bring a goblet of wine.

He allowed his coiling essence to loosen, letting the brambles fall to the ground.

Once she was free, Savine gave Morgan the glass. Morgan didn't hesitate to drink the wine in quick gulps.

"Did you or any Nepheli have any involvement with the disappearance of Avery Hollis?" Savine asked.

Morgan didn't fight her answer. She never looked uncomfortable as if she struggled against the tug to answer his question truthfully. She didn't even hesitate in her reply.

"I have no knowledge of her disappearance. This has nothing to do with King Rylo or any Nepheli."

Savine cursed. He had even less idea where Avery could be. He racked his brain for where she could have gone without her close companions. It wasn't like her to say nothing about a hike through the woods or a soak in their private hot springs. No, there was something very wrong.

If it wasn't Rylo, then Morgan's presence here really was for other purposes.

Savine felt his essence still.

But if it wasn't Rylo, then it had to be the Hunters.

Garnel approached Savine's side. He'd been sent to search the surrounding forest, while others looked in town.

Savine pressed his hands into his face. He'd failed Avery again. Let her be taken by someone who wanted to harm her. He'd thought she'd been safe with that crown on her head, but yesterday and now this proved that he was wrong.

"The Hunters took her."

"Darby is missing too," Garnel said.

Chapter 43

Avery

There was no way in hell Avery was being sent back to Earth like this. Avery kicked at the Hunter holding her leg in place as to her horror, Darby picked up the wooden bowl from the ground. As she twisted, she threw her head back, smacking it into the Hunter holding her upper body. The crunch of his nose on her skull reverberated off the humming of the portal.

It was enough to distract her captors and Avery gave one solid kick as the now bleeding Hunter dropped her upper body. She fell to the ground with a soft thud, landing in blood splattered snow. The body of one of the murdered guards was close enough for her to smell the metallic tang of his blood.

She didn't let his death distract her. Not now. Not when her survival counted on quick actions, and Avery's ability to save herself. No, she couldn't rely on Savine to always be there to protect her. Avery was the only one who could prevent her disappearance from Aeritis.

Avery ran at Darby, hands still bound behind her. The force she hit Darby with even surprised herself. Darby fell to the ground, the relic sinking slightly into the powder. Immediately, Darby was crawling toward the bowl. She knew exactly what it was.

Avery ran as fast as her body could go, sinking into the freshly fallen snow with every agonizing step. She made it to the relic first, but with her hands tied she'd need to secure the bowl and its magic before Darby could get to it.

She dropped to the powder, sinking her face into the snow as she grabbed the bowl between her teeth. Immediately, she felt a rush of power stir within the bowl. Thinking of how naturally the deep magic had flowed into her the previous day, Avery opened herself to the magic, despite being bound, despite the Hunters closing in on her.

The deep magic ripped into her like the icy waters of a rapid, tearing at the bindings and snapping them into tatters at her feet. With her hands free, Avery was *fucking done* with these creeps. Done being a victim, and done being seen as an enemy because of some arbitrary prophecy.

"Don't let her attack!" Darby shouted at the Hunters. Avery unsheathed the iron axe at her side. The axe that those cowards would never touch, too concerned about what that pure, cold iron would do to them if they touched it. Just as the day before, she let her magic flow into the weapon, buzzing with as much power as the portal at her side.

Then she unleashed the axe, watching it soar through the air in a perfect arc as it landed at her target.

Darby fell to the ground. Blackened blood and brain matter splattered into the already stained snow. Her body continued to twitch even with the magic infused axe lodged in her skull.

Good riddance.

Avery didn't have time to retrieve her weapon before the Hunters began closing in on her, corralling her toward the ringing of the portal behind her. This portal was different somehow, more accessible, like it had been tampered to always be open.

And now her deep magic filled body seemed to be drawn to the opening like a pair of magnets, forced to join.

She had to stop the Hunters before they pushed her into that portal, into whatever they had planned on the other side of that barrier.

"No!" Avery shouted, releasing a stream of brilliant light that struck with a force that sent shock waves through her arms. Two of the Hunters fell to the ground. One, the man with the injured nose, was sprawled in the snow, his neck at an unnatural angle as if the power welling inside her had snapped his spine like a brittle twig.

The other Hunter was crying out as he bled, painting the snow a brilliant shade of crimson.

Two more remained, their bodies thin and frail from the years of wasting away, depleting their essence in her world. All the time searching to end her, to never let her make it to Aeritis.

They charged her, and she felt the deep magic respond to the threat. What came out of her nearly stunned her.

Coiling thorny vines shot from her fingertips, burning her skin and blasting holes in her leather gloves. But she didn't back down from the pain. This, somehow, was a gift from her soulmate. The man she had no intention of leaving. Not today, and not ever.

The vines worked their way over and around the two fae, and Avery relished in the look on their faces as she let those thorns grow longer, sinking through their threadbare winter clothing, through their flesh. One screamed out in such horror that Avery *almost* relented.

Almost.

The fae fell to the snow.

If they wanted Avery to be the monster the prophecy made her out to be, then she'd do it. She'd tear this world apart before she let someone take her from Savine again.

The buzzing of the portal grew louder. Avery looked over her shoulder. No, it wasn't possible. The portal was pulling her in. She tried to run back from its tug, but her feet sank in the deep snow, trenching her toward the electric energy of the portal.

Just then, she saw two figures flying atop an eagan. Her breath escaped in a gasp as she saw Morgan and Susan bank toward her.

Morgan

The first thing Morgan noticed from the sky was the red streaks in the freshly fallen snow. So much blood, it looked like the site of a battle. Then she saw a slight figure in a coat far too large for her.

"Avery!"

Morgan directed the eagan toward the ground, but she kept her eyes locked on her sister as they descended. Avery was the only one standing, but there was obviously something wrong. She seemed to be battling an unseen force that was dragging her across the snow, sinking her body until it formed a trench that Avery fought against.

The eagan landed near a dead woman. Morgan and Susan both jumped off the bird and sank into the deep powder.

"Don't come close!" Avery shouted.

That's when Morgan heard the familiar buzz that had brought both of them to Aeritis.

"It's an open portal?" Her aching heart rattled against her ribs. She could go home. She could leave this place. The rattle in her heart was replaced by a queasy sensation. *Did she even want that anymore?*

Morgan wasn't sure if she truly wanted to go home any longer. Give up magic, give up all she'd worked on and learned, the goal of finding the relics.

Give up Rylo and all she'd promised him.

She shivered and shook the thought from her mind.

"Don't come close! The portal is drawing me in! There's some kind of trap on the other side!"

Morgan looked at Susan and Susan nodded.

"We can help you!" Susan called out. Morgan reached for the cool stones of the relic around her neck. Unlike the scepter, this one didn't flood her body with deep magic. It wasn't as in tune to her touch and needs as the scepter was, but as she grasped it, she felt the stirring of magic deep within its stones.

Morgan's shadows wrapped around and Susan grasped her hand. "We need to try to close the portal," Susan said. "Together. Unless you want to risk going through? Going home now?"

Morgan's voice was steady, her mind made up as she said, "It's not my time to go home yet. Someday, but not today. There will be other portals."

"You're sure?"

"Yes. I'm going to feed the deep magic into myself. Remember the undoing spell?"

Susan nodded and grasped Morgan's hand all the tighter.

"We're going to stop it, Ave!" Morgan shouted over the whir of the portal.

The deep magic fed into her, cold and heavy and she let it settle into her being, mingling with the shadows that wound around her furiously.

Susan began an incantation and Morgan followed along, speaking the words of undoing. They pointed their intention at the portal and released their combined magic in a steady, searing flow that rushed out of them toward the source of the ringing.

The world filled with shadows and light, water and earth as an eruption blasted *through her* and smacked into an invisible wall.

Immediately, the world was silent except for the panting of the three women's combined breathing.

Morgan let go of Susan's hand, collapsing in the snow. Her vision was blurred and everything hurt. She could barely make out Avery's small frame, crawling through the snow, the oversized coat left in a heap on the crimson snow. She reached Morgan's side, wrapping her body around Morgan. The familiar scent and feel of her sister near her brought tears to her eyes.

"If you want to go home, I think I have a way." Avery's voice was rough and raw, almost unrecognizable.

Morgan shook her head. "Not yet. I'm not done here."

She couldn't keep her eyes open as she let herself slip into sleep.

Chapter 44

Avery

Avery wrapped her arms around Morgan. She could tell by the steady rise and fall of her sister's breathing that she'd slipped into what could only be the dreamless sleep from deep magic burnout. Susan also seemed to sleep in the snow, red hair blending with the carnage on the ground around them.

Savine's cry for her shook her from the fog she'd drifted into.

Avery stood up, walking to the jacket in a pile on the snow, and wrapped the heavy coat around herself, tucking the bowl into the oversized pocket.

"Savine!" she cried, running to the ridge as best as she could through the deep snowfall. "Savine! Savine!"

Savine's tall, broad frame crested the ridge, fire in his blue eyes as he looked down at the scene in the ring of trees. She tugged on the bond between them and his eyes snapped onto her.

Never could she imagine that such a large, strong man could run across the snow with such speed. His feet *flew* across the snow, leaving hardly a print behind as he ran to Avery. She trundled through the snow, still making painstakingly slow progress to her soulmate.

Their bodies crashed together when he reached her. In one smooth motion, Savine scooped Avery into his arms, their mouths meeting in a tangle of teeth and tongue, the desperate need to be reunited pulsing between them.

Savine pulled back and looked at Avery with pain in his eyes. His voice was raw with emotion. "I failed you again. I don't deserve to be your mate, Little Flower."

Avery touched his hand with her broken gloves. "You make me stronger. You were with me when I defended myself. It was your essence that I used."

Savine shook his head, and she could see the bitter self-loathing on his face, but she cut him off. "Savine, you can't be with me at every moment, and I'm becoming stronger because you believe in me. Because Kyla and Rue make me work every day to be better."

"Did they kill Darby?"

Avery shook her head, not even trying to stop the small smile that stretched across her lips. "No, that was all me. She's the one who brought me here. She'd been working with the Hunters for years."

She didn't care that Darby had been like a mother to him; Darby had gotten in between Avery and Savine, and there was no space for someone like that in her life. To her surprise, Savine's face turned up into a smile.

He let her body slide down his, but opened her oversized coat and wrapped the front of the coat around himself, pulling her to his chest.

"Good. If she tried to hurt you, she deserves to die."

Avery looked at the bodies in the snow, her sister's sleeping form included. "The portal was pulling me toward it, and I almost went through. Morgan and Susan shut it somehow. I think they're suffering from burnout. We need to get them back to the King's Residence."

Savine nodded, picking up Avery and carrying her across the snow on nimble feet to where her sister slept. He whistled toward the ridge of the mountain and moments later, guards led by Garnel and Jay made their way down the steep slope.

"Do you trust Garnel with your sister?"

"Of course, but I'm still confused how she even got to me. Did you know she was in Orofine?"

"I did. She arrived shortly before you were discovered missing."

Avery looked down at her sleeping sister and noticed the scratches around her exposed neck. Bruising and rivulets of blood dotted her neck and Susan's. Dammit. Savine had attacked her sister and friend. She clenched her jaw as she tried to tamper her anger toward him. Avery still felt the remnants of the deep magic circulating in her blood.

"You thought *she* was the one who tried to take me, didn't you?"

Savine's voice had a growl to it, like he was frustrated with Avery. "She is working with Rylo. It seemed far too coincidental that you should disappear around the time that Morgan shows up, and knowing that I have not released Selene."

Avery turned her back on Savine. How dare he hurt her sister? "I can't believe you would think Morgan or Susan would hurt me!" Avery shouted. "Get the hell away from me!"

Jay and Garnel walked over to their side, giving her space as they looked between herself and Savine. She turned, walking away from Savine as she asked Garnel, "Will you please take Morgan and Susan to Hyacinth? If Kyla's up for it, could you let her know that they're here?"

"Of course, they're in safe hands with me." Garnel motioned for Jay to pick up Susan, while he lifted Morgan. "What about the eagan?"

Avery looked to where Garnel was pointing and shuddered.

The eagan was hidden in the treeline, one of the Hunters in his talons as he ripped shreds of clothing and flesh from the dead body.

She curled her lip and turned her head as entrails spilled onto the snow. "Let him eat. At least we won't have to worry about feeding him."

"Thank Althea we ride elk. That's disgusting," muttered Jay.

The two walked away, carrying Susan and Morgan's limp bodies. Savine turned back to her, scowling. Around them, guards lifted the corpses and began carrying them up the ridge.

"You're angry I reacted with my essence toward your sister and Susan?" Savine asked.

Avery turned from him, post holing through the snow over to Darby's body. She bent down and yanked the axe from her skull with a sickening crack.

Nausea threatened to make her sick, but she pushed it down, walking past Savine as she began trudging through the deep powder, the bloody axe slung over her shoulder.

"*You* just killed my mother's dearest friend, a woman loyal to me, and I'm not angry at you!" Savine shouted. Two guards passed her, carrying Darby's hanging body between them.

"*I* was betrayed by that woman! *I* heard her very thorough confession as she tried to send me back through the portal to some impending death. So excuse *me* if I don't see the two situations as the same."

"But they are!" Savine argued.

"Hell no, they aren't! You probably started strangling Morgan with your thorny vines before she had a chance to explain why she was in Orofine. You probably forced the answer out of her under duress. I protected myself from a woman who was trying to harm me!"

Avery continued to stomp up the steep, winter white mountain, past craggy boulders and spindly subalpine firs. There was no reason that Savine couldn't catch her easily, not with her slow, clumsy, human footsteps through the snowfall. New flakes clung to her braid and eyelashes. She could hardly hear Savine's deft steps behind her.

"Rylo could have been trying to take you again! I was afraid!"

Avery didn't reply as she tried to make distance between them. It was an impossible task at this steep incline and with these conditions.

"Please, don't ignore me, Ave!" Savine pleaded.

She let his plea linger on the wind before she answered him. "I can't believe you'd hurt them! All I want is to be with Morgan right now, so just give me some space."

Savine's steps slowed. She didn't need to look behind her to feel their bond growing taut with the change in distance and the hurt that washed over her.

Chapter 45

Morgan

Morgan's eyes adjusted to the warm, cheery firelight in a comfortable room. The scent of herbs hung in the air. On her left, Susan sat up in bed with a round, dark-skinned and dark-haired fae chatting contentedly with her. They were both drinking from an earthenware mug. Susan laughed harder than Morgan had ever heard her laugh and the other woman snorted back.

Morgan tried sitting up, but everything hurt. She and Susan had practiced their magic together for weeks now, but she hadn't tried utilizing deep magic and connecting her magic to Susan's before. The burst of power that they threw at that portal had nearly wiped her off the map.

"You're awake!" Susan said. The other woman turned toward Morgan.

"Morgan? It's nice to meet you," she said, grasping Morgan's shoulder in a tight squeeze. "I'm Hyacinth."

"Nice to meet you," Morgan croaked. Her throat was parched and she desperately needed a drink.

"Just one moment and I'll have just what you need to restore your constitution," Hyacinth said as she walked over to a kettle on a stove. She began pulling down bottles from her shelf, assessing each one in a manner that Morgan couldn't figure out.

"She can sense what you need," Susan said. "Hyacinth is the greatest healer in Aeritis."

"Now, don't be telling stories, girl! I'm good, but I'm not that good," Hyacinth argued.

Susan chuckled. "She's humble too!"

"I heard so much about you. It's nice to know I'm in good hands!" Morgan said. Her head felt heavy and she gave in to the desire to lie back down.

"She's the one I said could remove your scars if you want to," Susan suggested, a friendly smile on her face.

Morgan bit her lip. Her scars had fueled her rage against these fae for months now. The scars were an ever-present reminder of what they could do to her, to never let her guard down. They also were a testament to her resilience. But part of her did wish she could erase them. Break down those barriers she'd sealed around herself.

No. She couldn't do that yet. She couldn't let go of everything that had happened when that monster ripped into her face, carrying her in his jaws back to that tunnel.

Maybe someday, but that day wasn't today.

Morgan shook her head. "No. I'm good."

"We all must walk our own journey, child. Yours will be full of hardships here. Wear your scars like armor and I will be here when you're ready to remove that armor," Hyacinth said, stirring various dried plants into a mug of hot water.

"Thank you," Morgan whispered. She liked this no-nonsense, wise old fae already.

Hyacinth offered her the cup and Morgan sipped it, tasting notes of sage and juniper, clover and nutmeg, plus something else that she couldn't discern. "How do you know what to put in each mug?" Morgan asked, taking another drink of the soothing elixir.

"My essence guides my hand, and it's my essence that does the most healing. However, I can speak to what ails you in a way and the herbs or spices I choose for the cup reflect what your body craves. It makes taking the draught much easier to consume too."

Morgan immediately felt her body growing stronger, less exhausted from when she woke. "Do you ever choose something that tastes bad?"

"Yes of course, but the recipient needs to drink it regardless for the healing to happen. I also heal directly with my essence. Some more challenging cases need more work as well. Your sister was wrapped up in a paste and left to sleep with it overnight when she couldn't recover from her lung infection and fever. I dare say she didn't find it too pleasant!"

Morgan's eyes grew wide. "She was sick? How?"

Hyacinth bit her bottom lip. "I shouldn't say. I'll leave the story for her to tell."

A knock on the door startled the three women, but Morgan heard her sister's familiar voice and the unease disappeared. Avery walked into the room and went directly to Morgan, tugging her into a hug and kissing her on her scarred cheek. "I'm so happy you're safe and you're here!"

Morgan gave a weak smile and put her cup down before she spilled it in her sister's next embrace. Avery slid into the bed next to her, crossing her legs and leaning close enough to touch Morgan. "I've missed you, Ave. I'm sorry I left the way I did. I just—I couldn't stay here."

Avery took Morgan's hand in hers and gave it a squeeze. "It's okay. I'm sorry too. I should have listened to you when you said you were uncomfortable with coming here. I was being selfish."

"It's okay. I think we were both being a little selfish at the time. I shouldn't have abandoned you the way I did." Morgan squeezed her sister's hand back before bringing her fingers to the crown on Avery's head. She didn't even know what to think. Her irresponsible ski bum sister was now a queen. "Ave, wow."

Avery grimaced. "It's complicated, but basically this crown and the title of Queen was another thing forced on me by Althea. Don't make too much out of it, okay?"

Morgan nodded. "Okay."

"By the way, I'm sorry Savine attacked you when you landed here. I'm so angry at him, looking at him makes me furious."

Morgan gritted her teeth. As far as she knew, Avery had always just casually dated. Now she'd bound her soul to a fae king and was already angry at him. To be fair, Morgan would be ready to slice Rylo's throat if he laid a finger on Avery.

Hyacinth was already making a cup of tea for Avery with the remaining hot water from the kettle.

"Avery, dear, Susan shared that the portal nearly brought you back to your land. Did you consider going through and seeing if you could return back and forth?"

Avery shook her head. "I didn't want to leave, plus there was a trap set up on the other side for when they pushed me through the portal." Avery turned to Morgan, her mouth turned down. "We'll figure out a way to get you back. I think I know how, too. We'll need to return to Quartz Mountain after the snow melts. The quartz you gave me will guide you home."

Morgan sighed and pressed her head to her palm. "A lot has happened since we've been apart, and I'm not ready to go home until I finish some tasks I agreed to do."

Avery looked at Susan, then back to Morgan. "For Rylo? Did he send you here?"

Susan's face was turned up in a mischievous smile. Morgan didn't want her sharing that she'd become close to Rylo. She never liked sharing her private life with anyone, even Avery, and she didn't have plans to start now. Besides, Rylo was furious at her for not disclosing how Elio died, and would probably continue to ignore her after she returned from Orofine.

Susan finally replied, "We were sent here by Rylo. I think Morgan has more details than I do on the full extent of why we are here. But, we need to include King Savine and his council in the conversation. Where's Kyla? I expected to see her with you."

Morgan let out a sigh of relief. Susan hadn't disclosed her close connection to the Sun King.

Hyacinth let out a huff. "That girl is running herself ragged."

At that moment, the door opened. Kyla and Rue came in, expressions serious.

"Look at us! All back together again!" Susan said, standing to hug Rue and Kyla.

"This room is too tight for everyone," Hyacinth argued from the corner.

"I'd call it cozy, Hyacinth!" Susan called. She seemed so much lighter, so much more at ease, now that she was back with folk she knew. It made Morgan feel a bit envious of the way she'd seamlessly slid back into a familiar world.

Kyla spoke first. "I wish we could stay in here with Hyacinth, but I'm here to bring all of you to the council. We need to know why Morgan and Susan flew here, and what Rylo wants."

Rue turned her face from Morgan's gaze, her mouth set in a hard line. Morgan had never seen Rue look so angry. As they slipped from the room and into the stairway, Morgan wanted to ask Rue if she was okay. Wanted to reach out to her as a friend, but just couldn't. It felt invasive to ask her what was bothering her. For all Morgan knew, it could be something caused by her presence in Orofine.

Morgan followed the other women through the weaving stairs and open air balconies of the treehouse palace. They finally entered a comfortable apartment set far above the city. Was this Avery's new home?

She recognized the other fae in the room. There was Raikin, the white skinned fae, thin and tall with eyes as green as her own scowled at her and Susan as they took a seat. His soulmate, Jay, close by him with a cheerful smile and kind words for Susan. Kyla went across the room to her soulmate, Garnel. His size was still intimidating. Knowing that he could transform into a bear didn't help either, but Morgan respected Kyla and trusted that her soulmate wouldn't hurt her here.

As Morgan guessed, Avery took a seat between herself and Susan on a comfortable couch. Avery avoided Savine's obvious attempts at eye contact.

"Morgan, Susan, welcome to my home," Kyla said to Morgan and Susan. "The council of Latiah has gathered here to listen to your news together. We trust it is urgent, due to your unplanned arrival, but you are not the first to arrive unexpectedly from Nephel recently."

Susan spoke up first, and Morgan felt relieved she didn't have to address this group on her own. "I spoke with Selene before she left The Towers. I hope she's not being punished for seeking out her soulmate. The will of the Goddess has never been superseded by borders."

Savine spoke and Morgan felt the tension from her sister as he talked. "No harm has come to Selene, despite her always treating me poorly. I'm not one to come between the will of the Goddess, or a bond between soulmates."

Rue let out a stifled cough, her eyes searing daggers at Savine. Clearly he'd angered more than just Avery lately.

Susan's voice was unsure as she said, "That is good to hear. Now, for why we came all this way. King Rylo requests your military support against Goldoth." Susan's words were calm, authoritative in a way that Morgan didn't expect she possessed.

Garnel let out a snort.

"There must be some kind of misunderstanding!" Jay said between belly laughs.

"Indeed," Savine replied. "Last I spoke to the trees, rumors were that Rylo was going to Goldoth to seek an alliance." He looked directly at Morgan as he added, "And you accompanied him."

Morgan gulped and said, "We did. He had ulterior motives that supported Kyla's mission to find the relics. Things went badly there, but we escaped with one of the Divine Five. Now Rylo needs your help before Goldoth retaliates."

Savine raised his eyebrow. Nobody dared laugh now. The room fell silent, waiting for Morgan to share more. Avery reached out and squeezed her sister's hand as she said, "Can you provide more details than that, Morgan?"

Morgan took a deep breath, nodded, and began to explain what she and Rylo experienced in Onyx Cavern. No one interrupted her story, even when she paused to ask for a drink of water to help her parched throat. She left out no detail, sharing Rylo's story of the twins marked by Althea and their destructive power. Tears began streaming down her face as she explained how she escaped with the relic, even sharing that she used a spell to utilize Elio's essence, accidentally draining him in the process. How the mines are filled with human slaves, forced to spend their whole existence underground, working in brutal conditions.

Finally, she put her hands to her head, exhaustion overcoming her. Avery rubbed her back in comforting circles. This wasn't an easy story to tell, and Morgan felt thankful that Avery chose to be close to her before she began her story, supporting her without Morgan needing to ask for her support.

Avery continued rubbing her back as she whispered in English, "It's okay now, Morgan. You're safe. We'll help you keep Nephel safe too."

Savine's fingers pinched the bridge of his nose, head held low. "The trees can never report to me about the true whisperings in Onyx Cavern and their network of other caves. I had no idea what they held. I don't believe anyone outside Goldoth does."

Raikin's eyes narrowed. "Do we trust the word of a human, particularly one loyal to Nephel?"

"Don't do this," Avery said, her voice cutting with frustration. "Don't accuse my sister of lying because she's a human."

"It is a reasonable question, and convenient that Rylo sent humans to share his request."

Morgan shook her head. "Who else could he send? I was the only one who survived the mine! Rylo was alone when he saw the two witches' power, and as far as I know, he only told me what he witnessed. How could anyone else tell this story?"

"Perhaps we could test the validity of her story?" Garnel suggested. Morgan watched as Kyla gave his arm a squeeze, digging her nails into his bare skin.

Savine shook his head. "There is no need. Morgan, you have provided enough information. Thank you for sharing your story. I know that couldn't be easy for you to do. But, I need time to make a decision. There are many factors to consider before I commit to bringing my folk into another war."

Savine's answer was not surprising, but Morgan couldn't stay here waiting for him to make up his mind. Rylo could already be in danger, and she needed to be by his side. He came closer to her as she stood on wobbling legs. God, she was exhausted.

"Of course. Excuse me. I need to rest. Susan and I should head back to Nephel tomorrow morning while you deliberate. Will you have a way to share your decision with us?"

Savine's brows furrowed and he glanced over to Rue. His voice dropped low as he leaned in close to her. "Selene will deliver the message. Look for her in one week."

Kyla walked to Morgan's other side. "Let me help you to our guest room," Kyla offered as she stood and helped steady Morgan, guiding her down a hallway to a bedroom.

The fae lights illuminated a room with white washed walls and a wooden beam ceiling. The bed had large furs spread over a blanket and a mirror was on the opposite wall. Morgan looked at her reflection. The deep blue circles lining her puffy eyes. Her tangled black hair. She looked completely exhausted.

"I can help you sleep if you need some assistance," Kyla suggested.

Morgan was so bone tired she didn't think she'd need any help falling asleep, and shook her head. "I'm so tired, I should be fine. Thank you for the room though."

"If it means anything, my brother believes you. Even though he hates Rylo, he won't leave our borders threatened. It's not in him to abandon the helpless, and we all know Nephel's warriors won't win against the full force of Goldoth.

It's what Morgan hoped. She needed to return to Rylo with news that hope was on its way. If not, she'd be leaving all his folk vulnerable to an attack that she caused when she agreed to steal the relic.

Chapter 46

Kyla

Long after the men had gone to sleep, Kyla and the other women sat together in the darkness of night. Morgan and Susan had slept for a few hours before waking and joining the others in her sitting area. Kyla felt a sense of kinship with these three witches and Rue that she'd never felt with other women, their combined destinies so entangled it was difficult to not feel close to them.

She'd shared the news of her pregnancy with Morgan and Susan, and they'd celebrated her good news. Yet, the somber knowledge of the war loomed over their conversation. They needed to make the most of their time together before Morgan and Susan left for Nephel at first light.

Avery and Morgan sat side by side, arms touching as they whispered something in their home language. From what Kyla could sense, Avery didn't fight Morgan on her decision to leave Latiah. She looked sad, but resigned to let her sister return to the Towers.

Susan and Rue talked quietly, no doubt catching up about what had happened between them over the course of several weeks.

Finally, Rue said loud enough for all to hear, "I need all of your help. I need to get Selene out of here." The heaviness in her tone didn't surprise Kyla.

Kyla tried to give her a reassuring smile, but it fell flat. Rue must be sick with worry about Selene. "I saw to her care myself. She's being housed near Hyacinth now. I know the men aren't releasing her, but look at it from Savine's perspective. Selene is the person who caused him more pain than anyone else in this world—including Jasper. The bond will be respected, but he needs time to think."

"I promise Selene won't be hurt," Avery reassured her.

Rue shook her head. "I know you all may have different opinions on Selene, but she is my soulmate. I knew too. I didn't admit it to anyone because I was a bit ashamed, and now I feel like I have squandered my time with her."

Susan raised her hand up to get everyone's attention. She was much more soft-spoken, and Kyla wasn't surprised by this gesture. "I've never said I don't like Selene. She is fiercely loyal. Won't she join us to Nephel? Rylo depends on her, especially now that Elio—" Susan's voice cracked. Kyla could feel the emotional pain she carried like a fog creep through the room. Meanwhile, Morgan's shadows slowly slid around her, cocooning her legs.

"If Latiah allies with Nephel, Savine will release her. He has no choice since she's the only one Rylo trusts," Morgan said, leaning back in her seat and propping her feet up on the small table in the middle of the room. The shadows skittered back into her. Such strange behavior these American women did from time to time, it often caught Kyla off guard.

Susan snorted, hurt in her eyes. "That isn't true. He trusts *you*, Morgan."

Avery lifted her eyebrows, "Does he?"

Kyla saw the blush growing on Morgan's cheeks. Her pale skin changed from alabaster to cherry within a few moments.

"It's not what you think. He considers me like his pet or something." Morgan's words slid off her tongue in a smooth lie, almost so sharp that Kyla could taste it in the air. Morgan wasn't being fully truthful about her feelings for Rylo, or perhaps what she meant to him. But, Kyla would let Morgan keep her secrets. It wasn't her place to share what Morgan was hiding behind her lies.

"Savine was convinced I was his gift from Althea, so that's not too different. Are all fae men this possessive?" Avery asked.

"All *fae* are that possessive," Kyla said with a laugh, diverting the conversation to take the growing pressure from Morgan. From what Kyla understood of Morgan, she was a private woman who preferred to keep much of her thoughts and feelings to herself, rather than disclose them to a larger group.

Susan gave a sad smile. She'd suffered a loss since they were together in the Towers, and by her reaction to Elio's name, Kyla could see she was in mourning for him. "The exception would possibly be a Bayberry, but I believe my parents would tear the world apart if they were separated."

"At their age?" Avery asked.

Susan smiled, but it faded quickly. "Oh yes! They are very devoted to each other. I think my chance of that is gone now."

Avery looked concerned at their friend. "What do you mean?"

Morgan sighed heavily, putting her hands to her face before looking up at the others. "Susan, I am so sorry for Elio. I know we talked about his death, but I shouldn't have made you hear the details again."

Susan's face looked cracked with grief. "I know there are risks with magic. It's just we were only beginning to know one another. I've never felt so wanted, and I don't even know if we were soulmates. Now

I'll never know." Tears streamed down Susan's face and Rue pulled her close as Susan sobbed on her shoulder.

Kyla got up, her lower back aching from being in the same position. She let herself stretch her arms high overhead. The nausea she'd been experiencing had been growing more intense in the past few weeks, and she never knew a fae could feel so worn down as she did. It was well past her typical bedtime, but it was worth staying up late with her friends. She made her way to a cabinet and pulled out another wine bottle, topping off the other women's glasses.

She turned to Avery while she stretched. "I don't mean to intrude on your relationship with my brother, and I know you're still adjusting to life with a fae soulmate. It sounds very different from what relationships are like in your realm. But, please, don't continue to hold his devotion to you against him."

Avery frowned and shook her head. "He hurt my sister for no reason!"

Kyla sighed. She knew Avery was going to fight her on this. "That was wrong of him, but he nearly lost you today, and he still blames himself for your kidnapping, and your injury when you arrived at Orofine. He's going to make mistakes, but you are his soulmate." Kyla had to fight back her own emotions, thinking of all her brother had been through to get to this point. "You're his soulmate and he still can't believe that he gets to call you his. Please understand he will react if you are threatened. It's the nature of the bond between you, and the reason you reacted the same way with the Hunter."

Avery bit her lower lip, nodding her head. "No, you're right. I'll talk with him after Morgan leaves tomorrow."

Susan stopped crying as she rested her head against Rue's shoulder, and Avery broke the tension by telling Susan and Morgan more details of the Hunters, while Rue and Kyla pitched in.

Morgan frowned next to Avery. "So we've been hunted all our lives?"

"Apparently. They did a terrible job hunting us. According to the lists we found, there are still more out there."

Morgan looked tired, like she couldn't take on the burden of more bad news.

"Can we share something cool? There's been a lot of grief while we've been separated, but Susan and I have learned some amazing magic. Would that be okay with you, Susan?"

Susan nodded. "I think a distraction would be good. We could show them how we can connect mind to mind," Susan suggested. "But I think Rue and Kyla will be left out. It is probably only possible between witches."

Kyla saw how Morgan bit her bottom lip. "I was able to communicate with Rylo mind to mind, even when we weren't close in the caves."

Susan had a puzzled expression on her face. "I haven't actually tried with a fae, I just assumed we couldn't."

Morgan shrugged. "Let's show Avery first."

The room grew silent, Kyla watched Avery as her face lit up. "That's so weird!" she shouted, far too loud for fae hearing. Kyla cringed at the high-pitched tone of her queen. "What's the spell? I want to try!"

The women shared the words of incantation, and Kyla watched as Avery struggled to connect through to them mentally. Finally, a wide grin spread across her face.

"I guess they're talking to each other," Rue said to Kyla.

"Makes me a bit jealous to not be a witch," Kyla replied, keeping her tone light.

The three women continued to stare at each other with broad smiles on her faces. It was obvious that they'd managed to communicate together as one, and Kyla couldn't help but think how invaluable of an asset that could be if they go to war. She only knew of one other couple who could communicate through their minds, but they were soulmates. Their bond between them manifested itself through telepathy. Finally, Susan turned to Kyla.

"Can I try to connect with you mind to mind?"

"Of course! I was feeling a bit left out over here," Kyla replied, instinctively placing her hand on her abdomen

"What about me?" Rue asked.

"I can try to connect with you, Rue, if you're okay with it," Morgan suggested.

"Please do!"

Kyla waited for something to happen, for a pulse of magic to enter her or for a connection to be made, as she often felt when she touched a fae. There was nothing between her and Susan.

She looked to Morgan, who clearly was growing frustrated with her failure to cast a spell to Rue's mind.

"Perhaps if you touched me?" Kyla suggested to Susan, reaching out her hand to her friend.

Susan took her hand. Immediately, Kyla felt the effects of the wine on Susan's body, her senses and emotions slightly dulled. But there was also some frustration. Her brow looked damp with concentration, but still there was no voice in Kyla's mind. No telepathic connection with her witch friend.

Susan sighed. "It's not working. I can't find a connection to you."

Morgan and Rue approached the others. "I couldn't find my way into Rue's mind either. Well, we've done a lot of spell work outside of just talking to each other through our thoughts."

Avery added, "We need to practice magic together, but with you returning to Nephel I don't know how that will be possible. I'm not as talented as either of you, and I've gotta get caught up. I can't just stand on the sidelines of a battle and wait to heal folk. Have you used the deep magic together other than this morning?"

Susan replied, "That was the first time. It was—overwhelming in its power. I've yet to find any document that explains how the witches combined the deep magic with their own power. Could you imagine what it took to separate the realm into two?" She shook her head, fear in her eyes. "It must have killed them in the process. I don't see how anyone could survive such power."

"Well, we need to start practicing," Morgan said. "If that witch can raise the dead, we're going to need to be ready to stop her somehow."

A chill ran down Kyla's spine. That sort of power wasn't natural, shouldn't be possible.

"The other witch is basically a bomb. She can implode things with her mind, which is also terrifying. But according to Rylo, they've been abused all their lives. They are afraid and angry. We need to use that to our advantage."

Avery's eyes softened. "They never had a chance to know freedom. We can't really blame them for what they've experienced."

Chapter 47

Avery

It was early morning and Morgan and Susan were already flying back to Nephel on their own. It was such a short trip, Avery longed for more time with her sister and Susan, but they both insisted they were needed in Nephel. She still didn't know what Savine thought about the prospect of an alliance, but she was ready to do whatever she could to support Morgan.

She'd thought more about Kyla's words and knew she was right. She couldn't hold onto this anger for what Savine did to Morgan. It wasn't fair to either of them if she continued to hold a grudge.

"Savine?" Avery asked, stepping into his office. He sat at his desk, forefinger and thumb on the bridge of nose. His essence was still and he looked as though he'd hardly slept the night before.

"Ave," Savine said, quickly bridging the gap between them. "Did Susan and Morgan leave already?"

She gave a tiny nod, reaching out her hand to his. He took it greedily, the contact between them sending a jolt through her that she could never resist.

Savine tugged her close and knelt before her as he dropped her hand. To see this powerful, courageous man kneel before her, looking up at her with a mix of pain and longing, nearly took Avery's breath away. The intensity in his eyes made her stomach twist as he placed his hands on her hips.

"Avery, I never want to cause you to hurt. Harming Morgan and Susan was a foolish mistake I made in fear and anger. Goddess above, last night not having you close enough to smell, to taste, to share all the happenings of the day with you has been painful enough that I'll do anything for your forgiveness."

Avery could feel the hard wall of her anger cracking under his words, diminishing to a pile of rubble as his hands tightened against her waist and he continued speaking.

"Not touching you almost broke me. Every piece of me is yours. Every fragile shard is yours to shatter, and that's what you're doing to me. You're shattering me into fragments of myself. If that's what it takes for you to forgive me, then I'll let you crumble me to ruin. But just please, I beg of you, tell me that you won't stay angry."

With that, the wall crumbled into the dust and she placed her hands on his cheek, rubbing circles against his beard. "Savine, my love for you is strong and it's lasting. Even when I'm mad, I still love you and that's not going to go away."

"Do you forgive me? I need to know you forgive me."

Avery wrapped her hands around his broad arms and tugged him up to her. Standing there before her, she tilted her head up to look at him. His face was softer, but there was still the lingering doubt that she would continue to torture him. She didn't want that. All she'd even wanted was for him to say he was sorry. Was that too much to ask?

"Of course I forgive you. I love you too much not to," Avery said.

Savine let his body crash against her, pressing her back against the wall. She wanted to swallow his need, his thrumming desire for her up and never let it go. As his tongue slid against hers, Avery knew this man could do *anything* and if he met her on his knees she'd forgive him. She'd welcome him back to her again and again.

Savine pulled back and looked at her with darkened eyes. "I want you, Avery. I want to make you cry my name so loud that the whole city knows how forgiving you are."

Avery rubbed her thighs together, sensation building in her core and she quirked a smile at Savine. "Is that a challenge, old man?"

The tip of Savine's essence peeked out of his shirt and his pupils dilated so that the dusky blue of his eye was but a slit. "Do you accept the challenge?" Savine said, a wolfish smile on his face.

"Happily," Avery said.

Before she could draw another breath, Savine's nimble fingers were at the leather cord of her pants, unfastening them and tugging them down to her ankles. Avery gasped at the contact of his skin against hers.

Savine's knuckles brushed against her inner thigh, the roughness of his hands scraping her sensitive flesh. He worked his way up her leg, reaching her hot center. His finger pressed inside her and she cried out from the delicious pleasure of his touch. His touch against her innermost walls was so good as his fingers glided in and out of her. She couldn't stop her body from rocking against his fingers as tension coiled deep within her.

"Damn, Avery," Savine growled as he pumped into her harder than she thought she could bear. His nimble thumb found her bundle of nerves as he began making stroking circles, increasing the pressure as he felt her respond to him. She needed this, this connection to him that made her wild for the fae that had stolen her heart and her soul.

Savine kissed her desperately, seeking his need to feel her release just as much as her own. "You're going to come for me, aren't you?"

Avery let out a whimper that was meant to be a yes, but it died on her tongue.

"Is that a yes, Little Flower?"

"Yes!" Avery gasped out as Savine flicked her clit, making her see stars as her world exploded in light and heat and need. She didn't even notice how she screamed his name. He was wringing every bit of pleasure from her that her voice didn't even seem real anymore.

"Good girl," Savine said, pulling his fingers away, leaving her empty. "Now I want to be so lost in you that I can't remember my own damn name." Her pants were still tight around her ankles as he positioned her against his desk, ass in the air.

He tugged his pants down, exposing the thick, hard ridge of his cock, letting his leathers slide down to his feet. She could feel his erection rubbing against her entrance. She wanted him inside her. Needed to feel him stretch her and take her so deeply against his desk.

"I want you hard and fast, Savine," Avery said, her voice husky with desire.

He gave her exactly what she'd asked for. He didn't press into her gently or slowly. With both his hands on her hips, Savine slammed into her, filling her to the hilt. He stretched her, fitting so deeply, so tight at this angle, that Avery didn't know if she wanted to cry out in pain or bliss. She bit down on her lower lip, as he began moving in and out of her, the slap of their skin filling the room.

"There will never be anything that prevents us from being together. You know that, don't you? Not some fucking fae who wants to steal you from me, not a prophecy, not even our *pants* will stop me from being with you, Ave."

All Avery could do was whimper, "Never, nothing," as Savine crashed into her. He moved in a way that was meant to sear, to reclaim her as his own, as his mate, and she wanted him to. She wanted him to make her scream in pleasure and pain, to skirt the edge of that balance. Avery arched her back, letting him drive into her even deeper, harder as he drove her to the edge of her pleasure.

Savine sensed her spiraling closer to the edge of her release, and drove into her in a frantic rhythm, desperate to fall with her. The world around her ceased to exist. Nothing else mattered than their plunge into ecstasy together.

Avery gasped, leaning her head against the desk as Savine slid out of her and helped her find her balance.

"That was—" Savine didn't finish his thought as he kissed her neck and shoulders tenderly before he pulled up his pants. Moments later, he returned to her, kissing down her spine.

Avery smiled through the kisses. "That was some hot make up sex." Savine helped her stand as he knelt before her, resecuring her pants.

Savine wrapped his arm around Avery's waist and began guiding her to the chairs.

As he sat down, he pulled her into his lap, resting his head against her shoulder. "Avery, I needed you. Not just physically, but I need to know I have your support with the decision I come to concerning allying with Nephel. There are so many factors to consider, and I can't be impartial when it comes to Rylo."

"Tell me what's on your mind."

He shook his head, before running his free hand through his tangled hair, the crown not visible. "I just got Latiah out of a war. We haven't even begun to recover, and pushing my folk into a conflict that is not ours is wrong. Yet, I also know if we do not accept this alliance and act early, we will face the war on our own borders, and there are the relics to consider. What does it mean if Kyla doesn't follow the will of the Premier Goddess? If Morgan and Rylo gained one then that makes three relics found, only two left. It would be worth it to ally with Nephel just to find the relics."

Avery thought carefully about what Savine was saying. She understood how he would feel so conflicted, and yet, in her mind, there was only one path. Even if she hated Rylo for what he did to her, even if she never forgave him for the hurt he'd caused Savine, she couldn't imagine abandoning Morgan to a war against a more powerful enemy. But she didn't want to blurt that out. It was her natural instinct to say what was on her mind right away, but she was trying to change, trying to be a better listener.

"You're taking the right steps by considering the different possibilities that could happen before making a decision to ally with Nephel. Why don't we go to the trees for your answers?"

Savine nodded. "Thank you for listening to me, Little Flower. I think you're right." He stood, pulling her up to her feet. They went to their rooms and changed into thick winter clothing before venturing into the forests.

Savine

The horror that Morgan had shared with his council was nothing Savine expected, and it left him reeling with concern for his own folk's safety. If what Morgan said was true, Goldoth could travel up river from Nephel and be at Orofine's doorstep by midwinter. His newly reunited kingdom could be under siege by an outside nation before the Long Night.

"You believe Morgan, don't you?" Avery asked as they walked into the still and silent forest.

Savine knew he'd made a terrible mistake when he didn't trust Morgan upon her arrival at Orofine. "I have no doubt in my mind that

Morgan is telling the truth. I was wrong when I doubted her loyalty to you, and that won't happen again. She may choose to take a different path from yours, but she would never try to harm you."

Avery smiled up at him. "Thank you for believing her."

The day was sunny and cold, the sun's reflection on the snow stung his eyes as he looked toward the forest nearby. Avery covered her arm across her face. "I'm adding sunglasses to my list," she muttered to herself.

"Sunglasses?" Savine asked. Another human contraption, he supposed. Humans seemed to have an endless supply of gadgets to make their life more comfortable.

"Yeah, they block out the sun's rays. They're going on my list for when I figure out how to travel safely between our realms."

Savine chuckled. "What else do you plan to bring back with you?"

"More like what am I not bringing. But really, my winter gear. I'm tired of wearing a dead animal to keep warm. Toothpaste, a fresh toothbrush, human birth control-—that tea Hyacinth brews me tastes like dirt—tampons, and a ton of food. You're going to love coffee. Oh, and beer. Plenty of beer. It would be fun to bring my bike too, and skis of course."

He loved hearing her daydream of how to blend their cultures. He hoped her dreams came true and he could see her homeland, as well as bring back anything that she lacked in the fae realm. "I think I will need to start expanding our rooms sooner than I anticipated, just to accommodate all your human items." Savine pointed to a copse of pines and firs nearby. "We'll go to the pines there. They can begin relaying our message south."

Savine approached a tall ponderosa pine. He'd often come here when he needed to check on news quickly since coming into his throne. Using mycillious, he said, *"Hello friend, tell me of the stirrings beyond our borders. Send messages south toward the borders of Goldoth and the Wastewater."*

The tree began to slowly shake, stirring its high branches. *"What you ask will be long in coming."*

"How long?" Savine asked.

"Not until the sun sinks below the mountains."

Savine looked at the sky. It was still early morning.

"Very well. I specifically need to know what the Goldoth army is doing. If their warriors are on the move, what direction?"

"War stirs too soon on the throne of so young a ruler."

"Rulers often do not have the luxury to know when their rule will be tested. It appears the time is now." Savine said before he turned from the tree and walked to find Avery watching from a distance. She looked anxious as she eyed the tree, still stirring from his conversation.

"What did it say?" she asked.

"We should return home. It will be a long time before the trees have answers to what I seek." He slid his arm over her shoulder, thankful that he was once again touching her as they made their way back to the King's Residence.

Chapter 48

Morgan

The Tower of the Moon was silent; the dark, unlit halls eerily similar to the cave she'd fled only a week ago. A chill ran down her spine and she tried to keep herself from running. *Running from what exactly?* There was nothing there to chase her. Nothing threatening her life. Just the hall of the place that had begun to feel like home.

Morgan had left Susan at her own room, saying that she would see her in the morning. She knew she needed to check in with her early, but Susan seemed so weary Morgan hoped she would be alright alone for the night. Morgan was also bone-tired, but there was no way she could sleep without first seeing Rylo and reassuring him that she'd done what he asked.

She'd tried his private rooms, but no answer came. There were no guards nearby either, making her think he must be somewhere else in the Towers. She padded through the dark interior hall on slippered feet, tired of wearing the heavy leather boots and layers of furs to keep warm during her flight on the eagan. Morgan would give up and go to sleep if Rylo wasn't in his private library.

She found the hidden space that led to Rylo's hidden sanctuary, but she couldn't get in on her own. Despite all the time she'd spent in this room, she still depended on Selene or Rylo for entry.

Her heart skittered as she knocked against the empty wall. She could hear shuffling within the room and the entrance dissolved. Morgan stepped into the room. The smell of old books, leather, and dust hit her senses like a familiar friend. But it was the smell of honeyed spice that made Morgan's breath catch.

Rylo was there, dressed in a remarkably casual grey sweater and loose pants. He looked at her with a half smile and walked close enough to her that she could feel the warmth of his body on her chilled skin.

"You're back." Rylo's wings flared slightly, as they often did when he was close to her.

Morgan filled the distance between them, wrapping her arms around his slender waist. He seemed to hold back for a moment, not sure if he wanted to reciprocate her hug, then he tugged her close to him and she felt the feather soft touch of his lips in her hair.

"I'm back, and I think I got you an army," she whispered into his chest.

Rylo stepped back, taking her in. "You beautiful, witty woman. Of course you did."

His mouth was on hers before she could reply. A sweet, welcoming kiss that made her want to melt into the heat of his mouth. Rylo pulled Morgan into his arms, carrying her over to the chair in the small library. As he walked, she kissed along his smooth jawline, twining her fingers into the soft curls of his golden hair.

He sat down, placing her in the seat opposite his.

"Tell me everything," he said, crossing his legs as he gave her his full attention.

Morgan left nothing out as she told him about her experience in Orofine. What she learned of the Hunters and the discovered relic, that Savine needed time to deliberate, but he would release Selene with his decision. She shared that Selene wasn't in danger, only being kept away from the others while Savine decided what he would do. The only two details she left out were that Savine hurt her when she first landed and that she shared about Elio's death. She knew Savine and Rylo hated each other and she didn't need to make things worse by sharing how Savine had reacted when he thought she'd been involved in her sister's disappearance.

Rylo rubbed his chin, deep in thought. "I've rallied my warriors and the Towers have been preparing for siege. But perhaps if Savine brings his troops to the Wastewater, we can avoid a siege on the Towers. When will he arrive with his warriors?"

"He'll give us his answer in a week."

Rylo frowned. Was this going to be too late? "It will be close, getting his warriors to the Wastewater in time. What convinced him that you were telling the truth? Did he force the answers from you?"

Morgan's stomach tightened with nerves. She was going to have to tell him about Elio. Everyone else already knew and it wouldn't take long for word to reach Rylo.

"I guess I was very convincing."

Rylo pursed his lips. "You're keeping something from me, aren't you, pet?"

Rylo

Rylo could almost taste Morgan's lies in the air. She still wasn't being honest with him about Elio's death, and now he suspected she could be keeping a great many things from him. Storing and collecting secrets, spinning lies, and waiting to use her two remaining oaths against him.

"I don't know what you're talking about," Morgan muttered, looking anywhere but his eyes.

"When we woke up in the Wastewater, you continued to refuse to tell me what happened to my friend. Now I must wonder what else you're keeping from me. Did Savine actually kill Selene? How can you be so sure they will come to our aid?"

Morgan shook her head, but the look of concern on her face didn't go away. "No, she's alive and coming back to Nephel. Savine privately told me that he'd allow her to deliver his decision. Apparently she's really fast?"

Rylo let out a harsh laugh. "Savine has never had the stomach to take action when he had the opportunity to. That's why he needed a human to defeat his father, and that's why he'll never kill Selene or myself, despite how much he hates both of us. It's also why he needs a week to commit to an alliance."

"I think the only time he takes action is when Avery is threatened," Morgan said, touching her throat. Despite the low lights of the library, Rylo could make out the healing scratches along her neck, the slight purple of bruising in thin lines along her delicate throat.

Rylo clenched his hands into fists as he stood. His essence poured out of him like pure sunshine, and Morgan covered her eyes, the light intense and powerful in his rage.

"How dare he use his essence against you? I'll personally make him pay for every scratch and bruise on your body," Rylo's typically smooth voice was harsh with so much unrestrained emotion that it took him aback. He reached out and stroked the scratches on her throat. Unlike Savine, he was willing to take action, and he'd be sure to fulfill his pledge to make Savine pay.

He sat down, taking a steadying breath as Morgan's shadows danced up and around him, blocking his shining light from her.

"I apologize," he said, the honey returning to his voice. "I knew there was a risk that he could harm you, and I took that risk anyway for my nation. I shouldn't have done that to you."

Morgan didn't look scared, despite his rage slipping out of him. Of course she wouldn't be intimidated by seeing him when his essence burst forth from him.

"It's okay. It was all a misunderstanding anyway."

Rylo nodded. "I am still going to take it out of his flesh when he arrives."

That made Morgan look nervous. "Please don't. I don't want you to end up fighting a two front war."

No, there was no excuse for how Savine had treated her and he didn't care if it hurt Savine's ego when he harmed him. "He needs to learn that he does not have permission to harm what is mine."

Morgan stiffened. "What in the hell are we doing, Rylo?"

"We are discussing your brilliant international negotiation skills," Rylo said, and he couldn't disguise the smile on his face. He had no doubt that she'd won him an alliance with a man who hated him. With Morgan at his side, he'd be unstoppable in this realm.

"I mean between us. You were furious at me when I left, and then you kissed me with so much tenderness I could taste how much you care about me. Now you're threatening to hurt Savine because he scratched me," Morgan said, pulling her feet into her seat and turning her body to look directly at him.

Rylo felt called out by this woman whom he wasn't supposed to care about, and yet, despite his better judgment, he'd let her sink so far into his mealy, tiny excuse for a heart that he didn't know what to do with whatever emotion he felt when he looked at her. He didn't know how to stop the way his breath caught when she looked at him with her jade green eyes, or the moments he made her smile unexpectedly.

And yet, she was capable of lying to him. He already assumed she must have done something to Elio. Something so horrible she was unable to admit it to him. He already knew it in his heart that Morgan killed Elio.

But he wanted to hear her say it. He wanted to know that she was sorry for what she did; that she wouldn't hide things from him if he chose to give her his heart. And that was just what he was willing to do.

He wanted to give her his heart if she would have it.

But not until she could be honest with him.

Morgan looked at him through sleepy eyes, her head reclined on the side of the armchair, her body curled in around itself.

"I've often enjoyed the pleasures that come with being king. Women willing to bed me when I desired company. I'd never be as foolish as Savine to choose a vow of celibacy. I've slept with women in my court and foreigners. But I've never shared my heart with anyone. The connection has rarely gone beyond a physical relationship."

The scowl on Morgan's face was adorable, and he fought the urge to lick away the furrows on her brow as she said, "Why are you telling me this? I don't need to know about your past relationships."

"Yes you do. Because you see, I never trusted them. I never wanted to trust one of them. But with you, I feel myself putting up my guards and warning myself to not let you into my heart fully. But, don't you see? I'm always desiring to break down those guards and give you my heart on a platter. To shout that it's yours to take. To squeeze and devour as you please. Doing that requires trust. Trust that I want to have in you, yet I know you are deliberately keeping something from me. Aren't you, Morgan?"

Morgan buried her face in her hands, but Rylo caught the guilt in her eye as she hid her face.

He felt a cool wash of shadows caress his mind and he opened it to her, letting her into the bright warmth of a mind.

I can't even say it out loud, but I think you already know. I killed Elio. It was an accident. I used a spell that drained his essence while going after the relic, and I am forever sorry for taking your friend from you. It's no excuse, but I didn't know the spell would do that.

"I suspected you were responsible for his death."

Rylo felt cold inside, empty and hollow. This brave, intelligent woman was his friend's murderer.

He needed to give himself space, to be alone in his thoughts. He stood up, opening the door to the hall before walking out into the crisp air of the night without sharing another word with Morgan.

The stars were glittering above, a sea of gleaming beacons all calling to him. Elio's body would never be presented to the stars, as was the Nepheli tradition. Rylo said a silent prayer to the Goddess that his soul had been accepted into Arcadia, not left to wander in the infinite darkness of the caverns, or castaway to the Abyss.

He didn't notice how long he stayed in the chill of the night air, but when he returned to his library, Morgan was gone.

Chapter 49

Savine

"If you're going to war, I'm going with you, Savine. You can't make me stay back," Kyla argued. They'd been having this back and forth for far too long, but his stubborn sister didn't seem to understand that a battle was no place for a pregnant woman.

The north wind howled against the windows of his office and his essence swirled under his skin as he looked at the tiny bulge revealing itself from Kyla's flat stomach. "I can't believe Garnel would agree to this."

"Hyacinth has assured Garnel I'm just as capable as I was before being pregnant. And I let him know I wouldn't leave his side. We're better together. Now you tell me when was the last time that you won a battle without my skill set?"

She had him there. He'd always relied on Kyla's ability to manipulate the other side's emotions. That was partially why his newly unified army had so many former loyalists who looked at his sister with such fear. She'd forced them to live in their worst nightmares, just as his father once had done.

Two evenings ago, the trees had relayed information that Goldoth was amassing troops outside of Onyx Caverns. The thought of facing the Goldoth forces, along with any weaponized witches they harbored, terrified him. He'd carried the weight of the souls he'd lost for over twenty-five years, and the burden of their loss was something he could never forget. Moreso, how could he convince his warriors that this war was theirs to fight?

He'd yet to make his final decision as he analyzed the resources his warriors had at their disposal. It would be close—thanks to Jasper's personal stockpiles of supplies—he could ensure his warriors had enough to eat through the winter, but only if he no longer provided supplies to the folk still desperate for support. Every day there were folk coming to him in the throne room, seeking assistance as winter began settling into the steep river canyon. Abyss damn him, he'd even needed to turn folk away recently, knowing he may need all the supplies he had stored for the war with Goldoth.

If he chose war, he was choosing this conflict over the health of his nation. Yet, if he didn't act now, he would surely be bringing the power of Goldoth to his borders.

It felt as though there was no right answer.

"*If* we go to war, I want you to stay back with Avery. Who will be with her if you're not there?"

Kyla shook her head. "If you think Avery won't be at the front, then you're a fool and need to have a serious talk with your soulmate. She made it clear that she wants to help stop the Goldoth witches."

This was news to him. He'd planned to keep Avery back, just as he'd promised her at the Towers after her kidnapping. Savine told her that he would never make her face a battle again, and he meant it.

"What are you saying about me?" Avery asked, walking into his office without knocking. Behind her was Rue at her side. The shifter scowled at him. She'd avoided him since he decided to keep Selene separated from her.

Regardless of what was going to happen, he needed to let Rue unite with her soulmate. Although it had only been a few days, it was no better of him to keep Selene from Rue as it had been for her to take Avery away from him. Even with all the pain Selene had caused him, he couldn't do that to Rue. He made a mental note to personally escort Selene to Rue's room this evening.

"Kyla seems to think you will be fighting if we go to war," Savine's words came out coolly.

Avery came close enough for him to smell her sweet scent. "Kyla is right. The witches are needed in the battle. How else are we going to use deep magic to end the battle?"

"Ave," he growled.

"I am these warriors' queen. I'm not going to stand by while they battle a force more powerful than our own. Especially not when I can use deep magic."

The wind howled against the window, sending a chill into the room, despite the fire and the added essence to the King's Residence.

"I promised you that you'd never have to face another battle, and I'm standing by that promise."

Avery wrapped her arms around his waist, craning her neck to look at him from this angle. "Savine, sometimes things change. And I feel ready for this. Please trust me that I can do this with Morgan and Susan."

Savine sighed. "If we go to war, you are not leaving my line of vision this time. Do not burn yourself out. If you feel even a little bit over set we will both leave the battle."

Avery rolled her eyes. "Okay, old man. I know. Possessive and obsessive."

He pulled Avery closer, bending over to lick the rounded contours of her ear. "You have no idea just how possessive and obsessive I can be."

He felt the heat of Avery's skin flare, smelled her arousal. "And you like me this way," he murmured.

Avery gave him a knowing smile. "Too bad you're busy deliberating on whether to go to war or not. Where's Raikin and Garnel, anyway?"

Savine shook his head. Damn his responsibilities. "Raikin is completing inventory for me. Garnel and Jay have ordered the warriors to report. Typically, I give my warriors leave during the winter. Even in the winter encampment I wouldn't require as much service from them. Training would continue, of course, and everyone would pitch in to maintain camp. But, we weren't actively battling, thanks to the mountains dividing Latiah. I'd already released many of the warriors for leave this winter and many have chosen to be united with family rather than stay near the King's Residence. Both sides deserved a break after so many years of conflict."

"And now they may be facing another war." Avery shook her head, and Savine could almost feel the tension in her body. "It doesn't seem right to ask them to fight in another war when they've just returned home."

"Yet, the alternative would be to leave our borders vulnerable to Goldoth's attacks. If this war is inevitable, I'd rather fight it in the Wastewaters or Nephel than allow my folk to be devastated by war once again."

There was no easy choice, and Savine was running out of time to decide.

Chapter 50

Morgan

Not a single star shone through the thick cloud cover in the sky. The blackness of the night sent a tingle down Morgan's spine, reminding her of those dark places that haunted her dreams. The distant beating of drums that had chilled her to the core had stopped only an hour ago. Avery hadn't come. Tomorrow they would face an attack by Goldoth and her sister hadn't come to her side. She pushed through the fear, stepping back into her room and toward the silent hallway.

She'd promised herself she wouldn't be afraid of battle. She had spent the last few months developing the skills she needed to wield her magic, and with Susan at her side, they'd find a way to stop this conflict before it could decimate either side.

But there was this twinge of doubt that kept creeping into her mind. Despite hours of meditation and working through her nerves, Morgan couldn't get the thought that she could die with Rylo hating her from her mind.

He'd avoided her for days, keeping her at a distance, and choosing his words carefully. His coolness stung her more than she was prepared to admit.

Nobody stopped her as she walked on silent feet to Rylo's room. Two guards stood outside the door. When they saw her coming, one stepped into his room, no doubt warning Rylo of his guest.

But Rylo didn't come to her. The guard returned to his post, saying, "King Rylo is occupied at the moment."

Morgan could hear muffled conversation from his room. Rylo's slow drawl mixed with a sweet feminine voice. A pang of jealousy stung her chest. Maybe she really didn't mean anything to him.

"This was a mistake," Morgan muttered. Rylo's groan of pleasure came echoing into the hall, and she thought her heart might plummet to her feet.

This was a stupid, terrible idea. Another moan came from his room and she thought she might be sick.

"We have heard what you did to him," the guard muttered. "Be off now."

"What I did to him?" Morgan's voice grew louder than she intended. But even her voice couldn't muffle the sigh coming from inside the room.

"The bargain. Forcing his hand like that, then leaving Elio for dead." The guard shook his head in disgust. "You don't deserve his company."

At that moment, she heard Rylo's dry laughter mingled with the melodic laugh of a woman with him, followed by shuffling footsteps along the wooden floor.

"He's finished," a woman whispered as she snuck past the guard.

"Good, thank you for your work, even at this hour," the man said, slipping some coins from a pouch around his waist and handing them to the woman.

The woman had a sweet, heart shaped face and full lips. Her light blonde hair looked slightly mussed and her white wings shone in the soft faelights. She wore a revealing blue silk dress, cut low with a corset that accentuated her slender waist. The woman brushed past Morgan with a wink.

Morgan turned to walk away, her head pounding with emotion. Why did she think he'd even want to see her?

She heard the door open, but she dared not turn around. It was probably the guard going back in. Had she just witnessed Rylo being serviced by a prostitute? It all seemed very transactional. Nausea twisted in her stomach. She picked up her pace on the stone floor, the click of her heels against the stone echoing around her. Everything was so silent, so hauntingly quiet after the Goldoth drumming of the evening. The war drums had ushered in everyone's greatest fears. Goldoth would attack the Towers and the Latian warriors had abandoned them. Morgan had failed to secure an alliance, and she failed to even see Rylo before tomorrow's battle.

She felt defeated. She wanted more with Rylo, but had ruined that. She'd failed him when he needed her and betrayed him by forcing his hand.

As she turned the corner, she heard a voice she'd recognize anywhere, sweet as honey, but punctuated by its deadpan tone. "Where are you plodding off to, pet?"

Morgan turned, her foot slipping on the polished floor as she fell on her ass. She looked up at Rylo, golden hair perfectly placed. He was leaning against the corner of the wall, his arms were crossed and his smile was big enough to reveal that damn dimple of his.

She pushed herself up, but she noticed her dress was torn and her ankle stung.

Great. Not only had she been caught loitering outside his room while he paid a woman for sex, but now she was battered and disheveled before she even set foot on the battlefield.

"I wasn't plodding!" Morgan seethed at him. "I was just passing through."

Rylo walked over to her, his fur-lined slippers silent on the floor "I think you're telling lies again." He pulled her up from the floor and into his arms. She winced at a sharp pain in her ankle and failed to disguise the discomfort from her face. "Come into my room. You took quite a fall there."

Her heart thrummed in her chest as he looked down at her with golden eyes. No, she couldn't go in there. Not after what she just heard.

"I'll be okay. Thanks though," she said, disentangling herself and taking a step back from him.

Rylo reached out to her and tugged her close to him. She was close enough to feel the heat of his very bare chest.

"Don't go yet."

She tried to pull away, the heat of her embarrassment probably visible on her cheeks. "I'm okay, really. Just out for a late night walk."

"Morgan, look at me," he said, gently tipping her head up toward him. His voice was smooth and he smelled like clean skin and spice. How did he smell so damn good all the time?

"I was just thinking of you. Please join me in my room."

Morgan flinched and felt herself make a face in disgust.

"Gross. Please don't tell me you were thinking of me when you had a prostitute visiting you."

Now it was Rylo's turn to make a face at her. He wrinkled his nose and frowned. "A prostitute? What are you talking about?"

"I did lie. I came here to talk with you because, well, against my better judgment, I've missed you. But I could hear the noises you were making in there. Then I saw the woman that the guard paid. It was obvious what was going on."

"Goddess alive, woman! I was getting a haircut and a shave!"

Morgan snorted. "I don't know anyone who makes sounds like that during a haircut! And who gets a haircut in the middle of the night?"

Rylo pressed his fingers to his temples. "The noises? I admit I can be loud at times when I get a neck and scalp massage. She added that last because I told her I was struggling to sleep tonight."

She watched as he shivered. The Sun King *shivered*. It couldn't be from cold, not with the essence imbued in the Towers keeping the building at a toasty temperature, despite the cold dreary weather outside. Was he scared? Is that why he shivered?

Rylo reached for her hand, and she let hers slide into his. "Will you please come with me?" he asked.

"Fine! But I still don't understand why you were getting a haircut right now."

Rylo barked a laugh. "The stylist said the same thing. If you must know, I couldn't sleep, and the thought of dying tomorrow with stubble and mussed hair was the tipping point. That at least felt like something I could control before going into battle."

Morgan's heart sank. He was afraid. Afraid and alone and seeking something to grasp onto that he could control.

They walked into his room together. It was warm, the bed neatly made like he hadn't even tried to lay down for the night yet. As she walked, her ankle burned with discomfort. She didn't think it was broken, probably not even sprained, but it was definitely bruising.

"You're limping," Rylo observed as he steadied her.

"I'll be fine."

Rylo shook his head and moved closer to her, filling the distance between them. "Don't do that, pet."

He was close enough that she found her hands drawn to his bare chest, absorbing the heat of his skin and the hardness of the muscles underneath. Close enough that she could feel the warmth of his breath on her eyelashes.

He knelt before her, moving so quickly she couldn't stop him. "May I look at your ankle?"

Morgan gave her consent, slowly lifting her foot up to his outstretched hand. His hands trembled a bit as he traced his fingers along her ankle. With quick fingers, he unlatched the strap on her heel, letting it fall to the floor. His hands drifted upward to her calf.

"Rylo?" she whispered as he continued his exploration of her leg.

"Yes, Morgan?"

"What are you doing?"

Rylo let out a wicked laugh. "I'm making sure my kingslayer is in working order."

"You don't need to do that, really."

He worked his hands back down to her ankle, carefully tracing the purple bruise that was already appearing before going up going higher and higher until he reached the tear in her dress. "I can't risk you fighting on an injury, can I?"

Her breath shuddered as he examined the shredded dress, kneading his hands along her exposed thigh until he caught sight of the scrap of gold lace hidden beyond her dress.

He lightly blew a breath of sun-kissed air against the lace. Morgan's skin prickled and a tingle shot through her core.

"Tell me, do you wear undergarments like this daily or was this bit of fabric specifically for this purpose?" he said as he began unbuttoning her shirt.

Morgan bit her lip, her voice came out husky. "It's for you, Rylo."

His smooth voice roughened as he said, "I hoped so. It would be a pity if I'd been missing out on this each day."

Morgan's hands shook slightly as she placed them on Rylo's shoulders. "There's a chance we might die tomorrow. I couldn't die regretting never feeling you inside me."

Rylo's hands gripped her hips. "And have you had that regret for long?"

Morgan closed her eyes, as she breathed in deeply.

"Yes. Yes I have." She exhaled as she tugged the ties on the back of her dress, letting it fall in a pile of silk on the floor.

Rylo's eyes roamed over her skin. She felt wanted and alive and she wanted him to never stop looking at her like that. "You wicked, beautiful woman. Why have you been avoiding me?"

Morgan looked down at him kneeling before her, hands gripping her hips. "Me avoiding you? You have been so angry at me, and I know I deserve it."

"I hate so much of what you've done to me. You are my undoing. My weakness. And never is that more obvious than when I am pining for you to give me even a morsel of your attention."

The honesty on his face stung. He was speaking the truth. Free from games and tricks.

"Rylo," she whispered as she tugged on his shoulders, pulling him to his full height. "I'm so sorry I've hurt you."

He pressed his thumb to her lips, tracing the shape of them. "I have never tolerated such insolence in anyone," he said, shaking his head. "That is what makes you so dangerous."

He parted her lips with his thumb and she sucked it into her mouth, gently biting the tip.

"Abyss damn me!" Rylo rasped as he wrapped Morgan into his arms and brought his mouth to hers. His warmth and tenderness took her by surprise. She came here expecting anger, teeth and tongues clashing. A violent need that fulfilled her deepest desires for him. Instead, he kissed her with such a softness that when his tongue glided to hers, it was a pleading invitation to accept him.

Rylo lifted her into his arms before he placed her into the soft folds of the bed. He stood over her, a heated gaze taking in her body in the diminishing fae lights. "Kingslayer. That's what you are, you know? Slaying my worthless heart into shreds for you. It may be the worst punishment I could receive."

"Do you really hate me? I never meant to do that to you," she said in a whisper.

Rylo began making small circles along her arms, working toward her chest. "My hate for you is deep, but it's nothing compared to my need for you. My need for you, pet, is a bottomless sea of desire."

He worked his nimble fingers over the lace that clung against her breasts, nipples already peaked from the fire set by his touch, his gaze, and his words. His hot hands on her cool breasts made Morgan suck in her breath and lean greedily into his touch. The friction of the lace on her skin felt delicious.

"Maybe your desire will go away after you've fucked me. Then you can just hate me," Morgan taunted, but it was just empty words. She didn't want that at all.

Rylo smiled, that kissable dimple shining. "No Morgan, I fear this may be a lifetime affliction."

He let his robe slide off, revealing his sculpted chest and narrow waist, his legs covered by loose-fitting pants. How does a man who spends most his day reading and drinking tea even look like this?

The bed shifted with his weight as he slid beside her, leaning down and pressing his lips to her breast. His tongue teased and sucked through her lingerie, increasing the friction against her skin until she was moaning with a desperate need for him to touch her at the aching place between her legs.

Rylo looked up at her with a knowing grin as he slid his free hand down, skimming across the delicate fabric. He grasped the scrap of lace at her mound in his hands and ripped it in two, just as he lightly bit down on her nipple. Morgan cried out, the edge of pleasure and pain mingling. Cool air hit the heat of her core, but was replaced by Rylo's hot hands grazing her entrance.

"Ah," Rylo said, propping himself on his elbow. "I believe I've found the only hot place on your body."

He sunk his fingers into her depths, as Morgan closed her eyes and moaned out, "Don't tease me right now, Ry."

"Ry?" he said, the word husky on his lips. His fingers filled her with a steady, tantalizing rhythm that had Morgan squirming under his touch. "I wouldn't dream of teasing you. No, I want to unravel you and break you down just as you've done to me."

At that, he pressed her thighs further apart and angled himself between her legs. All the time, he continued drawing his fingers in and out, in and out of her, as she barreled closer to her release. With a wicked grin, he brought his lips down to her clit and sucked hard enough that it sent her spiraling over the edge. She came so hard that her shadows bucked out of her with her release, writhing and twisting around Rylo, his wings outstretched, shielding them from the darkness overhead. She screamed Rylo's name so loud it was probably waking the entire Towers up. Rylo didn't relent as he kissed and licked her most sensitive places, his clever fingers working in tandem with his tongue and teeth.

Finally, so agonizingly slow, the crescendo of her pleasure began to retreat, her shadows fading and she felt like she could finally speak again.

"Congratulations. You've unraveled me," she said, breathless from the pillow. He let out a huff of a laugh as he sat up between her legs.

"Oh pet, we've only begun." He slipped off the bed, leaving her exposed and boneless on top of the covers. She watched as he worked the ties on his low-slung pants, his cock tenting the front and the V of his abdomen making her bite her lip.

When his pants fell to the floor, Morgan couldn't stop the purr that escaped her lips. His body was like a marble statue, all hard edges and rippling muscles, and his cock—Morgan had never given much thought to what a truly beautiful cock would look like, but this was it. Thick and just the right length to make her mouth go dry with need.

She sat up, pulling the torn lingerie over her head and letting it fall to the floor. Rylo came to her side, palming her breasts.

"Is this really what you want? To feel me inside of you?"

"I came here with that as my sole objective," Morgan whispered.

Rylo kissed her neck, working up to her jawline and over the scars on her cheeks to the corner of her mouth. "And if I had rejected you?" he asked against her lips.

She sucked in a breath at the heat of his lips, the warmth of his sun-kissed skin against her cool flesh. He was going to make her catch fire, to burn to ashes with his touch.

"You would have broken me, but I would have deserved it," she said honestly as her heart thundered. He still could reject her. If his goal was to make her ache, make her feel his hatred, this would be the way to do it and she wanted him to know that truth. To give him that option. After all, hadn't she been taking his choices from him over and over again? She needed him to know that she'd accept his rejection, if that is what he really wanted. "Isn't that what you want to do?"

He pressed her flat on her back, her head sinking into the soft pillow behind her as he kissed her with a smoldering heat that threatened to consume her. "If only I could let my anger win against my desire. But, that is not what I want. I want to be your flame. I want you to burn for me and only me."

"Then consume me, Ry," Morgan rasped. Her words seemed to spark something feral in him, the permission he'd been waiting for.

He positioned himself between her legs, the tip of his broad length against her entrance as he entered her slowly, working himself in and out as her inner muscles burned and stretched around his cock. His length slicked out of her, nearly leaving her empty and writhing for him to come back before he drove into her again, this time hard and fast. He looked at her with claiming determination.

"You're mine, pet. Don't doubt it." His voice was rough and his face was agonizingly beautiful with desire.

"That's all I want." The words escaped her lips and he smiled at her like she'd given him a precious gift.

Over and over, he set a rhythm that made Morgan cling to him, dragging her nails across his back and pulling him closer to her.

The heat of his body against hers was so intense, she thought she might combust from it. His skin faintly glowed as his essence escaped him in his pleasure. She let her shadows pool out of her and wrap around him, bringing his face to hers. She kissed him in a crushing embrace, her tongue sliding in and out of his mouth to the beat of his thrusts. Her inner muscles began pulsing with the need to reach her release.

Rylo reached between them, stroking her throbbing clit as he growled into her ear, "Come for me, Kingslayer."

Morgan cascaded into her release, and Rylo followed, growling out her name as they were both consumed by the flame that had been fanned into a firestorm between them. The heat of his release filled her quivering inner muscles and she let her shadows wrap around them, plunging them into darkness.

Rylo's forehead pressed against hers as they slowly came down from their climax. He pushed her sweat-soaked hair from her face and slid out of her, the slickness of their release sticking to her inner thigh. Rylo turned her onto her side as he stared back at her.

The mask he wore so often was gone, and Rylo's expression looked soft and sated. Morgan traced the pointed tip of his fae ears before tracing her fingers down his jawline to his beating heart. She pressed her hand against his chest, feeling his heartbeat beneath her fingers.

"This damn heart beats only for you, pet. I tried to stop it from happening, but I am yours," Rylo said dryly.

Morgan quirked a smile at him and wrapped her leg across his hip. "This didn't relieve you of your need for me?"

She felt him growing hard again—so soon—against her inner thigh.

"No, Morgan, as I said, my need for you is a lifetime affliction." He pulled her on top of him, letting her enjoy every inch of his gorgeous body at her own leisurely pace.

She stayed with him that night, as they explored each other's bodies and drifted into sleep, only to repeat the process again and again. By the time Morgan slipped out of his room, drum beats had begun to sound across Nephel.

War was upon them.

Chapter 51

Savine

Savine had run out of time, and yet he still hadn't sent Selene with word on his decision. Today, he'd have to let Nephel know if help was on the way or not. There was no other option. Before he made his decision, he needed to hear an updated report from the trees. He'd been in the forest, seeking information from the trees more than he had in years. Not since the early years of the civil war. Even now, he didn't know what the right decision was. Either way, his folk could be hurt.

"What more information can they provide?" Garnel asked. "We know the Goldoth warriors are marching swiftly. We've already lost the opportunity to cut them off at the Wastewaters. In a few short days, they will be at the Towers."

"I need to know if there's any evidence that they will attack us this winter. If war is to come, perhaps more preparations are necessary. Alternatively, if there is a reason to believe they are seeking Avery then I will stop at nothing to keep them from our borders, and will do all that I can to keep her safe in Orofine."

Savine turned from Garnel and rested his gloved hand against a giant cedar.

"I am seeking updates on the Goldoth military. What rumors circulate on their location? Do they pose a certain threat to Latiah?"

The tree shook its boughs down, one brushed against the gilded bough of his crown. A clear move to put Savine in his place. He knew the trees were growing weary of his many daily requests. But he was desperate for clarity. Nearly twenty-six years ago, Savine had no choice but to put his nation on the path to war.

The thousands of folk affected by that decision still haunted him. He could never make the same rushed choices again.

After he requested information, he turned from the tree and walked to find Garnel. By now he knew the information he requested would take hours to reach him. His friend was already splayed out in the hot springs water, eyes closed, yet he must have sensed Savine's presence as he said, "Do you remember when we were boys and would sneak from the Residence to swim?"

Savine glanced toward the clearing with the agate headstone, not far from the pool. "Of course I do."

"I long for those simpler days."

Savine nodded and joined Garnel in the water. This was as good of a place as any to wait for the tree's response, and he would see the rustling of the branches. Garnel's soul had been heavy lately, and he needed to give his closest friend time. Even with the burden of war weighing down on him, he'd make time for Garnel. It was something he regretted never doing during the last war. Changing his habits was hard. Opening up, sharing when he needed support didn't come naturally to him. If he was being honest, neither was listening to his friend's worries.

He splashed into the water, skin stinging at the heat of it.

"Savine, I don't know if this pool is made for two grown Latian warriors."

"Then move over, brother. My bones are chilled and my heart is heavy."

Garnel sat up, moving to the opposite side of the pool from Savine. "Neither of us should have heavy hearts now. We ended the war. We stopped our enemy, and yet, I've never felt so empty."

"You still can't shift?" Savine asked, already knowing his answer. He'd avoided asking all these weeks, knowing that if Garnel could shift he or Kyla would tell him.

Garnel tugged on his red beard. "The feeling of my other half is fading slowly. It may be too late."

Savine noticed how Garnel's essence had faded to fine, dusky lines. If his essence was depleted, he would not be able to survive for long.

"We now know of three relics. We'll find the remaining two and Althea will restore your essence."

Garnel's face looked like it would crack, anguish cut through his voice. "What if we don't? What if my essence drains from me and I never meet my child? All because of one foolish mistake."

"Brother, I'll pull you from the goddess-damned Abyss myself before I let that happen," Savine muttered.

They sat in silence, the steaming water boiling their skin as dusk swept across the steep mountainous canyon walls.

The spiny branches of the nearest coniferous tree began to shake, and the forest came alive with movement, stirrings in the branches.

"The trees have an answer," Savine said, sliding out of the water. He walked barefoot through the snow to his clothing, letting his heated skin melt the snow underfoot. As he tugged on his furs over his slick skin, he heard the trees calling for him.

"*Prince of Chaos.*"

"*What is the news?*" Savine asked.

"*The armies are at the southern reaches of the Towers. They call for revenge against what was stolen. They want the witches of the north.*"

Savine cursed under his breath as dread built in his chest. "*Avery as well as Morgan?*"

The tree shook in the icy wind. "*They will stop at nothing to claim the witches marked by the Premier Goddess. They come north with a darkness that will overpower and destroy.*"

A chill ran through Savine as Garnel came over to Savine's side, dressed in his furs. "What was their reply?"

"We must prepare the warriors. We march for war."

Chapter 52

Rylo

The view out Rylo's balcony chilled his essence to ice. Maglar's troops had crested the southern mountain range separating his nation from the Wastewaters and ensconced themselves near the Tower of Stars.

It had been a week.

A week since Morgan and Susan returned with hopes of an alliance between Latiah and Nephel.

A week since he'd been certain he had an alliance on its way.

And yet, there had been no word. Selene still hadn't returned from abandoning her post in the name of her young soulmate. Her desertion could very well cause the Towers to fall in a single day. He could possibly succeed in holding off the waves of warriors with Selene, but he was a lost cause without her, even with the two witches and the deep magic on his side. They were both untested in battle, and after Morgan shared how the deep magic had ripped through them, causing her to burn out with startling speed, Rylo was hesitant to allow her to use deep magic for his sake.

Rylo turned and looked at the empty space where Morgan had been. She'd come to him last night, and despite the hurt she'd caused him, he couldn't regret spending what could be his last night with her in his arms. His need for her was like his need for the sun. Life wasn't worth surviving without her in it. He only wished he hadn't waited so long to have her. At least he had one night. That would have to be enough.

The beat of the drums was incessant. A constant pulsing in Rylo's ears as he prepared to meet Maglar and Mara. He would follow the protocol of war—a cordial meeting before blood was shed.

As he prepared to fly to his generals he heard a knock on his door.

"Come in," he called. Morgan and Susan walked into the room, both dressed in Latian leathers.

"What an interesting choice in clothing today," Rylo drawled, examining every curve the leathers accentuated on Morgan's body. If only there were some odds that would result in him surviving the day. He'd peel the leather from her, revealing the alabaster glow of her skin.

"Avery made sure we had some protection before we left Latiah." She pointed to a dagger at her side. From the gleam of its metal, Rylo knew it was iron. "I should have spent more time learning how to use these."

Rylo shook his head. "You don't need them."

She let out a sad sigh. "My magic. Right."

He didn't know if she thought of how her magic could cause such devastation with just a few words. How she could rip the essence right out of a fae and leave them devastated in her wake. He'd known she had the potential to be powerful, that was why he chose to make her his, and yet, he didn't know it would cost him so much.

"We've come to join you, King Rylo," Susan said, her voice shaking as she finally spoke up. "We may be the only thing to stop the witches if Goldoth brought them to battle."

The thought of Morgan fighting in this battle, even knowing her magical potential, left his skin clammy and his heart thumping in his chest. But he didn't have a choice. That's what she was here for, and he couldn't abandon his folk to protect her now. Even if all his heart demanded him to do was wrap his arms around her and flee to some far flung cave in the mountains.

"Yes, of course." His mouth felt too dry as Morgan moved closer to him. She reached out her hand to his and squeezed it.

"We can do this. Even without Latiah. Right? We'll make it," she said, her voice shaking.

He forced out a clipped nod. "We best meet Maglar and Mara." He turned and looked at Susan, still twining Morgan's hand in his. "I will have you stay near one of my generals during the talks." He turned back to Morgan, and couldn't stop himself from cupping her face in his hands, his thumbs rubbing the scars on her cheeks. "I want you beside me the entire time. I need to be able to fly with you if we need to fall back."

Her face had a determination about it that he always admired in her, yet her hands shook as she grasped his forearms. "I won't leave you. I'll never leave you, Rylo."

Rylo pressed his lips to hers, needing to feel her against him one last time before they faced the battle.

—-

Morgan

Rylo wrapped his arms around Morgan, lifting her close to his chest as he flew her out of his balcony and toward the far side of the river.

"Talk to me. Please," she said, her words catching in her dry throat. The cold mist seemed to cling to her face, her hair, anything that it touched.

Rylo didn't try to give her a false sense of security. He was direct, without twisting his words into half truths. "We'll meet with Mara and Maglar. They will provide their grievances, and we will share ours. I don't have much to go on, since I attacked the rulers of Goldoth and you stole their relic."

Morgan tried to hide her chattering teeth. Whether it was from the biting cold of the mist, or her fear, she wasn't sure. "Then what?"

"Most likely we won't reach any sort of agreement. We'll return to the Towers and prepare the warriors for battle."

Overhead and behind them, other Nepheli warriors followed close, including a general with Susan in his arms.

Morgan let her head rest against Rylo's collarbone, his hard armor kept her head at an odd angle. "It's all very organized for a battle."

"It's the way of things, at least at the beginning of the war. Or should be."

They began their descent toward a black tent placed just uphill from the Tower of Stars. Even from far away, the bald woman wearing a crown shone in the weak morning light. Like a diamond in the sun, her exposed head glittered. "Mara waits for us," Rylo said.

Maglar came out of the tent, hate in his gaze as he locked eyes with Morgan. It sent a chill down her spine. "Maglar looks ready to flay me alive," Morgan whispered.

"Don't say such a thing, pet. Not today," Rylo muttered against her ear.

Rylo circled overhead before landing next to his warriors. Even on the ground, his wings were wrapped close to her, his hand kept a vise-like grip on her waist.

Rylo's voice was chillingly calm as he said, "So it's come to this, Maglar? You chose to bring war to my own doorstep."

"We only seek justice for the insolence of the Nepheli king and his witch," Maglar spat as he pointed at Morgan, his hate-filled eyes boring into her. "That witch stole something sacred from us and killed or maimed hundreds of our slaves. King Rylo, your attack was unprovoked. We are well within our rights to demand justice for the insult brought upon our folk."

Morgan caught a flicker of something in Rylo's eyes as he said, "What is the cost you demand to prevent war between our nations?"

Mara smiled a bitter smile. "We want the witches. We know you harbor two witches, and demand them in exchange for peace between our nations, as well as our restored relic and any other relics the witches wield. We also want the witch's sister. The one in Latiah."

Rylo's typically indolent mask was gone, and his face was glowing in a harsh light. "That is not an option. King Savine will never willingly part with his soulmate, and I have already shared my personal attachment to my witch. Dare take her from me again, and my previous attack will pale in comparison to what I promise to do to you."

A chilling laugh escaped Maglar. "Then so be it."

Two tiny, thin women were pushed forward by fae guards. They wore nothing but thin rags, their pale skin and bare feet exposed to the cold. Both women squinted their unnaturally large eyes, so large they didn't seem to fit their faces. One walked with her head low while the other thrashed and screamed like a beast on her chains.

Rylo's wings stretched out, ready to take flight, but he didn't. Instead, he whispered in Morgan's ear, "They're here. These are the witches."

"Unleash the slaves," Mara said to the fae holding the two women's chains. The more subdued one didn't move as the collar around her neck fell to the floor. Morgan could feel a power stirring around them that made her want to run and hide, to flee from the terror that was this tiny creature. The other sister grabbed onto the warrior at the end of her chains, thrashing as he tried to remove her collar. Once the collar was off, she grabbed onto his arm and sunk her teeth into him. The man screamed as he attacked her with his essence.

"Don't harm her!" Mara hissed at the warrior. He stopped fighting the woman, even as she wrapped her hands around the man and squeezed, power penetrating her being and forcing itself into the man. He collapsed in a heap, his essence and his blood draining onto the wet ground.

"This is not how war talks are conducted!" a Nepheli warrior shouted.

"When one is attacked in their own home, war talks mean nothing," Maglar spat out.

The little creature turned from her kill, her enormous eyes meeting Morgan's before they rolled back in her head, becoming a hauntingly milky white. Another warrior walked forward, but there was something very wrong with how he moved. His gait was choppy, lacking that natural fae grace. Morgan gasped as the man looked at them. His rotting flesh clung to sinew and bone. The hollows where his eyes should be stared at her. The tattered grey feathers lay limp behind him.

"Elio!" Rylo shouted. His voice was filled with such pain, such grief it shook through Morgan like a laceration.

"I will not have *humans* ruling my northern borders! They are nothing more than slaves and by the end of this, you shall beg me to take them from you!" Maglar bellowed.

Rylo didn't hesitate to spread his wings, taking flight toward the river. His grip on her was so tight it would bruise, but Morgan didn't care. She looked over his shoulder far enough to see the other Nepheli warriors take flight, sending out their essence in a steady attack against the undead fae.

But it made no difference. Elio snapped his neck, looking at Morgan as wings exploded out from behind him and he took flight toward Rylo and Morgan.

Chapter 53

Rylo

The icy fog rushed past as Rylo broke through the thick blanket of clouds that ran across the river canyon. Morgan clung to him, crying out that she was so, so sorry. But Rylo didn't have time to think about her apology. No, he could feel the cold, unnatural presence of the thing that followed close behind them.

Rylo dared to take a look back. The undead creature that had once been Elio was gaining on them. Tattered pieces of flesh slapped in the breeze as he drew closer. "Morgan, I need you to give us some cover."

Morgan nodded as dark mist began to writhe and billow out of her, blowing around them and circling the sky into darkness. The mass of darkness grew and grew, the power of her shadows plunging not just them, but all of Nephel into night.

"Good girl," he purred, drawing her against his chest. Her arm held tight to his neck, clinging to him. "Goddess damn me, I love your magic."

She was looking behind them, past his wings to where the undead fae should be. "It's gone. Elio—I don't think he's there anymore."

Light filtered through the darkness, Morgan's concentration becoming distracted by their surroundings.

"Keep focused, pet. We need your shadows now."

They flew forward, hearing the sounds of battle behind them. But Rylo didn't stop, didn't go back to the front. All that mattered now was getting Morgan away from the Goldoths. They wanted to take her from him, to punish him through her, and he'd never allow that. First, he needed to get her back to the Tower of the Moon—to safety. Then, he'd unleash the full power of his essence on those bastards.

Rylo screamed out in pain as something tore across his face, ripping the flesh from him. He loosened his grip on Morgan for one moment, just a second of hesitation, but it was enough. A keening screech filled the darkness and he felt Morgan being tugged from him, torn from his arms.

"Rylo!" her scream sent his senses scrambling as he grabbed onto her arms. Another terrifying scream filled the air as Morgan's shadows thinned. Elio had hold of Morgan's waist, his jerking movements didn't stop him from yanking her away with unnatural strength.

This wasn't actually Elio. It wasn't his friend that he'd worked for so long to protect. It was just a shell of who he once was, and yet, it was him. His body was twisted into something that should never be possible. Filled with dark magic so unspeakable that Rylo growled in the face of the darkness. The undead fae plunged dagger sharp bones through Morgan's leathers, stabbing her in her soft midsection. Rylo could smell the tang of Morgan's blood in the air as she screamed in terror.

"Elio! Let her go!"

The creature hissed in response, beating his tattered wings in as he tried to fly away with Morgan's lower half.

"Make it stop! Make it stop," Morgan gritted out, tears streaming down her face.

Hearing her crying out in pain awakened something feral inside Rylo. His pet. His *person* was hurting. She was crying out for him to stop this threat. Her need for his protection, palpable in the air.

"Concentrate your shadows around you and close your eyes, love," Rylo said. Her shadows had thinned enough that he could see her do it before she became cocooned in darkness. He could target his essence directly at Elio, but the brilliance of it would leave permanent scarring on such a fragile being's eyes. He didn't hesitate to release the full force of his essence, channeling the heat and glow of the sun itself as he struck the creature that had once been his closest friend.

A blazing, screeching light filled the sky as Elio imploded into starlight and sun fire. Tiny bits of dust peppered Rylo's face and leathers. But he was gone, that shell that had once been his friend was dissolved into nothing.

"Rest easy, friend," Rylo muttered as he drew his attention back to Morgan.

Morgan, who was plummeting in darkened shadows toward the ground below.

"Rylo!" she screamed, her panic kicking his senses into hyper awareness. He tucked his wings tight into a plunging dive toward her.

Her body flailed as it fell toward the ground, shadows wrapping around her to protect her from the impact. He reached her and tugged her battered body tight into his arms.

"You came for me." Her voice was raspy from screaming, blood pouring from the punctures in her leathers.

"Always, pet. Always," he said, pressing a kiss to her lips. He could smell the hot blood from her wounds. So much blood, too much. He needed to get Morgan to a healer.

Below, he saw the Goldoth warriors working to breach the river. Others shot carved stones across the canyon, targeting the Towers. Already, the Tower of the Stars was overrun with Goldoth warriors as Nepheli warriors fought from the skies and ground to protect what was theirs. Priestesses of the Tower of Stars fought side by side with Nepheli warriors. The Goddess of Stars was alight in divine fury, burning stardust crashing and twisting around any Goldoth warrior in her path.

Rylo was almost to the Tower of the Moon. Morgan just had to stay with him a little bit longer. He pressed his mind to the shadowy depths of hers, sliding into her darkness.

Almost there love, stay with me.

Morgan gave no response as her head lolled from his chest into the crook of his arm, blood sticky against his hands.

As he looked to the north, he choked back the emotion that threatened to claw out of him.

Ebony wings shot through the sky, racing toward him.

Farther across the horizon, just below the heavy fog was the faint outline of elk and riders, dashing down the steep canyon trails.

There still was hope in the darkest hour.

Acknowledgements

First, thank you to my wonderful husband, Richie and my kids for supporting me as I chase this wild dream of being an author. I love you and love all our adventures together!

To my amazing accountability partners, AC Marholin and Meredith Kasian. You two keep me motivated every single day! I can't wait to have you join the published author party!

To my alpha readers: Dana, Ashleigh, Lydia, and Brianna. Without your thoughtful feedback, Sapphire Falls would still be a wide, shallow puddle. You all made me laugh, think critically, and ultimately made Sapphire Falls the book it is today!

To my beta readers: Marissa, Sara, Brie, Taylor, Whitney. Your feedback helped polish Sapphire Falls even further along. To my sister, Allie, I love how you're willing to tell me what's working and what's really not working. Please never stop being my sounding board!

To my editors Kay and Ambria, thank you for all your amazing work in making Saphire Falls the best it can be!

All my Street Team and ARC team members who encouraged me to make a Street Team, to sell signed copies of Quartz Mountain, and who just helped hold a newbie author's hand as I navigated my first release with Quartz Mountain and helped make Sapphire Falls release even better. I'd be literally lost without you! There's been so much to learn on this author journey and my community has been the very best.

Lastly, to you, dear reader, who choose to support indie authors and love our books. You literally mean the world to me!

Author's Note

Thank you so much for reading *Sapphire Falls!* I hope you loved reading it as much as I loved writing it!

If you enjoyed this book, please consider leaving a review on **Amazon** or **Goodreads.** As a new indie author, every review helps my book get into the hands of other readers! Your review means so much to me.

Looking for more of *The Lost Realm Series* world? Grab your copy of my FREE novella, *Golden Meadow.* This standalone novella takes place a few years before Avery travels to Aeritis, and features a fae warrior traveling to our world!

Finally, if you're excited about finding out what's next for everyone in Aeritis, consider joining my **mailing list** for information on new releases, pre-orders, and just fun updates on my works in progress!